BEDFORDSHIRE LIBRARIES

KE

KEMPSTON LIBRARY

Adams		.
Binner		
Munro		
Souter		
BEDFORD BOROUGH COUNCIL		
WITHDRAWN FOR SALE		
Price.		

BOOKS SHOULD BE RETURNED
BY LAST DATE STAMPED ABOVE

ar.
(1950), the story of two young Athenians who study under Socrates and fight against Sparta. Both these books had male protagonists, as did all her later works that included homosexual themes ove between men would

D1440340

By Mary Renault

Purposes of Love
Kind are Her Answers
The Friendly Young Ladies
Return to Night
North Face
The Charioteer
The Last of the Wine
The King Must Die
The Bull from the Sea
The Mask of Apollo
The Praise Singer
Fire from Heaven
The Persian Boy
Funeral Games

NORTH FACE

Mary Renault

Introduced by Sarah Dunant

virago

VIRAGO

This edition published by Virago Press in 2014
First published in Great Britain by Longmans in 1949

Copyright © Mary Renault 1949
Introduction copyright © Sarah Dumont 2014

The moral right of the author has been asserted.

*All characters and events in this publication, other than those
clearly in the public domain, are fictitious and any resemblance
to real persons, living or dead, is purely coincidental.*

All rights reserved.
No part of this publication may be reproduced, stored in a
retrieval system, or transmitted in any form or by any means, without
the prior permission in writing of the publisher, nor be otherwise circulated
in any form of binding or cover other than that in which it is published
and without a similar condition including this condition
being imposed on the subsequent purchaser.

A CIP catalogue record for this book
is available from the British Library.

ISBN 978-1-84408-955-0

Typeset in Goudy by M Rules
Printed and bound in Great Britain by
Clays Ltd, St Ives plc

Papers used by Virago are from well-managed forests
and other responsible sources.

MIX
Paper from
responsible sources
FSC® C104740

Virago Press
An imprint of
Little, Brown Book Group
100 Victoria Embankment
London EC4Y 0DY

An Hachette UK Company
www.hachette.co.uk

www.virago.co.uk

Contents

Introduction

At a white-tiled table a young girl was sitting, sucking a
bullseye and sewing a shroud ... She was nineteen, pretty,
undersized and Welsh; hideously dressed in striped cotton, a
square-bibbed apron that reached her high collar, black
shoes and stockings and a stiff white cap.

... the child who presently would wear the shroud was
lying with a pinched, waxy face, breathing jerkily through
a half-open mouth. An apparatus of glass and rubber tubing
was running salt and water into her veins to eke out the
exhausted blood. It was all that could now be done ... The
little nurse stitched doggedly away ... She had made plenty
of shrouds; the first few had made her feel creepy, but they
were just like the rest of the mending and darning now.

Mary Renault was in her early thirties when her first novel,
Purposes of Love, was published. That quiet but dramatic opening was also a mischievous one. Neither the young nurse nor
the child would make it past page two. Instead, the story is
thrown down a staircase, along with a heap of soiled laundry,
into the hands of Vivian, a trainee nurse, whose experience of
both hospital life and an intense relationship with Mic, an
assistant pathologist, makes up the core of the book. So far, so

hospital romance conventional. But it isn't long before a fellow female nurse seduces Vivian and we discover that Mic has had an affair with her brother. By anyone's lights, such a book, coming out in 1939, marked the arrival of a bold new voice.

For those who, like me, grew up gorging themselves on Mary Renault's historical stories of ancient Greece, it may come as a surprise that for the first twenty years of her career she wrote only contemporary novels. For others more attuned to the homosexual subculture that the Greek novels explored, or having read *The Charioteer*, published in the 1950s, it will be less of a revelation to learn that even as a fledgling popular novelist she was interested in issues of sexuality and sexual orientation, writing with a directness that made some people, including an early reviewer of *Purposes of Love*, wonder if the author's name might be a mask for a man.

In fact, Mary Renault *was* a pseudonym, but not one designed to protect her gender. She was born Eileen Mary Challans, the first daughter of a middle-class doctor, in 1905 in London's East End. Her early memories show an intelligent, strong-willed child with an independent streak, no doubt exacerbated by her ringside seat on an unhappy marriage. 'I can never remember a time ... when they seemed to me to even like each other,' she wrote later in life to a friend. Though her fiction often takes the knife to frustrated, resentful mothers – both classical and contemporary – she could also be understanding. In her third novel, *The Friendly Young Ladies* (the euphemistic title refers to two women in a sexual relationship), she dramatises elements of her own childhood, but not without sympathy for the wife who, though she is intrusive and manipulative, is also clearly unloved.

Mary's escape from her parents came through education: at the insistence of her university-educated godmother, Aunt

Bertha, she was sent to boarding school in Bristol and then went on to St Hugh's College, Oxford, subsidised by her aunt, as her parents considered the expense wasted on a daughter. An early love for history and literature would colour her whole life, allowing her later to meet the challenge of immersion in Greek history. She became involved in theatre, another passion that was to persist, but in other ways Oxford University in the 1920s was a conservative establishment, especially for the few women who went there, and there was no hint from her friendships with both men and women of the more radical way her life was to develop.

Her first attempt at serious writing came in 1928, when, during her last term at Oxford, she began work on a novel set in medieval England. J. R. R. Tolkien was perhaps an influence, as Mary had attended his lectures and clearly admired him. She was later to destroy the manuscript, dismissing the story as 'knights bashing about in some never-never land', but she was still working on it at twenty-eight when, looking for a way to support herself independently from her parents, she started to train as a nurse at the Radcliffe Infirmary.

It was to be another defining experience. Nursing was extremely hard work, but it offered the burgeoning writer a richness of experience that would have been well nigh impossible for a woman of her class elsewhere at that time. While others were marrying and starting families, she was deep in the business of life and death, meeting people from all backgrounds. It also gave her first-hand knowledge of the human body, in both its wonder and its fragility. All her fiction would drink deeply from these experiences. When she turns her hand to Greek myth and history she will confidently inhabit their overwhelming masculinity, celebrating athletic, erotic male beauty side by side with the heroism and agonies of battles and death.

Meanwhile, the dramas of medicine and illness would permeate all her early novels.

Purposes of Love, not surprisingly, draws heavily on the training she has just come through; even the novel's title is taken from the prayer that the nurses recited every morning. Peopled by a beautifully observed cast of minor characters ('Sister Verdun was a little fretted woman with an anxious bun, entering with a sense of grievance into middle age'), it plunges the reader into the gruelling physicality of hospital life, contrasting the drama of sickness and injury with relentless rules and routine. Near the end of the book we sit with a nurse in night vigil over the mangled body of a dying, but conscious, young man. The scene is rich with the authenticity of detail, but it is clever as well as upsetting, since we know the man much better than the nurse does, which makes her mix of professional care and natural compassion even more affecting. The novel was an impressive debut, and became a bestseller, attracting fine reviews both sides of the Atlantic.

Kind are Her Answers was published the following year. Mary was under considerable pressure to write it quickly as both publishers, especially Morrow in America, wanted it delivered before the outbreak of hostilities. In the end, it came out the week of the evacuation of Dunkirk, in 1940, which meant that it was largely critically ignored. Perhaps for Renault's long-term reputation that was no bad thing, as *Kind are Her Answers* is a much more conventional love story. It has its moments, though. Kit Anderson is a doctor locked in an unhappy marriage, who meets the woman with whom he will have an affair on a night visit to her seriously ill aunt. For a modern audience, the sexual passion is the most convincing part of the story. Their hungry young bodies make a painful contrast with the old woman's ageing, fading one and the adrenaline of risk and proximity of death adds to their abandon; during his unofficial night visits they must keep their voices down when they make love in case they are heard.

Return to Night (1947), which won Mary the MGM prize, a whopping £150,000, is a doctor–patient romance, though it cunningly inverts the stereotype by putting a woman, Hilary, in the white coat. The book opens with a riding accident and the time-bomb of internal bleeding inside the brain, which Hilary must diagnose in order to save a handsome young man's life. Renault had done a stint working on head injuries and the drama of the diagnosis and the tussle of wills between the complacent matron and the woman doctor is expertly played out.

In her fifth novel *North Face* (1949) nursing becomes character rather than plot. Inside a love story between two guests in a Yorkshire boarding house after the war, Renault uses two women in their thirties as a kind of spatting Greek chorus, ruminating on the morality (or not) of the affair. Already very much professional spinsters, one is a desiccated prissy academic, while the other is a blowzy, more down-to-earth professional nurse. Though the satire is at the expense of them both (at times they are more entertaining than the rather laboured love story), the nurse at least feels in touch with life. If Mary Renault had ever considered academia, this is surely her verdict on the choice she made.

But nursing did more than fire her fiction. It also changed her life. It was while training at the Radcliffe, living inside a set of rules to rival the most oppressive girls' boarding school, that Mary met twenty-two-year-old Julie Mullard. The coming together of their fictional equivalents after an evening tea party in one of the nurses' rooms is one of many perfectly realised scenes in *Purposes of Love*. Mary Renault and Julie Mullard were to be a couple until Mary's death. In England they mostly lived apart, often working in different hospitals, snatching precious weeks in holiday cottages or visiting each other under the radar of the rules. Then, in 1948, helped by the money Mary had won for *Return to Night*, they moved to South Africa.

Despite the fact that they would live openly and happily together for the next thirty-five years, neither would refer to herself as lesbian, nor talk publicly about their relationship (though elements of it are there to be read in Mary's fiction: the character of Vivian is clearly a mix of both of them, even down to the dramatisation of the short affair that Julie had with a hospital surgeon soon after they met). Some of their reticence can be explained by Renault's own personality: private and contained, with success she became more so. Some of it was no doubt a throwback to the difficult moral climate in which they began their relationship; the only contemporary public example of lesbian culture had been Radclyffe Hall's provocative *Well of Loneliness* and both of them found it 'self-pitying'. But it was more nuanced than that.

In 1982, a year before her death, Renault was the subject of a BBC film directed by the late writer and poet David Sweetman, who later went on to write a biography of her. I was a good friend of David's at the time and, like many gay men I knew, he was eloquent about the place Renault's novels had played in his life. When he asked her about the sexuality in her work, she had this to say: 'I think a lot of people are intermediately sexed. It's like something shading from white to black with a lot of grey in the middle.'

The words describe perfectly much of the shifting sexual territory Renault fictionalised in her first five novels. For the sharp-eyed, *The Friendly Young Ladies*, published in 1944, is a portrait of a sexual relationship between Leo(nora), writer of cowboy novels – Mary herself loved cowboy fiction – and

Helen, a lovely and talented nurse who has the odd dalliance with men. We meet them first through the eyes of Leo's young sister, who runs away from home to stay with them. Suffused with Mills & Boon sensibility, she sees only what she wants to see; Leo's tomboy manner and clothes, the shared bedroom and the domestic familiarity are all taken at platonic face value. A young doctor, full of his own psychological insights, is equally blinkered, trying his hand with both women (and being turned down more because of his personality than his gender). It makes for playful story-telling as it divides not only Renault's characters, but presumably also her readership. In the end, this cosy set-up is broken apart by the rugged American writer Joe, who has a night of passion with Leo that results in what feels like a conventional but unconvincing happy ending.

Interestingly, in 1982, when, on the recommendation of Angela Carter, Virago reissued the novel, Mary herself wanted to alter the ending. In a letter to the publisher, written barely a year before her death, she said: 'You will see I have marked a cut of several pages near the end, and will I am sure agree that this was a thoroughly mushy conclusion ... far better leave Leo's choice in the air with the presumption that she stays with Helen. The ending I gave it looks now like a bow to convention, which it wasn't, but it was certainly an error of judgement.' A compromise was reached, and instead of changing the text she wrote a new afterword, which is reproduced again now.

The same criticism of an imposed happy ending might also be levelled against *Return to Night*, where the heroine doctor falls in love with Julian, the young male patient she saves. Breathtakingly beautiful, emotionally quixotic and under the thumb of a domineering mother, Julian yearns to be an actor and a halo of sexual ambivalence hovers over him throughout the novel. Hilary meanwhile, eleven years older, in a man's job with what could be a man's name, finds herself cast as half lover, half mother. As they head towards the happily-ever-after of marriage you can't help thinking that they would both benefit from more wriggle-room to experiment.

Mary Renault was eventually to find that wider sexual and imaginative freedom in her Greek novels, but not before one last, extraordinary, contemporary book. Freed from the grey British skies of post-war austerity and culture, in 1951 she wrote *The Charioteer*, an explicit portrait of homosexuality during the war. Its rich backdrop is drawn from her experience nursing soldiers in a hospital partly staffed by conscientious objectors, and it tells the story of Laurie, an intelligent, introspective young man, who comes to understand his sexuality through a platonic but profound encounter with Ralph, an older prefect at his public school. Injured at Dunkirk, he goes on day release from hospital and is introduced into a homosexual subculture, in which Ralph, now a naval officer, is a player. The hot-house atmosphere of this hidden society is brilliantly, though not always flatteringly, observed (Renault had had experience of such a world in her early years in South Africa).

Laurie's continued self-analysis and his struggle as to how to live as a gay man, dramatised as a choice between his love for Ralph, who he learns had saved him at Dunkirk, and the growing connection with a young conscientious objector working at the hospital and yet to realise his own homosexuality, make up the rest of the book.

Reading *The Charioteer* now is to be blown away by its intensity and bravery. In 1953, when it came out in Britain, it was a cultural thunderbolt (in America it took another six years to find a publisher); reviews were overwhelmingly positive and Mary received scores of letters from appreciative readers. By then, though, she had moved on and was submerged in two years of research for her next book, which was to be something altogether different.

From the opening sentence of *The Last of the Wine* (1956), ancient Greece and the male voices through which she enters it burn off the page with an immediacy and power that will characterise all her historical fiction. Homosexual love, sacrifice, companionship and heroism abound in a culture which accepts, encourages and celebrates sexual diversity. At nearly fifty, Mary Renault had at last found her world.

Sarah Dunant, 2014

I

Approach from the North

The lane was deep – an outpost of Devon, which was within walking distance if one took walking seriously – and for a couple of hundred yards it ran straight between banks frilled with fern, higher than one's head. Towards the end, meeting trees made it a tunnel, from whose nearer end one could see at the other a round hole of twisted light. Until one emerged, the tower was wholly concealed; to a redundancy of dramatic effect was super-added the element of surprise. New visitors, if alone, would refocus their eyes in suspended belief; or, if not, would exclaim to companions with a certain personal pride. They were off the beaten track, discriminating individualists: their contempt for the promenade at Bridgehead, and even for the nearer cosiness of Barlock, knew no bounds.

The tower reared, sensationally, above the trees. Very naïve explorers took it for part of a ruined castle; the more sophisticated knew it at once for a Folly of the most extravagantly Gothick kind. Its grey battlements, patched with orange lichen, were flimsy; its ornate windows, with their decaying foliations of wrought iron, had never contemplated defence against anything but the drab realities of the Industrial Revolution. In its side was a door, from which a dizzy iron stair, like a fire-escape, went down to a lower ridge of battlements, whose teeth just showed above the trees. It was a thin tower; the upper room which it enclosed could not have been much more than twelve feet by ten, the rest would be filled by a staircase of whose decay the outer supplement said enough. Its pointed roof was topped by an ornate weathercock, knocked to a rakish angle like the feather in a desperado's hat.

The windows were dark, seeming to lay bony fingers on lipless jaws. One thought of walled-up brides; of mad old virgins fingering trousseaux from which the moths flew out; of heirs vainly guarded, till the predestinate birthday, from a Romany curse.

Feasting on these visions, visitors would press forward with the excitement of conquistadores. This coming sharp bend in the lane must bring them in sight of the house itself.

It did.

The very air, hereabouts, seemed printed visibly with outraged anticlimax. Neil Langton merely nodded his head, wondering why he hadn't anticipated it. It seemed to him almost mystically expressive and right.

Consulting his watch, he found that he was a little early. He cached his rucksack, which was heavy, in some bracken behind a field gate, and went off for a walk.

The house looked ready to approve of this nicety. It was two storeys high, with a glossy slate roof over squat gables to which Tudor-type woodwork was externally applied. There were lace curtains and ferns in the bay windows; the front door was painted to simulate wood-graining with a varnish the colour of fresh manure. A precise board on the gatepost said 'Weir

View – Board Residence'. Like a genteel spinster sitting in a disproportionately high-backed chair, the house adhered in smug insignificance to the residual wall, quite ten feet higher than the chimneys, at one end of which was the tower. The iron stairs linked them as a will does two incongruous legatees.

Neil, half turning as he went on down the lane, looked back at the stairs and came nearer to laughing than he had been in six months. Tonight he would be climbing them to bed. He felt as if a god with a mordant sense of humour had cocked a snook at him. Then the flat greyness came down over his mind again. He walked on.

Mrs Kearsey, too, from the concealed doorway in the roof, had just been looking at the tower. She had been to put sheets on the bed, and, among blue air and tree-tops ringed with a receding haze of moors and sea, had felt her embarrassment almost too much to bear. For thirty years she had been trying to live down the Folly by ignoring its existence, and felt now that she was begging a favour of someone with whom she was not on speaking terms. All kinds of people must have seen her on the stairs. They would say she was a profiteer, or, alternatively, that she must be going bankrupt, putting a guest up there; and, as such things were never said to one's face, she couldn't explain how scrupulously she had warned the gentleman in advance that all she had free was 'a small top room in a separate annexe', or that he had replied that this would suit him very well.

He had written from somewhere in the north of Scotland. It was said to be very bleak there, and the inhabitants very hardy; they had outside staircases, too, she had somewhere read. She had also a dim impression that they all went to universities, even the poorest, tramping for miles across the heather from remote crofts; so one could not tell, from a letter, what they might be accustomed to.

Even at the best, life had treated her hardly, she felt, in forcing her to terms with the Folly. Till now, she had always firmly implied that it had nothing to do with *her* house; it was merely something that happened to be left standing after a fire. In fact her father, a jobbing builder who hated waste, had bought up the ruin forty years before, and made use of the one sound wall. His wife and daughter had always felt keenly this parsimony so sensationally advertised. He would never move; after he had lost his savings in speculation he could not afford to, so they had stopped discussing it. Now, after his second stroke, he had clamped it finally round her neck. He would have known no difference, having only the needs of a blind baby, if he had gone to the Institution; but the disgrace was unthinkable, and the Home of Rest cost five guineas a week. Hence the tower. To her friends, she had explained that anything was better than turning people away, their first real holiday since the war and all the hotels full.

It was mainly to recover a sense of social security that she went straight from the roof to the Lounge. Here everything was modern and in nice taste; nothing frowsty, nothing queer. She had had it done up in '38, out of her husband's insurance money, at the same time as she had had the second bath put in.

She found two of her guests there: Miss Searle, who had a cold, and Miss Fisher, who had sunbathed all morning on the beach and, as she now admitted, overdone it a bit. 'It's my colouring,' she explained. 'I'm like it every year. No proper pigmentation.' Miss Fisher, a hospital sister, had an impressive vocabulary of words like this.

Mrs Kearsey liked Miss Fisher, while admitting to herself that Miss Searle gave the house more tone. With her Mrs Kearsey aspired to no communion, but felt her presence to be an asset against the liability of the tower. A sudden and sinking anxiety possessed her lest this Mr Langton should be one of those who didn't quite know where to stop in the way of fun. It was to Miss Searle that she said brightly, but with an undertone of propitiation, 'Shall I expect you both in to tea? I was just thinking of putting in some scones.'

'How very nice,' said Miss Searle, and added on inquiry that her cold was much better; Miss Fisher had most kindly given her something for it. They all discussed remedies. Mrs Kearsey's pleasure in the lounge was increased by their harmony; she had been afraid at first that they weren't going to hit it off. The Winters were out so much that they seemed scarcely to count; besides, they were leaving in a day or two.

'I'll bring tea straight in, as soon as the scones are done. We won't wait for Mr Langton. I can always make a fresh pot if he comes.'

She hovered in the doorway, studying effects. She had been seven years in the business, and had observed that unattached women, if their stay fell in with what she called 'one of the all-female spells', very infrequently booked another year. Financially, nowadays, this did not matter – she had refused three bookings only today – but she felt her prestige involved. Not, perhaps, that this would apply to Miss Searle, who though scarcely, if at all, past her thirties, had what Mrs Kearsey (quelled by the books she left about) vaguely called Other Interests. Sure enough, Miss Searle made no comment at all, but fished her handkerchief out of the sleeve of her cardigan and unobtrusively blew her nose; it was a little pink today, spoiling the well-cut profile which was just too regular to be what one would call distinguished. Miss Fisher, however, could always be relied on to pick up a cue. She was about Miss Searle's age, but dressed (not without some success) a good deal younger. She put up one hand to feel the screw of a floral plastic ear-ring, smoothed a wave in her reddish-sandy hair, and said, 'Got a fresh face for us today, then, Mrs K?'

She had called Mrs Kearsey this since the second day of her stay, when she had come into the kitchen to see to the maid's cut finger. Mrs Kearsey, who hoped she could tell a homely way from real commonness, rather liked it.

'Yes,' she said, adding, 'I do hope he'll turn out nice,' in a tone to establish sympathy, and disclaim responsibility, if he did not. 'A Scotch gentleman, I think. He wrote from Fort William; that's right in the Highlands, isn't it?' Because Miss Searle did not instantly reply, she was taken with sudden loss of faith in her geography, combined with a wish that, before coming in, she had changed her spotted rayon for her blue marocain. Miss Searle often had this effect on her.

'Somebody leaving today?' asked Miss Fisher optimistically; speaking, if she had known it, for Miss Searle as well. Miss Lettice Winter, a natural platinum blonde, was far too evidently aware of her own cinematic charms.

Mrs Kearsey had seen this coming. Attempting ease, and achieving a nervous trill, she explained about the Tower, recalling as she did so an earlier remark of Miss Searle's that it was 'a most interesting ruin', With what she hoped was a light laugh, she added, 'He seems to think he'll quite like it. Aren't men *funny?*'

'Well, they've got their uses, and that's about all you can say for them, eh, Mrs K?' Miss Fisher's fresh square face, her just-perceptible cockney overtones, were soothing as a pair of old shoes. She counted twelve stitches rapidly on her pale-blue knitting and added, 'Must be one of those with a head for heights.'

'He must, mustn't he?' said Mrs Kearsey brightly; but her good moment was over. A new and worse set of misgivings, their climax a coroner's censure headlined in the *Mirror*, seized her. Murmuring something about the oven, she hurried out to worry undisturbed.

Miss Searle had no kitchen in which to hide. She picked up her Trollope again; but Miss Fisher's clicking needles distracted her, not so much by their noise as by their reminder of an aimless, vacant mind awaiting conversation. It was like trying to enjoy a meal with someone else's dog begging beside the chair. She earnestly hoped that the new guest would be of a type sympathetic to Miss Fisher, that he would return her interest at sight, would have a car, and petrol, and would take her out every day. For the second time in an hour, Miss Searle reminded herself that she had come prepared for Miss Fisher, in general if not in particular. She had determined on a cheap holiday this year, in order to save for an unstinted one as soon as the Continent was open. It would, perhaps, have been more sensible to have stayed with Muriel; but after five landlocked years she had starved for the sea. She had not expected that this hunger would be so quickly appeased. She had bathed twice, and, shivering with the cold which had begun yesterday, felt indifferent if she never bathed again. She had seen the thatched white cottages, with the pink and blue hydrangeas, facing the little harbour whose smell of seaweed had ceased to excite. She had been to the top of the cliffs, where the bracken attracted flies, and impenetrable woods, clothing the faces down to sea-level almost everywhere, obstructed the view. She had seen a Norman porch and an Early English font. She had reached a stage in which she might even have visited a cinema: but Barlock was proudly unspoiled; she had chosen it for this.

Miss Searle had always considered boredom an intellectual defeat. She prepared to fall back on her inner resources, and got out her Chaucer (Skeat's edition, which she would be reading with the second-year students next term) and a new paper on Old French metrical forms. She had them with her now, in case Miss Fisher should go out; a diminishing hope, which Mrs Kearsey's promise of an early tea had finally destroyed.

Failing to concentrate on *Dr Thorne*, she would have liked to look up; but Miss Fisher would treat it as an invitation, and might embark on another hospital anecdote. Nursing was a noble vocation, but, tragically, coarsening. In Miss Searle's view, one made a sufficient contribution to realism by admitting that the Seamy Side existed. To dwell on it, if with feeling and intelligence, was morbid; if with humour, gross. Miss Fisher's last story had been quite definitely tainted with grossness.

She could have borne Miss Fisher (she often told students to whom other encouragement could not truthfully be given that the world needed Martha as well as Mary) if the whole house had not been like an extension of her. Choosing a moment when she was counting stitches, Miss Searle looked at the Lounge. She would have preferred to its mean little parodies of functional simplicity even the jungle of Victoriana which must have gone originally with the Tower. That would have had character, at least. (Miss Searle delighted in character, if it was safely uncontemporary; if not she called it eccentricity, obtrusiveness, or lack of proportion.) As for the bedrooms, 'done' with shiny rayon taffeta in orange, pink or electric blue – hers was pink – their hideousness made it impossible even to read there. She wondered, passingly, how Mr Langton would like his room in the tower. The thought of this Beckfordian eyrie, enclosing a perfect Tottenham Court Road interior, made her fine colourless lips move in a faint smile.

Miss Fisher's ball of wool rolled off her lap, and over to Miss Searle's feet. She reached for it as Miss Searle stooped politely.

For a moment their hands met on the ball: the hand of a scholar, meticulous, with fineness but no strength in the bone, taut veins blue under the thin skin at the back, the nails ribbed, brittle and flecked here and there with white; the other broad-palmed and short-fingered, with the aggressive smooth cleanliness that comes of much scrubbing with antiseptic followed by much compensating cream, the nails filed short and round, their holiday varnish spruce. Each woman was momentarily aware of the contrast.

When thanks and apologies had been exchanged, and Miss Searle had picked up her book again, Miss Fisher stole a look at her under sandy lashes which could not, like hair, be deepened with a henna rinse, and on which mascara would have been too obvious. It was a look which Miss Searle had once or twice intercepted with indefinable unease. It was more transparent than Miss Fisher knew; a compound of patronage with envy and respect. If she had been a Frenchwoman, Miss Fisher would have expressed the patronage in the words 'Miss Anglaise'. What Miss Searle felt to be mental and conversational decency, Miss Fisher saw as an iron curtain of spinsterly repression. With sincere conviction, she thought it more unpleasant than crudeness. Her own standards had been shaped by her work, in which from the age of eighteen she had learned to regard prudery as a social crime: young medical students must be helped over their first awkwardness, shy patients must find their confidences aseptically eased. She took all this so much for granted that she could not have found words for what she felt, which was that for a mature adult to force evasion on others was selfish, discourteous, and a mark of moral cowardice besides.

'Inhibited,' said Miss Fisher to herself, looking with sad wistfulness at the plain, perfect handmade shoes, recalling the worn hide case with the foreign labels, trying unsuccessfully to recall

9

elusive vocal cadences, the precision of vowels. In the presence of Miss Searle an old humiliation, like an irreparable bereavement, returned to haunt her: an occasion when walking back after a party a young resident, tender and sentimental and only a little drunk, had tried to talk to her about Housman. She had thought he said 'houseman,' and had replied humorously. He had turned it off with a hurt clumsy joke; the evening's promise had frosted in bud. A *Shropshire Lad*, which she had read next day against a return of opportunity that never came, remained with her like a scent with sorrowful associations, having no independent life.

Miss Fisher was not, in the ordinary social sense, a snob. During a spell of private nursing she had slid bedpans under a representative section of the British upper classes, encountering the usual averages of cheerful pluck and querulous selfishness. Their preoccupations had often differed from those of her own circles only in scale; they had soon ceased to have any mystery for her. Bound since she was eighteen to a routine of uncompromising realism, Miss Fisher craved for strangeness, for otherness, for all that eluded tables of measurement, more deeply than she knew. Hence the spell that intellectuals still worked for her; they had to be very disagreeable before she stopped making allowances for them. Ideally, she liked them unconventional and unpractical, but fairly clean in their persons and with a sense of humour; when she would describe them as Bohemian, her most distinguished term of praise. She had had initial hopes, soon dashed, of Miss Searle.

When Miss Fisher had time to daydream, which was seldom, it was of belonging to this race and of being accepted in it. Sometimes it had vaguely occurred to her that membership was a by-product, not a point of direction like a mink coat, but, like an adolescent who dreams of fame and will decide later for what he shall be famous, she willed the end, not the means. One day, at a party, on a bus, through some consequence yet hanging in the stars, a citizen of El Dorado would take her hand and lead her through the invisible doors, and, magically, she would be there. Meanwhile, she solaced the waiting-time by tuning in to Frank Sinatra, and reading the serials in *Woman and Home* which had good knitting-patterns as well.

Miss Searle put a marker in her Trollope and said, 'I do hope your sunburn won't give you a painful night.' It was impossible to read; she remembered Miss Fisher's kindness about the cold-tablets; besides, tea would be here at any moment now.

'It was more the headache, really, thanks. I took some APC and it's nearly gone.' Here, Miss Fisher felt obscurely, was an inheritor of the invisible key who let it rust on a nail. She thought, 'If *I'd* had her advantages . . . ' The tea came in; there was a polite contest of withdrawals from pouring-out; Miss Searle, who hated strong tea, allowed herself to be persuaded. A third cup was on the tray; it stood, a bland, blank question-mark, midway between them.

Miss Fisher, sipping her tea, wished that Miss Searle had thought to stir the pot; she had not liked to suggest it. Conversation faltered and died; she felt that it was her turn to revive it.

'I wonder what we've got coming,' she essayed politely.

Miss Searle, who perceived at once what was meant but did not feel equal to it, expressed silently a civil interrogation.

'The new PG, I mean.' Miss Fisher remembered Miss Searle's cold; it was on herself that cheerfulness devolved. 'This mystery-man that's going up into Rookery Nook.'

'Oh, yes, of course. I'm so sorry. Do have another scone. Mrs Kearsey really manages very well on the rations, don't you think?'

'Ta, after you. Well, hope springs eternal, they say, but I expect it'll be a case of a castle in the air, more senses than one, don't you?'

'I'm afraid I don't quite ...?' Would even Rome and Florence, Miss Searle was wondering, make up for the weeks spent in this mental slum?

'Well, I mean to say, with men in the short supply they are, if they've got anything *to* them they don't need to go to boarding-houses on their own. Mind you, it was different before the war. I've started out once or twice not knowing a soul, and had the time of my life. But not now; not unless you go to these holiday camp places, and goodness knows *who* you might pick up there. I'm afraid I'm too fussy who I go about with.'

'Yes,' said Miss Searle. 'Quite.' But the hot tea and her cold conspired together against her. She snatched at her handkerchief. Miss Fisher put down her terseness entirely to force of circumstances.

'Must be this side of sixty, anyway. Mrs K's pretty straight, she wouldn't have poked him up there without giving him some sort of hint what he was in for. Nice if he turned out to be a Raf type, demob, leave or something. But what a hope.'

'I don't suppose' – Miss Searle tucked back her handkerchief – 'that we shall see a great deal of him, in any case.'

'I follow you there all right.' Miss Fisher felt she was getting a response at last; she warmed. 'Not if that Winter girl sees him coming. Talk about a fast little bit—' With some presence of mind, she clipped off two consonants just in time.

'Oh? Miss Winter goes out so much; I'm afraid I've noticed her very little.'

This time, Miss Searle had managed a clear articulation. Miss Fisher bent over her plate; the scone she was crumbling made a film of margarine on her fingers. Her sunburned brow stung like fire. Miss Searle must have caught the word after all.

Rolling, obliviously, a greasy crumb, Miss Fisher relived, as rapidly as the drowning, the bad moments of a lifetime: the Housman disaster; the time when she had called a bishop Mister; the cocktail party to which she had gone in a backless evening gown. With it all, she felt an inarticulate sense of wrong. The Miss Searles got the last word so easily, by freezing explanation. She would have liked somehow to make clear that she had let slip a bit of occupational slang, whose specialised place she really knew quite well; that she wasn't interested in Raf types only because they made good escorts, but because some of them, when she looked in with a hot drink just before the night staff came on, had unburdened themselves of things not known to their mothers or their girls. All this struggled within her, hopelessly; she groped for her handkerchief and wiped her fingers clean.

'I see in this morning's paper,' said Miss Searle, relenting in victory, 'that we can expect some settled weather for the next few days.'

A couple of hundred yards up the road, Neil was folding away his map. The scale was irritatingly small; inch-to-the-mile editions showed no sign of reappearing, and his pre-war collection had not covered this unfamiliar ground. Well, he could make his own. Why not? He had nothing better to do, or, certainly, to think about.

Two-inch to the mile; it was unlikely he would get squared paper at the local stationer's. The nearest place ... Disturbed by a vague feeling that there was something he had better do first, he realised that he was hungry. The sensation had become, lately, so unusual that he was slow to recognise it.

Anyway, he thought, the air's good here.

As he disinterred his rucksack from the bracken he remembered that, having travelled down from the north overnight without a sleeper, he would probably be improved by a clean shirt. He swung the rucksack indecisively; but, like everything else nowadays, it didn't seem worth the trouble. Shrugging himself into the straps, he made for the landmark of the tower.

Mrs Kearsey received him at the door with instant misgiving. She had hoped against hope that he would be young enough to find it amusing. Forty-five, she thought, if a day; then subtracted a few years, for he looked very run-down, she thought, and shockingly thin for a man of his length and shoulders. Her spirits, which had sunk at the sight of him, were not raised by a Standard English accent which disposed at a blow of heather and outside stairs. Chattering with nervous brightness while she sought for comfort, she found some reassurance in the shirt. He couldn't be fussy; it was doubtful if he had even shaved today. (Neil owed the benefit of the question to the fact that his beard grew lighter than his hair.) He had forbiddingly little to say; he must have seen the tower as he came up the road. Unable to bear it longer, she committed her fears to words.

'That's all right. I saw it coming along. It'll be quiet up there.'

'Oh, yes, beautifully quiet. You won't know anyone else is in the house. And the bathroom's only just at the foot of the steps, quite handy really. They *look* a bit flimsy, but the builder's not long been over them and says they'll be safe for fifty years. You'll find there's a lovely view.' She paused on this. 'There's just *one* thing, Mr Langton, and be *sure* to tell me, for I'd make arrangements somehow if it meant moving out myself . . .'

'What is it?' asked Neil abruptly. The moment of suspense, the impending of a personal question, scraped like a rough thumb along his nerves. He had had an almost sleepless night in the train, besides.

Taking alarm, Mrs Kearsey dithered, prolonging his discomfort. 'It's nothing, really, only I know some people find ... I mean it's the *height*. Now please be sure to tell me if you can stand looking *down*.'

'Yes, thanks,' said Neil, speaking with rather more irony than he was aware. He had just spent some time on Ben Nevis, going into this question closely. Life had never been much disposed to hand him solutions ready-made.

Sure that she had offended him beyond repair, Mrs Kearsey launched herself into a stream of palliative platitudes; she had seen, too late, the clinker-nailed boots slung outside the rucksack. It took Neil, who was preoccupied, a few moments to realise what it was all about. Pulling himself together, he smiled at her.

'Of course not. Nice of you to worry about it.'

Mrs Kearsey underwent a relaxing process inconsequent to Neil, who was not given to mirrors. Becoming suddenly almost cosy, she showed him the bathroom and went off promising tea. The tapwater was hot; he quite wished he had taken his razor in with him. But never mind. It was after five; the dining-room would be clear by now, he would get a meal in peace.

The door of the Lounge was neither really thick nor quite gimcrack. Incomplete, filtered sounds of arrival had come through it: the bell, Mrs Kearsey's strained twitter, sliding down the register to an easier C natural; infrequent, low-pitched replies, feet, light and decisive on alternate stairs. The feet sounded young.

A conversation, about the difficulty of understanding Russians, drifted rudderless and ran aground. Miss Searle tried to tug it back into the fairway, but broke off to give a careful pat to her nose. Afterwards, she pushed her handkerchief out of sight into the sleeve of her cardigan, and smoothed out the bulge. Miss Fisher stretched her stockings out sideways, looked for rubbed places over the anklebones, and, satisfied, crossed her legs at the knee. They were American nylon; Miss Searle noticed this for the first time. She herself had on woollen ones, because of her cold. Crossing her legs at the ankle, she tucked them under her chair: she was quite unaware, in any cerebral way, of doing this.

Mrs Kearsey came in with tea, a large plate of bread and butter, and some more scones. She flicked at Miss Searle and Miss Fisher a concealed look which had something of con- science about it. Two minutes later she came in again, with a boiled egg.

'One shouldn't spoil them,' she said with guilty brightness. 'I warned him not to expect it again! But you know what the food is, travelling nowadays. I always do think the rationing comes hard on these tall men.'

Miss Searle said nothing. Years of comparison between the endowments of men's and women's colleges had left their mark. Miss Fisher gave a little smile, whether of irony or approval it would have been hard to say, and smoothed the hem of her dress over a stocking knee.

'*Now* I shall have to hurry him up,' said Mrs Kearsey, rapidly filling-in Miss Searle's rather palpable silence. It seemed, from the sound, that she had needed to go no farther than the foot of the stairs.

Miss Fisher thrust her needle carefully through a stitch, a little farther than one does when about to continue. Miss Searle picked up her cup, and had raised it to her lips before becoming aware of the cold dregs at the bottom. There was a tiny pause, like the moment in a darkening theatre when the rustle of pro- grammes ceases to be heard.

The door opened. They were exposed to the first reactions of a man tired, hungry, unkempt after rejecting the opportunity to be tidy, and not totally lacking in convention, who finds himself confronted with two strange women, to whom he must make conversation while eating alone.

It was not a happy moment for anyone. Neil was awkwardly aware that his face had slipped. His social conditioning had returned with force after a single glance at Miss Searle; he knew he must look as if he had slept out. Miss Searle, who in her early twenties had suffered agonies (now almost hidden from memory) at the dances to which she had dutifully gone, felt the aura of male negativism like a cramp in the back of her neck. Miss Fisher came off best. She had had to encounter many disagreeable and defensive people, and was interested besides. Her first instincts were clinical; she wondered what he was convalescing from. His deep tan, combined with his spareness, had suggested tuberculosis until she noticed that his condition was too hard for this. Provisionally, she decided he might have been a prisoner with the Japanese. There was a certain look about the eyes; and besides ... But, the occasion being a social one, she was as careful as Miss Searle not to take a second glance at his hair, in which, flattened by a hasty brushing, the dead yellow-white stripe across the forehead assaulted the eye as violently as a facial scar.

Introductions were exchanged; the visitor acknowledged them with stiff little bows, and apologised for himself; he had been travelling all night, he explained. Miss Searle almost said they had heard as much, but changed her mind; he looked so guarded that even this seemed too personal an intrusion. Aloud, she said that travelling nowadays was nothing short of an ordeal, and of course, they quite understood.

Miss Fisher, with one part of her mind, was thinking, The time he must have been repatriated, they ought to have put more flesh than that on him by now: nursed him in one of these makeshift temporary dumps, perhaps. He had no scarring from boils or jungle-sores, she noticed, and she left the diagnosis open; for her personality hung divided. The voice, the carriage, the travel-stained clothes which carried for her the stamp of a lordly indifference, pulled the secret cords of her imagination. Beyond its façade of washed tile and chromium, a casement opened in a mysteriously intact ivory tower.

Seized by an adolescent shyness, she remembered with comfort her nylon stockings, anchors of self-confidence in an uncertain world. Flexing her ankles becomingly, she extended them a little. Unhappily, it was only Miss Searle's eye which was caught by the movement. Mr Langton was looking, with an embarrassed formality, from the tea-table to Miss Searle.

'No, no; we finished long ago. That's yours.'

Feeling uncomfortable and inhibited, Neil dissected one of the scones, which would have been an easy mouthful if he had been alone. He cheered himself by remembering that, except for breakfast and supper, this was the last meal to which he need ever be in. Meanwhile, since he looked like a tramp, he had better make some effort not to eat like one. He resented this social necessity, as he had come to resent most others. Conscientiously, he asked them what the weather had been like in this part of the world.

Relieved, they informed him between them that he had just missed some terrible days, and that the local people predicted a fine spell now. Neil expressed pleasure; he was doing his best, and did not know that he sounded like someone receiving information about Patagonia. Discovering the egg, and at the same time losing all enthusiasm for food (this often happened now) he asked if the place were a good one for walking, just in time to avert an abysmal pause.

They were both aware, before they had carried this topic far, that the question had only aimed at embarking them on something which would need the minimum of concentration and reply. Most of the running was made by Miss Searle, who tried, by an intelligent impersonal manner, to dissociate herself from Miss Fisher's hosiery display. She was almost physically embarrassed by women whose manner altered in the presence of men. Owing to the bad weather and her cold, most of her information had been acquired at second-hand, and covered a radius of about three miles. It gradually emerged, from Mr Langton's civil replies, that his notion of moderate exercise was in the region of twenty. Conversation flagged again.

Suddenly finding her voice, Miss Fisher said, 'Do for goodness' sake make a proper tea. We had our turn making pigs of ourselves, before you came.'

'I'm doing fine,' said Neil, much relieved by her comfortable commonness; he had hoped that all his fellow-guests would be of this unexacting kind. It was past the season for well-to-do holidays. He had placed Miss Searle at once as a schoolmistress, and wondered what she was doing here at the beginning of term.

Miss Searle, who had failed to detect the signs of an even unconventional donnishness, was making the same speculation. She noticed his hands, long, bony, and, she thought, scholarly; failing to notice their rigidly controlled flexibility, and a tensile strength which reflected experience alone does not impart. Pleasantly conscious of the contrast between Miss Fisher's voice and her own, she said, 'One's really very fortunate if one can get away at this time of year. I was teaching in schools before I came back to Oxford, and I used always to feel very ill-used at being fetched back at the beginning of the September weather. It's so often the loveliest of the year.'

'Yes,' said Mr Langton. There was an awkward silence; he stirred his tea. In the manner of a man keeping himself up with difficulty to a resolution, he added flatly, 'I'm a schoolmaster myself.'

'Indeed?' Perhaps he was taking a grace-term. 'What is your subject?'

'Classics.'

His taciturnity, she thought, verged on the brusque. Having volunteered so much, he must surely expect some kind of comment; perhaps he was merely shy. She checked herself on the verge of asking whether he had been at Oxford; this would lead, inevitably, to dates, and Miss Searle often thought she had aged a good deal less than some of her contemporaries. She waited, expecting him to name his present school; but this he showed no sign of doing.

'I can't, I suppose, possibly have seen you at Winchester?' she asked, to remind him of this omission. 'I've a nephew there I visit now and again.'

'No. I think not.'

His face, and his voice, were simply a full-stop.

Not since her own schooldays had Miss Searle felt such a helpless sense of mortification. She opened her bag, and aimlessly looked inside it.

Suddenly he looked up, as if, by some delayed process, he had only just heard himself. With a difficult, painstaking smile he added, 'Perhaps I've got a double there.'

Forced as the smile had been, it had held something more than recollected manners; an instinctive kindness seemed to move in it faintly, like old habit overlaid. It restored to his mouth for a moment a guarded humour, and still more guarded idealism, which had, perhaps, once been characteristic. But it came too late for Miss Searle, whom the preceding snub had unnerved past all perception. She murmured something, without looking up, about her memory for faces being very poor.

'You won't have time for much of a holiday, will you, before the schools go back again?'

It was Miss Fisher, rushing blithely in past the warning signs. Her voice, however, had not the note of inquiry so much as of an instinctive solicitude. Perhaps for this reason, it sounded commoner than ever; when she said 'the schools', asphalt playgrounds labelled 'Boys' and 'Girls' leaped to the mind. Miss Searle, waiting, felt quite sorry for her in advance.

Mr Langton turned round. Relief showed in his face, relaxing the hard downward lines which were like, and unlike, the prematurely-ageing lines of work and worry in the very poor.

'Are you in the profession too, Miss – er – I'm sorry . . .?'

'Fisher's the name.' Her evident pleasure in the question, so clearly a red-herring, faintly amused Miss Searle. 'No, I'm not that brainy. I'm a nurse – a sister, matter of fact.'

He proceeded, promptly, to draw her out about hospital nationalisation. While he talked, a different personality emerged, like the reviving stuff of routine. He could be imagined dealing competently, but not without some genuine feeling, with the awkwardness of boys at Sunday tea-parties, the fuss of parents, the recurrent feuds of the staff. Even now, when the manner was quite clearly self-protective, it somehow failed to suggest an uncaring exploitation. Miss Fisher gave of her best. She had forgotten her stockings, and had crossed her legs indifferently at the calf.

Miss Searle's cold, which had only begun last night, began to advance into its second stage with the quickened tempo often observed in the evening hours. Her skin crept and winced, her back ached, a feeling of sodden thickness spread from her face to her brain. She had to get out her handkerchief, whose size embarrassed her. It was chilly upstairs, and her hurt pride flinched from open retreat. If she had been staying with Muriel, she would have had a bedroom fire and tray.

'What our boys are worrying about,' Miss Fisher was saying, 'isn't their pay and hours and all that. What have they got to lose? They're working round the clock for pocket-money, as it is. It's the way these Civil Service types gum everything up. It's bad enough now, waiting three months for a permit to build a new sluice, before they start on the patients. You can't fit an emergency into a buff form; and some of these forlorn-hope treatments, that *may* come off, are off the track and maybe expensive. By the time it's been pushed through a few in-trays and out-trays and passed-to-you-please, where's the case going to be? Fixed up tidily after the post-mortem, waiting for the flowers to arrive.'

'I suppose so. Excuse me; I have to unpack.'

The door closed quietly. Miss Fisher, who had not nearly finished, was drawing breath for the next sentence before she was well aware that he was gone. The displaced air of the room seemed to snap together behind him, as if at the contact of some hidden violence not expressed in sound.

Presently Miss Searle said, 'What an extraordinary man.' She spoke with emphatic disapproval, and at once felt obscurely that she had put herself at a disadvantage.

'Not what you might call forthcoming,' said Miss Fisher. Her feelings had been not less wounded than Miss Searle's before; the fact that, unlike Miss Searle, she partly blamed herself (for the professional feeling had persisted) made her feel no better. Suddenly the room enclosed a confidential warmth of female understanding.

'Your cold *has* come on heavy. You ought not to be up.' Miss Fisher felt that Miss Searle, who had established common ground, only to have it kicked rudely from under her, was the more deeply injured party. Her voice expressed this, and she felt that it was not resented. 'Why don't you pop into bed? I know how it is with landladies, you don't like to put on them; but I'll ask her for a tray and just run up with your supper myself. It's no trouble, truly.'

'Oh, but on your holiday. I couldn't think of it.' But she mopped her nose, encouraging further persuasion. The thought of facing at supper both a headache and Mr Langton's aggressive reticence, was too much. She yielded. Miss Fisher, who said she never used her hottie unless it got much colder than this, promised to fill it and bring it along.

She had intended to do this immediately, but paused to pick up the book which lay, forgotten, at the foot of Miss Searle's chair. She could bring it along with the bottle; but, seeing the title, she was fascinated by its bulk. Dimly recollecting a selected textbook at school, she had conceived *The Canterbury Tales* as a thin feuilleton. The archaisms within made her see Miss Searle with new eyes. A brain like that was enough to choke off any man; Miss Fisher's envy was for the first time mixed with a protective feeling.

Idly she continued to thumb the pages, finding odd passages which spelling and inflexion did not wholly disguise, and feeling pleased with herself for getting some sense out of it. This one, *The Miller's Tale*, seemed homely stuff enough. Presently she paused, startled; turned up a glossary she had discovered at the end; and read, incredulously, the passage again.

Well, said Miss Fisher to herself. Doesn't that show you? I've met *that* sort before. Sit talking to the Vicar all through visiting hours, but when they're coming round the anaesthetic, you have to keep the junior pro out of the room. And then she has the nerve ... It won't hurt her to let her

23

know I had a look inside. In hospital, I'd be running round on duty with a cold no worse than hers. Better take her temperature, though, I suppose.

Miss Searle, whom she found pottering in a dressing-gown, received the bottle cordially and got into bed. Waiting for the thermometer to register, Miss Fisher noticed the fineness of her white silk nightgown and bed-jacket; also their complete opacity and lack of moulded cut. They combined, mysteriously, the utmost fastidiousness with complete absence of allure. There was a faint scent of eau-de-Cologne in the room.

The thermometer read 97.8; Miss Fisher, rinsing it, decided that no more compunction was called for. She was just opening her mouth when Miss Searle said, gratefully, 'And you've even brought up my Chaucer. You *are* spoiling me. Now I've everything round me I can possibly want.'

Miss Fisher eyed her with mystified concentration. She knew more about human behaviour than about Middle English; this total unself-consciousness could only be genuine. A happy and charitable thought struck her. It was a long book; Miss Searle couldn't have got there yet.

'Is it an interesting book?' she asked, delicately sounding.

Miss Searle smiled, on the brink of a polite assent (there really seemed nothing else to say); but the *naïveté* of the question moved her. She scented in it a stifled intellectual curiosity, to which all that was best of the pedagogue in her responded.

'You'd hardly imagine that anyone *could* find it interesting, after going back to it again and again for fifteen years—' (Fifteen *years*, thought Miss Fisher; she must know it off by heart!) ' – but do you know, I never really get tired of it. Both technically and humanly, it's almost inexhaustible. The vitality, the fascinating touches of realism.' Gratified by the rapt stare in Miss Fisher's eyes, she went on: 'It seems unbelievable that for centuries his verse was thought to be irregular and crude. Because of the changing sound-laws, of course—'

Miss Fisher could hold herself in no longer.

'That's ever so interesting. I thought he was supposed to be – well – rather rude?'

'Well, of course,' said Miss Searle serenely, 'some of his humour has a coarseness that would be quite inconceivable in the present day. But . . . '

The pleasant, well-modulated voice ran on. Groping after enlightenment, Miss Fisher thought: She hasn't noticed that it's about *people*. It's poetry, in a book, with clever rhymes and all that, by someone who's dead. Advancing from this partial truth another step, she decided, It's her job, after all. Sort of smooths out one bit of you, and leaves the rest.

Miss Searle too, after her fashion, had been traversing a gap of understanding in the opposite direction. There was a hesitant little pause; neither succeeded in expressing what she felt.

Miss Fisher said, at length, 'It must be nice, being able to read it straight off. It looks just like a foreign language, to me.'

'It's so much a matter of the spelling. If you heard it read – but I'm keeping you.'

'No, do read me a bit, if your throat's not too sore.'

'Thank you, it's past that stage. But I'm afraid I shan't do it justice.' On an impulse, she put aside the *Tales* and picked up the *Minor Poems* from the bedside table. Something short and self-contained. A little concession to modern pronunciation would, she thought, in this instance be justifiable.

Miss Fisher listened languidly, content to have extended her olive-branch. It was the *Balade de Bon Conseil*. The opening seemed to her rather sententious. The even voice read on, with the slight increase of power which Miss Searle had kept in reserve:

'That thee is sent, receive in buxomness,
  The wrestling for this world asketh a fall.
Here is no home, here is but wilderness:
  Forth, pilgrim, forth! Forth, beast, out of thy stall!
  Know thy countree, look up, thank God of all:
Hold the high way, and let thy ghost thee lead,
And truth thee shall deliver, it is no drede.'

Taking Miss Fisher by surprise, a prickling made itself felt in the back of her neck, and a shiver in her throat. She blinked. The next verse was a short one; the poem was finished. She swallowed hard.

'Well,' she said. 'That was ever so nice. I hope your voice isn't tired.'

'Not at all. Do borrow the book at any time, if you'd care to.'

'Thanks ever so.'

'When this wretched cold of mine is a little better, perhaps we might go exploring together one day, if you're free.'

'I'd love to. We might go along to the coach-office and see if they've any good trips.'

As in many chemical reactions, while the precipitate settled quietly at the bottom of the vessel, the reagent, with a different specific gravity, floated at the top. It was falling dusk; a light defined the lancet windows of the tower. Having decided that he could not face any more civilised conversation today, Neil Langton prepared to slip out quietly for an early dinner somewhere, and get to bed.

2

Weather Report

Late sun slanted along the bracken, throwing every clump and curve into relief; deeply luminous towards the west, to the east richly shadowed; on the grand scale, the hills repeated the theme. Far ahead, beyond the thickly wooded cliffs which hid the shore, the sea lay in tiny glittering pleats. Every pebble and rut on the track seemed to yield up, under the loving exploration of the light, a separate rejoicing personality.

Neil's shadow, grotesquely lengthened, shot obliquely before him, playing in a spirit of good-humoured caricature with the limp from his blistered heel. Either his sock must be through, or he had darned it in a hurry; he must really get himself out of this. The pain should have offered a kind of distraction, but he was worried lest he should be too lame to walk tomorrow. 'Sometimes I sits and thinks, and sometimes I just sits.' The second alternative still remained an aspiration.

The lit bracken shivered, subtly, in a light breeze; a dark cloud-shadow caressed a hill in passing. Conversations were going on everywhere, in which once he had been included. It was foolish, he supposed, not to have been prepared for this destruction along with the rest. He should be grateful, perhaps, for the illusion that such things would remain; it had kept him alive for the first few weeks, till living had established itself as a habit. Besides, what was happening now would have happened anyway, he supposed, in another twenty years, though imperceptibly then, like the stiffening of muscles and the resistance of the intellect to new ideas. Little by little the spirit would have ceased to answer the eyes, the mind would quietly have taken over. A fine day, a temperate breeze, an interesting conformation there in the hills. 'I only have relinquished one delight, To live beneath your more habitual sway.' (William Wordsworth: *Ode on Intimations of Impotence in Early Middle-Age*.)

Perhaps it had been some inner reluctance to make the test which had sent him, when he left the school, to London. At the time he had only said to himself that no one attracted more than five seconds' notice there. From this point of view, it had been quite a success. His friends had well-defined orbits, easily avoided; he had existed for some months untroubled by any human contacts beyond those involved in saying 'Yes, thank you,' to a mercifully laconic landlady, and 'No, thank you,' to the varied assortment of prostitutes whom he attracted by a tendency to take long walks at night. They seemed to have a sixth sense for him (like flies for a carrion, he thought) but with practice were easily out-manoeuvred, except when they emerged from doorways in one's path. With all these assets, it was a pity that London had to produce its customary effect in the end. The half-felt surrounding swarm, the great skep in which it was a social distinction if one had space to breathe, began to affect him like the smell of a rank, sick animal in a room. When he took to staying in all night as well as all day, he knew that this could not go on much longer. Why should it? It was time now for the mountains. The matter of training would right itself; and at last, there, so would everything else.

He got there well aware that he was not fit to climb, and spent a week walking himself into condition. It took him another week to know what had happened, and several more to believe it.

If his nerve had gone, or his staying-power, he would have been presented with an object in life, and an unimpaired promise beyond it. Indifferent to death, he had been at the top of his form, and it had shown him the truth. The contact was broken. The technique was exercise; the route a mechanical problem; the summit a terminus. Two two-thousands of feet made exactly four.

Always when he had come to the hills happy in himself which was good, they had freed him from himself, which was better. When he had come with what had seemed at the time like trouble, they had lifted it and left him again with something fit to lose. What he brought them now was not acceptable; they handed him back to himself to keep. He had wrestled with them, for a blessing at first like Jacob with the angel, then in anger and for revenge. He had always hoped, when his time came, to die on a climb by some mischance not shaming to his skill. Now, taking meticulous care on increasingly severe routes, he refused to a treacherous ally the satisfaction of killing him; he could manage without this final humiliation. He did nothing unjustifiable by the strictest standards, except to climb alone. He did not feel qualified, now, to lead a party, and saw no reason why other leaders should be responsible for him on a rope. In their place, he would have preferred to pick someone else.

He might still have been there, defying emptiness, if he had not had the folly (or the wisdom) to repeat a climb fifteen years old; it had taken the measure of memory to show him that he was through.

He and Sammy had been twenty-five. On a night in May they had camped high, and in the first twilight done a short but exacting route, with one unexpectedly tense moment; reaching the ridge, they had confronted the sunrise on the other side. Above a world folded in every dark gradation of shadow, the sky rose in profound transparencies of green and blue; a vast wing of cloud, shaped like immortal speed, swept the zenith with a deep but brightening fire purer than snow. They had taken out their food, discussed, now that there was time, the awkward rock-fall in the chimney; and stopped talking to watch the sky. Presently, between two bites at a sandwich, Sammy had spoken with the factual simplicity of someone commenting on the weather. "'We will fall into the hands of God, and not into the hands of men: for as His majesty is, so is His mercy.'" Neil, continuing to eat in peaceful silence, had reflected in a remote kind of interest that at sea-level it would have been embarrassing.

Standing on the same ridge again, he had known that this must be his last climb. Considering, indifferently, where to go from here, he had found the Weir View address in his pocket-book. It was one of several he had noted four years ago for his honeymoon, but rejected as not being good enough. It seemed, now, that it would do.

His rubbed heel was growing tiresome; the blister must have broken. Perhaps after all there might be a tin of small dressings for this kind of purpose in one of his rucksack pockets; he had snatched it up, in the last stages of packing, and had flung in odds and ends on top of the debris of last year. He sat down with it on a bank of mossy grass, through which the ruins of a centuries-old stone wall broke here and there, and found that he was in luck. The tin was there, and heaven knew what rubbish besides. Something caught in his fingers as he fished about. He examined it; a small and very grubby handkerchief, edged with pale blue. It had been folded and pulled lengthways; two corners still showed the creases of an untied knot, and in the centre was a little brown stain, of the size that comes from a scratched ankle. One of the uncrumpled corners was decorated with the word 'Tuesday', and with a pink rabbit wearing a blue coat.

Beside him on the bank, between the roots of a thorn-tree, was a heavy moss-topped stone. He prised it up, brushed from the cavity with careful thoroughness the creeping things disturbed by the light; and, having pressed the half-handful of cotton flat on the earth, replaced the stone. Opening the box of dressings, he attended to his heel.

The plaster clung firmly; the pain of walking was relieved; the mind was left, less fortunately, disengaged. There remained the sometimes helpful expedient of Virgil. He began in his head, his feet marking the beat of the hexameters:

> Nox erat, et placidum carpebant fessa soporem
> corpora per terras, silvaeque et saeva quierant . . .

He broke off; that had too many associations already. It had been a comfort, now and again, to have sleeplessness resolved into so calm a universal. Perhaps, he thought, the more positive effort of translation? He decided on an early nineteenth-century manner, further imposing on himself the problem of rhyme. By the time he had reached the edge of the town, it had become a not unpresentable effort: the kind of thing Byron might have torn up on an off day, as an undergraduate, having

31

diverted himself while dressing for dinner. It had taken Neil all of two hours; but it had proved some sort of concentration to be within the grip of his will, which was something to go on with. Better still, during all this time the grey and gold hills, and the deepening sea, had ceased to trouble him. Except as a series of surfaces to be traversed, he had not been aware of the moors at all. He even passed the gate of Weir View without seeing it, and had to go back fifty yards. Preoccupied still as he walked into the garden, he did not see Miss Searle's deck-chair till it was too late to retreat.

Well, he thought, this was as good a time as any to begin recovering the social decencies. At the back of his mind, he recognised this moment as one of decision. If he failed to make the effort with which chance had confronted him, tomorrow would find him where he had been yesterday. In the end, the application to New Zealand would not be sent either; he had only a fortnight longer in which to put it off.

Walking quietly across the lawn, he thought at a nearer approach that she was asleep; the promise of reprieve made him feel, instead of pleasure, a weary sense of defeat. She was awake, however, looking out placidly across the open book sunk on her knees, at the visible strip of sea by which the house modestly justified its name. A good profile, he thought dimly: she could afford to do her hair in one of those piled-up styles that the wrong women always wear. Better not, though; she'd be one of those that leave a bunch of wisps hanging out behind, and look as if they'd screwed it up for a bath ... 'Nice evening, isn't it? I hope I didn't disturb you.'

'Not at all,' said Miss Searle. She was aware that she had given a startled little jump, and felt the half-conscious resentment of people surprised in what they have believed to be solitude, a resentment so much deeper than vanity that its origins are probably to be found in the jungle and the cave. However, this was the first voluntary approach that Mr Langton had made to anyone since his arrival three days ago. She smiled, and wished she had not ignored a vague prompting to tidy herself before tea.

'You've been very fortunate with the weather today.'

'Yes. Very.' His tone was flat: she took it as a comment on her triteness (he was, she thought, that kind of man) and it annoyed her; she was sensitive to criticism of this kind. Still, if he were bored there was no need for him to sit down, as he was doing, in the chair left by Miss Fisher a few minutes before. She decided, since he was so contemptuous of one's conversational gambits, to leave the next to him. This resulted in a perceptible pause.

Neil was in fact racking his brains. Their common ground was, obviously, shop; but this must lead either to personal details, or to the acute awkwardness of refusing them. In desperation, he began a long and detailed account of his day's walking. As scarcely any of his reactions to what he had seen were repeatable, the effect was a little colourless. Miss Searle, however, perceived in it a willing spirit. She asked him whether he had yet visited the Doone Valley. He had; they agreed that Blackmore had grossly romanticised this not very impressive coombe. At the back of her mind was the thought that Miss Fisher, when she went indoors, had said she would be back in a few minutes, and that Mr Langton was occupying her chair. One could hardly tell him so with civility, and no doubt if she came out he would vacate it. It was, of course, also possible that she would see him from indoors and stay away.

'But of course,' she said, 'this part of the country is soaked in literature. Not only *Lorna Doone*, but *Kubla Khan*.'

'Yes,' said Neil absently, 'I've been there too.'

'I beg your pardon? Oh, you mean to Coleridge's cottage, of course.'

Hastily closing a door which he had not meant to open, Neil accepted the correction. To forestall further details (since he had never seen the building and did not know where it was) he talked on quickly. 'I don't know whether you feel as sorry as I do for the Person from Porlock. It's a little hard, after all, to make an innocent call on legitimate business, and find you've walked into immortal infamy along with the lunatic who smashed the Portland Vase.'

'I'm afraid I've shared in the injustice,' said Miss Searle smiling. 'It's the kind of story children and students can be relied on to remember.'

'Yes. And they don't stop to think that if Coleridge hadn't rotted his will-power with opium besides giving himself spectacular dreams, he'd just have locked himself in and finished the job.' As soon as he had said it, he reflected that denunciations of this kind are characteristic of men who distrust their own strength.

Miss Searle's experience of men, though necessarily wide, was not deep. It had been conditioned (like much of her other experience) by the fact that she had been a very plain child, and had been encouraged to over-compensate for it by prowess at school. Since then the plainness had lessened a good deal; but she had got used to the idea of it, and sought no other remedy. So, now, she did not perceive, through Neil's over-emphasis, the underlying sense of failure. She took it at face-value, as an arrogant statement of virility; and somewhere within her a romantic schoolgirl, whom no one had encouraged to grow up, thrilled with admiration. The adult part of her reacted promptly with feminism.

'When people point out – quite truly, of course – that all the great masterpieces are the work of men, one can't help wondering what might have happened, if women who resented trivial interruptions weren't regarded as a species of monster.'

Neil found he had still the capacity to be irritated by this kind of thing. During term-time, there had not been one clear hour in twelve when he could call his study his own; by comparison, this woman's life must have been a cloistral peace. But he was not sure how his temper would behave in argument; and, besides, he remembered in time that as he hadn't produced a masterpiece, he could be held to support her point. Still, he did not feel like conceding it tamely.

'There's a good deal of force in what you say. But would you be hurt if I suggested that even with favourable conditions, women have – well, a natural tendency to diffuse their energies? Even within the subject itself, I mean?' Becoming momentarily interested, he was about to make the physiological analogy, but remembered in time that it would shock her to death.

Not since she was twenty-five (and far too nervous to take advantage of it) had Miss Searle felt her essential femininity thus underlined and appealed to. Neil had been anxious not to undermine his own confidence by impatience or rudeness; he had imposed on his naturally firm voice a careful courtesy and, unconsciously, something approaching charm. While Miss Searle's intellect sought a telling rejoinder, her cheeks became faintly pink, and her frame underwent an indefinable softening of its angles. A few minutes ago one would have described her as a thin woman: now, the spontaneous word would be slim.

'I'm afraid I do know what you mean. The trickle of print meandering over huge boulders of footnote.' His face was quite transformed when he smiled. She went on with decision, 'But I refuse to take that as typical. Think, for example—'

Neil thought, obediently, of her examples. Having asserted

35

himself to his satisfaction, he continued to say anything which would keep the conversation pleasant, and a going concern. He was enjoying it as people who have been some time in bed enjoy a first walk in the air, attaching little importance to the destination. Miss Searle thought him delightfully reasonable, even generous, in discussion, and reflected on the folly of judging by first impressions.

Neil, meanwhile, was forming an inward picture of Miss Searle as an undergraduate: the busy bicycle, its basket sagging with notebooks, shuttling from lecture to lecture; the leather jacket and tweed skirt which, in his day and no doubt hers, had been almost a uniform; the glasses which were lying now on the open book on her knee. He could have sworn to the exact place where a wispy bun would have bulged the black quadrangular cap, and to the kind of jug in which she would have brewed cocoa at ten-thirty. He felt a sudden sympathy for all her sisterhood about whom he and his friends had made the standard jokes; he could not find in himself, now, the Olympian perspective of twenty-one. Aware at this point that he had been gazing at her in silence for much longer than convention allowed, he sought for something to say, and bridged the interval with a smile.

The external part of all this, as it reached Miss Searle, added up to a long, intimate look of understanding. When he started to talk again, she found that she had lost the thread twice, and had to concentrate urgently in order to have a reply ready in time.

The conversation lasted another five minutes. Then, with what in such weather always seems startling abruptness, a bank of evening cloud swallowed the sun. Everywhere – in the bricks of the house which had seemed to reflect warmth along with the light, in the grass and the ragged late flowers – the golds changed to a tired sullen grey. The sea, lying lowest and extinguished first, looked like cold lead; the breeze, which had ingratiated itself till now, like Jove to Danae, with a seductive glitter, began to strike chill. Neil's nerves, which had recently been nearer to breakdown than he chose to recognise, made him vulnerable to such transitions. He found himself emptied of his unreal animation, as suddenly as a tilted glass. The woman in the chair beside him had shared in the sea-change; her pale-grey eyes no longer looked blue, her neutral-tinted hair had lost a gleam of gold. Everything had dissolved into a uniform flatness. Helplessly void of resource, he wondered whatever they had found all this while to talk about. At least he had done what he had set himself to do, and could decently make his excuses now. He did so, and went indoors.

Miss Searle remained for some minutes longer. It was really a very pleasant garden, not over-trimmed as it would certainly have been with labour available. She must come here another day.

Miss Fisher, meanwhile, had decided to change a little earlier this evening, and had done so with some care. It took her twenty minutes; considering, indecisively, a return to the garden, she saw that her deck-chair was no longer available, and retired to the Lounge. It was empty. She did not feel in the mood for knitting, and had nothing to read. Her library book was finished; she had concealed this fact from Miss Searle, who had already pressed upon her, once, an old-fashioned novel as long as *Gone With the Wind*, but much more difficult to get into. Now, glimpsing from the bay window, Mr Langton's face lit for the first time with an impersonal kind of enjoyment, she wished she had taken the offer after all. She could have skipped the first few chapters, and there was no doubt that a good book did make something to talk about. The chance was gone, however;

and, without wasting time in fruitless regret, she went to the sofa and began turning over the cushions. She had noticed, the evening before, that this was where Miss Lettice Winter put her copy of *No Orchids for Miss Blandish* when her mother came into the room. Miss Fisher had heard interesting accounts of it, and it might still be there.

The cushions concealed nothing but the art-damask uphol-stery of the sofa which missed their shade (something between puce and rust) by several tones. Footsteps in the hall informed her that her chair outside was again at her disposal; she half thought of going out, but she and Miss Searle had come this evening to the end of their conversation, and, though it was possible Miss Searle had been supplied with fresh material in the meantime, Miss Fisher felt no pressing wish to hear it. She sat down with a cigarette on the sofa. The seat, subsiding under her weight, presented her with a smaller book which had half slid into the crack at the other end. It did not look promising; indeed, she wondered at first if she could have dropped it her-self. It was an obvious technical handbook with rounded corners to fit a pocket, had a brown paper cover, and generally resembled a work known briefly to nurses as *Honor Morton*; but it was not Miss Fisher's habit to take her *Morton* on holiday with her, nor was its cover nearly as dirty as this. She opened it at random, her habituated eye still expecting something like 'GALL BLADDER: A reservoir attached to the Common Bile Duct.' What she read, however, was: '(4) Ascend the sixth pitch of Route 1 to the ledge and small belay immediately above the top mantelshelf.' She blinked for some time at this cabalistic formula before trying another page. Here the subject was somewhat clarified by a passage beginning: '265 feet. Very severe and exposed. For an expert party only and in dry weather.'

The fly-leaf, to which she now turned without delay, bore the erased name of a man unknown to her, and, below it, 'N. W. L. from S. R., Hadrian's Wall, 23.4.30.' There were also dim traces of a limerick, which had been rubbed out but retained the indentations of the pencil; she studied these hopefully in various lights, but (since the language was dog-Latin) without reward.

Miss Fisher gazed for some minutes, fascinated, at this mysteriously masculine trophy, before settling down in earnest to read it. Mainly incomprehensible to her as it was, the terseness of its factual detail pleased her. Her mental picture of climbing had comprised, till now, a line of alpinists strung together on a glacier. On one page she found a passage starred, and a note in the margin, 'Hand traverse variation.' Below the note, very finely drawn, was a little diagram. She was still trying to make something of this when the door opened and Neil Langton came in.

Before she had time to think, she had made an instinctive movement to stuff back the book where she had found it. Suppressing this, since it was too late, she said politely, 'I expect you're looking for this, aren't you? I do hope you'll excuse me taking a glance at it.'

'Of course,' said Neil with awkward civility. He had been relieved for a moment to find he hadn't lost it out of doors; but, immediately after, he had recognised with disgust his own lack of surprise. At the back of his mind, he must have known where he had had it last. It had never been a habit of his to lose things, in particular things like this. One did not need very much psychology to trace this kind of amnesia to its source. Why, for that matter, had he been carrying it about with him at all? It was bad enough that he should have felt the need to dig up this reinforcement from the past. It was unspeakable that his subconscious should have contrived somehow to plant it here, in the seat occupied every evening by that predatory little blonde. From their first moment of impact he had felt his revulsion to be psychopathic: he had had no wish to repeat the sensation, and for the last two days had had breakfast early, and dinner out, in order to avoid her. That this relatively harmless woman should have found the thing was embarrassment enough.

'I'm afraid,' he said, 'the FRCC guides don't make very imaginative reading. Are you stranded without a book? I've got some odd weeklies upstairs. Just a moment, I'll see what there is.'

He unearthed the salvage of his journey, and brought it down. Miss Fisher found it nearly as intimidating as the book she had declined, tactfully, from Miss Searle; but perhaps boredom had made her less exigent, for it failed to depress her.

'These will see me right through tomorrow. They'll make a nice change; you get a bit sick of all this happy-ever-after stuff. Not a bit true to life, really, is it?'

'I wouldn't know. They'll be a bit less arid going than the Guide, anyway. D'you mind if I take it with me, before I forget?'

'Yes, do, of course,' said Miss Fisher, keeping it, however, in her hand and turning a page or two. 'But I thought it was rather fascinating, in a way. All worked out step by step; almost like surgery, really. Of course bits of it are rather puzzling if you haven't the experience. All that I mean about not getting caught in the rain. I suppose, high up like that, you catch cold more easily?'

'Caught in the rain?' inquired Neil, his impulse to retreat yielding to a bewildering curiosity. 'Well, it can be unpleasant on some pitches, but I don't quite see—'

'It's always coming in.' She pointed to a paragraph ending:

'The climbing is very exposed hereabouts, but the finish is near at hand.'

Rigidly controlling his diaphragm, Neil reflected that a good laugh ought not to be wasted in times of short supply. When he could manage, he said, 'It's only a kind of jargon, you know. Comparable with boxing journalese. It just means you don't look down thereabouts unless you're quite sure you want to.'

'Oh,' said Miss Fisher. A light first dawned, then dazzled. 'You mean it's a terrific precipice?'

After suppressing a slight shudder (Miss Fisher would have felt much the same on hearing the words 'wonder drug') Neil gave a cautious and qualified admission that something on these lines was meant.

Miss Fisher's excitement mounted. She felt she was getting the principle of the thing. 'So, really, all this is a way of saying that it's frightfully dangerous?'

This revolted Neil's sense of the proprieties too grossly to be let pass. He sat down on the arm of the sofa, and gave her a short discourse on climbing ethics.

She heard him out with careful attention, and then said, 'Well, even if you only do what you feel you can manage, I shouldn't have thought it was frightfully *safe*.'

Neil found himself grinning at her. There was something bracing about her stolid common sense; he forgave her her assault on the niceties of what was, after all, a highly mannered convention. 'Neither is crossing Oxford Street,' he said, 'if you come to that.'

It was now clear to Miss Fisher that she was being treated to a series of heroic understatements. The fact that he had sat down was distinctly encouraging. A maxim of hers, seldom found wanting, was, 'When in doubt, get them talking about themselves.' She continued to pursue it.

41

'I should think it must be terribly hard work. No wonder they say "strenuous". Cutting steps in all that rock.'

'*Steps?*' said Neil dizzily. 'You didn't mean *cutting* steps?'

Miss Fisher hastened to retrieve her error; it was so long since she had seen the film. 'No, of course; it would take too long, wouldn't it? I was really thinking of those iron spikes you knock in to step on.'

Neil savoured, for a second or two, a vision of the Pillar Rock triumphantly scaled on a Jacob's-ladder of *pitons*. He locked all his muscles in resistance, but it was no good. He laughed, started to apologise, and laughed again, helpless with joy.

She seemed, he saw with relief, quite happy about it. A nice woman, and restful, he thought. 'Do forgive me,' he said at length. 'I think you've probably been reading Whymper,' and proceeded to lighten her darkness a little more. In the process, it emerged that he had been up the Matterhorn. Seeing her eyes dilate and her mouth open, he explained hastily that he had only gone up by the Zermatt route, to look at the view; but it was too late. Whymper or not, for her the Matterhorn was clearly established as the next thing to Everest, and there, unshakably, it would remain.

By now he was determined that at least he would leave her with some kind of distinction between rock-climbing and mountaineering. As he came to a pause after doing his best, he found himself thinking that he must really write and tell Sammy the one about cutting steps. It was about time he shed the habit of saving things for Sammy, after three years.

She was quick to pick up a point; from the first, he had not made the mistake of confusing her complete ignorance of the subject with stupidity. Feeling, with sudden embarrassment, that he was getting didactic (he had grown rusty in the small give-and-take of conversation) he dried up rather abruptly; but she took over at once, and they had a little gossip about the amenities of the house. She was much easier, if less stimulating to the intelligence, than Miss Searle. When she asked him if the view was good from his room in the tower, he pulled up just in time on the verge of offering to show it to her. There were other reasons, besides the risk of misinterpretation, why this would not do.

'I wonder,' she said, 'who we'll get instead of the Winters.'

'Why, are they going?' He did not attempt to veil his cheerfulness, judging from her tone that it would not give offence.

'Yes, tomorrow, so Mrs K said.' She added, regretfully, 'I don't know who's coming, she had to go before I could ask her.'

'Oh, well, we'll soon know,' said Neil, successfully hiding his indifference on this head. He was tired of having dinner in hotels, which was incidentally expensive, and of inventing excuses to Mrs Kearsey for his absence; he felt grateful for the information. They parted cordially.

Upstairs, hooking up the floral art silk which she had decided to wear this evening after all, Miss Fisher considered the all-day expedition which had been almost settled for tomorrow between herself and Miss Searle. It would be, the forecast promised, very hot; too hot, probably. Miss Searle had told her, once, that she was one of those people who never dreaded solitude, so it could not disappoint her to go alone. It would be nice, Miss Fisher had decided for her own part, to take a lazy day, just sitting about reading; or talking, at the most.

Downstairs in the Lounge, Neil, still anchored by indolence to the sofa, put his climbing guide safely in an inner pocket, got out his pipe, decided that there would not be time, and started a cigarette. He was tired, and bored by the prospect of going out again. The Winters, on their last evening, would almost certainly be out too; he would have stayed in if he had not told

Mrs Kearsey this morning not to expect him. He felt, too, an unacknowledged regret, as people sometimes do for a perverse sensation they have rejected. The dream in which Lettice Winter had appeared to him last night had been unpleasant, but irritatingly incomplete ... He gave his mind an impatient shake, and got up.

'Oh, Mr Langton, are you going to be in?'

It was Mrs Kearsey, looking disconcerted; her voice was pitched in the tone which, as the Latin textbooks say, expects the answer 'No.' He supplied it; adding with relief, 'But I shall be in tomorrow.'

She seemed pleased; he had thought she would be glad to save the food, but, realising that she must have begun to think he despised it, improvised a little flattery, which was well received. He liked people who took a pride in their jobs; perceived that her rather trying refinement hid a quite real sensitivity; and was sorry to have upset her. The result, however, was a little too good.

'Now I *knew* there was something I've meant to ask you,' she exclaimed in the conscious manner of one who has just thought of it. 'These people who are coming tomorrow; I didn't promise any definite room. I was thinking, you could just as well come down to Mrs Winter's room on the first floor. It's nice for ladies to be near the bathroom; but one of these that's coming is a gentleman, so I don't see, really, why he should have the choice before you.'

'That's extremely kind,' he said hastily, 'but I couldn't be more comfortable than I am.' His room in the Tower, furnished with Victorian pine displaced by the improvements below, was much less hideous than those he had glimpsed on his way downstairs. He liked, when he could not sleep, to look through the open door at the sky. Perhaps Mrs Kearsey, who had a passion for locking things at night, had noticed this habit and deplored it. He found her several good reasons for staying; and ended, as one often does in such a case, by finding one too many. 'Besides, if they're together I dare say they'd like to be on the same floor.'

'Oh, no, Mr Langton. There's nothing of that kind about it at all. They booked *quite* independently.' Neil listened with half an ear as she explained, with intricate circumlocutions, her feelings about what his former colleagues would have called 'the tone of the House'. He found slips of the kind he had just made very undermining; it had not been like him, once, to make clumsy *faux pas*. He was never sure, now, when his brain would slip a cog, or he would become too much enclosed in himself to measure other people. When she ran to a stop, he explained that he had thought they might be brother and sister, or mother and son. This was so readily, indeed remorsefully, accepted that he felt quite ashamed of it.

By the time she had gone, it was getting on for dinner-time. Without troubling to change the disreputable tweeds he had walked in all day, he went out to the *Barlock Arms*.

Miss Fisher, before putting on the floral crape, had found a bathroom free and taken her best bath-salts into it. Dusting herself afterwards with talcum powder, she looked in the mirror with a dim sense of injustice. Why was it, she wondered, that it was never till she got her clothes on that her hips looked too heavy, or her waist too thick? Her search for an answer to this recurring question had not taken her as far as the National Gallery, which she might have found comforting. But, humble before the proportions of *Vogue*, she had never thought of seeing in herself a Ceres with neglected altars in the reign of unfruitful Artemis. She only turned her smooth dimpled hips from the unkind glass, wishing they were of the kind to set off a pair of well-cut slacks.

As she opened her door to go downstairs, another door opened. She and Miss Searle almost collided on the landing. Miss Searle gave a little smile, and passed on. If Miss Fisher had known it, it was the smile with which Miss Searle would have acknowledged, if absolutely obliged, an undergraduate wearing a fancy pin in her academic cap.

The door of the Lounge had been open when, on leaving the garden, she had gone upstairs to change. She had had a brief but full view of Miss Fisher, whose manner had been not only ostentatious and crude but almost personally embarrassing. By it the little exchange of amenities on the lawn, which had been pleasant and civilised, was indefinably cheapened; at least, if a definition was possible, Miss Searle did not attempt it. Her inner censor was almost faultlessly efficient. Comfortably unaware of its activities, she failed also to define her pleasure in the fact that the roses on Miss Fisher's dress were crimson, and her ear-rings scarlet.

Allowing, by mutual consent, an interval of a few yards to separate them on the stairs, they entered the dining-room almost simultaneously. Miss Searle, who was last, heard Miss Fisher say, 'Well, this *is* a surprise,' and hung back distastefully; a repetition of this evening's performance, she thought, would really be too much. It was Mrs Winter, however, whom Miss Fisher had rallied in this friendly way. For the first evening this week, both she and her daughter were in.

Miss Searle disliked Mrs Winter for the reasons which had caused Miss Fisher to pity and like her. She was a comfortable matronly body who, determined to be a social asset to her family, had self-sacrificingly made herself smart. Miss Searle thought her peroxide and rouge and built-up stays both vulgar and ridiculous; Miss Fisher thought so too, but recognised in them also, as Miss Searle did not, the pious pelican's bleeding breast. Mrs Winter had once confided to Miss Fisher that she wanted to give her little daughter every chance, and it had nearly made Miss Fisher cry, when she had stopped herself from laughing. After years of drudgery in the Services, Mrs Winter had gone on to explain, it was time the poor child had a little fun.

The poor child was beside her now, her silk hair brushed back from a satin tan, her mouth, like red velvet, scroll-shaped in a face composed of fine flourishes and curls. She was leaning back in her chair, a pose which showed, under her cambridge-blue dress, breasts that lifted like those of an angel at the prow of a ship. Miss Fisher was ready to allow that she was fond of her mother. She was smiling at her now; a considerate, daughterly smile which seemed to say that nothing had really changed, that if the bedtime confidences had ceased these last few years it was only because there was, after all, so very little to tell.

Miss Searle, assenting politely to Mrs Winter's opinion of the weather, wondered why young women spoiled their natural charm with artificiality. She thought this quite sincerely; to her, naturalness in young women implied obliviousness of their sexual function, the more oblivion, the closer to nature. Consciousness was artificiality; emphasis she would have described as vulgar, her vocabulary not including a more exact term. It will be seen, therefore, that her estimate of Miss Winter (whose taste in dress was much better than Miss Fisher's) was quite a charitable one. Part of the blame, Miss Searle thought, attached to the mother.

It was at this point of her reflections that Mrs Kearsey, coming in with the sweet, said to the company at large, 'I wish I'd thought to ask Mr Langton if he was going to be late back. He tells me, you know, when he remembers, he's really very good about it. But he forgets sometimes, and then one doesn't know what to do about the locking-up.'

'He's been out walking all day,' said Miss Fisher, forestalling Miss Searle's diffidence by half a second. 'He didn't sound to me as if he meant to make a night of it. I shouldn't think he'd be long.'

Perhaps from an instinctive avoidance of one another's glance, they both looked across the table. Miss Winter had been displaying the suspended animation of fish when the water freezes, and highly charged young women surrounded by their own sex. Now, she did not look up or move; she was merely all there. It was as if a little light had been quietly switched on under a crystal shade. Her mother had not altogether missed it. One could see the pelican conquer, not for the first time, an unformed questioning. All was well, her eyes concluded; and, in fact, very nice.

Miss Searle got up, and went over to the sideboard. 'Miss Fisher,' she said, 'these gooseberries look delicious. Do let me give you some.'

'Thanks aw'fly,' said Miss Fisher with sudden warmth. 'I don't expect they've got enough sugar, though. Have a bit of mine; truly, I've got lots.'

Miss Searle had strong principles about eating the rations of others. She dealt with them, this time, by accepting gratefully and making lavish passes with a few grains.

'It must be a little inconvenient for Mrs Kearsey,' she said, 'not to know if she can get to bed.'

'Men never think, do they? It's just the same in hospital; waste an hour of yours to save two minutes of theirs, if you let them get away with it. These things *are* sharp. Do have a spot more.'

'Thank you, they're just as I like them, now.'

Lettice Winter was discussing a film with her mother. It seemed she had found it more stimulating than anything which had appeared in the conversation till now. At the end of the meal, she agreed that they must both have an early night in view of the journey tomorrow; yes, she would look into Mummie's room on her way to bed. She slid a hand into the hip-pocket of her blue dress, produced powder and lipstick, and unconcernedly applied them. When the two had gone out, looking like a Siamese cat strolling behind a Pomeranian, Miss Fisher and Miss Searle loitered, by some common impulse, behind.

'At the risk of being thought conventional,' said Miss Searle, 'I do feel that for a woman to make up at table is needless, and a little repulsive.'

'What I always say is, it's little things like that that give away the sort of homes people come from. Made their pile in the black market I should think, wouldn't you? *You* know the sort – sit down with real pearls on, eating fish and chips off the grand piano.'

'Er – very probably,' said Miss Searle faintly, but without rebuke.

In the Lounge Miss Winter got out her knitting, and Miss Searle her Trollope. Mrs Winter had already gone upstairs, for the early night or perhaps to pack. Lettice Winter, forsaking her usual sofa, had curled up on the divan at the other side of the room. It was, perhaps, more comfortable; it gave also more space, and a better light, to her long legs and silk stockings. Miss Fisher, who was an expert in these matters, decided that the stockings were from Cairo, and that Miss Winter had acquired them there. She had brought *No Orchids* with her from upstairs. Miss Fisher allowed herself a marked look from the book to Miss Searle, who, unable at that distance to read the title, which would have conveyed nothing to her in any case, related the look to Miss Winter's uncovered knees and gave a slight, corroborative nod. Miss Fisher liked her the better for this sporting admission of her lighter reading.

This little exchange made them both miss the sound of footsteps on the path outside. Both of them, however, heard the slam of the front door. A moment later Neil Langton hesitated on the threshold of the Lounge, gave a quick glance at the empty sofa, and came inside. It was a windy night, and he was a good deal blown about. He must, Miss Fisher thought, have decided to do a little more walking after all; he had the interior glow, and a dark shine about the eyes, which distinctively comes with this exercise at night. Perhaps for this reason, or because of the high-necked pullover he had put on under his jacket, he looked much younger than he had seemed so far. It was possible to surmise that he had been a not unattractive young man, at a date not so very far remote. One could imagine him, now, in his twenties, physically saturnine over a basic good-humour, and superficially unkempt over a basic respect for razors and soap. He was a little out of breath; when Miss Searle and Miss Fisher looked up from their chosen preoccupations, he distributed between them a smile which was nearly a grin.

'Whew,' he said, 'I thought I was sunk. Tried one of these spurious short cuts and had to spend half an hour picking my way out of a bog.'

'I'm told,' said Miss Searle, 'that some of them are really quite dangerous.' She felt, suddenly, almost protective.

'Well, they need watching up on the moor. There wasn't anything to this one but waste of time. It was Mrs K I was worrying about.' He had already picked up from Miss Fisher this abbreviation. 'She's a great one for knowing what to do about the locking-up.'

'She was asking after you,' said a cool, clear voice from the divan in the corner.

Neil turned round. His eyes had still the half-focused look of people who have come indoors from wide spaces and the dark.

Lettice Winter did not smile. She looked at him, quite pleasantly and with perfect self-possession, as one might look at a hat in a shop-window which may possibly do: one will need first to turn it round and then perhaps, if it seems worth while, to try it on. It was not an arrogant look, but almost purely a conditioned sexual reflex. It said, in a voice as clear as the one in which she had spoken aloud: 'Application received, state qualifications.'

It had never, probably, achieved so quick an effect. The relaxed casual air, which had given the brief illusion of youth, went out like sun in a room where someone has snapped down a blind. His loose stance changed, with a stiffening like that of age. No one would have taken him now for anything but a schoolmaster.

'Thank you,' he said. 'I'd better go and set her mind at rest.' The second sentence was addressed to Miss Fisher. He went out.

Lettice Winter turned a page or two of *No Orchids* and stifled a yawn. When, half an hour later, the door of the Lounge closed behind her, two mouths opened simultaneously, as if a starting-gun had been fired to set them off.

3

Novice

The wind had dropped, and the fumed-oak barometer in the hall was set at Fair. Barlock, sheltered from what little breeze there was in its half-basin of hill and wooded cliff, shimmered in an autumnal heat-wave. The only coolness was to be found in the water, or high up on the precipitous jungly cliff-paths and over-hung rides, approachable only through masked gaps in bramble hedges, beyond rough fields, after a hard, perspiring climb. Neil, who had discovered for himself secret miles of such territory, found himself developing an adolescent secretiveness about it, and went perdu there all day. For climbing in the technical sense there was not much scope; this did not trouble him, since he had come neither expecting nor wishing any. His map was coming on well. The steep woods rustled in a breeze unfelt below; he came upon a new gully, overhung by an interesting rock-face, which he found his mind filing for reference. The hours slipped by, marked only by the slow shifting of the light-spars between the trees, and by the first respites of an extroverted peace, brief escapes into a contentment too instinctive to be broken by awareness of itself.

Miss Searle endured without exaggerated grief the news of Miss Fisher's defection from the day-trip. She had been truthful in saying that solitude within reason did not bore her; she preferred it, at least, to company sought for company's sake. The effort to talk down to Miss Fisher's understanding, without offensive obviousness, had increasingly become a strain; she was unused to carrying on such conversations for more than ten minutes at a time. Miss Fisher had, besides, a habit of bursting into comment at the wrong moments; sudden graces of light or landscape were transformed, before one had time to assimilate them, into terms of the Beauty Spot or The View.

Miss Fisher, who had been shielded from these reactions by Miss Searle's good manners, watched her departure with a vague sense of guilt, which she did not acknowledge at a level conscious enough for argument. Still, in the guise of inconsequent thoughts, the arguments slipped in and out of her head. The trouble was that Miss Searle's refusal (as Miss Fisher saw it) ever to get down to realities, made her such pathetically easy game. She was the kind of woman who, with more than enough intelligence to play her cards well, would play them badly sooner than admit to herself that she was playing at all. On the other hand she had been given what Miss Fisher described to herself in all good faith as Every Advantage; her helplessness was therefore of her own construction. Miss Fisher, as she walked down to bathe, signalled a clear conscience by humming *Yours* under her breath.

The beach offered nothing of interest except itself and the adjacent sea. Indeed Miss Fisher had hardly expected it; the wet bathing-trunks always appeared on the tower steps at a discouragingly early hour. Miss Fisher's constitution was equal to a seven a.m. plunge; but her self-confidence, social and physical, was not. That morning, as usual, she had heard his footsteps passing her door, considerately quiet but without fussy tiptoeing, and had turned over regretfully for another nap. Breakfast had been, as usual, disappointing. With unaccustomed hope, however, she settled herself in the garden, after her bathe and coffee, to wait for lunch.

She was well-placed to witness the departure of the Winters, in an opulent hired car. After this nothing happened until the gong sounded, when she found she had the dining-room entirely to herself. The maid served her lunch with an air of patient reproach, on a tablecloth spread over one end of the table.

Miss Fisher put on her sun-glasses (the glare was beginning to be uncomfortable) and went back into the garden again. After all, she thought, the Winters might not have been leaving till after lunch; the afternoon would be the time for anyone to come back who might be hoping for a bit of peace. The end of the afternoon (she added to herself an hour later) in time for tea. The time passed slowly; she wondered whether the heat was making her wrist-watch lose.

Only one more event, however, broke her siesta before tea-time; and, somnolent with boredom and sun, she gave it the briefest attention. It was the arrival of a young woman with a rucksack and travelling grip, who crossed the garden to the front door. She was slight, with a fair skin and intermediately coloured hair; neither short nor tall, nor striking in any way. She had on a grey flannel suit, evidently worn to save bulk in packing; this had made her hot, and she had sought relief by opening at the neck a blouse not designed for it. Her hair was limp with the heat and falling across her forehead; a few highlights, bleached by the sun, saved it by a shade from being classified as mouse. The general effect was timid, neutral and untidy.

As she came up the path she saw Miss Fisher, and for a moment turned hesitantly towards her; shyness seemed to check her, and she passed on to the door. Miss Fisher took her at a first glance for twenty-one, and at a second for twenty-five; the expression, rather than the contours of her face, misled. It had something left of the adolescent's defensive uncertainty, which her carriage bore out; but whereas some women of this age seem to repel maturity with a religious conviction, she had an odd, wavering air of having somehow lost herself on the frontiers, as if a good push might send her either way. Her grey eyes, when they met Miss Fisher's, were direct, but turned away quickly. A fine skin, and a clear shapeliness of the cheek and jawbones, redeemed her from plainness: but Miss Fisher's verdict, which she arrived at without disturbing herself to full wakefulness, was 'Very ordinary'. She had been looking at Lettice Winter only a few hours before.

The girl had apparently come alone; as Miss Fisher settled down into torpor again, she thought this might be very nice company for Miss Searle; the college type; they could talk about books together.

In fact, when she came down for tea after repairing the effects of lethargy in the sun, she found them already in conversation. Miss Searle had said distinctly that she did not intend to be back till evening; Miss Fisher, whose afternoon now looked in retrospect more pointless than ever, greeted her without warmth. The result was a certain restraint between them, which both relieved by talking mainly to the girl.

She looked, by this time, a good deal more presentable and, indeed, she had evidently made some effort about it. She had changed into a plain dress of light green linen, had brushed her hair (its length, like so much else about her, was intermediate, reaching the nape of her neck) and had put a little

55

make-up on. The result was a freshness concealed before; she could have seemed delicate, even fragile, with a little poise. Now that she was less covered in loose clothes it could be seen that she had good slender bones, a well-shaped neck and neat little breasts above a small waist: but she was ill at ease (she was evidently very shy) and this had induced an awkwardness which had set her arms and legs in hard angles, cancelling all structural grace. By separate internal processes, both Miss Fisher and Miss Searle decided that by contrast with Miss Winter she seemed very pleasant and harmless. Her nervousness impressed them as a likeable quality. They proceeded to draw her out.

She was neither secretive about herself, nor particularly expansive. Miss Fisher's guess about college had somewhat overshot the mark; she had sat the entrance exam for Oxford, she told Miss Searle, but had been prevented from going up by the war. She had worked in an aircraft factory; she added that her mother (of whom she spoke in the past tense) hadn't wanted to be left alone.

'How extremely interesting,' said Miss Searle. 'Did you work in the drawing office, or at some kind of research?'

'No, I just worked on a lathe.'

Miss Fisher, warming at once, noticed that Miss Searle looked at a loss, and took over. It turned out that the factory nurse had trained at her hospital; the girl seemed shyly pleased by this link.

Tea came in, and was amicably taken. No addition to their number appeared. Both Miss Fisher and Miss Searle had almost forgotten to notice it. Each felt that she had gained in some sort an ally, a support not irritatingly intrusive, but comforting in reserve. At the same time each felt that here would be someone on whom the other could be dumped without difficulty or the creation of resentment. She had a foot, as it were, in both their camps.

It was only a step, from this, to recommending walks or excursions which they felt sure she would enjoy. Each was privately considering an invitation when better occupation failed, but awaited the absence of the other in order to avoid an awkward threesome. At this point, however, the girl's shyness seemed to descend with more than its first acuteness. She said she had brought a map and things with her, and had a few plans worked out. Her voice was suddenly like a civil boy's when his arrangements are intruded on by well-meaning adults. Had her nervousness not been so evident, they would have thought her rude. As it was, they renewed their efforts to put her at her ease.

Miss Searle, who had unearthed a remote mutual acquaintance at Oxford, was making the running, when Mrs Kearsey opened the door. She was talking charmingly over her shoulder, and patting her hair.

It may be that in Miss Searle's subconscious this gesture had formed one of those linked associations which Pavlov demonstrated in connection with dogs' dinners. Her voice trailed off. Miss Fisher, in whom the association was a fully conscious process, looked up with a smile already forming on her lips. However, the young man who followed Mrs Kearsey in was a stranger to both of them. He was thirty or a little less, fair-haired and buoyant; at the moment he was receiving Mrs Kearsey's promise of tea with warmly expressed thanks. One had immediately the feeling that servants would do anything for him. Miss Fisher thought he looked attractive and good fun. Miss Searle, used to moving in an unregarded ocean of young men, dissociated him from Oxford by some instinctive process of which she was scarcely aware. She had an open mind about Cambridge, and indeed about everything else. His good looks, which were not insignificant, rang no bell for her. He had not, in her view, an interesting face.

He acknowledged Miss Fisher and Miss Searle with graceful courtesy. It could somehow be sensed that he was a success with old ladies, too. Miss Searle did not take this in ill part; she liked good manners, and her work had inured her to deference from people not vastly remote in years. Miss Fisher was less pleased. Neither, however, had time to form conclusions; for the young man's next acknowledgment had resolved itself into a start of surprise.

'Well, it can't be! Ellen Shorland! I don't believe it. Don't tell me you're actually staying here?'

'Yes,' said the girl. Her shyness, Miss Searle thought with sympathy, was really quite painful; she had blushed to the roots of her hair. After a pause she added, 'Are you?'

'Just this moment arrived.' The young man swung himself with casual ease on to the arm of her chair. 'Don't tell me you're on the point of leaving, or I shall howl like a dog.'

'No. I came today, too.'

'Of all the coincidences. Well, look here, if you're not booked solid we simply must organise something. I'm quite non-attached; just came here on impulse, really. Don't know this part of the world at all.'

'I've got quite a good map. Inch to the mile.'

'Oh, good work.' His approval was just a shade too prompt and practical; he added quickly, 'I mean, they're hard to get; I tried everywhere. Can I take a look at yours, sometime?'

'I've got it here.' Before settling down to it he remembered to smile nicely at Miss Fisher and Miss Searle and to say, 'You will excuse us, won't you?'

'Of course,' said Miss Searle. 'I have to go out now, in any case.' It was true that she felt a little cramped after the motor-coach;

58

besides, they were a well-mannered couple and, she thought, deserving of tact. As she withdrew, she felt a little glow of selfless pleasure on their behalf. It must be delightful for them to meet like this, after the damping expectation of a holiday alone. Finding that Miss Fisher had followed her out, she said, smiling, 'One of those happy coincidences that often lead to an engagement, don't you think?'

Miss Fisher gazed at her, momentarily stricken dumb. One had grown used to making allowances for an almost unbelievable *naïveté*, but really! Of course, she was as blind as a bat without her glasses; but even if she had failed to see the look the young man had given the girl, just too soon, behind them, anyone who was all there would surely have felt it.

She remarked, with meaning, 'Quite a surprise for both of them, I'm sure.'

'Oh! But surely not.' It was the tone, not the words, to which Miss Searle replied. She felt, after the first start, both distaste and resentment; she would have liked to point out to Miss Fisher that her calling, noble and indispensable as it was, did make for a one-sided view of life. A friend of Miss Searle's, who was a welfare worker, often deplored the same tendency in herself; but *she* was decently aware of it.

'I don't think,' she said, 'that we really *need* to assume anything of that kind, do you? They seemed very healthy, natural young people, I thought.'

Miss Fisher was not given to the exact analysis of words, but Miss Searle's serene and definite use of these adjectives caused her to suppress a giggle. 'I wouldn't say no to that. The more health, the more nature, as you might say. But they'd better watch their step with Mrs K. She's very fussy who she has here.'

Miss Searle decided that the conversation had become definitely unpleasant. (She also thought that it had become lower-middle-class, but did not register this supplementary opinion.) With a marked absence of reply, she walked out into the garden, where the deck-chair of Miss Fisher's fruitless vigil still remained, looking restful in the late and relenting sun. Settling there comfortably and opening *Henry Esmond*, she entered a state where the wicked ceased from troubling. It was she, therefore, whom Neil greeted with half-absent friendliness as he came back, relaxed and momentarily released, from a day of exploration on the hidden cliffs. He was beginning to associate Miss Searle with the garden, like a summerhouse or a sundial, and to pause beside her as one might form a habit of pausing by a fountain to contemplate the fish.

To Miss Searle he came, quite genuinely, as a welcome surprise. She had been preoccupied first by the effort to cleanse her mind of Miss Fisher's innuendoes, and then by the concentration she still gave *Esmond* after however many readings. Now, by a happy prompting of instinct, she removed her glasses as she lowered the book; the effect that they were reading-glasses and unnecessary, even annoying, at other times, was quite realistic.

Her wide-brimmed hat masked the premature strain-lines round her eyes, and left to the light a sensitive, well-cut mouth. A civilised face, he thought, if rather a sterile one. He asked her what she was reading, and spent a comfortable half-hour with her discussing the novelists of the great age. Having had a strenuous day, he lowered himself on to the grass; Miss Searle considered offering her cushion, but refrained. What she believed herself to think was that it would break the flow of conversation; what she really thought was that, faced with a definite invitation to settle down, he would become restless and go away.

They had worked along to Anthony Hope and *The King's Mirror*. 'The psychology is so entirely convincing,' Miss Searle remarked. 'It makes one realise how needless some of these unsavoury modern delvings really are.'

'I agree with you entirely.' He spoke, however, with that slight over-stress sometimes used by courteous people to hide a moment's lapse of attention. Her work had sensitised her to such lapses; either this instinct, or a simpler one, made her look across the lawn in the same moment that he looked away. Ellen Shorland was standing at the end of the path. She had pulled on a white woollen sweater over her green dress. It was tight – with age and shrinkage, one could see, rather than by design, and indeed what would have been provocative on a woman more maturely formed only gave her slight body a schoolgirl's look. She had one hand on the garden gate and was swinging it mechanically to and fro. Miss Searle thought her lacking in animation, almost sullen; it was certainly a great pity that want of confidence made her so defensive. The young man had obviously a cheerful open temperament, and few powers of introspection; she should really correct her manner if she wished to attract him, and judging by her blush when they met, Miss Searle felt justified in supposing that she did. He came at this moment out of the house, and ran down the path to join the girl at the gate. He said something in his lively assured voice – the words at that distance were inaudible – and they went out together. At the last moment the girl returned his smile; but not, Miss Searle thought, with a really attractive spontaneity.

She was recalled by a nearer voice saying: 'We've acquired a honeymoon couple, I see.'

He had been talking, in the minutes before, with what for him was almost animation; she was a little jarred now by the dead emptiness of his tone. Probably he got enough of youthful spirits in term-time; she could sympathise with him in this. She was mainly concerned, however, with the unwelcome memory of Miss Fisher which his misconception had recalled. It lent emphasis to her reply.

'Oh, no. I believe little more than acquaintances. They met here just now, quite unexpectedly it seems. But the surprise was a pleasant one, I think.'

'I expect so.' His brief interest had evidently flagged. She tried, in vain, to remember where they had left the previous conversation; he was a man in whose presence pauses quickly became embarrassing. To bridge this one, she said, 'They'll certainly be late for dinner if they mean to go any distance. But perhaps they're taking it out.'

'Which reminds me that I'm not. It must be time I thought about cleaning up.'

The same thought had occurred to Miss Searle, and reconciled her to his rather abrupt departure. Fifteen minutes later she paused at her glass and, after a moment's hesitation, opened her handbag. The sun of the last two days was very trying to the skin. Her lips had become quite dry; she was glad she had remembered to buy a salve for them. This one, for the first time, was slightly tinted; but the assistant, a very helpful girl, had explained that though it was labelled as a lipstick, it was specially made for its soothing properties, in fact for practical purposes a salve; it was the type they called 'Natural' and perfectly unobtrusive.

Peering carefully into the mirror, she put some on.

4

Guideless Ascent

Neil had made himself a rule, which he had never broken, not to take medinal more than one night in three. Tonight was only the second; so at twelve-thirty he switched on the light again, and began work on a Torquemada crossword which he had saved for some such occasion. Without reference-books he would not finish it; but what he would do would take him longer, a compensating advantage.

There were three clues relating to his own subject, which he solved quickly. One from Shakespeare teased him with half-memory; he lay staring at it, and wishing it were the third night instead of the second. His rule was of some standing, and dated from a time when he could afford to stand no nonsense from himself. Now, as far as he was concerned, the box of tablets might as well have been in a safe of which he did not know the combination. He had had influenza in London and the landlady, growing alarmed, had sent for the doctor, who had prescribed the medinal – irrelevantly, Neil had thought, and had said so. When the doctor – an observant student of humanity – had assured him that medinal was not addictive, he had been very rude. The medinal had arrived next day without further comment. He wondered sometimes, though not oftener than he could help, what would have happened if it had not. Lately things had improved a good deal. Until the night before last, he had had none for five days.

He applied himself to Torquemada again. 'To lie in cold (eleven letters) and to rot.' Suddenly remembering, he pencilled in 'obstruction' and was stone-walled again. He had never been defeated so quickly before, and felt that he was not going full out. It would be useless now to attempt sleep before three. The mechanism that settled these things was like a separate entity of which he had intimate, but quite external knowledge; as if somewhere in his brain lived a petty bureaucrat, a smug devotee of routine, to whose schedule he had to conform because argument was too wearisome to be worth while. At least he had learned how to entertain himself while he stood, so to speak, in the queue; he had a silly feeling that this annoyed the bureaucrat, withholding from him the spectacle of bored frustration which sweetened his sense of power.

His thoughts had begun to fly off at tangents, not in the looseness of coming sleep but with the wound-up busyness he knew too well. He put on his dressing-gown, sat up in bed, lit a cigarette, and set about the puzzle in a more systematic way. The needed effort still withheld itself. It often did. He was passing the time; and one does not, without some inner resistance, adapt oneself in a few months to a process one has despised for thirty years. Besides, it pointed out an inconsistency: if one was willing to kill time piecemeal, why jib at killing it altogether? This logic, since it seemed unanswerable, he let alone.

The few books he had brought were beside him on the table. The two thrillers he had read; the rest were major classics, large parts of which he knew by heart. Looking at them he felt the anticipatory staleness that comes with fatigue. 'Very well then,' he said, almost aloud, as one speaks to an exasperating child, 'what *do* you want to do? Think? All right, what about? Careful, now.'

He had an answer to this one. He was becoming morbidly self-centred; what he needed was to interest himself in other people. The two spinsters, for instance, the don and Miss Whatsit. They were probably around his own age; the don seemed a little older, the nurse a little younger, but that was largely conditioning, he thought. To start with something concrete, he speculated whether they were virgins. The don, obviously. The nurse, more doubtful; women in professions of this kind lost so many inhibitions, they gave little away. If she had had experience it had probably been below her real standard (she was far from stupid) and she had too much sense to dress it up, but would probably repeat it. The don, now, looked the type to believe in soul-mates. Her imagination would work strictly on the day-shift. As for the rest, she would hope uncomfortably that it was all right if people really loved each other.

At this point, his mind was arrested by an unsought memory of the girl who had come that day, standing and swinging the garden gate. He recalled his own remark about a honeymoon couple, which had sprung from an instant conviction that they were nothing of the kind. Doubt and hesitation, and a decision still ahead, had been written all over her. He did not know why he had said it; to find out what the don would say or out of some casual protective instinct towards the girl, born of a guess that they would have registered under the same name. But, of course, there was this business now about identity cards. It must make things awkward. At this point, something caused him to consult his watch. One-fifteen. Well, he remarked to himself with a rather forced brutality, she probably knew all about it by now. He could not much admire her taste; an obvious type, like an advertisement for shaving cream. A pity to have chosen him for the first attempt; he looked too self-satisfied to take much pains with his routine. It would be too bad if she were let in for any serious dependence on him. She didn't look very well able to take care of herself.

Considering this prospect on her behalf, Neil had got outside his own concerns to a degree which deliberate effort, often attempted, had failed to achieve. Perhaps for this reason, his mind suddenly broke off. Everything he had been thinking grew unreal and remote. Something had happened, at a different level, while these surface reflections had been going on, which had nothing to do with them or with their subject. He had shaken himself free. It would not last; but, for the moment, the thing which had been a part of his blood and bones had become external. It was attached to him, but like something on a length of chain; not to be escaped from, but able to be looked at from without, and, if he wished, seen whole. He had known that this moment would some time come, had longed for it, and begun to despair of its arrival. Now that it was here, he wanted to pretend to himself that it was not. He had not foreseen, till it was on him, the strain and labour it would mean. Tomorrow, some other day. It was late, he was tired; it was no more the hour for it than for stripping off one's clothes to swim an icy stream. There are streams, however, which widen at each refusal, becoming impassable seas. He knew this; for a moment, idly tracing back the train of thought which had sprung this ordeal on him, he remembered with a grudge the girl at the gate. It was pointless, a delaying action; he dismissed her from his mind. Suddenly the ghost of exhilaration moved in him, like the tension he had felt sometimes on the first difficult pitch of a big climb. As if for a physical effort, he flexed himself, his arms behind his head.

His mind began to cast about in the past, backward and forward, seeking a point to begin.

He had taken up teaching without any sense of vocation, but not as a frustrated *pis-aller*. It was a thing he could do, within a reasonable distance of his own standards. It would not make him miserable, he knew, unless he continued trying to write. It was possible that he could have made a living by writing (he had had reason, since, to think it even probable) but at twenty-three he had allowed himself exalted ideas. It had not seemed to him worth doing, in its present phase of overproduction, unless one could hope to reach the level of the minor classics. At twenty-four he decided that his abilities were not, and never would be, of this order, and made one of those ceremonial bonfires one regrets ten years later. Having put it behind, he was determined not to let it go sour on him. Later exercises he regarded firmly as recreation. These included a few translations which had had a respectable press, of the kind neither to crush nor to elate. They had been a professional asset, and he had taken a prosaic satisfaction in this.

Having come to his work without high dreams or serious sense of defeat, he had avoided the pitfalls of the disillusioned idealist and of the unwilling hack. He liked boys on the whole, without depending for any indispensable satisfaction on their response, and retained a sense of humour about them. He stood no nonsense, not because he was an eager disciplinarian, but because he had no time for it. It pleased, but also amused him, to find himself the kind of master about whose ruthlessness rumours are spread by boys who stand well with him, from motives of conceit.

The gradual discovery that he was a success had, at some deeper level, faintly alarmed him. He had not set enough store by the artist in himself to allow it any dignities or rights; but, threatened with assimilation, the creature took fright and protested. By this time, however, he was sufficiently confident to help himself to as much escapism as he felt he could use. Into climbing, by degrees, he put most of what he had put into writing before. One of the few things that got on his nerves was to find stories about it leaking round the school. It appealed, of course, to the boys; it was an asset, and, unlike the translations, it was not a thing to be capitalised. He had developed the need of a private citadel.

Like many people whose choice of a career has been in the first place rather casual, he retained at bottom, mostly unknown to himself, the approach of an amateur. Until he was over thirty, school had seemed a place where he happened to be. The boys felt (and the more intelligent realised it) the absence of the parochial spirit; it was perhaps the main factor in his popularity. He saved money, partly because his tastes were simple, partly to retain for the unassimilated part of him its feeling of independence.

Then the war came.

Suddenly it all began to close in. He tried to volunteer in '39; but the Head pleaded with him, and as nothing much was happening it seemed unreasonable to refuse. One by one, as their age-groups were reached, the younger masters went; retired dug-outs took their places; the responsibilities of the permanent staff increased. With a sense of something like outrage, he began to feel himself classed among the older men. Imperceptibly he had begun to take for granted his prestige among the boys; he had accumulated, by now, an adventurous legend. In 1940 he went to the Head again. The Head, a not

68

insincere old man but also a clever one, unbent and told him his troubles. He went away, as he had been meant to go, feeling that to anticipate his call-up would be a subtle self-indulgence. In implanting this idea, the Head had soundly gauged his man. Without arrogance, Neil was sure enough of himself to believe he would do as well in the Army as the next. Climbing had accustomed him to physical danger and emergency, as well as to hardship; he had had no trouble in handling boys so anticipated none in handling men. He was still young enough to feel sometimes that it might be better not to outlive one's prime; and, though aware that war could present death in many disgusting forms, he did not fear death itself because its near approaches had always come, so far, at moments of self-sought effort and exhilaration. In common with many climbers at such times, he had never felt fear till after the crisis was over. He had far more dread of taking life than of losing it; but, with the confused conscience of the time, saw this as an egotism to be conquered by the will. All in all, he felt he had a good deal to lose by standing aside from the common experience; so, when thus appealed to, he stayed.

From this time, his sense of frustration mounted. He began to imagine that the boys looked at him differently. His temper shortened; he suspected even the old stopgap masters (who were in fact so dependent on his authority as to be jealous of it) of wondering why he was still there. Alternatively, he decided he was growing like them. It suddenly burst in on him that this war, which he had never believed would be a short one, would swallow the last years of his youth.

It was in this mood that he met Susan.

She had come as a junior nurse to the school sanatorium, taking the place of a trained one who had joined the forces. Susan herself was half trained. She told Neil all about it when, in the Matron's off-duty time, he called to inquire after one of the boys. She had simply loved the patients in hospital, she said, but she couldn't stand the red tape and all the stupid rules. Neil had never been in a hospital in his life, and his mental picture was of the dated kind which envisages nurses scrubbing floors, hounded by viragos. He readily believed that Susan couldn't stand it. She was twenty-three, with red-gold hair, a transparent skin, and the appealing way which makes incompetence lovable to all except those on whom the results actually fall. Neil, used to assessing people's aptitude for responsibility, realised from her first report on the sick boy that she must be bad at her job; but what she said about the boy himself was intelligent and amusing. She accepted and at once took Neil for granted as her own contemporary; not surprisingly, since he was the first man between eighteen and sixty she had seen since she came.

He came back for more of it, making sure this time of the Matron's off-duty first. Before long they were meeting for walks safely out of bounds. One day, when the Matron had scolded her, she told him that apart from the boys he was the only human being within miles; that she thought it marvellous of him to stay on here when he was longing to get away, just to hold the place together; that of course he was right, and that if he went the poor lads would have no one to keep them in touch with real life at all. After this he allowed ten minutes to elapse before proposing, the interval being for decency's sake. They were married in the summer holidays.

But for the war, Neil would have been a housemaster a year before; but the man who would have retired had stayed on. They took a small converted cottage just outside the school grounds. The Head was delighted. He had every intention of getting Neil's call-up deferred, took for granted that now there would be no opposition, and preferred his housemasters married in any case. He was a tough and determined old man with fixed ideas; his aim was to outstay his present deputy, and settle Neil as his successor. He never actually said so, but began now to drop Neil significant hints.

The Sanatorium Matron was also pleased by the match. Susan was the daughter of an Old Boy, and had been appointed through the Head; the Matron had begun to feel, despairingly, that it would be necessary to wait till Susan had killed someone before getting rid of her. The cut-glass decanter in the wedding display had the lavishness of a thank-offering. Neil was partly aware of this, but it only made him laugh.

The gaps were bridged now, the vacuums filled. He had not married for intellectual companionship, never having been intellectually lonely; if he did feel like talking from that side of his mind, she listened well and was never banal. She supplied a far more urgent need; she was someone with whom he could be foolish. For the first time (his only serious love-affair before had been in most ways unhappy and strained) he was let into the secret world of private mythologies and of the little passwords which are so excruciatingly funny when innocent outsiders bring them by accident into the conversation. More by a great deal than all this, she let him find himself as a lover. He was her first, though she had naïvely assumed on the strength of a few flirtations the airs of experience. Because he had awakened it, her frank sensuality seemed to him a tremendous compliment. She told him often that she could never endure to have another man make love to her as long as she lived.

He had meant to put off a child until the war was over; but she wanted one because she was afraid of being called up. When Sally was born, he found that his happiness had had, after all, room for an addition. She was an individual from the first. Her hair and skin were like Susan's; but as soon as she had grown to be more than an instinctive little animal, she turned most to Neil. He was idiotically proud of the fact that she would always stop crying when he held her, though he supposed it was only because she felt safer in a stronger grip. She was nearly a year old when Neil's call-up papers arrived. With an unpleasant sense of shock he realised that he had pushed the whole question into the back of his mind; he no longer wanted to go. He tried not to realise this at first, knowing that if he did he would let nothing stand in his way.

The Head, when notified, said that there must have been a clerical error. Neil realised suddenly that this might well be true; the Head had been pulling wires and saying nothing about it. He had influential contacts, and, in the staff situation, a pretty good case. Neil came back and told Susan that he would have to get going at once. They had their first quarrel about it. She had guessed his mental processes, and told him in as many words that he was sacrificing her, and Sally, and the school to his own pride. He could put up little defence to this; in a sense it was true. He tried to explain his own point of view, which was that if he stayed he would go downhill till he ceased to be worth keeping; she replied that if he had such irrational feelings he ought to be strong-minded and conquer them. They were wretched together until the day before he left, when she had a passionate fit of remorse which would have been lacerating enough if he had had no choice. He believed in his own work and thought it necessary; he was going, not from an abstract sense of right but because the particular structure of his self-respect demanded it. It was the kind of issue about which his mind worked clearly; he did not attempt to evade it. Since the thing was done, however, he prepared himself as best he could to do it well.

In all this he had reckoned without his hosts. The Head, dogged to the last, had had another pull at the wires. From his own point of view he failed; but he had driven home, quite successfully, Neil's qualifications. The Army Educational Corps opened its arms to him. When he resisted the embrace, he was told reprovingly that this was a specialist's war; the square-peg era was over. Didn't he want to serve his country where he could be most useful? Well, quite. He would therefore report at the training depot in the Midlands to which he had been posted. No; the schools of mountain warfare had their full complement of instructors by now: after all, the war had been going on for some time.

He remained at the depot, commissioned, comfortable, and not much troubled even by air raids, till the end of the war.

Two things lightened the first crushing weeks of anticlimax. The first was Susan's joyful relief. This struck him as quite illogical, for he seemed to himself to have justified all her strictures; he had simply got into khaki, and had been far less dispensable at home. The other concerned Sally. He hated to miss the years of her quick early growth; but her dependence on him had begun to grow alarming, and Susan had accepted it with disquieting placidity. She liked to please, but hated responsibility. He had wanted a child; she had given him one; he was satisfied: the uncomfortable interruption had justified itself. Neil, who did not fear responsibility, but had studied the psychology of children, had not been entirely happy about it all. Now things would adjust themselves.

The months crawled by and clotted into years. Draft after draft arrived, leaving when the dullards had begun to display gleams of interest, and the lively minds to turn to him as a friend. Between all of them and himself was a drawn sword with its edge turned away from him. An old boy from the school, happening to pass through his hands, wrote to a friend that Langers had got positively subdued, and looked quite a bit older.

He spent his leave periods with Susan in hotels. She had never found housekeeping easy even before scarcities began, and made it clear now that she could do with some leave herself. He did not doubt that her life was harder than his. Once, at his request, she brought Sally, but it was impossibly difficult and they did not repeat it; a sister of Susan's took the child in. He was not within reach of any climbing on a short pass; it had to go.

Susan, it seemed to him, was changing; but everything was changing or had changed. The twelve years between them increasingly appeared. He had hoped that the gap would narrow rather than widen; but he thought of the outgoing drafts, and his unhappiness seemed a self-indulgence. Things would straighten out when he got back.

All this was only the preface; it was a background over which his memory ranged at random, setting this in perspective or that. What he had before him tonight was to compose the foreground. This was the thing that had always defeated him, because much of it had to be done without the help of memory. The centre, which he knew, depended for its truth on a complex of lines and shades which only his imagination could supply; and always, when he tried to fill them in, they had toned themselves to the violent colours of his own pain. Helpless and exhausted he had forbidden himself to think about it; everything had been tainted by the knowledge that there was this rotten place, skinned over, in his mind. For the first time, tonight, he had felt emotion loosen its stranglehold; if he kept his will steady, he could use knowledge instead, and make deductions of the unknown from the known. If he could do this, it was possible that even from his own part of it he could stand a little away.

Getting out of bed, he opened the door that led to the iron stairs. There was a dark, deep sky outside; a three-parts-rounded moon had quelled the stars. The sea sounded, so faintly that it was only as if the silence stirred and said hush. He laid himself down again. Now.

It must have been a year or more after he left the school that the bulldozers came to the big meadow a couple of miles away, the pioneers followed, and the huts went up. The next move was the Head's; he convened a masters' meeting and moved the bounds half a mile in.

Marks and Canning, of course, would be the first boys to break them; returning like Joshua's spies with material treasures, electric torches and compasses and gum, pressed on them by their hosts to console them for the attempts of an archaic system to crush their enterprise. Fanciful rumours were ousted by glowing reports; if you seemed keen and didn't put on side, the Yanks would go to a lot of trouble to show you how things worked. Marks and Canning learned how to operate a search-light and (in theory) how to construct the framework of a skyscraper and drill for oil. They had acquired faultless accents and an impeccable use of idiom before, having displayed their accomplishments rashly, they were watched one night and caught.

All these events reached Susan distantly, in the cottage outside the grounds. They seemed at first to concern her no more than the building of a new lab. Sometimes she would see the Americans walk past, together at first, later with the village girls. After a while, when the camp had settled in, appeared the semi-professionals from the towns, little young-old harpies who saw no reason why the locals should get all the pickings.

The village girls were few, and soon acquired 'steadies'; the vivandières found it worth while to stay. Susan, considering these things with vague unhappiness, remarked to Neil at one of their meetings that she thought it was a shame.

Neil, his mind reverting to Plautus and Juvenal, agreed a little wearily that since two thousand or so B.C. it had always been a shame. Susan's eyes looked disappointed; he could feel her thinking that his mind was growing academic and dry, though it was his own boys in training about whom he was trying not to be foolish. Rousing himself, he said that the Americans must have precious few amusements, so far from a town; the staff ought to get up some sort of a do, and ask them over.

In the end, however, it had been Sally who had set the wheels moving. During one of Susan's frequent lapses of attention she had gone wambling out of the open front door, down the path and into the road, where the driver of a jeep, scorching his brakes and narrowly missing death in the resulting skid, managed to avoid her by inches.

The driver was a good deal more shaken than Sally. He picked her up and asked her where she lived.

Sally had forgotten Neil, by now, as a human presence; he had passed into her pantheon, along with Gentle Jesus and Santa Claus. But, like many girl-babies, she adored men and could never have enough of them. She embraced the driver confidingly. When he asked her if she would like him to bring her a box of candy, she made sounds of pleasure and clung round his neck.

The driver happened to be detailed for duty next day; but he had children of his own and wouldn't for worlds have disappointed the kid. He combed the camp for someone to deliver the candy. His two delegates called next afternoon. They were

76

straight from college, the lean, boyish, gangling kind; very diffident, conscious of their ambassadorial function, courteous and sincere. They explained the candy carefully to Susan, calling her Ma'am. Their youth and their gravity moved her heart; she thought of the harpies dawdling round the camp gates, and asked them in to tea.

Rigidly curbing their appetites (they knew about rationing) they told her how swell of her this was, and how good it felt to be inside a real home. They got out their wallets, and showed her the snapshots of their folks. Susan said that of course they must come again. Sally (to whom the news that candy meant sweets came as a delightful surprise) seconded the motion.

One of them did come the following week, with a different friend. He was about Susan's own age, and as charming as the others, though he knew a little more about it. He rang Susan up next day, and asked her to a dance at the camp. She went out with him several times, while the help from the village sat in with Sally. He was a good-hearted though not an inexperienced young man. Privately, he thought the girl had a tough break, married to some dusty old professor or something; but as she seemed fond of the guy, he wouldn't be the one to bust it up. He told her so. He had a girl himself, back in Cleveland. A few friendly kisses would keep them both in training, and do no harm to anyone. He kept his word. It was only pardonable vanity which, when some of his friends formed a wrong impression, kept him from correcting it.

The friends, unoccupied and intrigued, felt themselves challenged. If Pete's find was as willing as she was pretty, they saw no sense in leaving him a monopoly. One of these, setting out in this spirit of light-hearted competition, fell very nearly in love with Susan; the thing became serious, for him, before long. Susan, for her part, was getting to appreciate the practised approach; the charming boys, with their snapshots of the back porch, began to seem a little insipid. She had been bored and unsatisfied since Neil went away; and, when she did see him, he appeared to be losing his sense of humour. She did not tell him about these developments in her social life, in case he should not understand. He was a little old-fashioned, she was beginning to think.

Now, reconstructing it all as fairly as he could from his broken scraps of knowledge, he accepted a probability he had not admitted to his consciousness till now: that the man who had assisted at her first infidelity had not known he was the first. She liked to please, to avoid awkwardness, to be the kind of person her companion wished her to be; she always affected a little more sophistication than she had.

Whoever the man had been, it would have been the same. She was one of those women to whom the first step is decisive, the rest as easy as a greased slide. If Neil had stayed with her she would never, perhaps, have found it out; habit, sentiment and convention would have reinforced her warm, shallow love. Once these cables were cut, there was nothing in herself to hold her. He did not know, even now, how many men there had been later: perhaps three or four, perhaps half a dozen. He did not know if they had all been from the American camp. It made, in the essentials, little difference after the first.

Matters had stood like this for more than a year when Germany surrendered, and Neil's training depot became surplus almost at once. The Head wrote that he was applying for his immediate release; the news brought him, now, nothing but pleasure and relief. He was out of the Army just in time for the start of the spring term.

From the first he had known that things were wrong; but for a length of time he found it hard later to believe in, he had not guessed the cause. The truth was that for three years his frustration had been mounting to a pitch of inferiority where he found for every doubt and uneasiness an explanation in himself. When colleagues were constrained in his presence, or treated him with an awkward excess of consideration, he thought they were pitying the slowness of his adjustments; as, indeed, in a different sense they were. Even when he made love to Susan he did not guess. She had acquired in this language a vocabulary of clichés and vulgarisms which physically shocked him; but he thought she was trying by nervous improvisation to bridge the gulf of absence. His previous experience of women, which had never been commercial, did nothing to enlighten him. He had missed her very much, which made him uncritical.

It was Sally who, if he had not been armoured in self-distrust, would have been the first to tell him the truth. When he came back, still in uniform, she had looked from him to Susan with a sidelong glance that was almost sly. 'Hullo, Sally,' he had said, much shyer with her than with Susan, 'do you remember me?' She considered him and seemed, with unknown reservations, to approve him; but her smile, little more than a baby as she was, had a kind of affected babyishness, an air of playing to the gallery. 'Hiya,' she answered. He took it for a childish slurring; as he soon discovered, she was very backward in her speech. She had spent increasing time with the village help, who was the leavings of the call-up; kind by her lights, but little more than a high-grade defective. More disquieting facts emerged one by one. The child's clothes were unmended and half-washed; 'She gets through them so quickly,' Susan irritably explained. Before long he could see the reason for this. 'Surely,' he asked, still made uncertain by his own loss of confidence, 'a child of her age ought to be house-trained?' Susan said he had better get in touch with life again, and find out what running a house was like. He could not bear to see the child's dinginess; she had always been so crisp and fresh. When Susan was out (she often was) he washed Sally's things himself.

After he got back into mufti, Sally changed. She seemed suddenly to re-discover him. In dim memory or uncertain trust, she began to claim him again. When he was at work in his study, she used to slip quietly in, making few demands or none; in her sensitiveness to his concentration, and her patience, she was more like an old dog than a young child. With him she dropped her edgy cuteness and her affected lisp; natural talk was almost like a secret between them. She never spoke of anything that had happened when he was away; her memory was too short perhaps, or perhaps she had the child's sixth sense of something wrong. Her favourite game was to be hoisted to the top of a bookcase or of the garden wall, when she would say that she was climbing mountains like Daddy; it was always the highest mountain in the world.

With her he had the only complete happiness he had experienced since his return; but, before long, he saw that Susan was as ready as ever to leave her entirely to him. At this age, he saw more risk than ever to the child's emotional balance. At last he forced himself to speak to Susan about it. She flared up quickly; the boredom she had been suppressing was close to the surface. After that, the real quarrel was a matter of days.

He realised, after, that it had supplied Susan's conscience with some kind of sanction or permit. She persuaded herself, probably, that he no longer loved her, or, possibly, that he had got even with her while he had been away. At all events on the following evening, when a masters' meeting guaranteed his absence (the Head's meetings were never brief), she rang up the latest of her men and asked him over.

From this point of the story, there were no more gaps for Neil to fill in with imagination or inference. He knew the rest. If he could get through it clearly and sanely, and somehow without re-living it, he would have done.

The American camp had sent much of its strength home, or to Germany, since the European armistice, but a reduced force was still there. Susan had met this most recent man only a month or two before. That evening, having made clear to him that Neil deserved no more consideration, she took him up to the small guest-room at the top of the house. They were there some time.

Before this, Sally had been put to bed. She must have wakened, and been frightened by silence or by sound. When no one answered (the cottage was an old one, the walls and doors thick) she fumbled her way downstairs, in her nightgown, to Neil's study. It was empty; but there were warmth, interest and company in the fire, banked to last and burning brightly in the grate.

That night Marks and Canning, seniors by now but un-regenerate, were breaking bounds. The novelty of the camp had worn off, their special friends had left, and they had gone back to poaching again. They were on their way tonight to set snares for the rabbits which, tomorrow, they would skin and cook in the furnace-room under the labs, a useful supplement to tea. They went carefully, for they had been cautioned last term, and a threat of expulsion hung over both their heads. When they passed the cottage, therefore, they kept well down behind the wall, concerned not to be seen rather than to see.

The screams from inside had not held their attention at first; they assumed a fit of temper, and crept on their way. After the first few yards, something in the sound made them feel uncomfortable; they stopped in their tracks. No answering voice was audible; the shrieking mounted, intolerably. They looked over the wall, and saw through a window a flame running about a room.

A long career of lawlessness had made them resourceful. They scaled the wall, smashed the window, which was locked, with their muffled fists, scrambled in bleeding, and caught up a rug. By then the curtains were alight as well. Marks singed off half his hair, and Canning's hands were scarred for life. When the flames were out, they lifted the rug again and looked inside. Canning turned faint and had to lie on the floor; Marks, who did not feel well either, picked up the telephone quickly. He knew about the masters' meeting; their expedition had been timed for it. He dialled the Head's number.

Through the broken window the final screams must have carried farther than the others; they penetrated to the spare room upstairs, at the other end of the house. There was a pause, a tension; Susan got out of bed and felt for her slippers. The American, who had seen service and knew the value of time, flung on his trousers and ran down barefoot and stripped to the waist. Marks and Canning were past astonishment; they were glad to see anyone. Susan was a little later. She opened the faintly whimpering bundle, screamed, and clung to the American's neck. They were standing like this, with the green-faced boys behind them, when Neil and two other masters, who had run the quarter-mile from the Head's house, came in at the door.

Sally lived for nearly twenty-four hours. Neil sat all night by her cot in the hospital; she had had morphia, and only moaned dully now and again. Beside the cot some contraption of glass and rubber tubing ran fluid into her through a needle. A grotesque mask of white lint, with holes cut for her mouth and for one eye, covered up her face. Around him, hidden by the screens, children cried and murmured and were fed and changed. In the morning the night-nurse brought him tea, and the convalescent children started noisy games. The day went on. At some point in the early evening, he saw through the mask Sally's eye open. Half the iris was turned up into the drooping lid. He spoke to her, softly. The eye moved, and turned vaguely towards him. Something stirred in the other hole, the one for the mouth.

'Hiya, big boy.'

The eye moved again, upward. Nothing showed, now, but an arc of bluish-white, and the lid was still. After a little while, Neil went and told the nurse.

He spent some hours walking, he could not afterwards remember where. He had told Susan by telephone, and hung up quickly. From now they must find the sight of one another intolerable; this was self-evident, like the fact that he must leave the school within the next few days. There was nothing to add to it, certainly not the littleness of reproach. At present she was his responsibility, and he blamed himself for being gone so long. A woman might be driven to anything after this, he thought, and he hurried the last part of the way.

Susan too had been preparing for this encounter. She began at once, giving him no chance to speak. None of this would have happened, she said, if he had been man enough to stay where he was needed, instead of bothering about what people would say. She didn't suppose he had been a saint himself all that time; men always thought it was different for them. He listened silently (it had all seemed increasingly distant and unreal) while her voice mounted and sharpened. He had a blurred impression that she said the same thing several times. She seemed frightened; as he had said nothing, he could not see why.

Her concluding point was that she would have come

downstairs sooner – she had thought she heard something – but Dan (or Mike, or whoever he was) had said it was nothing and held her down. Curiously, this wakened Neil to an active loathing of her which all the rest had left unstirred. He had seen the man. They had been a foot away from one another, bending together over Sally in the first moments when there had been room only for one thought. He remembered the swarthy, blunt-angled face, stripped of its protective hardness, simplified by emotion like a child's. While Susan spoke, this face seemed closer to him than hers, and, though he hated it, more real. He went out, and left her talking.

He had a choice of two rooms to spend the night in; Sally's night-nursery, and the spare room upstairs. He spent it in his study on a chair.

The story was complete now, except for the epilogue.

It was two days later, the day before the funeral, that the flowers began to arrive. Neil, who had kept mostly in his study after giving the Head his resignation, scarcely noticed them at first. There would of course be flowers; he could acknowledge them in *The Times*. But soon there seemed no interval in which the door bell did not ring. Flowers poured in; wreaths, crosses, cushions, sheaves, flowers that would have been extravagant before the war. The room to which Sally had been brought back was so piled that he could scarcely reach her without crushing them; the cottage smelt like a hothouse. He looked at one wreath incuriously; it had no card and he could not trouble with the rest. When he reached the church next day he was still unprepared.

There was only a handful of mourners, his nearest friends on the staff; but, out in the churchyard, it was impossible to see across. There must have been nearly two hundred of them; a mass of olive khaki, silent as a wall. They had done, and were doing now, all they could find to do. Many of them, to whom Susan was only hearsay, had known Sally; she had liked to play in the garden, to talk and show off a little to strangers over the wall. Some were there simply for her sake; some for the honour of their corps, in a groping effort to dissociate it by this gesture from what had happened; some in a vicarious remorse. The only man left on the camp's strength who had a personal concern in the matter was miles away. Neil had been beyond knowing any of these things. He only guessed at them now, six months later, in a seaside boarding-house at three in the morning. Then, as the first patter of gravel had sounded on wood, he had looked away at the rampart of flowers that made the grave look as little as the graves that children dig for a dead bird. He had seen only a crowd of sensation-seekers, making banner-headlines of his suffering and his public shame. Like a gangster's funeral, he had thought. All that money can buy.

When he got back to the house, Susan had gone.

She left a letter for him. She was sorry, she wrote, for everything that had happened, and for the unkind things she had said; but he had frightened her. She had not been herself for some time. Now that he didn't love her any more, it was better to tell him the truth. She had not been sure when he first came back, and later she could not make up her mind what to do. Mike (or Dan) had said he would take her to town to have something done about it, if she wanted; but now he didn't want that any more. He wanted to marry her, and as his last wife hadn't had any children he would like to keep this one. She knew Neil would rather not see her again, so to go now seemed best for everybody.

Susan had always liked to please.

After this ... But suddenly he realised that he had got to the

85

end. Towards the last, his concentration had been so complete that he had not seen it coming. He was there. The smoke from his third cigarette curled in a thin scarf through the open door, catching a pale luminescence from the hidden moon. Against an almost black sky scattered only with the brighter stars, the denser mass of a hill showed faintly a ragged crest of trees. A soft wind blew in, heather scented from the moors, with a tang of salt.

No, there was one thing he had left out; strange how the mind, pretending to give everything, will hide, like Ananias and Sapphira, the last pennyworth of shame away. That night, going up to bed, something had caught his eye as he passed a mirror. It was the stripe in his hair. He did not know when it had begun to turn; it stood out already, perceptibly grey. Everyone at the funeral must have seen it. Alone, with two sleepless nights behind him, this last little thing had hit him like the last axe-stroke to a toppling tree. The only thing that had been left to his pride was the fact that he had maintained, outwardly, some kind of self-control. Now even this was gone; it was as if he knew now that he had shed public tears. He had been able to go quietly in memory over all the rest; but this, seven months after, he could not remember without finding he had crushed the end of his cigarette so that nothing would persuade it to draw again. It was quickly over; he had everything now. It wasn't so sensational, after all. Walking about London, he had seen several heads, on men and women, much the same. If we haven't learned in the last five years, he thought, not to be self-important, there's not much hope for us.

Slowly his thoughts fell away from the scoured hollow he had cleaned; a beautiful emptiness gave way to the inconsequence that precedes sleep. He thought vaguely, Something must have started me off on this. What was I thinking about before? That new girl today; no connection there. Things happen when they're ready, like birth. The girl's got her night's business over too, I suppose, by now; I hope it wasn't too disappointing.

It was the smell of the sea that directed the beginning of his dreams. As he fell asleep he was in Skye with Sammy, marking out a route on Sgurr Alasdair.

5

Moderate Rock-climb

A patch of morning sunlight, strengthening as it moved, crept over Neil's eyes; he woke, discovering with a pleasant surprise and sense of achievement that he had slept late. It was the first time, since he left the Army, that he had recovered the knack of compensating for a short night.

It was now nearly nine, he found; if he wanted breakfast (he certainly did) he had better waste no time. Still he fingered a few minutes more, reluctant to move, not from lack of energy but because his sleep had been deep and had left behind it, as deep sleep often does, an inexplicable sense of freedom, as if in one's unremembered dreams wisdom has been liberated in oneself, or given from a source out of one's waking reach. A pity it didn't last. He got out of bed and dressed, feeling the past strengthen its hold on him again. Shorn of the indignations which last night he had painfully stripped from him, and of the remnants of self-pity unacknowledged but simultaneously destroyed, he felt lightened, but with a long hill of effort still before him, and little to beacon him up it but the solitary goal of self-respect. The wisdom of the horn gate receded; he took a more immediate comfort in thinking of that rock-face above the second gully. It could hardly be dignified by the name of a climb, which was all to the good perhaps; but it had looked tricky and interesting. There was no sense in not keeping one's hand in.

Mrs Kearsey met him on the stairs and told him that she'd saved an egg with the rasher for his breakfast. Her voice was conspiratorial. Guiltily aware of favouritism, but glad about the egg, he thanked her with suitable emphasis and went into the dining-room. The sunny window looked cheerful; he walked across to it, and had been looking out for some moments before the clink of a cup informed him that he had not the room to himself. He turned, his eyes still blurred with coloured patterns of light; and saw, at the other end of the table, the girl who had arrived the day before. The remains of food, attempted but mostly uneaten, were in front of her; she had just poured herself out another cup of tea, and was drinking it with her eyes to her plate. She was alone.

Neil said 'Good morning,' because to omit it would have been more noticeable than to speak; and, when she had replied, turned back to the window again, to show that he expected nothing more. There had been no need to hear her voice, or see her eyes which had moved, in a perfunctory and unwilling social gesture, vaguely upward without meeting his. Both had said 'Let me alone,' but he had known to do that as soon as he became aware of her; and he had, for his part, no wish to do anything else. His recognition of misery behind a slammed and bolted door had been immediate; but he was so hardly removed from this state himself that he could not see it objectively; it called forth the resistance he would have felt if it had been his own. He reacted instinctively against a pity which, if he admitted it towards her, would come back on him like a boomerang; besides, on the principle of do as you would be done by, he knew it for an unwanted commodity.

All this he felt as he stood at the window, while the outside of his mind registered only a general discomfort and a wish that he had come down ten minutes later. Presently Mrs Kearsey would be here with a good breakfast, which he wanted and would be a fool not to eat; and this living reminder of his own worst moments would preside over the board like the admonishing death's-head at a medieval feast. He would feel a brute and be irritated with himself for feeling it. There was, obviously, nothing anybody could do.

Just then, with as much promptness as if he had turned round and put all these points before her, the girl got to her feet and went quickly out of the room. Neil looked at her cup, which was still half full, and regretted again that he hadn't come down later; she probably needed it. He liked several cups himself after a bad night. I hope to God, he thought, I've never looked as obvious next morning as that.

His reflections were broken by Mrs Kearsey, with an extra rasher as well as the egg. Neil found himself unusually talkative. It did not strike him as odd that he should be working to deflect her attention from the littered plates she was collecting at the other end of the table. The reflexes of a long self-defence were still active in him; the situation called them forth so naturally that he was scarcely aware they had been transferred from himself.

He was a moment too late, however. 'That sounds very nice, Mr Langton. I never seem to have time to walk that far ... You would think, wouldn't you, if people didn't want breakfast they'd say, not let you cook good food just to waste it all over the plate.'

Beside the immediate disapproval in her voice, there was an

overtone. Neil thought, She's noticed something. With a fluency to which he himself listened in detached fascination, he remarked, 'As a matter of fact, I rather think it was a bit of misdirected tact. Miss – I don't know her name – was saying she'd had some sort of bilious attack in the night; something she ate on the journey, but she was afraid you'd think she was blaming the food here if she mentioned it. Don't tell her I passed it on, or my name will be mud.'

'Oh,' said Mrs Kearsey. 'Oh, I see.' Her voice had an ascending note of enlightened relief. 'Well, of course, that would account for it. I did think I heard someone moving about.'

Left with his bacon and egg, he found his mind reverting to the young man who, in retrospect, reminded him of a shaving-cream advertisement more forcibly than ever. Really, he thought, she's not an unintelligent-looking girl, she should have had more sense. She seems to have learned the hard way ... Of course, there may be a reconciliation later. A good job, I suppose; we shall have some cheerful evenings if they're not on speaking terms.

At this point the post arrived, with a business letter for him which, having been delayed by forwarding, must be answered at once. It took him an hour of irritable semi-concentration, during which the bell rang again, a telegram this time. He went out into the hall to look, with the reasonless dread of those who have once received sudden and disastrous news. The wire, however, was for one Phillips; this, he now remembered from something heard last night, was the young man's name. Neil looked at his watch. There was a call-box just down the road, convenient for anyone anxious to send himself an early wire. So, whatever had happened, there was no doubt about it. Neil found himself unsurprised; the young woman had struck him as confused, but not irresolute.

He finished his letter, collected in his rucksack his lunch and the other oddments he needed, and started out.

Now that the sun was well up, it had turned out a sweltering day. He reached the cliff-top with his shirt sticking to him; even when he got down into the woods, the shade was warm and still, what slight breeze there was came from the land. He picked his way downward; the old track, since the day of smugglers and wreckers never repaired, was broken away here and there; roots had humped up into it, stones from its outer wall, fallen in remote years, were bedded deep and mossed over like the rest; here and there a fallen tree lay across. All the timber here lay where it fell at its natural death; the slope was too steep and overgrown to make retrieving it worth the labour. Often a bole hung precariously, its dead branches caught in those of a living neighbour or lashed to them with ivy; even a slight wind brought from somewhere the solitary, eerie creak of limb sawing on limb. He might have been a hundred miles from the next human being. He was too high up, on this calm day, to hear the sea; where the cliff below was steeply broken he caught sight of it, the waves turned by distance to faint creases that seemed not to move.

A day or two ago he had seen hereabouts, through the funnel-like perspective of a gully, a narrow glimpse of stony beach. Since half the morning was gone, he decided to fill in the rest by trying to make his way down to it for a bathe; his little climb could wait till the afternoon. The fact that he had brought no costume wouldn't matter in this almost inaccessible solitude, and it would be pleasanter without one.

The whole semi-precipitous slope was honeycombed with tracks. He worked along them to take in the gully; the excitement with which he had first discovered it had not worn off yet. When Miss Searle had mentioned *Kubla Khan* and he had incautiously answered 'I've been there,' it was this that he had meant. Discount the Oriental trimmings, the magnification of opium, and it was all here; the deep romantic chasm plunging down through immemorial trees; the brooding silence which only the noise of water broke; the cascade disappearing under the great boulder placed, heaven knew how or when, to form a monolithic bridge. Coleridge had lived only a mile or two off; his temperament, and the cult of the period, being what they were, he could scarcely have kept away. If anyone else had discovered this place, Neil hadn't heard of it; his childish pleasure in his little secret had been a turning-point of recovery, since when he had made progress every day.

He stood for a little while listening to the water, and taking another look at the rock-face he had ear-marked for the afternoon. He could trace two possible ways up; but that would keep. He found a promising track, and followed it down.

It took him so close to the edge of the gully that at one point he could see along it, under its cave-like roof of trees. It was rather like looking down a huge telescope from the wrong end; a round patch of sunlit pebbles ended the perspective, a glimpse of the beach. A mixed splash of pale colour among the stones puzzled him; he looked again. It was a pile of clothes, a woman's.

Neil said 'Damn,' and then, suddenly, on an indrawn breath, 'Oh, God.' The pale green of the dress had been familiar; he remembered now. The girl at the breakfast-table had worn that colour.

The path here was easy going. It was not till he had almost run himself over a straight drop, and checked himself with a tree, that he questioned his own impulse, and referred it to common sense. This melodramatic surmise, he told himself savagely, would occur to no one but a neurotic drawing on his own experience. Whatever had been the matter with her (and it might really have been a bilious attack for all he knew) it was fantastic to assume ...

The pile of clothes meant, of course, nothing either way. Even if one had not a friend or relative in the world, simple pride would prompt one to arrange an accident. Reaching another gap, he looked again. No towel. But that proved nothing either, he had none himself.

He was now only about seventy feet above sea-level, thinking as he went; the next glimpse he got showed him, as well as the beach, a patch of sea. There was a head in it, no great way out but moving away with a purposeful rhythm.

'This,' said Neil furiously to himself, 'is too bloody ridiculous.' He had a scarifying vision of taking a dramatic plunge, in his clothes or stark naked, pursuing a young woman to whom he had said 'Good morning' without the benefit of an introduction, and hauling her in from an innocuous bathe. She would probably take him for a sex-maniac and proceed to drown both of them in self-defence. Or one could bawl politely, from here, 'Excuse me, but are you committing suicide? Sorry if I'm wrong, but I thought you looked like it at breakfast.'

The trees, at this level, were getting much thinner; they opened at a new point, giving him an extensive vista of beach and sea. The girl, who must have put her feet down on the bottom, suddenly stood up in the water. It only reached her waist. She was quite unclothed.

Faster than he had ever done it on an Army course, Neil dropped flat into cover. His embarrassment and self-exasperation were such that if she had had a fish's torso instead of a woman's, he could scarcely have sworn to the difference afterwards. He had lain there some minutes, telling himself that people went to psychiatrists with minds less disorganised than his, when a further thought struck him. The girl had shown every sign of being about to wade in; as soon as she came through the bushes that fringed the beach she could not fail to see him, lurking in the brake with a furtiveness that could only bear one interpretation. The situation, seen for the first time in this light, raised the hair on his neck. He was right on the path she must go up by; she would be certain to hear him if he went crashing about among the trees. All he could see for it was to get down into the gully till she had gone. He eased himself down through a patch of brambles, landing ankle-deep in the stream.

Neil had been a schoolmaster too long to enjoy making himself more than reasonably ridiculous; as a doctor would put it, he had a low threshold to indignity. He had also a scratched hand and a torn shirt. Climbing out of the water on to a wobbling stone, he cursed the young woman with silent concentration; recognised, unwillingly, the injustice of this; cursed himself; and suddenly started to laugh. It overtook him so unexpectedly that he only smothered it just in time. His recent tension, though brief, had been acute, and he was feeling the reaction.

The cover, if highly uncomfortable, was good; he could just see part of the path, and would have to wait till she crossed it. Since his Actaeon-like situation carried none of Actaeon's privileges, there was no saying when this would be. She would probably decide to eat her lunch.

Evidently she did, for he was there twenty minutes; ample time, if he had known beforehand, to have got comfortably away. He did not enjoy his vigil. Besides having humiliated himself by a panic which now looked hysterical, he had time to reflect on the loss of his private wilderness. This wretched girl, who was clearly in a state to seek solitude, would probably haunt it for the rest of her stay; a stranger, to whom he need not speak, wouldn't have been so bad. He knew the tracks and could no doubt avoid her; but the fine edge of enjoyment would be gone.

With relief he heard her, at last, on the path below. Presently she came into his line of vision, at the steady plod of one with a long climb ahead. Her profile was turned to him; it was, he saw, clear and good, with a short straight nose. Her mouth and jaw, set in some private resolution, had a firmness which much improved their line. The pleasure of getting rid of her made him feel more kindly disposed; her methods of exorcism had his sympathy. He might as well get down to the beach himself now, and have his own lunch in the sun.

It was pleasant there, with an interesting miscellany of bleached driftwood to poke about in; he quite forgot her, till the heat again reminded him that he had meant to bathe, when it occurred to him that she might still be about somewhere. So what? he thought, pulling his shirt off. Let her do the worrying, for a change.

He had his swim, his lunch, and a cigarette in leisured peace; dressed again; and, feeling much better, recalled his plan for the afternoon. The climber's approach to a climb, even a short one, is nearly automatic; he made his way up the tracks to the steep part of the gully at a leisurely, energy-saving slouch. There was plenty of time. The sun was still high when he reached the cascade.

He had brought a pair of binoculars with him, to look for small holds near the top where he knew them to be scarce. As he unslung his rucksack for them, something caught his eye; another rucksack, loosely filled like his own but smaller, was lying on the path. He looked up. Half-way up the face, poised motionless in a pause of her progress, was the girl.

It was with some effort that Neil refrained from swearing audibly. This time he did not rebuke himself; it would have been, he felt, too much for anyone.

Clinging close to an almost vertical slab, she had not seen him. He gazed up at her, nursing his resentment. Of course she had taken the specious-looking route, so inviting from the bottom, which he had rejected in advance; she had just got to the point where he was pretty sure it petered out. When she found that it wouldn't go, perhaps, she would clear out and leave it to people who knew what they were doing. But he was sick of standing second in the queue for all the local attractions; besides, if he were here when she came down, he would have to talk to her. He might as well write it off.

He picked up his rucksack again, taking another look at her. Why the hell doesn't she get on with it, he thought. You can't dawdle about on a pitch like that. She had not moved hand or foot for nearly a minute. He saw her head turn, first to the left, then to the right. A new thought struck him. He fished quickly in his rucksack for the binoculars and focused them. He wanted detail. With them he could see her as well as if she had been a few yards away. Her feet were badly stanced, on little more than toe-holds, and her hands looked as if they had nothing very adequate either. They were cramped, and the knuckles showed white in the clear eye of the lens.

This, thought Neil, is the last straw. The fool of a woman's got herself stuck.

Dropping his gear, he walked up to the foot of the cliff. She was fifty to sixty feet up, with nothing to check a very unpleasant fall. The path itself was narrow; she might well bounce off it and go on into the gully, which, here, was deep and choked with thorn.

Raising his voice just above talking pitch (a sudden shout, if things were as they looked, might be more than enough) he said, 'Hullo. Are you all right up there?'

Her head moved, but not far enough to see clear of the rock. Anyone in good balance, he thought, could have managed that. He noticed, too, that she did not try to look down.

'Who are you?' she said.

Of all the damn-fool questions, Neil thought. Shall I go back and fetch someone to introduce us? 'My name's Langton. We met at the house this morning.'

'Oh, hullo,' said the girl. 'I'm all right, thanks, I'm just resting.'

Neil, whom this had rendered speechless, thought, Resting! She must be off her head. This is a nice proposition. His mind, however, was moving rapidly under conditions which had given him practice in rapid thought. The significance of her first question suddenly got through to him, with a muffled but hideous shock. She didn't believe he could do it. Too old, or did he look like a crock?

Hating her now without reserve, he looked at the rock again, and took off his shoes.

'Hold on,' he said. 'I'm coming up.'

'No, wait. Have you ever climbed before?'

'Good Lord, yes,' he shouted. 'Keep still and don't fuss.' This elementary cause for her doubts had simply not occurred to him. She had the best of reasons to know that it was no place for a beginner. The surrounding scenery suddenly looked much better arranged. As he wriggled up round an awkward bit of overhang at the bottom (it was this, no doubt, which had put her off the sounder route) it occurred to him that not many women in her situation would have bothered to ask.

A rope would be nice, he remarked to himself. There were plenty of trees at the top to belay to, and abseil her down if she had got to the paralytic stage. Having none, he might as usefully consider levitation. Pausing on a good stance at twenty-five feet, he studied the rock again. As he had thought, the route he had picked out was practicable all the way; but now the problem was altered. He would come up ten feet to the right of her, and in order to do anything would have to traverse along. The prospect looked unpromising; but till one was there it often did. The crack immediately ahead was good enough; too narrow to get the feet into, but as one edge projected it would do for a layback. He hooked his fingers in sideways, braced with his feet against the other side, and began to work upward. It was some years since he had had occasion to use this arduous trick, in which the arms bear the body's weight and leverage as well; by the time he got out on to a ledge, the sweat was running into his eyes. He had been facing away from the girl; now, nearly level with her, he was able to look again, and could see a series of small holds which would get him there. Whether they would get her back was another thing.

By this time he had got into her restricted line of vision, and took advantage of a good handhold to pause and give her a casual smile. The easier he could make it look, the better. She smiled back, with a strained hope and (he was pleased to see) a rueful respect. He perceived, though, a quivering movement in the hem of her dress where the sharp edge of colour showed it up. It was hardly surprising that, tense as she was, she should be starting a tremor: he had better lose no time. In a rational way, he knew the situation was a very sticky one; yet, curiously, the more he realised it the more his confidence grew. The fact was good and there was no time to examine it. His intimacy with the rock, the feeling that they belonged together and knew one another's ways, was so natural and familiar that he did not welcome it back as a lost happiness; he simply accepted it, like the air.

'Shan't be long now,' he said. 'Let's see what it's like your end.'

'The ledges don't go all the way.' He heard for the first time in her voice the tautness of desperation.

'Too bad.' He affected a more cheerful scepticism than he felt; there was, as he had noted, a nasty hiatus. 'We'll give it another look.'

The footholds were there, but they were narrow; socks had given a good friction-grip at the crack, but he wished now he had stopped to put rubbers on. The girl, he was pleased to see, was wearing them. With boots, she might have been tolerably secure; as it was, without the bite of nails or the support of leather, her muscular tension must be getting intolerable. She must have lost her nerve badly; there was a good little crack in reach of her nearer hand, but, clearly, if she moved she expected to fall off, in which case she very well might. He got to the last foothold and measured the distance. For him, it would have been an easy stride; she could do it, he was sure, if she could be made to think so.

'You're all right,' he said. 'Look. Use that crack and come along to where I am now. The holds are fine this way, right to the top. The crack,' he repeated distinctly. 'A foot to your right.'

'There's nothing in it to grip on.' There was still reason in her voice, though panic was not far from the surface.

'No, I know. It's a jammed-fist hold you want. Don't you know that one?'

'No.' Her eyes looked dilated. If she made a false move now, however slight, she would certainly fall.

Neil reached up with his right hand. It found what he had

hoped for against hope; a beautiful incut notch, a straight pull-up, perfect. He closed on it, the sense of security it gave running all over him. Giving it his weight, he stretched out his left hand; it just reached her wrist. He gripped it, pinning it against the rock.

'Let go with this hand,' he said peremptorily. 'You don't want it now, it's only a balance. I've got a hold like a house up here. Come on; do as I say.'

She let go slowly, keeping her eyes on his. She looked a little like St Peter walking dubiously on the sea. The part for which he had cast himself seemed suddenly rather overwhelming.

'That's it,' he said firmly. 'One good hold and you're OK. Keep your hand loose while I move it – all right, I've got you – and clench your fist when I tell you. Now.'

She closed it obediently. In this shape it wedged firmly, like a chockstone, into the narrow crack. Neil drew a silent breath of relief.

'Right. No need to worry now; you can put everything on that if you want to.'

He had got her just in time; she wasn't paralytic yet. Through the stretched lines of her dress he could see clearly the steadying of her muscles.

'Good. The other hand up there. Come along, now, get going. I'll tell you when to start fussing about your feet.'

'Cigarette?'

He rolled over on the dry grass and held the case out to her; convention seemed rather belated, and he could do with a rest.

'Have you enough?' The girl, who had been lying on her back in a stupor of fatigue, tilted her head limply on one arm. 'They're hard to get round here.'

'Plenty.' He rolled a little nearer, and gave her a light. Her face was flushed and her forehead damp after the last gruelling pull; she hadn't learned to let her balance work for her arms. She looked like a schoolgirl just off the hockey-field, and the competence with which she drew on the cigarette seemed precocious.

'I don't smoke out of doors as a rule, but I did need this one ... The thing I feel worse about than anything is that I asked you if you'd climbed.'

'Why? It was very ethical of you.' He smiled at her. 'Punctilious, in the circumstances, I thought.'

'It was no more than decent in the circumstances,' said the girl abruptly. 'I'd never have done it, if I'd thought anyone was about.'

She spoke in the manner of one who makes a reasonable statement, and suddenly looked uncomfortable. It gave her the look of a tongue-tied adolescent so strongly that he knew it must be deceptive; but he lacked energy to go into the matter.

'I've got some chocolate,' he said drowsily, 'but it's downstairs.'

'Mine is too. I want a drink more; do you think the stream's good?'

'I not only think, but know, that it drains at least two farms. Try sucking a pebble. Did I miss a step in the reasoning just now?'

'No.' There was a pause. 'All I meant was that it's not like a mountain. If I'd fallen it wouldn't have matt— I mean it wouldn't have meant a risk for anyone, to pick me up.'

'Pick you up? It's ten to one you'd have lain there for days. How many people do you meet in here?'

'I thought of that later ... One doesn't expect, in this kind of country, an expert to come along. I was afraid of someone thinking they ought to do something, and then ... You know, if I could start fresh I believe I could do it, now, after watching you.'

'I'd give it a miss for the present. Twenty feet of layback's a bit strenuous for a woman. That's the way you ought to have come.'

'You've done a great deal of climbing, haven't you?'

Anyone whom this could please, Neil thought, must be softening up. 'I used to,' he said briefly, 'before the war.'

'Whereabouts?'

'North Wales and the Lakes. Scotland mostly. The Dolomites; and a time or two in the Alps.'

The girl looked up at the trees for several seconds in complete silence. Then she said, so flatly that it sounded brusque, 'I was only learning when the war broke out. My young man was trying to teach me. But he's dead now.'

'That's bad luck,' said Neil unemotionally. He had had, indeed, no time to feel anything; and this seemed to be what she had intended. Her lack of expression, which could have passed for callousness, gave him no sense of affront; he felt curiously at ease with it. He said, 'The man's dead that I did most of my climbing with, too.'

'I'm sorry.' She pulled up a tuft of grass on which her hand had been lying. 'Jock was shot down over the Channel, in 1940.'

He said, in the same impersonal way, 'I suppose there are worse ways for a climber to go. Sammy Randall went down in a submarine.'

'How horrible.' Startled imagination put, for the first time, feeling into her voice. Suddenly she said, with a queer, suppressed eagerness, 'You don't mean S. J. Randall, do you?'

'Yes. Did you know him?'

'No, but Jock talked about him so much. He had all his

books; not only the one he made his name on, the early ones too. Once he very nearly met him. Some man was going to fix it up, and then at the last moment he was ill – the friend, I mean – and it fell through. I'd never seen Jock so disappointed over anything since he was thirteen.'

The words had come pouring out of her, like something dammed up for years. She spoke, not with unhappiness, but it seemed with a kind of pleasure at finding herself able to speak. Neil, to whom time was not likely to bring this indulgence, felt a stab of envy. He only said, 'You must have known each other a long time.'

'Since I was born.' She seemed ready to say more, and to be checked not by constraint but by a fresh thought. 'It's selfish of me to ask you, I know. But would you mind telling me something about Randall – any little thing, it doesn't matter. It's only that Jock would have liked so much to talk to someone who'd climbed with him.'

Neil wondered whether she had any idea how much she had said. There seemed nothing, now, about her look at the breakfast-table that morning left to be explained. He began to talk quickly, lest she should realise this herself.

'He was a deceptive type to look at. No physique on the surface at all. I don't know where he kept his muscles; he climbed on nerve and balance mostly, but they were there when they had to be. You'd never have guessed what a reach he had, either, because of the way he stooped. I remember him taking a bet once at a pub in North Wales—'

At the end of the story, before he had time to go on, she broke in, 'Your name's not Langton, is it?'

'Yes. I'm afraid the introductions were a bit sketchy just now.'

'Did you tell me? I'm sorry, I was past taking it in. Mine's

Ellen Shorland. But he writes about you, of course. In the first book, and—'

'Yes, I'm the hero of the dead sheep episode. Sammy always did have a fourth-form sense of humour.'

'Are you?' It was the first time he had seen her smile. It revealed one of those triangular dimples which surprise sometimes in a thin face where there seems no room for them, and one noticed the delicate springing arch of her brows. 'I wasn't thinking about that, though. It was the part about—' She fumbled with the Welsh.

'Clogwyn d'ur Arddu? I did that one with him, yes.'

'Oh, I *wish* Jock were here!'

She had spoken with complete simplicity, as of someone delayed by a missed train. What showed in her face next moment was not remembered grief but a hot embarrassment. Grief, as he guessed, was too familiar to have any ambushes left for her; she only felt ashamed of having betrayed a habitual way of thought. 'I mean—' she stammered, and blushed with the glowing transparency of snow at sunrise. The flush of physical effort was no longer there to disguise it; she turned quickly away.

Affecting an unobservant casualness, Neil said, 'It's funny you should say that. Only just now I heard something I thought would give Sammy a laugh, and I nearly sat down to write to him before I remembered. Some people take you that way. It's too bad they didn't meet; I should think they'd have got on.'

'Was it a good story?' He heard the quick relief in her voice, and what sounded like genuine interest as well. Discovering a solid enjoyment in sharing it, he told her about Miss Fisher and cutting steps. It had an immense success. Sammy himself could hardly have laughed with simpler enjoyment, or pursued the theme to more primitive depths of farce. For a few minutes she seemed about fifteen. Then she said, 'It's a shame, though, to laugh at her. She's a rock of good sense really; and people like her always lay themselves open because they're too much interested in other people to watch their dignity. I'd be glad to see her walk in at the door if I were ill, wouldn't you?'

'If I were too ill to mind being bossed about.' He was thinking what an odd mass of contradictions the girl was; her perceptions were those of a grown woman, her looks gained rather than lost by analysis; yet she seemed curiously cut off by a glass wall so that the last reaction she inspired was the natural one. He decided that it was this very negative quality, making her harmless but not uninteresting, which caused her company to seem unexpectedly easy. At the same time, he decided that all this had gone on long enough. He had more than a fortnight to go here, and must take care not to drift into anything that would prejudice his freedom for the rest of the stay. Tomorrow to fresh woods, he resolved, and pastures new. Immediately, he would see her back as far as the edge of the town, and then slip off; civil, but indefinite.

'I suppose,' he said, 'it wouldn't be a bad idea to get moving before we stiffen up.'

'Before I do, you mean,' she said smiling. She flexed her arm; an angular gesture which had so nearly been graceful that it was oddly irritating. 'I'm starting to creak already. Thank goodness it's only an artificial climb and we can walk down.'

'Not strictly artificial.' They got up and dusted the ground from their clothes. 'That applies when—' He went into the definition; and then, because she knew enough to ask intelligent questions, slipped into illustration. It was pleasant to talk of these things again; but, as he reminded himself, to her it was all a kind of keepsake, like the flower her grandmother might have pressed in a book. Exchanging ideas with women was always an illusion; they tagged everything on to some emotion, they were all incapable of the thing in itself. 'I suppose the final fascination of Everest is—'

He did not notice, in the end, when the first bungalows came in sight, and only remembered to excuse himself within a few hundred yards of the gate.

6

Route Abandoned

'Such a shame,' Mrs Kearsey had said to Miss Fisher that morning, 'the very first day of the poor boy's holiday. And I'm sure he could do with it; his work's very responsible, from what he was telling me. But it seems his father's subject to these attacks; blood-pressure, you know.'

'High blood-pressure,' said Miss Fisher automatically. These lay people! She'd be talking about a gastric stomach next. 'Had a haemorrhage, I suppose.'

'Something of that, I reckon.' In conversation with Miss Fisher, Mrs Kearsey was apt to relax her diction comfortably, as one kicks off tight shoes. 'I gave him back his advance booking, I mean you can't help illness and there's plenty of inquiries this time of year. He was lucky not to be with Mrs Parsons up the road; he'd not have got a penny back from *her*.'

Miss Fisher said that she hoped he appreciated it. For a moment, moved not by malice but by the mere impetus of gossip, she was on the point of touching upon the goings-on last night; but the girl, it seemed, was staying, and whatever she might have asked for there was no need to add to it. Miss Fisher discussed instead the amenities of Bridgehead, where she was going to spend the day. She had decided after breakfast that Barlock, though a pretty little place, was so slow that too much of it got you down.

She hesitated in her room, wondering whether to suggest that Miss Searle might like to come too; it seemed just possible that she also found Barlock slow. She had looked a little dim at breakfast. Unless, of course, she had had a disturbed night? Miss Fisher had been on the verge of asking her; but it wouldn't have done. There would be no harm, however, in telling her about the dramatic recall of Mr Phillips. Miss Fisher had the journalistic feeling for a scoop.

She waited till she heard Miss Searle's door close, and overtook her on the stairs. She was dressed to go out; but, Miss Fisher thought, half-heartedly. Having established the fact that it was worth the rain, to get a spell of weather like this after it, she produced her news.

It fell disappointingly flat. Miss Searle, happening to come down, had been an eye-witness of Mr Phillips's departure. Having volunteered this, she seemed to hesitate. Her evident deliberation began to interest Miss Fisher.

'His father had a stroke,' she remarked, 'or so he told Mrs K.' She added, after a significant pause, 'Funny his girlfriend not seeing him off. I should have thought, by this time, they knew each other well enough for that.'

'Perhaps,' said Miss Searle, 'she had a bus to catch.' She spoke with marked reserve. Miss Fisher was right in believing her to be a light sleeper. On the other hand, her room was on the opposite side of the corridor to Ellen's, whereas Miss Fisher's was next door. Miss Searle had heard enough to breed painful surmises, but not enough to create certainty. At the time, she had stifled her misgivings, partly because it was a Christian duty not to believe the worst of people, and partly because, had she continued to entertain them, they would have ruined her night's sleep. She had never, knowingly, been under the same roof with this kind of thing before; the thought that it might be repeated on other nights had been quite horrible, and the Phillips exodus had come as an immeasurable relief. Now she wanted to brush the whole matter from her thoughts, and had almost succeeded in doing so until the look in Miss Fisher's eye had thrust it back again. It settled her doubts. She became convinced immediately that nothing suggested with such vulgarity could ever have had lodgment in her own mind: she had examined the idea, it now seemed to her, only to dismiss it on the spot. This conviction gave poise and dignity to her reply. 'A tragic interruption to a holiday. I hope the poor man will find his father still alive.'

'Let's hope so, I'm sure. It's funny how many grandmothers turn the corner even after the funeral, round about Cup Final day.'

'Indeed?' said Miss Searle. She pictured Miss Fisher on a wooden seat, eating something out of a bag and squired by a person with a cloth cap, a rosette, and probably a hand-rattle as well. Her face showed this all too clearly. Miss Fisher, who as a matter of fact thought football (except hospital rugger, of course) very common, was deeply resentful.

'I've got my own reasons,' she said, 'for what I think, and good ones too. But,' she concluded with dignity, 'least said soonest mended, perhaps.'

'I do so agree with you. After all, sickness and bereavement are serious matters, to the people concerned.'

This gently stated truth reduced Miss Fisher to a strangled silence. If she did not feel literally capable of killing Miss

Searle, she understood how murders happen. A swift panorama went through her mind's eye of the crying women, and tensely silent men, to whom she had brought cups of tea in her little office, turning out herself when she was busiest to leave them in peace; of the recurring effort to say with conviction her lines about a peaceful passing and feeling nothing at the end. She never forgot that though she had played her own role a hundred times, theirs was new and terrible to each of them; she dreaded getting mechanical. How dared this bloodless, desiccated woman, who'd have run a mile from five minutes of it, assume that she had no feelings just because she wouldn't hide her head in the sand like an ostrich? Anger made her, for once, almost fully articulate.

'You're not much use to anyone that's in real trouble,' she said, 'if you're afraid to look at life as it is.'

She had intended the 'you' as an indefinite pronoun. Miss Searle, however, chose to take it as a personal one. Her face grew rigid.

'We should all take care, I think, not to generalise our professional outlook. The whole of life is not necessarily a case-history.'

'Nobody said it was.' Miss Fisher had worked up, at last, to the voice she used when she had words with the night sister. 'And if we all called it a case-history every time a healthy young couple jumped into bed, the world would be a dirtier place than what it is, and that's saying a lot.'

Feeling better for this, she watched Miss Searle's face with some curiosity. The little patches of colour had congested, in an ugly stagnant mauve, on her sallow cheeks. It made Miss Fisher uncomfortable; but she honestly did not see that she had been needlessly cruel, or that her assault had been aimed at the defenceless. Twenty years of hard fact had narrowed an imagination that had been willing, but never very subtle: she could sympathise with pain, with loss, with the fear of death, with the simpler frustrations of ambition or love. She could sympathise with the fear of difficult thinking; she had often felt it herself. She could not sympathise with the fear of truth, or think of it as being in any way conditioned: she thought of it merely as she would have thought of another nurse who refused to dress a septic case when there were no gloves.

Without compassion, feeling only that she had taken down a pretentious arrogance, she stood, her stocky figure firmly planted, and watched Miss Searle walk down the garden path to the road.

Miss Searle, for her part, made her way unseeingly down the lane till a furious hooting, and a sound of grinding brakes, roused her to a sense of her surroundings. A van-driver, who had had a more unpleasant half-second than she, was swearing at her in the reaction of relief. She caught two of the words as he passed. The whole world seemed to have become obscene. Now to her previous sensations was added that of acute physical fright. Her legs were shaking under her. When she reached the sea-front, she sank down on the first seat she could find.

She felt not only defiled, but a victim of the bitterest injustice. She believed in love, and in preserving a high ideal of it. To confirm her belief, she had herself been in love twice, experiencing on each occasion some years of romantic secret unhappiness. Each time, she had realised she was in love shortly after becoming certain that the object, once by a vow of celibacy and once by approaching marriage, was placed for ever beyond hope. She had never doubted that these facts represented the will of God, and that her spiritual development owed much to their uncomplaining acceptance. Often when she looked about the world she wondered how women she knew could endure the makeshift, unbeautiful relationships to which they so inexplicably abandoned themselves. She concluded that they must be naturally insensitive, and preferred to leave it at that. With the passing of years, she had come by unnoticed degrees to feel that the elementary emotions were in themselves signs of an aesthetic deficiency, and especially so when they were strong. The only modern novels that found permanent room on her shelves were about women of exquisitely refined sensibility, to whom a dozen unkind or tasteless words, a moment's falling away from perfect tact by a loved one, were lethal, the end of the world. They reinforced her faith that she was herself adjusted only to relationships like this. Her own loneliness had become for her simply the proof of a discrimination to which nothing was tolerable but the best.

This assurance enabled her after a short time to forgive Miss Fisher, as she would have forgiven a tramp for being unwashed in view of the lack of facilities. She pitied her, a blade whose edge had been blunted on humanity's necessary chores; there was a place in the world for such instruments, adapted to work on which a finer tool would break. She felt compassion also for young Mr Phillips, still in anxious suspense on the train, and for Miss Shorland, deprived of a promising friendship and slandered besides. These exercises soothed her mind; but her nerves still felt much upset; it would be better to take a brisk turn along the front, to blow the cobwebs away. She rose. A boy and girl on the other end of the seat, who had picked one another up only twenty minutes before, watched her off, discerning the relief in one another's eyes with hope and delight.

At this rate, thought Miss Fisher, the queue wouldn't be in before the big picture began.

The pavement outside the cinema, in a windless angle of

street, was hot underfoot; inside it would be stuffy. Cinemas always seemed to upset one's complexion for hours afterwards; she had thought, this morning, that this was one of her better days.

'Double at three and nine,' said the commissionaire.

A couple who had been standing farther back in the queue walked briskly past her. The woman's self-satisfaction seemed to be printed between the shoulder-blades of her disappearing back. The film would have been going for ten minutes or so at this rate, and it probably wouldn't be worth seeing round. She had dangled it in front of herself like a carrot in front of a donkey, to give herself an interest; an artificial carrot, she thought.

Her mind reverted to the morning, when from her window she had seen Mr Langton starting out. He had had on an old khaki shirt and old, faded grey flannels, with a battered rucksack, three parts empty, hung on one shoulder. As he went down the path she could see that he still had the loose easy stride of a young man. He had looked up at the sky once or twice as he walked, and she wondered for a moment if he would discern some unfavourable sign and turn back; but he had hitched his other shoulder into the rucksack and walked on out of sight. Now she suddenly knew – as if the moment had been a photographic film, standing in developing-fluid till the image appeared – that this was the moment in which she had given up hope.

She did not recognise it with any sense of drama; it had happened before, and she dismissed it now with the kind of joke she kept ready for such occasions. There must be something the matter with me, she thought, the way I always go for these brainy types. She puzzled over it, unaware that the queue had shifted a little, so that the man who had been standing just behind her was now at her side. It can't be genuine, she thought, or I'd go in for deep books and that in my spare time, like some of these new nurses do. Let's face it, the only way I like it is hearing a man talk; and what's *he* going to get out of that? Her own aspirations struck her as laughable to the point of farce. She had never entered the homes of any men engaged in creative work; the thought that she might find them, not infrequently, held together by women of temperament not unlike her own, never crossed the threshold of her humility. She dismissed the fading of her birthright, saying to herself that she was too old for such nonsense.

'Double at four and six.'

The queue trickled up, sluggishly. Was it worth waiting? With an irritable little sigh, she looked at her watch.

'Excuse me, but might I trouble you for the right time?'

'Ten to three.' She took in enough, in an inconspicuous glance, to decide on making it just more than a statement, touched with a note of friendly commiseration. Why on earth, she wondered, hadn't she noticed that this was happening? It was so unlike her to be dense.

Five minutes later, as she turned her back on the queue, she felt her own shoulder-blades flouting the unescorted. You can throw your whole life away, she thought, sitting around for a miracle to happen. Makes you an old maid before your time. I've had enough of *them* today.

She kept Miss Searle's face, defiantly, in front of her mind. It was easy, through that window, to renounce and deny the lost enchanted land.

7

Running Belay

'Look, I've found a perfectly good broom.'

'There's a fresh lot of drift on this beach every day,' said Neil. 'It's an inshore current from down channel, I suppose.' He watched her turning over the bleached wood, feeling irritated with himself. He had seen her, from above, before she could possibly have seen him, and could easily have gone his own way. At the time, he had decided that if he appeared it would prevent her from monopolising the beach by undressing there again. Now he had involved himself in a conversation, and could see no excuse for getting away. Since he had brought it on himself, he might as well be civilised about it. He walked over to inspect the ship's broom, and agreed that it was well-preserved. He himself had just found half a cork life-jacket, but did not spoil her fun by mentioning it.

'It's quite hard to buy good brooms now,' she said, inspecting the bristles. 'I wonder if Mrs Kearsey would like it.'

Reflecting that if she decided to drag it home, he could

scarcely do less than offer to carry it, he said hastily, 'It would fall to bits if it were used, I expect, after being in the sea.'

'I suppose it would.' She laid it down meekly. She had sounded a little damped: he wondered if she had followed his train of thought, felt rather ashamed of it, justified it by common sense, and experienced a silly urge towards rehabilitation. 'What do you think of this?' he asked, producing a specimen of his own. 'It's been subjected to pretty intense heat, by the look of it. Queer stuff.'

She straightened up, shaking a lock of soft brown hair out of her eyes. He showed her the thing, a brittle metallic lump, honeycombed by the pressure of expanding gases; she pored over it, and took it from him to turn it over. She had rather pleasant hands, cool and slim, with nails decently kept but otherwise as nature made them. He hated varnish.

'It looks like nothing on earth,' she said, and then, with a naïve eagerness, 'I tell you what, I wonder if it is.'

'Is what?'

'Nothing on earth. Do you know any geology? I don't; it was only an idea.'

'Speaking from a complete ignorance of the subject, I was wondering if it could be meteoritic myself.' For no reason he found himself wondering if he had said this like a schoolmaster; she seemed encouraged, however, as if she had half expected a snub. It was odd, he thought, that a good-looking girl (woman, rather, if one could remember it) should not have more confidence. The recent Mr Phillips, no doubt, had not done much to help. Continuing to stare absently at the piece of mineral in her hands, Neil thought, He seemed to have passed through some kind of orthodox school. God knows what schools let these types through without doing *something* to deflate their egos.

'I expect,' the girl said suddenly, 'you're thinking much the same as I am.'

'Well—' began Neil in a good deal of embarrassment, before reflecting that this was very unlikely. He smiled quickly and changed it to 'Well?'

'How long it will be before something like this is all that's left of us too. Perhaps this is part of some other planet that grew a dangerous animal in its old age.'

'Yes,' said Neil unwillingly. Like the pang of an old sickness he felt again, mocking his struggles, the deadening sense that his own trouble and effort were meaningless dust in the path of a cosmic disaster. Since he had ceased to believe collectively in humanity, the only answer he could see was beyond personality altogether, and, so far, beyond his strength. He did not see much profit, or pleasure, in discussing all this.

'You might as well forget all about it,' he said, 'and go on picking up shells. You can't do anything; you're young. No one gets power till they're half rotten. What does Leonardo say in one of those jottings of his? "I thought I was learning how to live, while I was learning how to die."' He had not meant to say so much.

'I don't suppose,' she said a little impatiently, 'that I'm so much younger than you are. No one's young, who was more than a child when this began.'

Considering what they were discussing, his momentary pleasure struck him as a fantastic comment on human vanity. Well, he thought, they dug up coupled skeletons under the lava at Herculaneum. He glanced at the girl; she looked too shy and vulnerable to be thought at in this way, and he talked on rather to protect her from his own mind than in any wish to share it.

'It's a drift,' he said, 'like sand drifting into a ravine. You put out your hand, and it drifts through your fingers. Men in the mass are a dead weight, like shale. Take them separately, most of them know not to kill, or steal, or say "My people are better than yours, so clear out". But put a dozen together so that they can say "Of course, I'm not doing this for myself" ... Talk about the Truth Drug. They didn't need to invent that, while they could watch a mob.'

'What do you mean by a mob exactly?' She had looked up; she had grey eyes, faintly streaked with brown in the centre.

Neil smiled without amusement. 'Where two or three are gathered together, there am I.' He had wanted to shock her, and, as soon as he had done só, could not imagine why. 'I'm sorry; there's no particular need to be blasphemous about it.'

'It's all right,' said the girl quietly. She did not speak as if she were smoothing a rebuke, but as if he had apologised for an involuntary sound of pain. He wondered why this did not make him angry.

'The way I think of it,' she went on, 'is that all these people who are running things are like a man who's been told that he'll die unless he knocks off drink. He believes it in an abstract kind of way; but each time he pours out another, he says to himself it'll be all right if he knocks off before the next, and this one can't be really decisive.'

'You're optimistic if you relate this kind of process to any individual personality, even the worst. Hitler was probably almost human, till the first time he got a cheer. No, it's a drift, like sand.'

She looked at the bit of clinker in her hand, as if he were telling her something about it; then straight into his face.

'Well – what ought we to do?'

He said, wearily but not unkindly, 'My dear child.'

'You mean it's too late already?'

'It's a lovely day,' said Neil gently. 'Here we are at the sea-side. Why not enjoy it?'

She dropped the meteorite on the pebbles, where it fell with a dry brittle noise. 'But isn't all this because everyone's saying that?'

'Of course,' he said indifferently, more concerned with watching her. 'Human drift is the most powerful force in the world. It wiped out a city of seventy thousand, only the other day. The people we think are controlling it are drifters too; just conspicuous pebbles lying on top.'

'Very well.' He could see a tension in her body like that of a stretched bow. 'Perhaps it's no good. It was no good last time, and people wondered why they'd wasted so much effort, and started tired. But what I think is, we've got to go on caring, and swimming against the stream, to keep alive. I mean, to keep alive until we die.'

'You're right,' he said slowly. 'But you're young.'

She said with a half-hidden and what seemed an old bitter-ness, 'All right, you needn't keep rubbing it in.'

'I'm sorry,' he said a little blankly.

'You don't have to take any notice of that.' She turned away towards the sea. 'But anyhow, you can't back out by just pre-tending you belong to the older generation. You know that yourself.'

'That's a courteous rebuke.' He found himself exerting his will to make her turn and meet his eyes.

'Was I rude?' she said, turning. 'I didn't mean to be.'

He smiled at her without saying anything. It was hardly fair, for he had known she couldn't cope with it. She blushed faintly – she was getting tanned, but clearly and evenly, so that it still showed – and, picking up a pebble, did a duck-and-drake with it on the sea. In spite of the ripples, she managed to make it bounce once.

Neil found a flatter one; not without satisfaction – he had not tried for at least twenty years – he got his to bounce twice.

'Talk about katharsis. We must have unloaded enough to make room for lunch. Let's have it on this raft, or whatever it is.'

It was roomy, and had one gunwale intact, making a good back-rest. They explored their lunch-packets; Neil, who did not like cake but had always lacked the nerve to tell Mrs Kearsey so, swapped his portion with Ellen for some bloater sandwiches. She assured him earnestly that he was losing in food-value as the cake had dried eggs in it; but she ate the sweet stuff with childish enjoyment. He stopped himself just in time from saying that they must repeat this practical arrangement another day. He would probably not feel like company tomorrow, and would be sorry if he had landed himself with it.

'No, thank you,' she said afterwards. 'I really never smoke out of doors.'

'I used not to either.' He lay down to protect his lighter from the wind, and feeling too lazy to get up again, stayed there. A gull mewed, close overhead. He realised he had been as nearly asleep as made no matter, and ought to apologise. He turned his head to do so, still feeling drowsy and regretting the need to start conversation again; with relief he perceived that she was nearly asleep too. The position into which he had turned himself was more comfortable than the one he had left; he would drop off again in a minute. A faint drone of insects came from the edge of the woods above, and the sea made a sleepy plashing and sucking against the stones.

She had curled sideways, half away from him, an arm locked round her bare knees. In the strong sunlight, her brown legs had a film of golden down, flat and silky, which had been invisible when she stood. It reminded him of something; he pursued the likeness with the obstinacy which accompanies a flight from serious thought, and presently remembered the pale silk that some rock-growing plants have on their leaves. In the satisfaction of one who has tidied something up, he relaxed again; but the desire for sleep had become less pressing. A few minutes later he told himself, sharply, This is ridiculous. I'd better wake up before I start taking it seriously.

'I nearly went to sleep then,' said Ellen without moving.

'So did I.' An undeveloped child, he thought. Oh, well, it happens like weather. Take no notice and it goes off.

'They say lettuce has bromide in it,' she remarked.

'Mm – m?' She did not answer; she had settled again, thinking he did not want to be disturbed. This, he now perceived, had been his intention. He sat up quickly.

'The water looks nice today. Mind if I go in?'

She stirred idly. 'Have you got a swim-suit or shall I clear out?' She might have been talking to a brother; she was a contradictory mixture, he thought.

'No, of course don't move, I'm all equipped. Plenty of trees.'

'I've brought mine too. Thanks for waking me up, I'd have wasted the whole afternoon. You take that end and I'll take this.' She fished a towel and costume out of her rucksack and strolled off.

Neil was first in the water. It did not take him long to realise that it was a most unpleasant beach for bathing at low tide. The stones, which were smallish at the top of the slope, got progressively larger, developing into boulders; and the tops of what looked like full-sized rocks were visible farther out. As he picked his way uncomfortably into deeper water, where it was still unsafe to swim, he thought, She might have been drowned, bathing here on her own.

'Look out for the rocks,' he called when she came out of

cover. 'You won't manage any swimming. I'm going in in a minute.'

'All right,' she said cheerfully, and ducked down to wet her shoulders. From where he was she looked very young, awkward and angular, edging about in the ungraceful way which is inevitable with sharp stones underfoot. He was glad to be doing something active; already he was wondering what it had all been about. Finding a fairly clear stretch of water, he got in a short swim. A sharp little cry halted him, followed by a splash. He was still in his depth; feeling for a flat surface he stood up. She had disappeared.

The next few seconds, during which he was floundering over, felt like several years. Speed was impossible, one could neither walk nor swim. He used hands and feet indiscriminately on the rocks, nearly falling several times himself. Recovering from one of these slips, he saw her standing safely a dozen yards away. For a moment, in his relief, he felt angry. 'Are you all right?' he shouted, out of breath.

'Yes. Sorry; I slipped on some seaweed. I only bumped my knee a bit. There's not much point in this, though, is there? I think I've had enough for today.' She started to walk shorewards.

'So have I. Not a very good idea of mine.' He lingered to let her get ahead. When she got near the water's edge, however, she checked, and stood still, looking down. I suppose, he thought, she's found some more rubbish she thinks might appeal to Mrs Kearsey.

Suddenly she turned, and started walking out to sea again. He looked at her curiously; she was going as if she could not see.

'What is it?' he asked, coming towards her.

In a voice as blank as her face she said, 'Don't come this way.'

Neil came over – the stones were easier here – and walked past her to the place where she had been. At first he thought it was a long boulder with weed on it; he found himself anxious to go on thinking this. His next step fell on a loose stone; he stumbled, and pitched forward almost on top of the thing. He just saved himself; but he had seen more than enough, and only took a second look because he knew that she must have seen everything. Half the skull was missing; there was slime in it, and, as he looked, a crab scuttled out. Part of the clothing remained, some kind of overalls; the arm was gone from inside one sleeve. His stomach heaved; he would have felt better if he could have vomited, but forced it back somehow, remembering the girl.

When he turned back to her she was still standing much as before, except that she seemed to know he was there. Making his voice as commonplace as he could manage, he said, 'I'm sorry about that; it's not very nice, is it? Come round this way with me.'

He put out his hand for hers, but she did not move. He saw that her face was the colour of vellum. Her body leaned forward, slowly; he reached out just in time to catch her.

She was slippery with salt water, and her dead weight almost slid through his arms. He managed to gather her into a transportable shape, and carried her up to the beach, the stones which he could not see cutting his feet. The raft where they had sat was partly sheltered; he laid her on the sun-warmed boards. Something rang as he put her down; it was a little gold St Christopher medal, hanging backward from a chain round her neck. He fished it up lest it should constrict her breathing, and saw the Air Force wings on the other side.

She looked as if she were dead, and he could not see her breathe. He felt for her wrist, but failed to find the vein. It's only a faint, he told himself; don't be a fool. All he knew to do for it was to throw water; and she was dripping wet already, even her hair. People did die of shock, he remembered suddenly; and, pulling down a shoulder-strap, he felt for her heart. Her breast was light, firm and cold, and pale like her lips. It was not till he had found the slow pulse under it that he had time to think what he was doing, and covered her again quickly.

She must have been shaken already by her fall among the rocks (he noticed now that her knee was grazed) and the other had happened within minutes. Warmth was the thing for shock, he remembered; but he had no idea where in the dense woods she had left her clothes. He had better fetch his own. As he was about to get up, she opened her eyes. Her face looked, now, both vacant and terrified. As a boy he had gone off once himself after a fall, and remembered the nightmare struggle to re-create oneself out of nothing. He rubbed one of her hands (the nails looked disconcertingly pallid and blue) and said, 'It's all right now,' hoping it sounded rather less ineffectual than it felt.

The drowning look passed, and her eyes began to wander. When they found his face, they rested there in a dim relief. In the thin uncontrolled voice of a sick child she said, 'I'm cold.' Her teeth began to chatter, turning her breath as it passed through them into a sobbing noise; there were blue-brown streaks under her eyes. 'Of course you are,' he said. 'Just a moment, I'll get you something.'

He ran off to the trees, found his shirt, slacks and towel (it had been too hot to bring a jacket), ran back and bundled them round her. She ought, he knew, to be got out of her wet costume without delay. In her present state she would hardly notice it, but she was too shy a creature not to be horribly upset afterwards. As he was wondering which consideration was the more urgent, she plucked uncertainly at a fold of the shirt and sat up.

'I am *so* sorry.'

The abject apology in her voice affected him queerly. He said, 'Don't be silly, lie down for a bit,' and put her back again.

'No, I'm all right. Please have your clothes.' She held the shirt shakily towards him, setting her teeth to keep them quiet.

'I'm not cold; it's a hot day really, you know. Look, tell me where your things are and I'll bring them over.'

She roused herself to give him a landmark, and he found them without much trouble. She did not look fit yet, he thought, to leave. 'Can you manage?' he asked, trying not to feel an awkwardness which would communicate itself to her. 'I can give you a hand, it doesn't matter.' He tried to think up some further reassurance, but each phrase as he considered it sounded more offensive than the last.

'No, I can, thank you.' She spoke with as simple a courtesy as if he had offered to carry a parcel for her. He felt the same shiver of compassion that had moved him when she said that she was sorry. 'I feel quite all right now. You go and get dressed yourself.' It was clearly impossible to convince her that she, and not the air, was cold; he left her in peace.

He was relieved to find, when he got back, that she had had a woollen sweater in her rucksack. She still looked very pale and pinched; but as soon as he got there, she scrambled to her feet and said, 'Let's go.'

'Not yet; it's too long a climb. Stay in the sun and get warm again.'

'Climbing makes you warm. I'd rather go.'

Neil looked over his shoulder; the tide had receded, and the thing at its edge was almost exposed. He moved himself into her line of vision. 'All right. We'll rest on the way.' He picked up the rucksacks and, to keep her from looking round as much as to support her, put his arm round her waist. Most of his thoughts were elsewhere. He had just remembered something she had told him at their first meeting, and was wondering what, if anything, could possibly help.

When they reached the track, which was too narrow for two, she freed herself and went ahead. 'Don't go so fast,' he said, for the pace she was making would have been foolish for anyone perfectly fit. She said absently 'Sorry,' and slowed down for a few yards, working up to the same speed again. A couple of hundred feet up, they came to a grassy shelf where the trees opened, and a splash of sun came through. He caught her arm.

'That's enough, now. Sit down.'

She settled herself obediently on the thin grass, panting a little. The beach was hidden from here; a rounded recession of tree-tops showed only a silvery strip beyond them, bounded by the far grey coast of Wales.

'Why not break the rule,' he said, 'and have a cigarette?'

'It isn't a rule.' She smiled quite convincingly. 'I'd like one in a minute. I think I shall have to do my hair first. I'm sorry to be so messy; but the tangles dry in if you don't.'

'Carry on,' said Neil. He began to add, 'I'm used to it,' and changed it to 'I don't mind.'

A comb was certainly urgent. She flung the rat-tailed mop forward over her face, and worried through it with dogged concentration. If one had planned for her a pose to underline her most immature aspect, he thought, it would have been this. The combing, on top of the salt and damp, left her hair darkened and almost straight. Nothing but a serge gym-tunic was wanting to complete an illusion which Neil, from his own angle, would have been ready to accept. The last half-hour, however, had shifted his perspective; his own angle had lost importance.

When she was ready he gave her the cigarette; he noticed that she could hardly keep it steady against his lighter. They smoked for a few minutes in silence, looking out at the trees and sea. After all, he thought, interference was futile; what could anyone do? Nothing except perhaps harm. Better leave things to their own movement. But in the half relief which this thought engendered, he knew that it was his own movement, or lack of it, that he wanted to let alone; that this had become in most things his attitude of mind. She had told him this morning what she thought of it; it seemed a little ironical that she should be exposed to the first effects of her own advice.

He took a quick look at her profile, remarking again how a certain delicate strength, integral to its structure, was spoiled by an unfinished look which suggested not arrested growth but a kind of defeat. Pausing still irresolute, he considered the hopelessness of words: words which are the strait-jacket of the imagination, the sandpaper blunting all fine edges; which trample out ecstasy like a heavy corps-de-ballet dancing *Giselle*. Words, the supreme anaesthetic, he thought; and remembered the failures and aspirations of his youth. From this he came to the idea that it worked both ways; now was the time to make an asset of a liability. She would think him a thick-skinned moron, of course. But never mind.

'We shall have to see the police about this, I'm afraid,' he said. She looked round; he could see that this external fact came strangely to her; he had expected it would. 'Don't worry, though, it's only a formality and I expect I can do most of it. You'll have to make a deposition, that's all. They're used to it, on a coast like this.'

She leaned back, easily, against a slab of rock behind her.

'Yes,' she said with brisk naturalness, 'of course, they must be. I think I'd better come along with you; they're sure to want me sooner or later; we may as well get it tidied up straight away.'

Thank God, Neil was thinking, I didn't let this go. He did not pause to examine his own sense of urgency, which was born of a realisation that she was not the Sensitive Type. He had been in love with one of these in his early twenties, and it had taken him eighteen painful months to discover that she could get over anything in half an hour, by the fortifying process of covering everyone in range with a guilt-laden sense of their own inadequacy. It had been like the enormous mount which lets no one forget that the small, weak etching it encloses is Art. This was something else. This determined cunning, as of an injured animal trying to hide itself in a protective back-ground, was something he recognised. He knew it, too well.

The bracing strain of responsibility, which he had almost lost the feel of, tightened in his mind; but he did not notice it. He felt misunderstood and lonely, as people do when they must pick up and handle a hurt animal that only knows the pain.

'I'll see them first,' he said, 'and find out what they want. Then you can do your stuff if you have to. There can't be much to investigate, though. He had on his parachute harness. Must have been posted as missing weeks ago.'

She looked round at him quickly; he had been ready for it, and met her eyes. 'Hard luck on the poor bloke; he probably flew through the war without a scratch.'

He wondered what he had better do if at this point she simply got up and walked off; he would probably have done it himself. Instead she said, with a flat kind of submission, 'The war hasn't been over very long.'

'Too long for that,' he said. 'Much too long. I've no special knowledge but I know that much.'

'I forgot I'd told you.' She seemed to re-discover her cigarette and drew on it, looking away.

'You know, don't you, there's no conceivable possibility?'

'I suppose not.'

'There's no supposition about it,' said Neil sharply. In his determination to convince, he used his disciplinary classroom voice; she looked, for a moment, almost startled. 'Sorry,' he said. 'But you've got to snap out of this, you know.'

'Please,' she said, 'you mustn't bother about me. I've been enough trouble already. I can't think why every time I run into you I have to make such an embarrassing nuisance of myself.'

'Now look here.' Neil was getting unconsciously into his stride. Boys too have their painful reserves, and piercing them had sometimes been his thankless but necessary job. 'You can drop all that stuff. I'm supplying all the nuisance-value at the moment. I know that. You're wondering why in God's name I haven't the elementary tact to shut up, and I know that too. But—'

'Of course I'm not wondering,' she interrupted him. 'I'm not such a fool as that.'

In the presence of this quiet comprehension, he felt the master's-study approach jolted somewhat out of gear. 'All right, then, we know where we are. I want to bust this up for you before it has time to sink in. The more flat-footed I am about it all, probably the better. Put it down to obtuseness or what you like, so long as it works.'

She sat forward hugging her knees, as if she were fighting her own listlessness. 'No, you're perfectly right. And you're right in what you haven't said, too.'

'Such as?'

'That all this personal stuff's completely insignificant.'

'I haven't said it, and I wasn't going to.'

'No, I know you weren't, because there's no answer. We know it's true and it's at the back of everything, now. This – this feeling that one hasn't the right to feel.'

He was shocked into momentary silence; she was too young for this. Presently he said, 'My dear, that's the sickness of the age. Let's stick to the personal, where we can do something, even if it isn't much.'

'You can't do that after you've seen the other.' She locked her hands more tightly round her knees; he thought that she was shivering and said, 'Are you cold? If so we'll move.'

'Not really; the sun's quite hot here. You want to make me talk about this, don't you? Well, I will, why not? What's happened is that I've seen a corpse in the water, and it happened to have flying kit on or something that seemed like it, so now I know how Jock looked.'

'Yes, go on.' He only spoke to give her some feeling of human company.

'Well, what about it? A few years ago I could have felt it was rather out of the way; the sort of thing that makes you say to yourself "I mustn't see life like that, I must get back to normal." Only now it is normal; it's trivial even. Someone who'd been tortured at Dachau, or crawled round the ruins at Hiroshima with their bone-marrow rotting away, would say I didn't know what trouble meant. And they'd be right. A little thing like this is just enough to start your imagination off, and you can go on till it stops and still there's more. And if it had even taught people anything ... but already they're deciding in what circumstances they'll go on to something worse. How can one cope with oneself, or try to get straightened out, when it's not worth taking seriously? What can one do?'

'I don't know,' said Neil slowly. 'The nearest thing, I suppose.' He moved up to her, sat back against the rock, and drew her into his arms. 'Don't worry about this. You're cold and I haven't got a coat to give you, that's all.'

Except for the first hesitation of adjusting her balance to his, she made no resistance at all. She accepted him as she might have done the coat for whose absence he had apologised. She was cold, as he had guessed, with the deadly devitalised cold of nervous exhaustion, and he was warm like any other healthy animal on a day like this: he could feel her absorbing the warmth as instinctively as a starved cat does milk, and when he held her more tightly it was only to be sure that she got enough of it. She felt a little like a cat, he thought, with sharp slender bones under a supple coat of flesh; presently she began to relax, as a cat does that has been brought in out of the weather.

'I don't make much of a Brains Trust,' he said. 'You ask for bread and I give you stone, or the next thing to it. And if I'd had a double whisky handy, I'd have given you that.'

'I know you would.' He could hear a dim smile in her voice.

'If I'd realised the state you were in I'd have done something about it sooner. You still feel like a fish; come over a bit more.'

It was no surprise to him, now, that she took it so simply. She was too drained for anything as vital as a sexual impulse to have any reality even in her imagination, and it had none for him either because of this.

'I felt so awful,' she murmured with vague apology, 'and you're so beautifully warm.'

'You want a hot drink inside as well. We can get some tea at that farm on the top. Comfortable? You know, none of this is as new as we think, all you were saying; the scale's altered, that's all. It's all in *Hamlet* and *Lear*. Lear was old and rotten with power; he took one good look and broke up . . . I'm only talking for the sake of it, go to sleep if you'd rather.'

'No, I shall keep thinking, anyway. Don't stop.'

'Hamlet was young, with phenomenal guts. He turned down every possible way of escape one after the other, beginning where Lear left off. The rest was silence. It still is. But we've been escaping into louder and louder noises for three hundred odd years ... If our trained nurse, Miss Whatsit, could hear this conversation, she'd tell me I ought to be shot.'

'Perhaps she would. But she'd be wrong for once.'

'Hamlet moves in on all of us at last, like the ghost of his own father.

> '"Do you not come your tardy son to chide,
> That, laps'd in time and passion, lets go by
> Th'important acting of your dread command?"'

'You didn't talk like this on the beach,' she said.

'No? I must be doing it now because it's so obviously the ideal moment, when you're all in and need to rest.'

'It is a rest, somehow,' she said. 'I don't know why.'

A cloud crossed the sun, and by contrast the air at once seemed cold. It caught her just as she had stopped shivering and made her start again; and, as instinctively as she might have pulled a coat together, she pressed herself against him. He held her firmly, and continued to hold her after the sun was out, and her shivering had ceased, and the contact of her body had begun to be warm instead of chill. Suddenly it became apparent to him that the present arrangement was outlasting its workability, and had better stop.

'I'm going to take off the blanket now,' he said, 'or we shan't make this farm in time for tea.'

'Yes, it must be getting late.' But she was leaning too far off her balance to move until he let her go. He had forgotten this when he spoke; or perhaps remembered it.

'Feeling warmer?' he said.

'Yes.' In the second's delay which he had meant should not happen, he felt the sudden, startled thumping of her heart. He got to his feet quickly, pulling her with him.

'Come on. If we're lucky we might get an egg with it. They gave me two once. The riddle of the universe works out quite differently, after a couple of eggs.'

8

'The Expedition has aroused public interest . . . '

'Good morning,' said Miss Fisher briskly.

'Good morning.' Miss Searle's voice was so remote that it reminded Miss Fisher, at once, of yesterday's strained relations. She herself had had, as she said to herself, something better to think about. The encounter in the cinema queue had been, of its kind, quite a success; she had arranged to repeat it. On her way downstairs she had looked forward to dropping the kind of hint which would indicate that her time was going to be less at her disposal. But, she thought, it seems we're not speaking this morning; fancy anyone being so touchy. Passing behind Miss Searle, however, on the way to the steamed haddock, Miss Fisher saw that she was only absorbed in a letter; perhaps there was no ill-feeling after all. One place at the table had been used already; but Miss Fisher was used to that by now, and had decided in any case not to waste any more time on foolishness. A bird in hand was the thing.

Miss Searle, reaching the end of her letter, turned back and ran over the essential part again.

'I was so interested in your mentioning the schoolmaster, because Denis knew his name at once.' The paragraph went on for two pages, and turned back to the middle. 'One does see how distressing it must have been for the Headmaster and *very bad indeed* for the boys, but Denis says he thinks it was *too much* covered up. He was there for Speech Day shortly after his demob, and feeling very *remote* from school of course, and said that the wildest rumours were going about, especially among the younger ones. Quite a number were saying that Mr Langton had *shot* this soldier and that the Headmaster and the Camp Commandant had conspired to hush it up! I am sure it would be quite impossible to do anything of the kind! Boys do so love sensation, it seems there is another rumour, which *everyone* believes, that his hair went white in a night! Denis himself was quite upset about it all – I think when he was there himself Mr L was rather a *hero* of his, though he is much too grown-up now to be reminded of it! It really is terrible how quickly time . . . '

'Excuse me, would you mind passing the pepper?'

'So sorry.' Never, thought Miss Searle, a moment's privacy. One should always open letters in one's own room; it was impossible to know what might be in them. Nothing was more unpleasant than to be stared at as if people hoped to read the contents of one's private correspondence reflected in one's face. She put the letter back in its envelope.

'Too good to be true, isn't it,' said Miss Fisher, 'the way the weather holds?'

'Yes, we're being very fortunate.' Miss Searle had another letter; she opened it and stared at it with fixed aloofness.

Miss Fisher's spirits, which had been bouncing on the up-current of the morning sunshine, lost a little of their buoyancy.

She had looked forward to the little vignette which, with the right emphasis and omissions, she had meant to draw for Miss Searle. In the process of telling, the memory would have grown into the picture; it would have acquired a dash of sophistication, a little colour of romance. Now memory had to manage alone, without the gin-and-lime which had helped last night. Miss Fisher had a good memory for a face and a voice; hundreds of patients and their relatives were assimilated into it each year. It showed her now a face a little glazed with gin and lime, and a voice, rather maudlin and self-pitiful, making significant generalisations about marriages where all the give and take was on one side.

Miss Searle laid down her second letter (a short note from the Bursar) and reached for the marmalade.

'I hope,' said Miss Fisher, brightening, 'I didn't disturb you last night coming in.'

'No. No, thank you.' Miss Searle considered picking up the note again; but it lay on the table, its six typed lines incautiously displayed. She put it resignedly away.

'I was a bit nervous Mrs K might have locked up and gone to bed, and she'd wonder where I'd got to, not knowing I was getting a lift by car. You know how time flies when people get talking, and it was such a lovely night it seemed wicked, really, to come in.'

Miss Searle, shut in her room, had found the night swelteringly hot, and had not slept till one. She had longed to get out to the coolness she knew must exist at the edge of the sea; but it would have been ill-advised to go alone, one might be subjected to annoyance if nothing worse. A waft of Miss Fisher's talcum powder reached her across the table, making her feel quite nauseated.

'Yes,' she said, with unmistakable finality.

Miss Fisher scraped margarine defiantly on to her toast, fighting her own sense of deflation. She hadn't expected eager curiosity; only some routine opening like 'Oh, you met a friend.' Almost anyone in hospital would have unbent that far. Her memories began to form again, with unwanted clarity.

Miss Searle finished her coffee, after which it was her intention to excuse herself and rise. She wanted to go to her room and read her letters again. She was already rolling her napkin when the door opened.

'Good morning,' said Neil cheerfully to the room in general, and went over to the sideboard for food.

Miss Searle's table-napkin was in her hand, half-rolled but still out of sight on her knee. Her fingers hovered over it, indecisively. The letter beside her plate seemed to be burning a hole in its envelope. She had taken for granted, when she came down, that as usual the used place at the table was his. The white streak in his hair always looked more startling when newly brushed. Now it was shocking to her, the concrete manifestation, crudely real, of ideas she was only used to receiving when they had been safely sterilised by literature. A strange and painful disturbance prickled in her back. If only she had saved the letter till later! She decided to go at once; but, at the moment of resolve, noticed Miss Fisher's eye wandering towards her with hopeful calculation. Really, she thought, the woman was a harpy, there was no other word; it would be too inconsiderate to leave a quiet, reserved man exposed all through breakfast to her undiluted vulgarity. Rising, Miss Searle cut herself a small slice of bread.

Mr Langton's reserve seemed, however, less in evidence than usual. He was positively talkative; and, taking casual charge of the conversation, kept it easily on common ground. Neil himself was not aware of making any particular effort. He had waked with an unanalysed sense of well-being, had experienced, for the first time in a long while, not the least discomfort at finding himself in the company of chance people, and was behaving as he might have done in the common-room when he had nothing better to do, blending the inharmonious elements with what (if he had thought about it) he would have felt to be very elementary *savoir-faire*. As often happens when people experience a radical change of mood, he felt quite naturally himself and unaware of producing a marked sense of contrast in others. Miss Fisher and Miss Searle each accepted the change as a personal tribute; each wondered when the other would become aware of her redundancy. The front door bell rang, but no one paid attention.

It was followed, however, after a few seconds, by the appearance of Mrs Kearsey. She looked distinctly shaken, and seemed to have some difficulty in finding words; directing at Neil, meanwhile, a glance compounded of doubt, reproach, and a determined hoping for the best.

'I'm so sorry, Mr Langton. But there's someone – asking to speak to you outside.'

Neil got to his feet. 'Is it the police?' he asked briskly.

Mrs Kearsey's assent fell into a silence which was heard even by Neil, who, having got through most of the routine yesterday, had thoughtlessly associated everyone present in his own sense of the commonplace. Gazing at the three faces, he wanted almost uncontrollably to laugh. Confused by this into a vague idea that he was explaining everything, he remarked, 'It's all right, they had me yesterday. It'll be Miss Shorland they want now. I'll just run up and warn her.'

They heard his feet taking the stairs in threes, then a tap on a door. 'Hullo, it's only me. They're here. Would you like—' After that the door must have opened, for his voice dropped, and only a general tone of solicitude could be heard.

Mrs Kearsey broke the silence with a polite nervous laugh. 'There are so *many* regulations nowadays, aren't there? I mean, really, nobody knows *where* they are, in a way. I must say, I do wish it could have been seen to without their coming here. Neighbours are so *silly*, you know.' Catching Miss Fisher's eye she added with relief, 'And spiteful, well, you'd hardly believe.'

Miss Fisher said, 'Well, I must say,' but the compulsion seemed to evaporate, for she said nothing more. At this point Neil came back into the room; his offer of support had not been taken up. The atmosphere hit him squarely, like a blast of conditioned air in the Tube.

'I'm so sorry,' he said to Mrs Kearsey, 'that you've been bothered with this. It's only about a body we found yesterday.' Seeing Mrs Kearsey's eyes protruding, he added, 'Washed up, I mean, on the beach.'

'Oh,' said Mrs Kearsey, settling. Through her little urbanisms, one could suddenly see in her a woman of the coast. 'That's the first since the war. It's a nasty thing for anyone on a holiday.' Neil felt remorse for his initial carelessness.

'I'm very sorry I didn't think to warn you, particularly as I'm responsible for their coming here. It shook Miss Shorland up a bit. I asked them to leave her over till she'd had a night's sleep; she found it first, it was a bit of a jar.' A little awkwardly, but feeling it to be necessary, he added, 'I don't think she'll want to talk about it very much.'

'Naturally not,' said Miss Searle formally. It was true that he had not looked at her; but she resented being included, even by accident. Her resentment was sudden and sharp, and surprised her by its force.

'I'll put on the kettle,' said Mrs Kearsey forgivingly, 'for some fresh tea. Miss Shorland will be able to do with a cup, after going over it all again, I'm sure.'

Miss Fisher, saying nothing, was remembering the first thing she had seen in hospital which had made her feel ill. Everyone had been too busy to notice. She had gone out into the sluice by herself, sat down on the bedpan steriliser, put her head between her knees for a minute, and gone back again. No one had missed her but the Sister, who had snapped at her for not being on hand when she was wanted. She had just turned eighteen.

When Mrs Kearsey had left for the kitchen, Neil hovered indeterminately for a minute, trying to think of a casual remark. His last had had, he felt, a touch of proprietorship which in retrospect made him feel foolish. Both the women at the table were looking at him – speculatively, he thought. He felt one of those waves of irritation which sometimes signal repressed shyness in people of adult intelligence. Briefly and pointlessly he said, 'Well, I suppose it'll be in the papers tomorrow,' and went out into the garden. He could see from there when the policeman left.

In the dining-room, there was a short but crucial silence. Neither Miss Fisher nor Miss Searle was fully aware of the processes with which it was occupied. They merely experienced them, and reacted. Miss Fisher, trained to prompt reactions, finished first.

'I'm sure,' she said, 'that when I read the papers, it isn't to look for things like *that*.'

A sudden wave of sympathy invaded Miss Searle. She had been hypercritical, she thought. Nurses must lead an extremely trying life, thanklessly giving their best while the doctors (Miss Searle pictured the doctors as exclusively male) stood about with unroughened hands, taking all the credit. It was enough to make any woman bitter and a little hard.

'It seems to be generally accepted among men,' she said, 'that women's interests are either trivial or sensational. It's a very convenient theory, of course.'

Miss Fisher could, she hoped, take a friendly advance in the spirit in which it was meant. In the manner of one continuing the main thread of the conversation, she replied, 'Talk about deep! No one would have guessed they knew each other to speak to, hardly. It just goes to show, doesn't it?'

'It does become a little clearer why the young woman elected to stay on.' Miss Searle was a little surprised to find she had said this, but felt no inclination to withdraw it.

'More fish in the sea. Well, she seems to know her stuff all right.'

Though the expression was deplorable, Miss Searle could not find it in her to condemn the sentiments. 'Really,' she said, 'men are as simple as children in many ways. There seems nothing so obvious that they're incapable of ignoring it when they wish, and a trained mind appears to make no difference whatever. The type of woman who can persuade them that she is helpless and sensitive and in need of protection ... it would be quite comical, if it didn't so often end in tragedy.'

'It's a pity,' said Miss Fisher significantly, 'his room's so out of the way. If he'd been down in our corridor the other night, he might know different.'

Miss Searle felt, as she so often did with Miss Fisher, that the safe surface of the conversation had turned to a quicksand from whose depths she shrank. In unthinking haste to shift her ground, she said, 'One would think a man used to keeping discipline would be a better judge of character; particularly when he has made one similar mistake already.' It was actually not until Miss Fisher's being had resolved itself, before her eyes, into an erect point of interrogation, that she remembered she had not recalled a matter of common knowledge. She had always hated anything upsetting to happen at breakfast. Surely Miss Fisher would realise ... But Miss Fisher was already saying '*Really?*' and waiting for an answer.

After all, thought Miss Searle, there had been no request for confidence in Madge's letter; nor had anything been done to place one under obligations in any other quarter.

'I know very little about the circumstances,' she said, 'so perhaps it was thoughtless of me to mention it. Most unlike me; I suppose this sudden invasion of police ... I simply heard from mutual friends that Mr Langton's marriage was rather ill-judged and turned out most unfortunately, I gathered.'

'I had a feeling all the time that there was *something* in the background.'

Beneath the crudeness of the words there moved an instinctive kind of humanity. It relieved Miss Searle, unawares, of the sense of pure vulgarity which would have made it impossible to go on. Besides, though she did not know why, she longed still to be talking, not yet to be left alone.

'Yes, she was apparently a girl a good deal younger than himself, and I should imagine—' She checked herself in confusion. She had been about to add '– from quite a different class; the school nurse.' In her anxiety to cover all trace of this, she told much more of the story than she had meant to tell.

'My God,' said Miss Fisher, 'what an awful thing.' There was a genuine compassion in her voice; but there was also, inevitably, the satisfied response to a strong sensation which is hard to avoid by people who have become indurated to minor ones. It made Miss Searle feel, for a moment, as if she had been standing with arms akimbo gossiping over a fence. Her sense of humiliation roused, in reaction, her instinctive defences. They were powerful ones; for more than ten years she had held a position in which it was most unsuitable to be in the wrong.

'Yes,' she said. 'Very dreadful indeed. Luckily men seem able to console themselves, and find distractions, much more quickly than most women would think possible.'

Shades of doubt, and a confused struggle with ideas, were reflected in Miss Fisher's face as she thought this over. Finally she said, 'Well, we're all of us human, I suppose.'

There was no depth of meaningless generalisation, Miss Searle thought, which would not pass for philosophy among the half-educated. She did not attempt reply. Miss Fisher, who never felt much at home herself with abstract thought, said, 'I should hope he divorced her, after that.'

'I believe so. One imagines it would hardly be made absolute yet.'

'Well,' said Miss Fisher, her voice suddenly sharp and practical, 'seeing he's the innocent party as they say, he'd better watch his step.'

A startled look fixed, for a moment, Miss Searle's pale eyes. She had never been forced to consider the technicalities of divorce. One either recognised it, or one did not. Her own position was, by heredity and conviction, that of the high Anglican.

'If he is a Churchman, he will probably not consider himself free to re-marry, in any case.'

Miss Fisher's mouth opened, remained parted for a moment, and closed again. She had heard that tone of voice before; you might as well beat your head on a wall, she thought, for all the use. Giving it up, she looked out of the window.

While they had been talking, the police must have left. At the moment when Miss Searle's eyes followed, involuntarily, the direction of Miss Fisher's, Ellen came out of the front door and joined Neil in the garden. Sound carried clearly in the still air; though the sentence with which he greeted her was not wholly audible, there was no doubt that it had included the use of her Christian name.

Miss Searle turned and smiled at Miss Fisher. It was the kind of smile which can be felt in the works of Jane Austen when she describes some piece of behaviour too ill-considered to admit of true levity, but too trivial to merit a paragraph of serious prose.

'I expect,' she said, 'you must become very tolerant of human nature, in work like yours.'

'Well, it's a fact you don't have many illusions about it.' A moment ago, Miss Fisher's own system of defence had prompted a little flourish on her next trip to Bridgehead, which had suddenly taken on in her mind the bright colours of defiance. But it was not Miss Searle she wished to defy; it was a little mean, perhaps, rubbing it in to someone who hadn't had the luck. In any case, it wasn't till tomorrow.

'It's going to be a lovely morning. I suppose you wouldn't care to come down for a bathe?'

Out in the garden, Neil had produced a map from his pocket; to study it better, he and the girl had spread it out on the lawn and were poring over it, like children, on hands and knees.

'I think,' said Miss Searle to Miss Fisher, 'that's a quite excellent suggestion. I can really think of nothing I should enjoy more.'

9

Bivouac

Neil glanced at the doubtful sky, felt a causeless but unshakable optimism about the weather, considered it realistically, and put his mackintosh in his rucksack.

Ellen's door opened as he passed it on his way down. She put her head round it, keeping the rest of her person twisted out of sight.

'Are we climbing?' she asked.

'I shouldn't think so. I doubt if there's anything there.'

'Right, I shan't be a moment.' Her head withdrew.

They had climbed yesterday, in a mild way, after the police had gone. It had appealed to him as a simple means of taking her out of herself, no more than a neighbourly duty; it would have been brutal to leave her alone. The plan had answered well. He could not remember, now, what had led up to making a fixture for today as well, only that it had seemed to follow quite naturally at the time. As he went down the last flight of stairs it occurred to him that she had been listening for his step while making up her mind how to dress. A vague pleasure at being consulted on this decision added itself to his diffused cheerfulness, but was altogether too silly to find lodging in his surface thoughts.

She came down a few minutes later, in a blue linen shirt and a grey skirt, pleated, which swung a little with her step.

'What sort of state is this castle in?' she asked as they left the last houses behind.

'Pretty ruinous, I expect. It's marked in Gothic on the map.' Both spoke as if they were continuing a current conversation, though they had said almost nothing since they started out.

'I think,' said Ellen, 'I like the ones that haven't been kept up and lived in the best; they're more themselves.'

After this very female generalisation, he was surprised to find, presently, that she had read Froissart, Villehardouin, Joinville and Malory, not conscientiously but, it was apparent, greedily, as if they had been novels. She was diffident about it and he had to drag it out of her piecemeal.

'Have you always been a medievalist?' he asked.

She looked quite alarmed. 'Oh, it's only for fun. I liked it at school, and in the last few years I've gone back to it a bit. It was a change,' she added apologetically, 'from the factory.'

And, Neil surmised, from much besides. As if she had anticipated his thought, she said, 'It seems all right till someone utters the word "escapism", and then you feel like a secret drinker.'

'It's an overworked word. No one can live, for instance, without a certain amount of sleep. I'm expecting to hear that labelled escapism any day now.' He was feeling a revulsion from his own phase of unrelaxing struggle; his first rejection of the doctor's sedative had been tiresomely characteristic of his whole effort, he thought. Now as at several other times, he did not recall the fact that she had had as many years to make her adjustments in as he had had months; trouble has a way of leaping at parallels

147

and discarding the rest. She looked so young that the thought would have been, in any case, hard to make real.

'Sometimes,' she said, 'it isn't as escapist as you'd like it to be. Nowadays, I mean. It was hard to imagine the cruelty once; now you can. Froissart on De Foix reads awfully like some journalist dealing politely with a successful dictator, except that the style's better.'

More used than he had realised to the scholastic angle, Neil was enjoying this personal approach, and feeling thankful that for once he hadn't to ruin it with injections of what the examiners required.

'I don't recall the gentleman,' he said, 'but I gather you dislike him.'

'Who, De Foix? After that story I should think only God wouldn't dislike him. One ought to pity him, I know, but ...'

'I'm classics, not history. I wish you wouldn't assume I know everything. Come on.'

'I'd spoil it.' They had reached high ground between the cliffs and the moor, which lay before them in a shimmering lavender haze of coming heat. It looked timeless and still, with the latent fierceness of a sleeping lion.

After he had persuaded her, she said, 'Froissart's terribly nice about it all, on the surface. He'd been entertained like a prince for three months, of course, in the castle; but De Foix impressed him too, I think. He did everything magnificently, peace or war; too much of a gentleman to read or write, but a great patron of the arts. The handsomest man of the age, as well. His bastard sons were all on the same scale and lived with him in state; the Countess doesn't seem to have objected, not that I expect it would have cut any ice if she had. She could afford not to, though; she was the King of Navarre's sister, and her own son was the most magnificent of the lot.

'Everything started when this King swindled the Earl of Foix over somebody's ransom; it was a sort of Big Business then, you know. He thought it would be a good idea to send the Countess to make her brother pay up. When she couldn't, she was afraid to come back. The way Froissart puts it is, "She knew well the Earl her husband was cruel where he took displeasure." She must have known, because she stayed in Navarre for years, while her son was growing to marriageable age. The Earl married him off to an heiress at fifteen. He seems to have been more interested in his mother, though, because after the wedding he asked to go and see her. The Earl gave him leave, but he wouldn't send a message, and when the Countess heard that, she was still afraid to go back.

'The King of Navarre had his own ideas about all this. The day the boy was due to leave, he had him in for a private talk, and said that if he really wanted his mother home again, it could easily be arranged. And he handed over a little bag with powder in it, a love-philtre, he said. The boy need only slip it in his father's food and he'd not only forgive his wife but love her for ever, provided no one was told about it, which would spoil the charm. The lad was terribly grateful, and hung it round his neck to have it ready. He was very careful not to tell anyone when he got back; so when one of his half-brothers saw it and got curious, it ended in a fight. The little brother lost and went away crying, and happened to meet the Earl, who asked him what was the matter. All the child could say was that Gaston carried a purse of powder round his neck, and he thought it was something to do with his mother coming back. "Then the Earl entered into imagination," Froissart says.

'That evening the boy was serving his father's place at table. In the middle of the meal the Earl called him over, and suddenly ripped open his coat. The boy just went dead white and stood in complete silence. The Earl took some of the powder and gave it on bread to a dog under the table. It took one swallow and died at once.

'The boy still stood there fixed on his feet. The Earl would have killed him at the table, with his dinner-knife, if the courtiers hadn't got in the way. There might be some explanation, they said, and besides there was no other legitimate heir. At last the Earl agreed to lock Gaston up while he thought it over. While he was thinking, he tortured all the squires in his son's household to death. There were fifteen of them, about the same age as the boy. He said they must have seen the purse and they ought to have reported it. There's still no record of the boy's saying anything. He was put in the keep, in a room without a window, and no one saw him but the jailer who brought his food.

'As soon as the news got about the demesne, deputations poured in to beg Gaston off; he seems to have been a friendly lad whom everyone knew. Someone even went to the Pope at Avignon, and a Cardinal was sent to go into things. He got there a bit late, though. The boy lay on his bed in the dark for a fortnight, with all the food he was brought lying on the floor beside him. The jailer got worried, and finally went to the Earl. It seems to have made him angry again, the boy taking things into his own hands. He went to the keep, walked up to the boy's bed, ordered him to eat, and when nothing happened, took him by the throat and shook him. He was weak by then, so he died.

'The Earl was always very correct about etiquette. He went into black and shaved his head. All he said that's recorded is, "I shall never have the joy that I had before."'

The lane had turned to a high trackway crossing a hill; there were sparse oaks here, stunted and leaning towards the land.

The only tall trees were a few Scotch firs, which strained and murmured against the wind.

Neil said, after a little while, 'And you don't think civilisation's advanced in the last five hundred years?'

'Do you?'

'"I shall never have the joy that I had before" ... He wore a hair shirt under his armour, I suppose, and was afraid of hell fire. Perhaps he was even afraid of himself. So much painful remorse, just for having liquidated an anti-social element. We do things better now.'

'I suppose we're all tarred with it, in the last few years. One had to disinfect things with generalisations sometimes, not to go crazy. De Foix did have his confessor. What have we?'

'Nothing at all,' he said, 'if we want to live.'

'Do you mean that?' said Ellen, looking at him; whether in curiosity or appeal, he could not tell.

'I suppose not. I mean no nice warm huddle of solidarity. People get together in this century like insects under a stone, to sanction all their more disgusting emotions and waste most of their good ones. If you can't live without a bit of group-ego, go to a party and get tight. That's honest anyway, you keep your own hangover and the damage to your mind is mainly physical. The Greeks knew that; that's why they honoured Dionysus as a god. The good shepherd who led the beast in mankind into the woods till it was tired, and kept the altars of the immortals pure.'

'The immortals?' she said. Her voice sounded bitter; but with the kind of bitterness which contains, unknown perhaps to itself, the longing for an answer. It stirred something in him, the residue of his faith: the irreducible something of whose survival he had, till this moment, been unsure. He thought of the Crito. But Socrates had not had the benefits of an English public school education; words like Truth, Beauty and Good had slid with Mediterranean shamelessness across his tongue. Neil said, 'Oh, well.'

Curiously, Ellen received this reply as if it were not entirely negative. All she said, however, was, 'My father used to say that to describe one's fellow-creatures as The Masses was the ultimate insult.'

They had reached the main road, and the board which marked the bus stop.

'Your father's dead?'

'Yes, when I was fifteen.' There was a pause which Neil filled with one of the conventional noises. As if following some interior conversation she said presently, 'Though I suppose to rely so much on another person can't ever be good.'

'No,' said Neil, and was at once shocked by his own self-centred brutality. Without sign of affront she said, 'He never took advantage of it.'

'Of course not. I'm sorry.'

'There's no need to be; he'd have said the same.'

'And your mother?'

'She died last year. She was never very well after she got buried, when our house was hit in '41. I was working on the night shift, so I didn't know till I got back next morning and found them digging for her.'

'What have you done since then?'

'I had some war-damage money, for our house, and a little my people left me, so I went up to London and did a secretarial course; I'd never trained for anything, you see. I've just finished it. I thought I'd have a holiday first, and then look for a job. I don't think I'll go back to London, though, if I can help it. I don't like it very much.' She spoke rather apologetically, evidently prepared for him to rally to its defence.

He said, 'Don't you either? Why not?'

'I suppose there are just too many people. You have to keep running to stay in the same place, like the Red Queen. And things cost money that ought not to, like peace and quiet and something to look at out of the window. After a time, the people you meet all seem to have tired cross faces, and then you know it's really you.'

'What part of London were you in?'

'Belgravia – the shabby part. I had a room in one of those decayed mansions, all plaster mouldings and alcoves for palms, and huge windows on the stairs blacked out with paint; they'd scraped a few holes in it after the war and left the rest. The other people were mostly Indians, and queer old women who didn't like strangers. The rooms had been divided up, so that they were about twice as high as they were wide; it's odd how a room that shape never seems to get friendly. Have you ever stayed in one?'

'I've just come from one. In Pimlico.'

This simple statement cost him an immense effort. As soon as he had made it, he felt a curious lightening within. He had carried the solitude of those months with him ever since; this moment's breach in their loneliness seemed not to belong to the present, but to be an alteration of the past.

'Pimlico?' she said. 'Why, that's only just round the corner. I often walked round that way, going to look at the river.'

The same stretch of Embankment, he thought, must often have seen them both in the same twelve hours, him by night and her by day. Neither said, 'We might have met,' because to each it seemed now that they had.

'What did you do with your spare time?' He felt a reasonless assurance that he could ask such questions without fear of their rebounding.

153

'The ballet sometimes, when I could get in. Once or twice I got asked to parties; a lot of the other girls lived in London, of course. Or I just used to read, and pretend I was somewhere else.'

He imagined her, at times when he must have passed her door, small and quiet in the well of her dingy room, its forlornness closing like well-water high over her unresisting head, herself withdrawn to Arabia, or China, or old France. In childhood, he thought, she must have been much in her own company; but, lest she should feel herself being intrusively analysed, he did not ask. He thought of the tall houses with their pillared stucco porticoes, the bomb-gaps like missing teeth, their lost look of an exploded security and permanence; now, while he talked, they still enclosed a thousand diverse solitudes which drifted helplessly past one another, without touching. The memory fell away from him; he lived there no longer. Half a dozen spoken words had done what the mountains had failed to do.

'And now?' he said. 'You're quite alone?'

'I suppose so,' she answered consideringly, as though he had presented her with a definition. 'But then, who isn't? Hullo, look, here's the bus.'

It turned out to be fairly full, and they had to sit separately. Neil, sharing a seat with a woman whose hat occluded most of the window, could see more easily the back of Ellen's head. The soft curls at the nape, bouncing with the bus, looked from behind like a girl's of seventeen. He sat thinking of Lupus Street and the Embankment with a memory unalterably changed, but still wishing not to think of them at all; till some kind of impalpable, transferred discomfort made him realise that he had been staring unseeingly at the woman in the hat. Ineffectually (the seat was narrow) she was trying to edge away;

no doubt she expected to have her knee squeezed any minute. Damning all women, he offered his seat with relief to the next who got on the bus.

Ellen was supporting in her lap the legs of a large sleeping baby held by the farmer's wife beside her, and looking down, in intense interest or deep abstraction, at its pink woollen feet.

'Sorry,' he said, as a lurch of the bus threw him forward at her shoulder. 'There's no handrail. I won't do it again.'

She looked up, her face startled into complete blankness. 'It's all right. I thought you were sitting at the back.' A slow, deepening blush, beginning at her throat, travelled up into her hair.

Some more people got in, pushing him beyond her. Standing, he was too tall to see out of the window at all. Suddenly the bus seemed intolerably crowded, and the contact of its other occupants a furious irritation. Their bags and parcels in the rack, on a level with his eyes, were extensions of them, and seemed to look at him with interest.

The outside air, when they emerged at last, was by contrast delightfully cool. They wandered round the small market-place with its stone-roofed cross, and fell into step together; or, rather, into that irregular but pleasant rhythm which, for people of different heights, can produce the same effect.

'How long have we got here?' Ellen asked.

'Until four-thirty, I think. It seems an idiotic time for the last bus; only gives us about two hours. I'll take a look at the board and see if there isn't a later one.' The table was fixed on one of the columns of the market cross; he returned with the news that there was, after all, a later one at six-thirty. This would leave them plenty of time for the castle, without prejudice to their tea. Relieved of the need for haste, they pottered about and presently found the lane that led to the castle. It was a green tunnel with a high roof of elms, and a grass verge wide enough to accommodate, at one point, an encampment of gipsies. It was past the season for the wild-flowers that gipsies hawk; but one woman gazed at them, from under her down-turned shapeless hat, with an interest that hinted at calculation.

'She looked,' said Neil when they were past, 'as if she wished she had something to sell us.'

'Yes, didn't she?' said Ellen, quickening her step. She had met gipsies before, and knew their line of sales-talk.

The lane ended at a wooden gate. There, beyond it, was the massive shell, the roofless keep and part of the wards. Much was there beside; a gaggle of voices, shrill and incessant as the chattering of starlings, though much louder, and a moving vista of round, identically trimmed hats. A tired young woman was trying to be everywhere at once; her face, denied the persuasions of art which would have helped it to something like prettiness, proclaimed her calling as loudly as a slave's collar. A House, thought Neil, noting the assorted age of her charges, not a form.

He swore, and apologised. 'Out of every day in the week, I would choose this one.'

'You couldn't help it,' said Ellen reasonably. 'It's an Act of God, like a thunderbolt.'

He could see, however, that she was disappointed. Neil shared the touching belief of all men that there are other, more victorious men to whom this kind of thing never happens. 'If we had tea early,' he said, making the best of it, 'they might have gone.' Provided, he thought, they haven't brought it with them.

'They're sure to have gone by then. There's lots of time.'

They turned back down the lane, enjoying the shade leisurely, since it was too early yet for tea-places to be open.

'Lovely lace, lady. All hand-made.'

Oh, *no*, thought Ellen, a wave of helpless protest crawling up her spine. Temporarily blinded by her own preoccupations, she had not seen the approach of the gipsy, who seemed to have materialised out of the hedge. The lace, of that very coarse kind which is a staple product of gipsies, dangled enticingly from her dirty brown hand. She had chosen a point where the path narrowed; it was impossible to get by without pushing her aside.

'Not today, thank you.' Next moment she realised that the only sensible move would have been to buy the stuff out of hand. But she only had a few shillings on her, and the older-established caution had had first word. It was too late now.

'Beautiful lace, sir. Only five shillings. You'll not see lace like this in the shops. It'll be lucky to you, sir.' Her soft, sweet, cadging voice dropped a tone, stagily confidential. 'Something for the young lady to remember you by.'

'Let's look at it,' said Neil. Though he knew rather less about lace than about conic sections, he picked up the bundle and looked at it searchingly, as if he had travelled in it for years. He hoped this would lead the conversation into technical channels.

'*Please* don't,' said Ellen, fatally interrupting just as this seemed about to succeed. 'I never put lace on things, it tears in the wash.' A new and formidable embarrassment leaping on her at this point, she added, 'I mean, of course, not for me.'

'Tear in the wash, lady? Hand-made lace? Why, it'll last you and your children out.' The gipsy had stopped smiling, Ellen saw in alarm; her black eyes sparkled. If she turned awkward everything so far would be, comparatively speaking, bread-and-butter. Ellen almost offered for the lace at once; but it was too late now, it would only seem that she was asking him to buy it for her.

'Look lovely in your bottom drawer.' The dark eyes smiled again, boldly, sure of themselves now. 'Come, now, sir. It'll turn your luck, and the young lady's too; you'll never regret the day. See, now, I'll make it four shillings, to a courting couple.'

'All right,' Neil said. He paid the money over. The confusingly violent protective instinct, which had suddenly possessed him, made him vague about the transaction; he handed two half-crowns. The gipsy clutched them and stowed them away in the pocket of her torn skirt, firmly deflecting his eyes by holding them with her own. They had an opaque polish, like agates, under their heavy brows.

'Thank you, sir, bless you, and good luck to you. There's a red-haired woman crossed your path for sorrow, but there's happiness before you if you've got the patience. Take care of high places, and you'll live to a fine old age.'

'Thanks,' said Neil mechanically, starting away. The gipsy, however, had not quite done. She had turned to Ellen; the professional cajolery had given way to an air of sudden enjoyment as of one who now pleases herself.

'You're a grown woman now, lady, and you'll spoil your luck if you don't remember it. From now on your troubles will be your own making.' Her voice dropped, skilfully, into another penetrating aside. 'And mind what I say, you've a gentleman there you can trust. He'll never bring you to harm, for he's one that's known more trouble than you have. You remember that, lady, and your luck will hold.' She went off through the bushes with a stride like a man's, her draggled skirt swinging over broken shoes.

Neil gazed at the lace in his hand, painfully conscious that he could not go on inspecting it much longer, and had better think what to say next. Meanwhile he observed that the stuff was of a thickness which, as even his inexpert eye could see, would outweigh any fabric thinner than calico. There appeared to be some yards of it.

'Well,' he observed at length, 'the notorious Warning seems to have got into reverse.' This somehow failed to hit the authentic note of farce. Trying again, he added, 'Sheds a light on the ballad, doesn't it? Awful results of sales-resistance.'

'They do it on purpose,' said Ellen. A tenuous hope, that her voice would emerge sounding casual and blasé, did not survive the moment of speech.

'Shock tactics.' The fatuity of this overcame him; he dried up.

Ellen straightened her shoulders. A little rush of anger, with the gipsy and with herself, broke the stranglehold of her shyness. He had been left to cope with everything, she thought; it wasn't fair.

'Look here,' she said, bringing it out quite strongly, 'we'd better get used to the idea that it's just one of those days. The stars are in the wrong house, or something. I mean, if we make up our minds beforehand, we shan't mind. There's sure to be one thing more – they always go in threes, like breaking china. We'll just have to be tough.'

Neil laughed, not without gratitude, and partly because her face saying 'tough' had looked funny. 'Does breaking china go in threes?'

'Oh, yes, always.'

'Can you do anything with this stuff?'

'Just because that old witch blackmailed you into buying it, you don't have to give it to me.' She struggled obstinately with a return of shyness. 'I've no house-linen, I live in digs. Someone who had might be glad of it. It – it would do for pillows or something.' She was grateful that he didn't look at her. It was terrible, she thought, what things slid out when one was running on in an effort to sound natural.

'Well, there's Mrs K, I suppose. She goes in for fancy mats.'

He turned the lace over in his hand, as if considering this in detail. 'I can't think of anyone else, if you don't want it. I'm living in digs, too.'

A bird flew across the lane in front of them; the sun made a fringe of gold in the thin edges of its wings.

'Oh,' said Ellen. 'Well, thank you very much. It's sure to come in for something; and it does last a lifetime, as a matter of fact.'

'You'd better have it; she might call the luck off. I'm feeling a ready prey to superstition just now.' He gave it her, and they smiled at each other in an incautious happiness which neither was quite in time to disguise. It was with something of a shock that they found they had emerged meanwhile from the castle lane and were in a street. The local constable, who did not look busy, had stopped his bicycle with one foot on the kerb, and was eyeing them with kindly toleration.

'Excuse me, sir. That lace the lady has there – may I ask if you bought it up the lane?'

'Yes,' said Neil. 'Not on coupons, is it?'

'That's all right, sir; that is, you've not committed any offence. But if you've been subjected to any annoyance, or the lady, I'd be glad to hear of it. We've been getting complaints.' He fished in his pocket, where the corner of a notebook appeared.

'Annoyance?' said Neil reservedly. 'No, I wouldn't say that.'

'Nor the lady?' The constable thumbed his notebook, with diminishing hope.

'Not at all, thank you,' said Ellen firmly. She put the lace in her pocket, where her hand gently retained it. 'I was glad to have it; you know, it's hard to get.'

When law and order had cycled away they caught one another's eyes, hung for a second on the edge of a laugh, and funked it at the last moment.

The Wheatsheaf Hotel had not received the benefits of modernisation. The façade was Georgian, but inside one could stand in the Tudor hearth and, looking up, see a square of sky. The service was leisurely, the bread fresh; they were the first comers and had the placid low-ceilinged room to themselves. They talked books, the kind of pseudo-impersonal conversation into which scraps of personal detail filter easily, without the need for acknowledgment. After the meal, they pottered round the church, and found that by a pleasing oversight the door to the tower had been left unlocked. Climbing past the sleeping bells, they stood on the warm leads, looking at the little town spread like an illustrated map below them.

'I suppose,' said Ellen, 'all over the world there were places like this, which people couldn't believe would ever change. Nothing seems solid, now.'

'Nothing ever was.' Neil looked at the stone of the balustrade, roughened and pitted by weather so that it was no longer possible to trace on it the mark of human tools. 'Once it was easy to forget it, that's all.'

'Perhaps it's wrong to accept it. Fatalism doesn't help.'

'It depends what you mean by accepting it.' He felt no resistance against sharing his thoughts, but some trouble in finding words. Things had come to him while he was by himself in the woods, real, but as glimpses of light and colour are real, of which one can say little more than 'bright' and 'blue'. Their shapelessness in terms of speech had not occurred to him, at the time. 'I mean, letting go of things need not be an act of despair, I suppose. Sometimes one feels freer, and even the things one lets go of are better than they were. Sorry to be so vague.'

'No, you're not. But—' She had drawn a little away; he saw

in her face a look of frightened resistance. 'It's inhuman,' she said at last. 'There are some things one *must* hold on to.'

He had no answer to this: it was not a point of discussion, but as if she had said 'I am cold' or 'I can go no farther'. Leaning over, he watched the tiny foreshortened figures crossing the market square. In its far corner was a shape like a long black-beetle sleeping against a diminished tree. 'Perhaps,' he said, 'we ought to be getting down. That looks like the bus.'

'It can't be that time yet! And we still haven't seen the castle.'

'You can see it from here,' said Neil. 'I was keeping quiet about it.'

She followed his eye, and laughed. 'How funny they look from here. Just the hats weaving about. What *are* they doing – playing rounders? Never mind, the church was quite as good.'

'We'll come again.'

When they got to the bus, they found themselves in sole possession. This inspired superiority at first, followed by a gradual misgiving.

'I suppose,' said Ellen, 'it *is* the right one?'

'It's the only one, so it can hardly not be. It's probably well known in the district for starting late.' After another ten minutes, however, he walked round to the front of it, where the direction board, turned half-way up into the frame, kept its secret still. 'We'll give it five more minutes, and if nothing happens I'll go and find somebody who knows.'

They were fortified, however, before this by the arrival of a stout, placid woman with several baskets and a hat trimmed with grapes, who settled herself in the front seat and began to knit a pink bed-sock with reassuring contentment.

'They must have altered the time,' said Ellen in an undertone. 'She looks all set for half an hour.' At the sound of her voice the woman looked back at them, with benevolent curiosity. Neil took advantage of this to ask her when the bus was supposed to start. This seemed to please her; she lowered the sock and sat round conversationally.

'Would you be wanting to see Mr Lambourne? He won't be long now.' She added, as one who removes the last ambiguity, 'I'm Mrs Lambourne.'

'How do you do,' said Neil with fogged politeness. 'This is the Barlock bus, isn't it?'

A look of deep satisfaction settled on Mrs Lambourne's round face. She speared a needle into her wool. 'There. That's just what I thought. The moment I saw you I said to myself, "Now I wonder if they've taken this for the Thursday bus to Barlock?"'

'Where *does* it go, then?' Neil was still not quite in touch with developments.

'You mean *this* bus? Why, this one, it doesn't what you might say go anywhere. Just back to the garage. My husband and I live up by there. He always picks me up on a Wednesday, when he drives the bus back. I thought as soon as I seen you there, "Now I wonder if they've got in by mistake."'

'Oh,' said Neil. 'Thanks very much.' He and Ellen got up. 'Perhaps you could tell us where the right one starts from?'

'The Barlock buses, they start from by here. But they don't run after four-thirty, only on market day.' Simplifying this further, she added, 'Thursday, market day is. Today's a Wednesday.'

Having agreed that this was so, they thanked her again, and left.

'Good thing you asked her,' said Ellen quite cheerfully. 'She must be wrong about there not being another. Summer timetable, I expect.'

'I'll have another look,' said Neil, with spurious ease. In his experience, country dwellers were rather more accurate about the local bus service than about sunset and dawn. Before he got to the board, he had guessed what he would see there. He was right. Beside the figure 6.30 a small letter t, which he had overlooked, gave reference to a footnote: 'Thursdays only.' A glance at his watch told him, further, that it was nearly seven. He walked back to Ellen, assimilating all this.

'I'm afraid we've had it. I'd apologise if there were anything to say.'

He braced himself for tact. She would say it was a mistake anyone might make, as she often did too; and he would see her looking alert, ready in future to rely on herself.

Instead she exclaimed triumphantly, 'There! What did I tell you? I said it always went in threes.'

'The fault, dear Brutus, is not in our stars. I didn't read the marginalia.'

'If it hadn't been that it would have been something else. It's a gremlin. It'll be all right now we've worked it off.'

She often used, involuntarily as he knew, these scraps of Air Force slang. This was the first time it had been followed by a moment's constraint between them. 'It looks,' she went on quickly, 'as if we'll have to walk. Oh, well, we've had quite a lazy day.'

'Walk? It's more than twenty miles, and the sun will be down in half an hour. No, it won't come to that. There must be a car for hire somewhere. Come and have a drink, they'll know in the pub.'

They went back to the Wheatsheaf. 'No, you don't,' he said, when she told him that hers was a beer. 'I owe you a drink and you're having one.' He gave her a large sherry; himself, he felt he could do with a double. The barman was encouraging: Mr George, in New Street, had a car. Neil settled Ellen in a corner with some *Tatlers* (it was the kind of place that has *Tatlers* in the lounge bar) and went off to see about it alone. He supposed it would be fairly expensive; she was the type who, given the chance, would worry about this.

Mr George, surprised at supper, came to the door wiping his mouth. He displayed interest in their predicament, and a sympathy that filled Neil with instant misgiving. Mr George was sorry. Late as it was, he'd have taken the car out again, seeing how things were; but he'd been out with a party all day, and hadn't above a gallon of his petrol allowance left. No, there wasn't another car for hire, not hereabouts. He returned, with a civil good night, to the kippers whose smell had followed him to the threshold.

Neil turned back into the street. Already the sun was on the horizon. The situation, reduced to its now inescapable essentials, accompanied him quietly on his way.

Just as he was telling himself that at last there was nothing worse left to happen, he heard his own name called, on a note of jocular disbelief. By the time he had traced the sound to its source, it was too late to do anything.

Templeton was an old colleague, a mathematician of (Neil had been assured) brilliant abilities. In less specialised matters, he displayed a mental age of about ten years. They had not met since 1940; Templeton, who had been doing something statistical in the Army, had declined reinstatement and gone impressively City. He now pumped Neil's hand up and down (he was also a great arm-gripper and shoulder-tapper, eking out a limited vocabulary by these means) and announced that this called for a drink.

Neil meditated escape; but it would look odd, and an anxiety not to be commented on was too firmly rooted in him, nowadays, to be shaken off quickly. He could do with a drink, besides. Vividly aware that the only decent hotel in the place was the Wheatsheaf in which Ellen was waiting, he looked about, saw, across the street, the lights of a fly-blown little pub, and with desperate bonhomie steered Templeton into it.

The story of Templeton's war took some time; but, though fond of talking about himself, he did not push it to fanaticism. He was quite out of touch, he said; how was the old place? Anything sensational happened lately? Templeton supposed not, it never did, though by God, when you were in that rut, if the Head lost his spectacles in chapel it seemed melodramatic. Never again, said Templeton, who was looking prosperous and had put on a significant amount of weight. And what was Neil (dark old horse) doing here on the loose? Shaken off the old harness too? That was the stuff. (His gaze filmed tactfully from Neil's jacket, which was very pre-war.) When, by the way, had he acquired that *mèche blanche*? It must go over big with the women, Templeton surmised. 'Distinguished,' he added, after a profound choice of words.

This seemed to Neil a good moment to go and fetch another round. Returning with it, he urged Templeton back into autobiography. It worked so well that he repeated it several times, after which the worst seemed to be over; it was now only a question of getting away. He relaxed, leaning back in the recess where they had found a rickety bench to sit on. The little bar was thick with a rich Somerset burr, as soothing as the *roucoulement* of wood-pigeons. Templeton, who had reached the phase of nostalgia, was telling an interminable story of how he had once got the better of the Modern Languages master about time-tables for the Senior School. Listening to one word in six, Neil reflected that another drink would have been one too many, but that he needn't have another now; Templeton was well away. As for himself he was just at the optimum, a peak of beautiful, untroubled lucidity and peace.

It was at this moment that someone at the bar said, solemnly and sententiously, 'No denying it. It's a happy release.'

'Who wants to deny it?' said Neil. He smiled up at the electric light shade, which had the insignia of a brewing firm painted on it in three colours. There was, he thought, something apocalyptic about it.

'Eh?' said Templeton. 'Didn't get that.'

'I didn't say anything. I was listening to you.' A happy release. He knew where he was, and could not imagine why he had been denying it so long. A happy, very happy release.

'Yes,' he said, when Templeton wound up. 'That was the term when by some queer coincidence all the boys sang the same variant of the school anthem, and all the parents heard the words.' After which he made his excuses briskly, relying on the strategy of surprise, and found himself suddenly alone in the little street, his hand still retaining a tactile impression of Templeton's hearty but curiously inadequate hand-grip, which felt as if the bony structure had decomposed into brawn. Above him was a red and green sunset, whose perfect composition looked most improbable; and the certainty which remained clear and apart from it all, like the single star which came out as he looked.

Ellen put down her third *Tatler* as he came in. It felt odd to be seeing her among all the little accidents of reality: a strand of hair loose from her slide, which he hadn't noticed before, a splash of mud across one sandal. A long-haired tabby kitten, which had picked her up in his absence, lay sleeping along her lap, its nose with a lop-sided white patch (distinguished, thought Neil) dangling between two white-gloved paws over the point of her knee. A mediocre sporting print hung slightly askew on the wall above her head.

Seeing him standing before her silent, she said, 'Never mind. It can't be helped, anyway.'

Neil pulled himself together with a quick jerk. This, of course, was what he ought to have been thinking of all the way here. The difficulty now was that it was so hard to realise he hadn't communicated it all to her already: Mr George's regrets, Templeton's smugness, the technicolour sunset and the star. To begin now seemed no more than a perfunctory form of words.

'I'm sorry I've been so long,' he said, sitting down beside her. 'I met a fool I used to know and couldn't lose him.' He broke off, discovering with a sudden shock that the forthcoming conversation wasn't in the least perfunctory, and the sooner he convinced himself of it the better. 'I'm even sorrier to tell you there seems to be no transport at all. I don't know where to begin apologising for all this.'

'It's all right,' she said. 'There's a peace on. Things like this are happening all over England.'

She spoke quite naturally; and, remembering how easily her shyness came to the surface as a rule, he guessed she must have been preparing this effort for some time. 'We've broken our third plate, anyhow,' he said. 'And Crown Derby at that.' It was an excuse to smile. Almost any other would have done.

'Well,' said Ellen briskly, 'we swore to be tough about it, however embarrassing it was. The first step is to admit it *is* embarrassing, I suppose.'

'You're telling me.' They had both, however, relaxed in their chairs. The kitten, dimly aware of some change in its resting-place, shot out its prickly claws and sheathed them again.

'I suppose,' she said, 'it's definite now that we'll have to put up somewhere here?'

'I don't see what else. It wouldn't be so bad if Mrs K were on the 'phone. The fact that she'll probably sit up for us till midnight, voicing her fears aloud, is going to give us a build-up we could do without for a start.'

Ellen stroked a finger down the kitten's spine; an electric ripple of fur ended in a twitch of its pointed tail. 'After all, we're never likely to meet any of them again.'

Neil forbore to tell her that this was one of humanity's less reliable bits of wishful thinking. Her determined cheerfulness had stirred something in his mind. It was incredible he should have forgotten; but there had been so much else to think about. There had been, besides, something about the transient Mr Phillips easy to forget, a certain essential inconsequence. It was unlikely, though, that anyone else at Weir View would see it in that light. ('*Two* men, my dear, in one week . . .') He looked up, refusing, for a moment, to accept the fact that there was nothing one could say. Their eyes met.

'Look here,' she said, 'please don't worry about this. It doesn't matter. It never really matters what people think.'

'I'll look after all that. I've had a certain amount of practice in making people see sense.'

'Of course it's all right. I'm not bothering about it at all. What's really on my mind is that I've hardly got any money with me. Can you lend me some?'

'Well, Good Lord,' he began, 'seeing this was all my fault . . .' and stopped; of course he couldn't settle her hotel bill for her. There must be any number of people, he supposed, who would carry all this off without batting an eyelid. He felt an intimate, secret pleasure in the fact that she wasn't one of them. 'We'll fight that out later on,' he said, and gave her a couple of pounds; at which point they both became aware of the barman, watching the transaction with interest. Suddenly, helplessly, they both began to laugh. The kitten looked resentful, and bicycled with its claws.

'I can't help it,' said Ellen presently, and then, 'I wonder what happens if you meet a gipsy and *don't* buy any lace?'

'God knows. It's too good to be true, isn't it?' What he really meant was the diabolic perfection of the timing; they were neither one thing nor the other, and too much could be understood between them, but not enough. It was, for a moment, purely exasperating that he couldn't remark on this point to her.

'By the way,' he said, 'I'd better order dinner.' He did so, and came back with a couple of sherries. He had forgotten all about Templeton by this time, and only remembered when he started his drink and found that it didn't feel like the first of the evening.

Ellen, looking doubtfully at her own, said, 'No, but this makes three. You left me with one, and I had another while you were gone because the barman looked as if he thought I should.'

'Good. Let's drink to the gipsy. We haven't tried that yet.'

'I feel much better already,' said Ellen presently.

'So do I. If we'd had any sense, we'd have got down to this sooner.'

They smiled at each other; the half-amused private smile of people who are aware of being a little lit-up, but not too much and in company so trustworthy that it cannot matter. The exchange of this confidence made them finish their drinks absently, and evolve a number of small jokes in order to smile again. It was not for some time that Ellen remembered she had not been to the desk yet about a room.

'I fixed that for you.' Once again he felt the unreality of explanations. 'That was all right, because I'm not staying here myself. I meant to have told you. I'm waiting for a divorce, and – well, the law needs a long spoon, like the devil. It's better to give it a bit of a margin.'

She had been playing with the kitten, which now curled round her hand, all teeth and claws, to point out that it was being neglected. She let it worry her fingers as if she did not feel it.

'And you've spent all this time,' she said, 'bothering about me.'

'Well, naturally. My part's purely technical. Besides ...' What he had been about to say he was not sure, but this was not the moment to say it. He unhooked the kitten from her hand instead. 'I fixed up at some bed-and-breakfast place I passed on the way here. It seemed rather an idiotic-looking manoeuvre to leave unaccounted for. I was going to tell you, though, in any case.'

Ellen stroked the kitten, which was too young for a soothing technique and resented it; she seemed a little insensitive to its reactions. 'It must be hateful, feeling you're living under suspicion, as if ... How perfectly disgusting it is, the whole principle of the thing.'

'I suppose it is. It hasn't arisen much with me. But the thing's almost through now; and apart from me, it would be a bit hard on my wife if it came unstuck.' Finding it didn't matter now, he went on, 'They want to get married before the baby's born.'

'Oh, I see.' He could feel her struggling desperately with her own inadequacy, and was unhappy not to be able to help. Presently she said, 'You haven't any children?'

'Not now.'

'I'm so sorry.'

'I don't think about it much. One has to cut free of things when what's left is mainly destructive. It's like surgery, I suppose.'

She said, half to herself, 'If one can'; and it was then that he noticed for the first time today (probably because it was the first time he had looked for it) the chain he had seen round her neck on the beach, just showing inside her collar.

Not hearing till too late the hardening in his own voice, he said, 'Even a limb becomes destructive, you know, after it's dead.'

For a moment something showed in her face which was not far from anger; but almost at once it changed to gentleness and remorse. Wanting neither to accept it nor to hurt her by rejecting it, he found a resource in the kitten. It was getting fractious, by now, from too much notice and sitting up past its bedtime, and responded to his advances by darting up Ellen's arm and scrambling about precariously on the back of her neck. They laughed, the tension broken; Ellen fumbled after it, wincing as its claws caught in her hair.

'He'll scratch you. Here, let me.'

He came behind her chair, and got hold of the creature round the middle. Its little body was soft and wiry, helpless and furiously vital. Her hair tangled itself round his fingers; its human texture, set against the feel of fur, an oddly exciting contrast different from any separate touch. When he had disentangled it, managing not to pull, she said, 'Thank you. How strong they are for their size,' and took it from him. It squirmed crossly, impatient at being suspended so long in their meeting hands.

'We'd better do something about this meal,' he said, 'before everything eatable's gone.'

He ladled the kitten into the chair he had left. It stretched on the warmed cushion, closed its hazy blue eyes, sighed through its nose, and poured itself into the benign slumber of infancy. Neil gave it a grateful stroke as they went.

In the dining-room they ate submissively what there was, talked a great deal about things of no importance, and had some lager, the house having run out of almost everything else. It was light, but added a certain gentle persuasiveness to what they had had already. The waiter, a sociable soul whose life was on the whole a dull one, became noticeably attentive to their table; and, getting a little above themselves, they played exhibitionistically up to him. During one of his enforced absences Neil said suddenly, 'Good God. What on earth are we eating?'

Ellen concentrated dimly. 'Pink blancmange, I think, with something mixed in. Semolina, is it? And bits of cake.'

'But the taste.'

'It's not exactly a taste. More like a smell that gets in your mouth. Perhaps they used bath-salts to colour it with.'

'Where's the menu gone? I collect the names they think up for things like this. I hope it's in French.'

'Charlot Russ,' said a helpful voice over his shoulder. 'You shouldn't have sat about out there till the pruins was off. I was wondering how soon you'd become alive to it, as they say.' Studying Ellen's face, Neil suspected that the waiter had given her a benevolent wink before departing.

Over the coffee, Neil was visited with an inspiration. 'What about the castle? After all, it's what we came to do. There's a moon up, now.'

'It will be locked up,' said Ellen; and then, 'still, the outside would look nice by moonlight, I expect.'

The little town was almost asleep already. In the square a few decorous couples were ritualistically walking-out. A cat shot across a road in the agoraphobic way of cats, becoming leisured and graceful in the shadow of a wall. It was growing cool; Ellen, when she went up to her room, had put her white sweater on. Her hair was freshly brushed; in the colourless light she looked very virginal, slight and young.

A last band of tarnished gilt still hung in the west, so that the dim oil-light in the houses below it looked like the sky shining through. It was a still evening; scents of hidden roses and of box hung about the gardens in motionless clouds; one walked through edges of scent as one walks through the edge of shadows.

They were silent at first. This was partly because the fresh air had been rather revealing, and they were going through private tests to be sure that they were sober enough for nothing to show. The outward aspect of this inquiry, at least, gave satisfactory answers. ('I can stand well enough,' thought Neil, hazily recalling Cassio on a like theme, 'and I can speak well enough. This is my right hand and this is my left.') The moon did not seem, like the sunset, too good to be true; it was what one had a right to expect, indeed obvious and inevitable. It was the past, not good enough to be true, which was receding into fantasy. ('God's above all ... For my own part, no offence to the General, or any man of quality, I hope to be saved.') The tree-roofed lane to the castle opened before them like a cave.

It became evident, when they were inside, why the courting couples in the square had been so circumspect and prim. The others were here. They lined the track, in an avenue as regular as that of the trees, invisible against the hedges till one was within a yard or two; motionless, and so silent that the rare murmur of a monosyllable sounded overt. But the lane, like the square, stood for a definite gradation in the progress of love; all the interlocked shadows were vertical. In this small, quiet town there were none of the makeshifts which, in city spaces, contrive to look at the same time furtive and defiant. For those who wanted it, the dark countryside offered the same shelter as to the foxes and the birds; the lane had a prestige.

Ellen, picking her way over unseen ruts which the dry weather had hardened, wondered whether when two couples met coming or going they acknowledged one another, or preserved the convention of solitude which was clearly the rule of the place. Tonight, though, strangers were present; something indefinable, like interruptions in an electric current, made her aware that as they passed all the regular members broke off their silent concerns and, in deeper silence, stared. When she found that this caused her no real discomfort, she knew that she shouldn't have had the lager, but didn't care.

Her foot turned on a sharp edge of hardened mud; she gave a startled gasp as she got her balance again.

'Careful,' said Neil softly, and slid his hand under her arm.

This was not only more comfortable, but, as she at once discovered, much more decorous and correct. She no longer felt conspicuous when they passed the next radar-beam from the hedge. It seemed natural too that his voice had dropped to just the same pitch as the infrequent voices between the trees.

The track widened; there was a smell of wood-smoke; against a gap in the trees a block of shadow showed, the roof of the caravan. From inside it came suddenly the thin crying of a baby, and a blurred murmur; then both died away. Involuntarily Ellen faltered in a step, and hung back.

'It's all right. They've turned in.'

He had whispered – not to wake them, perhaps – and had tightened her arm in his, pulling her against his side. When, presently, they met the first ambulant couple returning down the lane, the silent circumnavigation, the convention that they had not seen each other, followed exactly the etiquette that she had imagined.

The walk had become rather forgetful of its destination, and it was with a sense of abruptness and surprise that, rounding a bend, they found themselves at the wooden gates of the castle grounds. The lane led nowhere else; hence its popularity.

Beside the gates was the cottage lodge where the caretaker lived. Ellen, feeling shy again, slid away to try the catch of the doors.

They were locked, of course. There was an interval of uncertain pause. To accept defeat at once meant a clear choice between walking back again, and adopting with no more pretence the ritual of the lane.

On Neil's side, this was complicated by something more positive. Not to put too fine a point on it, he wanted to show off. He had not altogether stood out today for practical efficiency; now, under the influence of the lane, the moonlight, emotion and several drinks, he wanted to compensate for this, not by being practically efficient but by some lawless defiance of circumstance and fate. Pushing self-criticism overboard, he ran an eye, calculatingly, along the shadowy line of the wall.

Though it was high, it looked like child's play. Most of it was simply the old outer rampart of the castle, the broken upper courses filled in with dry-walling. The old wall (they had begun by silent consent to prowl along it) went in many places right to the top. Its stones were massy, often the size of boulders, and roughly joined.

'Look at that,' he whispered. 'There's nothing to it. Let's take a chance on a private view.'

Her eyes met his, a faint shine in the shadows. They squeezed through a thin place in the hedge, and followed the wall into a field. Out of the trees, it seemed nearly as light as day; the fissures between the stones were etched in inviting relief.

'It looks all right here,' he said.

She stood close up to him, surveying the wall. He did not try to touch her; imperceptibly the mood had shifted, it would have been out of key now. It is quicker to respond to these changes than to define them. He did not think that they had become boy and girl, reverting to the first sexual responses of daring display and shocked admiration; he merely adapted himself to it, without knowing with which of them, or in whose instinctive need, it had begun.

She said, 'If it's as good on the other side ... It must be frightfully illegal.'

'I'm going up first in case there's barbed wire at the top. Wait till I get down again.' The note of command dropped, without jar, upon an admiring submission.

'For goodness' sake be careful,' she whispered below him as he began to climb. 'It's very dangerous to slip on wire.'

'My college,' he said over his shoulder, 'had ten-inch iron spikes. I went over them about once a week.' He paused to add, 'Tight, too, as often as not.'

The cracks were smaller than they had seemed, belying the false emphasis of the moon; but he went up quickly, pleased to know she would discover that it was trickier than he had made it look. There was no wire at the top, but, on the other side, a very convenient tree with a limb almost touching the top of the wall. He came down and reported.

'It's a bit awkward in the middle. Stand on my shoulder when you get there.' There was no real need for this; it was, in point of fact, the lordly generosity of the schoolboy impressing the female with her dependence; but it felt quite natural. She said that she hoped she wasn't hurting him, and he said, 'Good Lord, no. Take a good shove off.'

On the broad top of the wall, he steadied her while she reached for the branch to swing herself down. It was springy, and just right for her weight. 'Marvellous,' she said at the bottom; and pleased by this, he launched himself off with casual ease. The branch, strained already and charged with an additional three stone, broke with a crack that splintered the night, leaving the last five feet of his descent to the uncompensated force of gravity.

'Are you all right?' He had come down on hands and knees, and she was tugging urgently at his arm. He straightened, grinned at her and sucked a graze.

'Is it bleeding? I've got a handkerchief I haven't used.'

'Sh-sh,' he said, and pulled her into the shadow under the tree.

The sound of a door opening and shutting had carried clearly in the quiet from the cottage a hundred yards away. They flattened their backs against the wall; it was largely from a sense of drama that he gripped her round the waist. Trying without success to hold their quickened breath, they waited till everything was quiet again. It had the awkward thrill of young experiment; and they pretended afterwards that it didn't count, as the young do at such times.

Stepping forward out of the shadow, they seemed to pass also out of time. On a gentle knoll, whose sides were still cleared for a bowshot round, the castle stood in full moonlight, secret and solitary, too far lost in its own stillness to resent intrusion; a deep sleeper does not lay a finger on his lips. It could never have covered much ground: a small courtyard, a hall into which the solar above had dropped two hundred years before, and the keep, standing like a hard core from which the fruit has fallen away. It was Norman; thick and narrow-eyed: forty feet of wall were still perfect. Now that the accretions of Plantagenet and Tudor had had their four or five centuries of ephemeral life and passed, like the comparative frivolities they were, the keep was the hold, as it had been in the beginning. Once it had been choked with ivy; later guardians, to save the fabric, had axed through the arm-thick roots, and there were no leaves now to reflect the moon, but the skeleton fingers still meshed the walls like giant lace.

Neil and Ellen walked up to it softly, remembering it in the afternoon. What jolly communal squeals, what private giggles, what heart-searching confidences must have littered the air: no print was left on the silence. Expanding like a night-flower, the personality of the place had spread and extinguished them. Neither period nor picturesque, but again a hard, cold mentor of the countryside, the stump of the keep squinted out through its slit eyes, as its hard Norman builder had squinted past the nose-piece of his helmet; a strong warden, but bad to cross. It was in some such place as this, Neil thought, that the boy in Ellen's story had starved himself in the dark, without consolation or hope, dying at last as his father shook him like a dog. At the time, trying to know the teller through the tale, part of his mind had been away; now it was easier to imagine than a contemporary atrocity sterilised by newsprint. For a moment his hair prickled.

The cruelty of the keep added that spice of danger which, even if only imagination supplies it, is needed to sharpen an escapade. They had come to the remains of the inner gate; a notice board, half legible in moonlight, announced that the penalty for something was five pounds. They looked at one another with a silent laugh. (The keep, too, which had helped to enforce the Angevin game-laws, was concealing perhaps a dark, sardonic Norman smile.)

Inside the courtyard the grass was mown and rolled, like a pile carpet under the feet. This part was fourteenth century; its maimed proportions were still courtly and gracious, presenting the other side of the picture; Aucassin and Nicolette, goldwork and lutes and missals, velvet and vair. The two invaders were becoming increasingly separated from reality, feeling the night, and the castle, theirs by right of conquest. It offended them, when they reached the round-arched doorway into the keep, to find it closed with a wicket of ash-stakes, strongly bound with wire. There was no room at the top to climb over. Neil, who was long past a sane inference that these precautions might relate to the state of the masonry, examined the padlock; but the blade of his knife was too broad to go in, and a hairgrip of Ellen's (the sole support of her front hair, which at once tumbled forward into her eyes) was too flexible. He explained this, leaving it to be presumed that if he were equipped with the tools to which he was accustomed, no lock could withstand him. The hair-grip was done for, and had to be thrown away.

They explored the outside of the keep, discussing it in stealthy voices, like a surprise-party at a siege. Even the lowest arrow-slit was twenty feet from the ground. Neil observed, however, a deep fissure, caused perhaps by subsidence in the earth, zigzagging down the wall, half masked by the brittle skeleton of the ivy. The moonlight mapped it, enticingly. To his somewhat overcharged imagination – now ready for anything but anticlimax and defeat – it seemed ideal. Ellen followed his look. The enjoyable fright, with which she had responded so far to his exhibition, changed in her face to something much more real. He was concentrating, and did not notice it.

'That looks fairly feasible,' he remarked. 'Do you mind if I have a crack at it? It won't take me long.'

'Please don't. I don't like the look of it.'

He noticed that her voice had altered, and thought that she didn't want to be left alone in the white silence, under the menace of the tower. Secure in a godlike sense of his own immunity, he said kindly, 'Look, I'll still be in call. I only want to see how it goes.'

'I don't think it's safe. I've got a feeling about it. If you go up there, I think you'll fall.'

'That's just atmosphere. I know what I'm up to.' He saw her eyes dilated with fear under her loosened hair. 'Not still got the gipsy on your mind? After all, we've broken our third plate.' He turned to the keep. Weathered in old blood and death, massively indifferent, it drowsed under the moon.

A hand caught his sleeve.

'No. You're not to. I know you'll be killed.'

He turned back again, quickly, and before she had been ready for it. The light irresponsible froth settled in his mind, leaving the reality from which it had risen, strong, clear and still.

'All right,' he said quietly. 'I'll pass it up.'

In the suddenly tautened and expanded silence, the whistle of a train sounded miles away, and, nearer, the flutter of a half-roused bird deep in leaves. He heard her draw in her breath; her voice, shaken and unsteady, began snatching at words. 'Well, anyone could see—'

It stopped at the first touch of his hands on her shoulders.

'There's nothing to be frightened of,' he said.

Like all first kisses, it tried to do too much: to explore and explain, demand and persuade and reassure; to satisfy the spirit and the blood. Like the rest it struggled with its incompleteness, losing its way among confused impressions, the surface coldness of lips and hands, the structure of bone under flesh and flesh under clothes, momentary distractions in the touch of hair: and, when it was over, both love and desire protested that they had been caught unready, and that everything had left off before it had begun.

Afterwards, because they were both people condemned to make life more difficult, if also more interesting, than is strictly necessary, they looked at one another. It is small wonder that the second kiss so commonly follows the first with a promptness that owes as much to cowardice as to passion. But these two, overtrained to effort, and unaware in the simplicity of their hard experience that they were doing more than human beings must, scanned one another's faces in the moonlight, getting no answer, since each was wholly absorbed in questioning; and not pausing to reflect that they were being what comfortable people call 'intense', and had brought it on themselves.

They were still standing embraced, however; and their bodies, which had found no difficulty at all from the beginning and had only needed a breathing-space in which to get used to one another, began to ask impatiently what the trouble was. Suddenly, their exchange of confidence and of trust seemed answer enough. The seeking eyes grew vague, the intent faces cloudy and still. He touched her lips lightly, a moment of prelude, and there was a little pause in which they held their breath.

It was at this point that they became aware of something disturbing the peace of their closed eyelids. They opened them protestingly, and found themselves neatly picked out in the beam of a powerful torch, directed from a few yards away. The sudden glare, striking their unaccommodated pupils, was so painful that they had not, for some seconds, even the wit to let one another go.

An apocalyptic voice, righteous and affronted, said, 'Here, here, now. We can't have none of that in here.'

Moving instinctively, Neil put himself between Ellen and the light, and squinted into the halo of impenetrable blackness it had created round it. The light continued to focus him, relentlessly, full in the face, and to deliver judgment.

'Closed to the public, these grounds are, since seven o'clock.

You're committing an offence under the bye-laws.' The light appeared to gather moral indignation; it wobbled a little. 'This building here's National Trust, open the proper times. I got enough to do in the day, seeing the public behave, without no one breaking in at night for carryings-on. There's places outside for that ... anyone wanting to do it decent.' Clearly feeling that nothing could be added without spoiling it, the light left it there.

Neil for his part had received some benefit from the sermon. It had given him a moment for recovery and, even more valuably, informed him that it wasn't the police after all. He had discovered, besides, that tonight there was practically no human contretemps which could get near enough to him to make him feel a fool.

'Sorry,' he said. 'But the place *was* a bit congested this afternoon, wasn't it?'

The light seemed to find this not quite what it had expected. Its beam described an uncertain arc, and settled on the ground. Its attendant genius could now be dimly seen, with pyjama-lapels showing under some kind of greatcoat, and a general air of grievance in the joints. Neil took advantage of the relative darkness to reach back and give Ellen's waist a reassuring pat.

'That don't make no difference,' said the light, clinging to its dignity, 'what it's like in the day. No one's got no business in here, this time of night.'

'I'm afraid,' said Neil sympathetically, 'we got you out of bed. The least we can do is to pay our entrance fee.' He advanced to the light, finding behind it a waxed sandy moustache, steel spectacles, and an open, not unreceptive palm.

'Well ... that'll be all right then, sir, this time.' The light, which had begun with an air of accident to move exploringly towards Ellen's ankles, went to ground again. 'But you can see we got to enforce the bye-laws, or we'd have all sorts in here.' Civilly, but with inflexible rectitude, it added, 'If you'll come along with me now, I'll let you out the proper way.'

In the open, where the torch was quite redundant, it continued to function; it seemed to be *ex officio*, like a truncheon or a mace. Neil, who had not had a chance to look at Ellen yet, fell a pace or two behind. She smiled at him; she was evidently determined to be very tough indeed. He gave her a quick squeeze and whispered vulgarly, 'Like a couple of cats being put out for the night.' The light paused, in a marked manner, for them to catch up.

It was a good job, Neil reflected, that the guardian of decency and of the keep hadn't stayed to inspect the branch which had given the alarm. It might just possibly have added up to the statutory five shillings' damage, and a joint summons. The local press notices would have gone down wonderfully at Weir View.

Arrived at the gate, the caretaker produced a massive key, and paused, like one who feels it his duty to improve an occasion. 'Any time you want to see the castle, it's open ten till seven summer-time, four in winter. Conducted tours at three. It's very historic, if you got the interest. Books about it there's been written. You'd find it very educational, and the young lady too – for its own sake.'

Having paused lest so delicate a rebuke should be entirely missed, he set the gate open; slanting the torch, at the last moment, to sweep Ellen comprehensively from top to toe. As the gate shut, the light behind it narrowed to a thin blade, like that of the sentinel angel at Eden's door. The unparadised sinners went hand in hand, with wandering steps and slow, out into the lane.

*

There was a certain tall rhododendron-bush, shaped in two buttresses with a cleft between. As if it had grown in conformity with local custom, the shelter it offered was strictly vertical; but very dense. Its assets were well known to the regular members, so that it was always taken up early, and sometimes vacated early also; thus, on a busy evening, it might have a second tenancy or even a third. One late-arriving couple, who had hoped to secure the reversion, had drifted towards it encouraged by stillness; but, hearing a murmur at the moment of approach, moved silently and correctly on. The voices, low-pitched instruments in a muted orchestra, continued undisturbed.

'You don't let me hear you. Say it again.'

'It must be time we went back.'

'Say it and we'll go.'

'I – I did.'

'You ought to grow out of being so shy.'

'Let's not talk.'

'Why not?'

'We're – not being ourselves.'

'God, who wants to be?'

'Promise not to remember, and I won't either.'

'All right. Shall I tell you something? Come here . . . '

'My – my dear. I'm sorry, oh, I know—'

'You're not asked to be sorry. Say "So would I."'

'Please don't let's talk.'

'It's not much, just to say it.'

'It is, and—'

'You don't have to think about it. Say it, that's all.'

'No, don't make me.'

'What are you frightened of?'

'I – I'm afraid of seeing you tomorrow. We're not like this really, and—'

'All right, then, we're not ourselves. Say it . . . I couldn't hear that. Again.'

'So would I.'

' . . . Oh, God, you're right, let's go back. No, just . . . '

'My darling, my— Neil, let me go. I tell you I'm not like this. I don't want us to remember. You don't understand.'

'Never mind. We won't remember.'

Soon afterwards, the next prospecting couple found a site to let. The outgoing tenants passed them within a yard; but the etiquette of the lane was well observed. Ghosts of different centuries could not have treated each other to a more perfect oblivion.

10

Party Overdue

The sound of the sea was creeping inland with the stillness of night. Moths bumped and fluttered against the uncurtained window. The garden gave off the changed scents which are extracted by dew. Miss Searle and Miss Fisher sat in the chairs which they had pulled up to the window a couple of hours before, to catch the first coolness after the heat of the day. A picture of the scene would have been a composition in evening quiet. Filling the room, yet quite separate and irrelevant, the powerful voice of a young man was raised in the climactic speech of a play. It climbed skilfully, dropped at the crucial moment, and finished in a dynamic undertone. A shot sounded. A woman screamed. All this noise had an odd effect of living to itself, privately, in a different dimension.

One of the moths, finding the open part of the window, flew in and dashed itself on the electric-light bulb in suicidal passion, a theme from Byron in miniature. The play had finished. A self-assured, reasonable voice stated, 'Well, I've just returned from three months in the British Zone, and the most vivid impression I've brought back ... '

'Do excuse me coming in. I thought I'd wait till the play was over.'

Miss Searle sat up in her chair, and looked at the wireless set with sudden attention. 'Of course, Mrs Kearsey.' Turning to Miss Fisher she said, 'Do you want to hear this talk?'

'No, thanks,' said Miss Fisher. 'Politics or something, isn't it? Do come in, Mrs K. We're just off to bed. If that play's finished, it must be after eleven.'

'Yes,' said Mrs Kearsey significantly. 'I *know* it is.' She came in, and sat down.

Miss Searle, who had been putting her bag and books together, let them go. It would be impossible now to escape upstairs without rudeness. Mrs Kearsey and Miss Fisher were looking at one another; Miss Searle saw in their faces the look of two women walking circumspectly – like sniffing dogs, she thought with the sudden vividness of disgust – round a sensational theme. The hideous appointments of the room seemed to crowd in on her; she could see, as if her eyes had pierced the ceiling, their counterpart in the bedroom to which she would presently go upstairs.

'I really don't know *what* to do,' said Mrs Kearsey to Miss Fisher, 'about the locking-up.'

'Somebody not back?' Miss Fisher believed in minding her own business until she had been given the entry to other people's in the clearest terms.

'It's *both* of them.' (The eyes seemed to be adding, 'Yes, by all means, do come in.') 'I know they're together, as it happens, not that I pay any attention how people spend their time, I mean that's nothing to do with me so long as I know what meals to expect them in for. But Mr Langton asked me to give them a light lunch early because they had a bus to catch, and he said they'd be in to supper the same as usual ... That's the only reason I happen to know today.' She pulled her dress straight across her lap, looked a little self-conscious as if she had seen Miss Searle's face with the tail of her eye, and added, 'I really don't know *what* to think.'

Miss Fisher looked out. The moon had risen above the trees; in the lighted frame of the window it looked more than usually secret and remote. Turning back to Mrs Kearsey she said, 'Well, I don't know, I'm sure. It's quite dark, now.'

'There aren't any buses round here run later than nine, not even from Bridgehead, and no trains, only the main line. And it's dark soon after seven.'

To walk in the dark, thought Miss Searle, would obviously delay people; why not say so simply and naturally? There was nothing significant in darkness, she thought with distaste; in winter it was dark at four.

'It doesn't seem a bit like Mr Langton,' Mrs Kearsey was going on, 'to lose his way. He never goes out without a map. And he'd surely find the right road again before it got dark like this.'

The dark again, thought Miss Searle; almost medieval. It did not occur to her that her own mind was contributing anything to her associations, except by way of criticism. Her attitude to its literary contents had been for years that of a curator.

'Of course,' Miss Fisher was saying, 'they might not have noticed how the time was getting on. It does seem to get dark so suddenly, this time of the year.'

They will be positively disappointed, said Miss Searle to herself, when this turns out to have some quite commonplace explanation. What purpose do they imagine they are serving by staring out of the window like this? We have surely established the point, by now, that it is dark . . . She was used to the classified specimens in her mind, on their proper shelves. She could enumerate their beauties. It was a long time since any of them had stirred in their places: she had quite forgotten that they were alive.

'I really don't like just to leave the door on the latch, with everybody in bed. There seems to be such a lot of funny people about nowadays. I think I shall just wait up for a bit longer. You can't settle, really, knowing you may be got up again any minute.'

'Well, it seems a shame, Mrs K. You're the one that's been working all day. You run along, and I'll make myself comfy down here on the sofa. A lot better than night duty.'

'That's very kind of you, Miss Fisher, but I couldn't think of it . . . Of course, Miss Shorland has always kept herself *to* herself since she's been here. She's nicely spoken and doesn't make trouble, but I don't feel I know much *about* her, really. But it isn't like Mr Langton not to be considerate. I don't know, I must say.'

On the contrary, thought Miss Searle, it is very like Mr Langton to be inconsiderate, at least about the times of meals. During the first few days he was here he was late for three, and missed two for which he was expected. Women of this class always prefer a morbid explanation to a straightforward one. The type that forms queues outside the Old Bailey for unsavoury trials.

Suddenly Miss Fisher turned back from the window. Her voice had lost its politely nebulous quality. She might have been speaking to a muddled probationer on her ward.

'Did they say where they were going?'

'Not that I remember,' said Mrs Kearsey. 'Only on a bus.'

'Mr Langton's a mountaineer. That's how he spends half his

time, climbing about on the cliffs. And this Shorland girl goes in for it too. I've heard them talking.'

'Oh, dear.' Mrs Kearsey's face changed; it grew simple, almost childish in distress. 'I never thought of anything like that. And here it is half-past eleven, and nothing anyone can do this time of night.' With a child's inconsequence she added immediately, 'What shall we do?'

'Seeing they went by bus,' said Miss Fisher, 'they may be any-where. There's nothing to be done now, before the morning.'

Her voice had a flat, deliberate kind of hardness. Miss Searle had a curious illusion that she had grown in stature. She had seemed to reach for the voice, as for an essential object of defence kept at hand for a familiar necessity. Miss Searle, taken by surprise before her own defences were up, had a sudden per-ception of what Wordsworth, in a different context, called 'unknown modes of being'. Dimly she sensed the daily knowl-edge of grief, pain and death, and the pressure of urgency which makes it irresponsible to feel too much. An uncomprehended feeling of affront and invasion stiffened her. First scandal, she thought, then melodrama.

'I don't think it likely,' she said quietly, 'that there's been an accident. Mr Langton and Miss Shorland were shouting to each other as they went downstairs; one could hear them even through a closed door. I remember their saying that they didn't intend to climb; in fact, though I was paying very little atten-tion, I believe Mr Langton said definitely that there was nothing which could be climbed where they were going.'

'Oh, well,' said Miss Fisher, 'that's one thing off your mind, Mrs K.'

'I'm glad you happened to hear that, Miss Searle, or I *should* have worried.' Mrs Kearsey looked at Miss Fisher. The moment of selfless humanity, which had given a goodness to their faces, was no longer there to unsettle Miss Searle. 'In that case – well, all I can say is, perhaps they missed the bus.'

Miss Fisher looked at her watch. 'It's nearly twenty to twelve. If I were you, Mrs K, I wouldn't waste my sleep waiting up now.'

Rising irresolutely, Mrs Kearsey went back to the window. (Not *again*! thought Miss Searle.) 'I don't think I will, really, now that it's got so late. It wouldn't be like Mr Langton to try and cross the moors; I mean by himself he might, but not with a lady, after dark.'

Miss Searle rose. 'Transport is very unreliable nowadays. No doubt we shall find that's the explanation. Let's hope they were able to find accommodation at such short notice.' With separate, formal good nights, she left the room.

Miss Fisher's eyes followed her to the door. She found that she had almost said, 'Don't go yet, Miss Searle. Stay for a bit and keep me company.' It was too late now; Mrs Kearsey, with an air of relieved liberation, was getting under way. It wasn't like her to be deceived in people, she confided; usually she could tell the very first day if they were that sort. She gave examples.

'Well,' said Miss Fisher absently, 'doesn't that show you?' She remembered that she had had an invitation for this evening; if she had had the sense to accept it, she would still be out, with business of her own to mind. She wished she could go out now, even alone. She would have been miserable, she supposed; and where was the sense of being miserable on your own, when you could have a bit of company? There was enough trouble in the world, without working up more; and yet, it would have been quiet down on the shore, empty and still. It might not make one more sensible about things, but one would be differently unhappy. Groping to explain this to herself, she thought that it would seem, somehow, like an old story, as old as the world; it would take one out of oneself. She could get no nearer than that, and gave it up.

If Miss Searle had stayed in the room, Mrs Kearsey wouldn't have let her back hair down like this; she was always very careful with Miss Searle, quite the lady. People always thought there was nothing you couldn't say to a nurse. It was all very well, in hospital; but off duty, there were times when it would have been nice to be able to walk, aloof and unquestioned, out of a room without anyone thinking it odd and wondering whether something had upset you. Yes, thought Miss Fisher; if I had a kid of my own, I'd see she had every advantage, even if I had to stick ten years' private nursing to make the money. It gives you a chance to keep yourself to yourself when you need to. And if you feel a bit low about something, you can read a book where it's all put beautifully about someone hundreds of years ago, and think, after all, other people have been through it, old queens and ancient Romans and all that, and it would make you feel better; instead of listening to this stuff ... well, why take it out on Mrs K? She's got her job to do and her worries, same as anyone.

'As far as that goes,' she said, doing her part, 'the things that go on in hospital sometimes, you'd be surprised ...'

A stealthy arm of moonlight, creeping over the pillow, took ten minutes to reach Miss Searle's face. In enormous space the moon hung, burning-cold and still. One side of the pillow was still screened from it; she moved her head away.

She had taken two aspirins, after praying against the sin of uncharitableness on behalf of Mrs Kearsey and Miss Fisher. The aspirins should be acting by now, but the light from outside was very disturbing. Even at the cost of ventilation, she had better pull down the blind. Getting up, she went to the window. A broad avenue of glittering light divided the sea, aimed at her like a pointing sword. Even the birds seemed half awake. No doubt it was this which was making her brain overactive; should she read a little? No, it would be foolish now not to give the aspirins a chance. She stood with the blind-cord in her hand, thankful to have escaped in time from the sordid and (she was quite certain) baseless gossip downstairs. A tiny breeze ruffled the water; the blade of moonlight shivered. Moonlight ... a shore ... a discarded sword. These vague associations were always irritating till one had tracked them down. But of course: it was too stupid to have hesitated over so hackneyed a passage.

> *In such a night*
> *Stood Dido with a willow in her hand*
> *Upon the wild sea banks, and waft her love*
> *To come again to Carthage.*

Extraordinary how frequently, even by the literate, the 'in' was misquoted 'on'. But it was getting chilly, and after aspirins one should keep warm. Besides, one had only oneself to blame for being unable to sleep, if one were foolish enough to take one's work to bed with one.

I I

Difficult Crack

'Could we – please – not go so fast?'

'I'm so sorry. I don't know why I have to walk at such a lick as soon as I start thinking.'

'I was afraid you were angry.'

'As a matter of fact, when I'm angry with women I always beat them to death. Just killing them with exhaustion strikes me as rather pansy.'

She laughed, stammered, and said, 'You are a fool.'

'Try again. It isn't difficult really.'

'I'm still out of breath.'

'Stop a minute. We'll be on the main road when we cross that stile.'

They were on the last lap of the journey back, walking from the bus-stop to the house, across the high downland that over-looked the sea. On a springy mat of heather between the gorse-bushes they sat down. The humming of bees mingled with a distant bleating of sheep, and the Æolian harping of wind in the telegraph wires. It was a hot, bright, blowy morning.

'Now,' said Neil, 'have another try.'

'What at?' She picked a bilberry from a clump beside her, tasted it, and made a face at its sharpness.

'The suppressed epithet you'd have come out with just now, if you hadn't remembered you didn't know me well enough.'

She was searching in the bilberry-clump and said, without looking up, 'After all, we don't know each other very well yet, do we?'

Poor child, thought Neil; of all the bloody-awkward ways to start the day ... The only bus of the morning had left at nine. They had had just time to finish their separate breakfasts, meet in the lounge of the Wheatsheaf, and dash to the square. It would have been much better (as he had realised when it was too late) if they had not managed to sit together. They were a good way now from the phase of unconstrained silences; he had found the effort to maintain a flow of bus-worthy conversation pretty trying himself.

'To go back a bit,' he said, 'is there really much sense in saying we'd better not start thinking about it yet? We have started, and we both know we shall go on, whether we talk or not.'

'I know. Only ...' He waited, but she made no effort to continue.

'My solicitor's taken it up as a Service case, which means it'll jump the queue. The legal time was up about a fortnight ago. I could hear any day, a few weeks at the outside. Should I have waited and sent you a letter? "Dear Miss Shorland, Circumstances beyond my control have forced me to dissemble; it may take you by surprise when I confess that the feelings I have entertained for you are not those of friendship alone ..."'

'I can't think,' she said brightly, 'how you keep it up. Haven't you got a headache or anything?'

'Now look here, my dear. I know this is all rather soon; but you know why. We were both a bit tight last night. I had to let you know that as far as I'm concerned it would have happened anyway. Well?'

'You see' – she was still poking in the bilberries, with averted face – 'I don't think you really . . .'

'I did before that, and I do now.'

'What I meant was, I – don't think you remember properly.'

'No doubt you know best.'

She looked up. He saw that she was crimson; and, sorry for her distress though he didn't quite understand it, took her hand. 'For heaven's sake come out with it, whatever it is. I shan't eat you.'

After a considerable struggle, she said, 'You know – there isn't any reason why you ought to marry me. People get a bit mixed up sometimes. I wondered if you – if you thought there was.'

'Good God. So *that's* what . . . My dear girl, I was no more than a bit happy. I surely didn't give you the impression—'

'No. No, of course you didn't. I only . . .'

'Not a very experienced drinker, are you?'

'I suppose I'm not.'

'Well, for your information, we were a comfortable Stage Two. I must take you to Stage Four sometime, just for reference. Lord bless you. Did you think I was trying to remember whether I ought to make an honest woman of you? You wonderful child.'

'Don't laugh at me. You make me feel a fool.'

'So you should. You've gravely insulted me. What are you going to do about it?'

'I'm very sorry. Please forgive me.'

'Darling, you'll kill me before you're done. Come here.'

He had kissed her once already this morning, as soon as they were alone, and had been neither surprised nor discouraged to find her response so much more constrained than it had been last night. What with the bus, the time of day, and her natural shyness, he had expected nothing else. During the night (he had shared a room in a lodging-house with a young man on a cycling tour from Manchester, who had had a piercing, intermittent snore) he had reflected that a good deal would depend on how he managed things today.

He was careful, now, to begin gently and not to hurry her. She submitted to his touch with an immediate, instinctive trust, and in the first moment he felt them completely together. It would not have been strange if he had let things go a little, but something warned him against it; and though last night's unsatisfied desire was still, he found, very close to the surface, he reminded himself not to alter the pace. Quiet as they were, there was an instant of unmistakable, electric communication; and then immediately, without resistance or withdrawal, she seemed to deaden; the current went off as if at the turn of a switch. She was only waiting now for him to let her go. He did so, easily and without haste as if nothing had been wrong. There was plenty of time, he thought.

Just now, in one of the long pauses while they sat in the bus (it had been taking a hill on bottom gear, making conversation mercifully impossible), he had made a summary of all the reasons against the step he was going to take. They were all very good ones, individually conclusive. He was in a phase, for instance, mental and physical, where such decisions ought to be avoided at all costs. He had made besides, a day or two ago, a radical and precarious change in his future plans, which he did not mean to cancel; he had no right to take on commitments in any case. This particular commitment would be a risky one in itself – a fact of which he had never been in doubt – exposing him to strain where he had become most vulnerable, and putting the test too soon. As if all this were not enough, she must be anything up to fifteen years younger than he was; and why this did not settle the matter out of hand, God alone knew if the psychiatrists didn't. (It must be becoming a syndrome, he supposed; or some other expensive term which settled everything and solved nothing.) He imagined some other man coming to him with all these points and replied 'Don't be a fool. You knew the answer before you started; why ask me?'

He had lost the trick of dealing softly with his own emotions. Considering them now, he observed that he not only wanted her, but found it fatally easy – what with her muddled innocencies, her shyness, and her loneliness – to become sentimental about her. If one were looking for a combination of factors deadly to sound judgment, here it was.

All this added up to a large total of impossibility. Perhaps it was the mere mountainousness of its proportions which made him obstinate. He could only feel it as the price of what one must have, and can with management afford. Through her he was learning to discover himself; she was the answer, not to what he had been, but to what he had become. Her uncertainty and candour, the blankness of her expectations, made her fears easier to him than another woman's certainty. Quickly alarmed by little things, in the essentials she took him as she found him; afraid of everything, she was afraid of nothing in the last resort. Her trust once gained, she would not draw back at the dark corners; they would be one kind of strangeness among many, and as fit as any for love. She would accept the dark love with the bright, because for all her inexperience there was in her too a darkness which his instincts had found already, not an inbred morbidity but something imposed and resisted, like his own. For a little while they had shared it, and released one another. Now she was in flight from this meeting-place, to which he was determined that somehow they should return. In this there was twisted a strand of perversity, which he did not hide from himself. It was there, and would have to be taken and dealt with as it came; but he felt that the main strength and substance of the cord was truth, not only for him but for her also.

'Well,' he said, 'now that we've cleared up this delicate misunderstanding, what about it? You're not a believer in two-year engagements, are you?' He smiled at her.

'My last one went on for ten. I had the ring out of a cracker, on my ninth birthday.'

She had returned his smile; he could see that she had wanted to carry it off lightly. But, against her will, her smile had shadowed with a secret pain. She was leaning a little sideways, so that the gold chain had slipped into view across the opening at her neck.

'That was only meant to be a joke,' she said quickly. 'Everyone laughed about it.'

'That's all right.'

She put her hand on his, but before he could take it, moved it away again. 'What I was really meaning to say is that I don't think I should be any good to you. I'm not good with people in bulk; I tried in the factory and I was hopeless. I could talk to them one at a time, but I never managed to be social. I know I'd be the most deadly failure as a schoolmaster's wife.'

'You never will be a schoolmaster's wife, if I can help it. Not unless it's that or starvation.'

'But . . .'

'No, that's nothing to do with this. I'd decided already. For one thing, I should be reminded of a good deal I'd rather forget; but it's more than that. I've been long enough in teaching. It's had what I've got to give it, and I've had what it's got to give me. I've seen this happen to other men. Either you get out while you're still young enough to make good at something else, or you stay in and wait for the dry-rot.'

'What do you want to do?'

Neil, who had dashed into this explanation without much thought, found himself swamped by a diffidence exceeding anything he had felt as an undergraduate in his first year.

'As a matter of fact, I should rather like to have a shot at writing.'

'Why didn't you tell me you wrote?'

She sounded quite cross about it. It made him feel better at once. He had been keyed up for the note of nervous kindness which this admission is apt to evoke, as if one had confessed to one of the more esoteric religions, or to a very peculiar kind of love-affair.

'I don't,' he said, 'yet.'

'Oh, nonsense. You're not the kind of man who decides to write because he thinks it must be nice to be a writer.'

She had become, in these few seconds, entirely adult. She even looked different. All at once he was talking easily, without tentativeness or uncertainty.

'Yes, you've a right to know this, of course. I know you'll keep it under your hat. Sammy told quite a few people himself, I believe, but that's different. Besides, it was all quite simple if you knew him. What happened was that he brought his first thing along to me when he was giving it a final lick-over; partly because I'd been with him on a lot of the climbs. Well, you know how it is, you talk till two and then you can't remember which idea was whose. The place was littered with notes on scraps of paper, and he said the very thought of getting down to it all again made him spew, so I just threw the results together, having the time. We worked like that on the next two as well.

The last one was a bit different. Sammy didn't write that to amuse himself, he needed the money. Not for himself; to finance a Himalayan expedition he was planning. In 1940, it was to have been. This was in '38, of course.'

'Yes, I know. I had it for Christmas – the book, I mean. I've got it still.'

'Have you? . . . He had quite a responsible job with a firm of architects, I expect you know. One of the partners went sick about then, and they started piling one thing after another on Sammy. He never wrote fast, at the best of times. The thing had been promised the publisher by a given date, and he was getting in rather a state about it. The upshot was he turned over his notes to me. The stuff was all there, just as he'd scribbled it down in pencil at the end of the day; a bit like a series of telegrams from Mr Jingle, but, as I say, the actual material was—'

'Yes, of course. You didn't do anything, except write the book. I can't imagine, now, how I didn't know it the first day I talked to you.'

'You see,' he said quickly, 'it was all right if you knew Sammy. It wasn't that he hadn't the ethics of an artist, but he couldn't spread them. He was a climber first and last. He'd as soon have drawn diagrams as written, if that would have given as full a record. He told me so, in those words, when we were working on the first one. About the last thing that would ever have occurred to him was that there could be anything in his own personality worth recording. When it came to this last one, he said, "Shove in anything you think of that seems likely to make it sell." He meant funny stories, I think. He thought about it as one of the chores of the expedition, like ordering the stores: if you're prevented from doing it, you hand over to whichever of the party you think can cope. He loathed lecturing, too. I often wished the audience could have plugged in to some of his language afterwards.'

'And what about you?'

'Oh, I was all for the money too. I was hoping then to go with him. Only, when I got down to it, it turned into something different ... Looking back, I don't think I ever did believe he'd live to grow old. I always imagined him finishing somewhere like Irvine and Mallory – oh, well, war hasn't very much sense of design. It was rather amusing, just as a problem, trying to slip him across between the lines without affronting his essential lack of exhibitionism. I was grateful to him for giving me the chance.'

'If he cared so little, why couldn't you have signed it?'

'It wasn't my story. Besides, Sammy had the sales-appeal. He'd climbed on Everest. His name's nearly as big a draw as Shipton's or Smythe's.'

'Yes,' she said. 'It is, now.'

'Let's get back to brass tacks. What I'm leading up to is this. Sammy never married. When he was killed, it turned out that he'd left the royalties and all the rights to me. It sold about fifteen thousand, and they're reprinting when they can get the paper, I believe. You don't generally ask a woman to marry you, and tell her you're chucking up your means of livelihood, all in the same breath. That's the reason I brought all this up.'

Disregarding the conclusion, she said, 'You'll never get away with it. Hasn't it occurred to you that you've got a style? I'd know it anywhere.'

'That was eight years ago. It's different now.'

'You've been writing since?'

'I had a rather uneventful war, you know. It'll need a good deal of going over before I do anything with it; how I've got the gall to ask you to take a chance on it, I don't quite know.'

She was looking at him, and had been for some time, with a clear unself-conscious directness; she seemed to have forgotten about herself so that this reminder still passed her by.

'And if you hadn't wanted to explain about money, I suppose you'd never have told me.'

'About Sammy, you mean?' He thought it over. 'Hard to say. I've told no one else. Human nature being what it is, I dare say I should have intended not to tell you, and eventually spilled it out in bed at three in the morning.'

Feeling so much at home with her now, he had run on without thinking. Her startled blush, and sudden shrinking into herself, pulled him up with something of a jolt.

'Sorry, my dear,' he said. 'That wasn't meant for a pass. Just a train of thought.' She had turned it now into something more; but there was no need to tell her that.

'I know.' With what he could see was a considerable effort, she looked up again. 'I should never do for you. You – you're far too straight.'

'Look, darling, forget that for now. It was just a manner of speaking. I'm not trying to run you off your feet. We've still got a bit of time here, to start getting acclimatised. Camp Three.' Uncertainly, she returned his smile. 'I won't ask you again for a day or two; we'll just take life as it comes. All right?'

'All right.' Breaking off a piece of heather, she twisted it between her fingers; then threw her hair back (there had been no time, this morning, to replace the broken slide), and said with such difficulty that it made her voice sound almost gruff, 'I'll tell you one thing. I shall never marry anyone, if I don't marry you. I know that. I couldn't have known you, and marry another person.'

'May I have that, please?' said Neil. She had been playing unconsciously with the heather in her hand, and only seemed to become aware of it when he took it from her. She watched him with a blank kind of interest, as if she expected him to botanise on it, or perform an experiment. When he put it in his pocket-book, it seemed to take her entirely by surprise.

He wanted to say, 'Do you love me?' He had been sober enough, through last night's foolishness, to be afraid of asking her then. Now he was afraid she would take it for an attempt to commit her, and a betrayal of the truce he had just declared. In the end he only said, 'Better be going, I suppose. If we're late for lunch, we shall just about put the lid on it with Mrs K.' He got up, and pulled her after him.

As they walked on, she began again to talk about the book. She evidently knew it well. He would have had more pleasure in this if he had not guessed whose gift it had been, but tried not to let himself think about it. In any case, something else had come into his mind. It was true that she was the first person he had told; the first without exception. In a moment of abrupt revelation, he understood why. He had trusted Susan with everything of his own, and it had seemed final, at the time. He had never owned to himself the instinct which had kept him from trusting her with something of Sammy's.

They had come to the stile. He was about to step over, to give Ellen a hand from the far side, when she caught him back by the arm. Roused from his thoughts, he turned to her quickly; but she did not move towards him, and he dropped his hands.

'I know we ought to get back,' she said. 'But you told me something, and there's something I ought to tell you. Not the same kind of thing. I wish it were.'

Neil leaned back against the stile. He found his hand had closed on the wood in a betraying grip, and loosened it quickly.

'Yes?' he said evenly. 'What is it?'

'It's about the man who was here the first evening I came.'

Before he thought, he had said, 'Oh – that.'

She looked at him questioningly. 'What did you think it was going to be?'

'Nothing. I'd no idea. Carry on.'

'We pretended when we got here that neither of us had known the other was coming. That was just to look better. Really I was going to – to have an affair with him.'

'Well, I knew that, of course.'

He had thought this would help her along; but she looked so lost that he added, 'Don't worry, though; you put it over all right with the others. The don believed it implicitly.'

She said at last, 'You knew all the time?'

'Why, yes.' He put an arm round her and settled her against the stile beside him. 'You know, I saw you next morning, too.'

'Yes, of course. You know I – I didn't, in the end?'

'I hoped not, for your sake. Stop shivering, darling. There's nothing to get in a state about.'

She said, slowly, 'Are you telling me now that you weren't sure, and yet ...'

He wanted to tell her that he had been grateful for being given something outside himself to think about, but found that he could not begin on that; he doubted if he would ever be able to. 'I knew that whatever had happened it couldn't have been more than a – well, a painful irrelevance. That's the essential, I suppose.'

'I wish I could make you realise,' she said under her breath, 'that you're too good to get mixed up with me.'

'Do try not to talk such—' In the stress of the moment he used an Army word, and hastily apologised; but she only laughed, as people do when something lowers their tension. 'Don't tell me the rest unless you like,' he said. 'It doesn't matter.'

'I'd rather finish it now. You see, after Jock died, I found that – that I couldn't feel anything about anyone.'

He looked away. It had not been only for her sake that he had said she need not go on.

'I wasn't proud of it, don't think that. Jock wouldn't have let himself go if I'd been killed; he was too much alive. Besides, other people had put up with worse things and not thrown in their hand. I thought I'd better try and get over it. No one had taken notice of me, before Eric did; men don't when you're quite uninterested – unless you're a beauty, I suppose. I was trying not to be a dead loss at some party, and he started then. He's attractive, on the surface ... You needn't make a face, I wasn't expecting you to agree. It seemed to me that if I ran away from this without giving it a chance, it would be rather defeatist. So in the end I agreed to come away with him here platonically ... No, you can keep that one too. I know it's very funny if you've read Plato, but Eric hadn't, so he knew what I meant.'

'Don't tell me you took one good look at him and thought he'd stick to it.'

'No, but I thought he'd be straight. Of course there was a kind of understanding left open that if it went really well it might end differently. But what happened was that the first night, he turned up in my room as a matter of course. He thought I expected it.'

'Oh,' said Neil. 'I see.' He remembered her wretchedness, and wished desperately that he could see the event as anything but an embarrassing, trivial contretemps. It was no use; he was like a man who, after swallowing Indian curry, is asked to pronounce on a light wine. As an actor struggles to get into a part, he tried to make himself twenty-five, twenty-one, nineteen. 'That must have been bloody,' he said.

'I knew you'd understand; a lot of people wouldn't. It was finding out that I'd got as far involved as that with someone who not only didn't know if I was speaking the truth, but simply didn't care. It was like suddenly knowing one had some squalid disease. To have come down to that – and then to remember.'

This, he realised now, was what he had been waiting for from the start. He said nothing. His face was well trained, and reliable.

'I tried to laugh it off in a way that wouldn't hurt his feelings. But he felt I'd let him down, and said ... Well, I can't tell you that. I didn't guess till then how a lot of people live. I shouldn't have said what I did to him afterwards – one finds it hard to believe that anything *can* get through. He didn't mean any harm, as he saw it. I expect the fact was, he thought I was used to it.'

'A perceptive type,' said Neil, suddenly angry.

'Don't let's talk about it any more. It seemed worse than ever after I'd met you.'

This time she was not passive to his kiss; she returned it, with an inexperienced attempt at ardour. At first he tried to believe in it; but last night had been too real to let him make mistakes afterwards. She was grateful for his understanding, and determined to reward it. Again he could not tell the quality of her inward resistance. It was not repulsion, nor indifference; such certainties do not admit of error. Rather it was as if she took fright at the first stirring of passion, not in him but in herself, and killed it wilfully, unhappy at failing him but by some stronger compulsion continuing to fail. He had a moment's impulse to try and force a response from her; but his wits came to his aid in time, and he let her go. As he released her, she reached up and gave him a swift, parting kiss. It felt like an act of expiation.

She moved off towards the stile; but he checked her with an absent movement, while he thought what to say. It was simple enough, after all.

'This seems to have brought us to another thing we'd better get sorted out. I think myself that the idea of trying it out before marriage has a good deal to be said for it. Not that it tells you everything, God knows, but I've watched one or two disasters among people I know that it might have staved off.' She had been facing him when he began, and she continued to face him. Suppressing a moment's temptation to tell her that he wasn't a firing-squad, he went on, 'But in case you're wondering, after this other thing, what to expect from me at any moment, I'm telling you now so that we'll know where we are. This whole divorce racket is just a joke in bad taste; but all the same, I'm seeing it through till the official deadline. What I want to avoid is any chance of a situation in which our future – and three other people's – is going to depend on my committing perjury. The idea doesn't attract me, and I shouldn't be very good at it. That's all. I just thought you might like to know.'

Her strained suspense had made all this something of an effort. Now, without warning, her face crumpled. He had forgotten, among the morning's difficulties, how charming her smile could be when she was really amused.

'Thank you,' she said, 'for telling me you wouldn't be very good at committing perjury.' She hesitated, and put a shy hand on his arm. 'Darling, you are a fool.' He reached for her, but she was too quick for him, and went smartly over the stile, leaving him to follow.

They both walked the next quarter-mile of road in a certain degree of abstraction. Presently, however, Ellen remarked in rather a subdued voice, 'We're almost there.'

'Good Lord. Yes, so we are.'

Their pace became perceptibly less brisk; presently, by tacit consent, they stopped altogether.

With an air of authority which he did his best to make convincing, Neil said, 'I think it will be the best plan if you go and have lunch at the hotel. I'll meet you afterwards of course. Then—'

Ellen stood back on her heels. '*Really*, Neil. What *do* you take me for?'

'There's nothing to it. You might just as well show up when the excitement's died down a bit. Only common sense. Why not?'

'Why not! If you think I'm going to lurk in a hotel while you take on all those women single-handed—'

'Well, we can't both talk at once, in any case. Seeing it's my job, you might just as well leave it to me. Can't you trust me not to make a mess of it?' This struck him as distinctly subtle.

'Of course we shall make the most ungodly mess of it, together or separately. It – it isn't as if we could *feel* like casual acquaintances who've been annoyingly stranded, is it?'

'No,' said Neil, wishing they were on the downs again; cars were passing at ten to the minute. 'But all the same—'

'Besides, I don't want to have lunch by myself when I could be having it with you. Come on, or we'll be late.'

After this conversation, it was natural that they reached Weir View in a state of heroic resolution, each privately at concert-pitch and determined to carry off the situation with brilliant aplomb in support of the other. Fate was unlikely to resist such a target for anticlimax. The hall, the dining-room, the Lounge, met them with indifferent emptiness.

'Of course,' said Ellen with determined reasonableness, 'people do go out, this time of the day. I don't know why we should expect them to be all lined up in the hall.'

The room vacated by Mr Phillips had been taken, the day after he left, by an old gentleman of retired military cast, an overflow from the hotel where his family was staying. He had all his meals there, and had thus remained a complete stranger to the Weir View guests. He now made a leisurely progress down the stairs, keying up their expectation (for he was a little man with a light tread) for several long seconds before he appeared in sight. Seeing them standing-at-ease below him, he gave them a courteous but rather dissatisfied inspection (as if, thought Neil, they had been foreign troops whose deficiencies had to be treated with tact), acknowledged with clipped correctness their tardy greetings, and trotted out, leaving final deflation behind him.

The clock made it, after all, only ten minutes to lunch-time.

'I suppose,' said Ellen at last, 'we'd better go and get tidy.'

Neil completed this process rapidly (his room-mate of the night had generously lent him a razor in the morning). Feeling firm and resourceful, though a little underhand, he hurried past Ellen's door and made his way down to the back of the house. He had never been, so far, into the kitchen. Perhaps the last five minutes before lunch might not be the perfect moment; but it was the man's job to break the ice, and he was going to do it.

So many sounds of activity were going on inside that he could not be sure whether anyone had answered his knock. His hand on the door-knob, he paused, seized with sudden misgivings about having shaved; involuntary castaways should manage less neatly. Fortifying himself, he decided that this was not the kind of thing a woman would think of. He went in.

Afterwards, he was never quite successful in recalling all the details of the interview. He tried several times, moved by anxiety to convince himself that it had gone off perfectly. He did remember, however, that Mrs Kearsey had been running to and fro, at what seemed to be high pressure, between the gas cooker and the table, and that her face, as he appeared, expressed less of moral censure than of frenzied irritation. He was also vaguely aware that she had been rebuking the little maid in a voice rather different from the one she used in the Lounge, and that he had entered in the middle of it. She had on an old chintz apron, none too clean; this she hurriedly and reproachfully removed, while he put over his opening speech. During the rest of the dialogue, the maid was scuttling in and out with trays; and Mrs Kearsey turned round, every time she came back, to watch her activities and correct them in a distraught *sotto voce*.

Resolved not to be put off by any of this, Neil stood his ground, and affected an imperturbable, easy charm. He had res-urrected this manner from the days of his first appointment, where the Head's domineering wife had responded to it fairly well; and did not pause to reflect that he had not tried it on Mrs Kearsey before. She seemed at least to be looking at him with awakened interest, and (after the maid's activities had sub-sided) to be hanging on his words. When he had run himself to a standstill, she replied briefly to the effect that she *had* been a little worried last night, but that accidents would happen, and that she was glad to know they were safe and sound. Detecting a note of reserve, and anxious to leave no telling point unmade, Neil assured her that he would have rung up last night to explain, if she had been on the 'phone. With a noticeable drop in temperature, Mrs Kearsey replied that it *was* a convenience, if it hadn't been for the war; but that one couldn't have every-thing nowadays the way one had been used to. Of course not, he agreed a little too hastily; no, quite. There was a pause. Mrs Kearsey rushed to the cooker, where a saucepan connected with the next course was boiling over. Having dealt with this and finding him still there searching for an exit-line, she remarked, with the air of one stating the obvious, that it was a pity she hadn't known in time to get lunch for them, but after having kept supper hot for two hours last night, she really hadn't known what to do, and she expected they would have made arrangements. He assured her they had, with an air of one accustomed to take charge of such situations, which almost convinced himself. Mrs Kearsey said that in that case she would expect them for supper, and returned to the saucepan. He became aware that the interview was over.

He went out into the corridor, wiped his brow (the kitchen had been like an extension of the oven) and said to himself that as she hadn't asked them to leave she must evidently have been satisfied. The thought visited him that landladies cannot easily expel guests who behave themselves on the premises, whatever they do elsewhere; but he did his best to dismiss it. He had better find Ellen, and take her along for a meal. Their public debut would now have to remain in suspense till supper-time.

Ellen was not in sight; but he heard voices, just inside the door of the Lounge. She must be there; they had caught her unprotected.

He strode to the door.

Just before he got there, a voice reached him. It was Miss Searle's, full of well-bred sympathy and understanding.

'*How* awkward for you. I remember something very similar happening to a colleague of mine, on a walking-tour in Dalmatia. But the British Consul was very helpful.'

Then he heard Ellen. She was stammering. In the grip of her intractable shyness, she sounded like a schoolgirl having a session with the better kind of house-mistress.

'Yes – and of course we hadn't anything with us, not even a toothbrush; if I hadn't had a rucksack I don't suppose the hotel would have taken me in. And there wasn't any s-soap; it's awful trying to get clean with just water. And it was even worse for Mr Langton; he had to go to an awful little place in a back street, and didn't even have a room to himself.'

It was the perfect approach. She couldn't have done better if a producer had coached her in it for weeks. When Miss Searle crossed the hall in response to the gong, Neil stepped unobtrusively out of sight.

12

Overhang

From the arm of the harbour, the lamps of the whitewashed cottages made snaky ripples that seemed to wriggle nearer across the lazy sea. There was a smell of tar and seaweed; the infrequent mew of the gulls had the different note of night.

'Did you mind coming out and giving them a bit more to talk about?'

'No. I like it here.'

'Supper didn't go off too badly, did it? Though the don takes a dim view of me, I'm afraid. She'd think twice before she gave one of her students late leave to go out with me. Miss What's-her-name was a bit subdued, I thought.'

'Miss Fisher doesn't miss very much.'

'Well, we didn't give them much to go on.'

'Look, there's a ship out in the channel.'

They stood together, watching the port light which seemed scarcely to move against the irregular beaded points that picked out the coast of Wales.

'Come here a moment.'

'I am here.'

'I'd like to be sure.'

'Neil.'

'Yes?'

'If I'm going to think this over, you must too. No, I'm serious now. I've not known you very long, but I feel all this isn't like you. If you were starting a climb, you'd want to find out more about the mountain first than you know about me. Whether the rock was good, or – or rotten. And if you started and then found it wasn't justifiable, you'd turn back. You can now; you can any time.'

'This one's either justifiable or impossible. Is it impossible?'

'I wish to God I could tell you. I think it would be fairer if I said yes.'

We ought to have this out, he thought. Here and now. Every instinct told him that retreat from this moment would have to be paid for. But there were parts of his own experience that he still felt he would never be able to talk about as long as he lived; it seemed both cruel and unjust that he should ask more of her than of himself.

'You don't have to worry about me. I know what I'm doing and I've got no doubts about it. Incidentally, you don't find out what rock's like by standing at the foot and guessing.'

'I don't know how you have patience with me.'

'My dear, we're both grown-up. I've made a headlong assault on you when you clearly weren't ready. It must have been pretty obvious to you that I simply let go because, one way and another, I was bloody sick of holding on. You had patience with me.'

She said, half aloud, 'I didn't need any.'

The spume blowing in from the sea had left a thin, cool film of salt on her lips. She would not open them when he kissed her; but he felt her hand touch his hair and quickly fall away. She turned her face aside; seeking for her mouth he found her cheek instead. It was salt as her lips had been, but slippery and warm.

'What is it?' He felt a sense of power and a certainty that not only the night was on his side. 'Tell me now.'

'Ought we to stay much longer? Mrs Kearsey may want to lock up.'

'What is it?'

'Oh, nothing. I'm afraid of all this.' She pulled one arm away to gesture vaguely at the night. 'It looks like a canto in *Don Juan*. One can't help it. It isn't real.' Feeling his arms loosen she clung to him again; he could feel the catch in her breath. 'Listen, Neil. Don't risk anything on me. Never give me a chance to hurt you, even in little ways. I'm not worth it. Why do you have to do more than amuse yourself with me? I don't mind if you do; I'd rather. I won't be awkward, I promise; I won't be any trouble to you at all, if only I know you're not risking anything on me that matters.'

'Thanks for the thought; but I can look after myself without a nannie.'

'I've not been fair to you. I've let you give me too much. There are some people who are more – more involved by giving than by taking. If I hadn't been utterly wrapped up in myself I'd have seen it before.'

'My dear child, we could both play at this game till kingdom come. Why not stop talking like a book and give living a chance?'

He took her back again. This time she was, as she had said just now, no trouble at all. Below the sea-salt, her mouth tasted by contrast sharply sweet. But, as before she had been too difficult, now she was too easy; her answers had a fluid kind of helplessness, like that of water moved by wind. Her mind was not in it; it stood, defeated and self-accused, somewhere apart. It made no sense to him that they could share this awareness without being able to overcome it. He let her go with disturbed senses and a spark of anger in his heart which, because he would not justify it, he would not own.

'Take it easy, my dear,' he said. 'Take it as it comes. It'll be all right.'

They walked back as they had come, his arm round her waist and her hand on his, holding it there. The sea still made its soft plashing against the jetty, and a hushing noise on the shingle of the beach. The stars brightened. They were silent, and separate in themselves, for the rest of the way.

Miss Fisher looked up from the picture-postcard on which for the fourth time she was trying to vary the phrases. All four were going to colleagues who would probably compare them; but she was finding it hard to give the problem her whole mind.

'I'm not one to be hard on anybody,' she said. 'People are only flesh and blood, is what I always think, and they make a nice couple, in a way, you can't deny it; a nice contrast if you see what I mean. As for having proof, that's hardly likely, now is it, when you come to think? But I've got my own eyes, and that's good enough for me.'

'My own opinion,' said Miss Searle, 'is that when an inno-cent explanation has not only been offered, but bears every mark of probability, the least one can do is to be charitable. Don't you think so?'

'I should say it depends what you mean.' Miss Fisher found it hard to find a fulcrum for her sense of injustice. Far from lack-ing charity, she felt herself to be reacting with toleration, even with some generosity, to a self-evident fact. 'I mean when a girl can't even pass a man the butter without blushing up to her ears—'

'I can understand her embarrassment,' said Miss Searle tartly, 'even better now than at the time.'

' – And when he says "Thank you" one minute as if she was a perfect stranger, and the next "Will you have a biscuit" as if he was the family doctor pepping up an urgent case ... well, that's only *one* thing. I mean, well, there it is.'

'From the little I know of Mr Langton, I should imagine he would feel responsible for the girl's very awkward position, and sensitive to her shyness about it. I can't see, myself, that any other explanation is necessary. Or kind.'

Unexpectedly, Miss Fisher felt an aching behind her eyes. Blinking it away, and not trusting herself to speak, she asked herself protestingly whether she wasn't behaving like a good loser; hadn't she taken people as she found them, even wished them luck; what effort of kindness greater than these was required? She licked a stamp, fixed it, swallowed, and said, 'Well, everyone's got their own opinion, and you can't say more.'

'I'm sure that's much the best way of looking at it.'

'And another thing,' said Miss Fisher, nature suddenly rebelling, 'he tried to squeeze her foot under the table, only she'd got it tucked up round her chair.'

'The table?' asked Miss Searle, pouncing on the syntactical error out of disgust for the rest.

Flicked on a tender surface, Miss Fisher paused with another licked stamp congealing in her hand.

'I ask you,' she said bitterly. 'It's pitch dark outside. What do you suppose they're doing *now*?'

'I have no idea. And I hardly feel it concerns either of us.

219

Oh, dear, it seems to be later than I thought; I must really get to bed. *Good* night.'

Miss Fisher, giving her attention to pulling the sticky stamp from her fingers, did not respond.

13

Fixed Anchor

'What is it now?' asked Neil.

Ellen looked disconcerted. With his back to an old ash-tree, he was looking straight out across the moors; it was she who had been watching him.

'Nothing's the matter. Why?'

Neil got out his pipe, cleaned the bowl with a twist of dry bracken, shook it out, and began to fill it. The silence became a contest of wills.

'When I said nothing, I meant nothing I could tell you without feeling a fool.'

'If you say so. I wouldn't know.' He got out matches, and turned over on his stomach to shelter the flame.

'You'll never do it, in this wind.' She picked up her sweater from the grass, and, kneeling over him, held it beside his head for a screen. He thanked her; but she saw that he had already got the pipe drawing without it. She drew away again, and arranged the sweater to sit on.

There was another pause; then Ellen spoke again, in a

sudden rush. 'Well, you asked for it. It's just that there are times when you frighten me.'

'That must be thrilling,' said Neil moderately.

'I knew you'd make me feel a fool.'

He put the pipe down on a flat stone, and moved towards her.

'No. Not now. It stops me from thinking.'

'We mustn't do that.' He began coaxing the pipe again.

'You made me tell you; it isn't fair to make it so difficult. I don't mean frightening in a simple way. You're always kind to me, when anyone else wouldn't be. When I know I'm being stupid and – and disappointing, you put up with it—'

'Blessed are the meek.'

'You're the least meek person I ever knew. That's what I'm trying to say. You're kind for my sake partly, I know, and it's good of you. But at the same time it's as if you said, "You see, you can't touch me." You put it up all round you, like a wall.'

'In heaven's name, Ellen, what *do* you want?'

'I don't know. You shouldn't have made me say anything. It's just a way you have of looking sometimes – suddenly shut up, and not wanting to be interfered with.'

'I suggest you try the door and see if it's locked.'

'I do, and it is.'

'My dear child, if it makes things any simpler, I was looking at the colour of those hills over there, and comparing it with something I saw near Delphi once.'

'Yes, it would be something like that ... Neil, what do you want with me?'

'Silly of me not to have told you. I was thinking I had.'

'You've never told me. You've picked me up like a stray cat out of the rain, and dried my fur and stroked me. You've said you loved me, but that can mean a lot of things. Neil, I must talk to you. Please don't mind this. You've – had a bad time, and you've been a good deal by yourself, and I think it's made me seem more important to you in some ways than I really am. I don't think it would last with you. That's all.'

Neil considered her for a few moments, with narrowed eyes.

'Look, my dear; there's no need to do a sort of verbal Dance of the Seven Veils. Are you trying to say that I've been carried away by the fact that I want a woman, and you happen to be on the spot?'

'No, of course not.' She blushed fiercely, through all the predictable stages.

'What do you mean, of course not? Any man proposes because he wants a woman. If you don't mean any woman, what's it all about?'

'I don't know.' She was doing something to one of her shoes.

'That does occur to a man for himself, you know, if he's past twenty-five. The procedure is to make a strong effort of the imagination, if it's important, and decide how she'll seem at eight in the morning after you've been sleeping with her for a week. By the way, do you wear curlers in bed, or one of those bags?'

'I don't wear anything.'

'That's fine.'

'It – it grows like this. I just tie it back.'

'And do you put thick grease on your face, or thin?'

'It isn't grease. You'd be no wiser if I told you.'

'Oh, one of those light things. Yes, you would. Shall you mind my shaving while you're having a bath?'

'I have it at night.' She took her shoe off, shook out a piece of grit, and put it slowly on again.

'Well, I'll need to shave at night, I expect, with a skin like yours, or you'll be changing over to grease. But let it go. What are you in such a flurry about? You wanted to know if I'd looked any farther ahead than getting into bed with you. It's quite a reasonable question. D'you mind my talking like this?'

'No,' she said under her breath. 'That's the . . . '

'What did you say?'

'I said No.'

'After that?'

'Nothing. I mean it wasn't what I meant, so I didn't say it.'

'Anyhow, I've answered what you were trying to ask me, haven't I?'

'Yes.'

'Haven't you ever talked straight to anyone about these things before?'

'I suppose . . . well, only to women sometimes.'

'Still, you'd rather we just talked things over sensibly, without my making love to you and putting you off?'

'Yes, of course I would.'

'Darling, you shouldn't let people have you for a sucker. I've been making love to you for the last five minutes. Rather sadistically, too.'

Ellen finished fastening her shoe and looked up. 'You think I've got no sense at all, don't you? If you really wanted to be cruel you could do better than that; you don't need to tell me. Whatever I'm afraid of, it's never that.'

Neil's face altered. Sliding along the soft turf of the bank, he came beside her and took her hand.

'What is it, then, stupid?'

He turned her hand over – he was lying on one elbow a little below her – and kissed the palm. She said, 'It must be awfully grubby,' and tried to slip away.

'What is all this?'

Looking past him, she said, 'You only want to do things for

me. You don't need anything . . . I mean only . . . not anything really, and you wouldn't take it if you did. You're too proud.'

His mind went back, involuntarily, over seven months of effort towards personal survival. Trying the word curiously, he said 'Proud?'

'You don't think it's true?'

'More likely it's just hardening of the arteries. At high altitudes the symptoms get worse.'

'Can't you ever stop laughing at me?'

'I'm sorry. It's one of those things where there's nothing to do but laugh. We can do damn-all about it. It's a kind of acquired reflex, like learning to swim. You may learn it on the ideal holiday, or you may get a push in the canal. But you don't unlearn it again; and no one but a suicide ever wants to.'

Presently she slid her fingers gently out of his; and he stretched out on the slope, in the sun and out of the wind. Her hand came down on his hair so lightly that he did not feel it till it moved. He flicked a quick, suspicious glance upward, to see what she was looking at; but she was looking at the hills whose colours had reminded him of Greece. Her slow, preoccupied touch was pleasant; he relaxed again.

'You must tell me any time,' she said at length, 'if I come pushing in on you when you want to be alone.'

'It doesn't make any difference . . . God's truth, what do you think I am? Greta Garbo?'

'You still don't say why you want to marry me.'

'To knock a bit of sense into you,' said Neil with restraint, 'I shouldn't wonder.'

He saw a little laugh ripple down her body, under her blue linen shirt. Putting an arm suddenly behind her, he leaned up and kissed the base of her throat, where the light golden tan shaded down to white. For a moment he felt her fold herself round him, shy and warm. Then something hard struck softly against his face. The gold St Christopher, as she leaned, had swung forward on its chain. He stiffened; and, feeling his movement, she lifted her head from above his, and withdrew her arms.

'Oughtn't we to be getting on?' she said.

'I should think so, if we're going to get any tea.' He got out the map. Ellen dusted, carefully, the grass from her sweater, and put it on.

They kept up a conversation for the next five minutes or so; long enough to make it clear to one another that no constraint existed. In a little while the silences grew longer, and presently they walked on quite enclosed in their own thoughts.

Ellen's mind had travelled inward to the fringe of its central trouble; and, retreating again, was wandering about the periphery, pausing at all those secondary uncertainties and failures of nerve which were easier to think about than the source from which they spread. Surely, she thought, she could force herself at least to master the small change of living, the trivial details that needed management and address. If not, she ought to be thankful that her ineptness amused him; and, indeed, she often was, as for instance that he had laughed her into stating baldly when she wanted to disappear behind a hedge. She was useless, she thought, she could neither give nor take with grace, willing neither to be carried nor, in the last resort, to stand on her own feet.

The footpath had divided into parallel tracks; they had taken one each to avoid walking single file; and, as often happened when he was preoccupied, he had lengthened his stride and got ahead of her. She did not hurry – he would notice in a moment – but looked at his back, a relatively unfamiliar view. He moved without any appearance of speed, evidently in his natural rhythm, with the loose slouching walk which, over a distance, reduces effort; an impetus from the hips, suggesting to her mind the swing of the heavy climbing-boots which she had not yet seen him wear. It was impossible to imagine him in uniform; in any uniform, physical or mental. His long dark head, slim neck and narrow hips made the unbroken width of his shoulders more impressive from behind than from the front: the two superimposed isosceles triangles, the broad above the narrow, the elementary male diagram of the life-class, fitted him with scarcely a modifying curve.

He's a snob, she thought, if you care to look at it like that. Perhaps what's wrong with snobbery is that it's so many centuries since it was applied to the right things. It needs revising, in an age where a whole school of advertising lives by blackmail, trading on people's wretched little fears of having less expensive gadgets than the Joneses or too few dates, and a whole school of propaganda tries to scare people into believing that it's antisocial to have a personal sense of right and wrong. The man who owns his own soul is the natural aristocrat, like the man in the old West who owned his own horse; a *caballero* among the *hombres*. What is it but the cream of snobbery, to risk your life over years, perfecting an art that has no audience, unless it's one or two fellow-artists whose standards are as strict as your own? And he's honestly surprised when one calls him proud.

'Sorry,' he said, stopping and turning back to her. 'I will do it. You just want to shout Hi.'

'It's all right. I'm only lazy.'

'I've rushed you till you're pink in the face. Throw something next time. Take it easy; look, here we are.'

The townlet they were making for had come into sight beyond the hump of the moor; soon they came down to hedges, then to lanes and roads.

'This,' said Ellen, 'looks like the kind of shop where they sometimes have hair-grips. I think I'll try; I'm down to my last one again.'

'Blaming me? I like it without. Still, you've as much right to the use of both eyes as the next, I suppose. I'll wait for you here.' He sat down on the low whitewashed wall of a cottage garden, on the other side of the narrow street.

Ellen went into the shop, which sold a little of most things, but mainly mineral-waters and sweets. A deliberate old man was helping a woman with five ration-books to choose a month's supply of acid-drops and peppermints and liquorice all-sorts. The conference seemed endless. Ellen wandered round the few square yards of space, glancing at the boxes and cards, and sometimes, for variety, out into the street through the open door.

Neil, waiting, looked at the ubiquitous hydrangeas in the front gardens, remarked the similarity of their pinks and blues to those of litmus paper, and decided to ask the next scientist he met whether they responded to reagents in the soil. Not that modern scientists ever knew such things; universal curiosity had gone out with the seventeenth century.

These reflections were disturbed by a snuffling sound, a couple of yards away. Looking round, he saw a girl child of five or so, her blue west-country eyes, under a thatch of pale Saxon hair, blurred with indecision and distress. Her nose was running; she sniffed again, ineffectively. She was a clean, well-kept little girl, and evidently felt her position keenly. Hesitantly she picked up a fold of her pink cotton dress, looked at it in conflicting agonies of conscience, and dropped it again.

In a habit-formed response, which he could not arrest in time, Neil's hand went to his pocket. She padded up to him, looking hopeful and relieved.

'Shall I blow it for you?'

'Yes, blease.'

He shook out the handkerchief; accuracy was usually tricky. As always, the indeterminate scrap of nose was lost among the folds; but he managed to track it down.

'Come on, then; blow.'

She planted her feet apart, leaned forward, and threw into play every muscle of her body except the ones directly concerned.

'That's no good. You blow with your nose, not your knees.'

It ended with his doing all the work himself; it always had. She emerged crinkled with laughter.

'Didn't blow with my knees.'

'It felt like it. Run along, now; they'll be looking for you.'

'I'm playing in our garden.'

'Better get back there, then.'

He picked her up under the armpits to lift her over the wall. Under sliding layers of cotton, her round, firm little body wriggled between his hands. She scrambled with her feet on the top of the wall and stood up. He had to go on holding her, to keep her from falling.

'You've got funny hair.'

'Yes, I know.'

'What you put on it?'

'Nothing, It's striped.'

'Like our kitty?'

'That's right. Over you go.'

'Don't want to. Why's it striped?'

'Ask your kitty. Heave over.'

'No. Jump me right up high.'

'Not now. I'm busy.' Suddenly he remembered having said this, too, before.

'What you doing?'

'Oh, all right.' He stood, and tossed her up; she squealed in delicious fright, eight feet from the ground.

'There. Now you're going back.'

'Don't want to. I wants to stop here. No – o!' With the incalculable suddenness of her years, she started to cry.

'Don't be silly,' said Neil helplessly. 'Your nose'll run again.' This was already happening; he was obliged to deal with it. Feeling insecure with one of his hands engaged, she steadied herself on the wall by grabbing two fistfuls of his shirt at the shoulder. He felt, without seeing, the familiar drag in the familiar place.

'Listen,' he said with sudden resource. 'Do you know what sweet coupons are?'

'Yes.' Hope mingled in her eyes with contempt for a silly question.

The vague little street ran to a dead end; there was no traffic in it. 'Take these, and this, and run across and buy some sweets. But only if you go straight back and eat them indoors. Promise?'

She squirmed eagerly down between his knees, and away. His arm and side felt cold when her vivid warmth had gone. Getting to his feet quickly, he glanced at the sweet-shop door. Ellen was out of sight, and couldn't have seen anything. Relieved, he walked away down the street. She could catch him up.

At a round, marble-topped table in the dark end of the shop, Ellen was drinking a glass of fizzy lemonade. It was all she had had time to think of when, her business done, she had found it impossible to show herself outside. It was a highly gaseous brand, and made her choke a little. The woman with the ration-books had remembered something else, and was still there.

'Hullo, Rosie my dear,' said the shopkeeper. 'What can I do for your mother today?'

'Please, Mr Bates, I want some choclit.'

'What's this, then? You had all your ration this month, you know that.'

'Gentleman give them me.'

'Did he now? Starting young, isn't she, Mrs Tanner?'

The woman with the ration-books looked round sharply.

'Now, Rosie, that's naughty. Your mum would never have that if she was to know. You don't want to get talking to strange men and letting them give you things, not when you don't know who they are.'

'Why?'

'Never you mind why, you ask your mum.' There was a muttering across the counter; the audible tail-end was '. . . some poor little innocent soul only in last Sunday's paper.' The child listened, with grave curious eyes. 'You go straight back in, Rosie, and remember what I said, or me and Mr Bates will have to tell your mum of you.' The woman picked up her shopping and went out.

When Rosie, looking doubtfully at her chocolate bars, had gone too, the shopkeeper said, 'It's a fact, you have to be careful, times like these.'

'Yes,' said Ellen. 'I suppose you have.'

'We'll be getting the still lemonade in next week. Not to everyone's taste, the mineral isn't.'

'It's very nice. It's just that it gets up your nose rather.'

'A bit strong for you, like?'

'Just a bit.'

She groped in her pocket for her powder, and looked in the glass. Alienated by this loose modernity, Mr Bates went away into the shop parlour. It was the kind of luck which was rare in

Ellen's experience, and she was duly grateful. When she was presentable again, she went outside.

'Any luck?' said Neil, strolling back to meet her.

'No. Only pink fancy ones. He thought he had, though, and I had to help him hunt all over the shop. That's why I've been so long.'

'Never mind. We haven't got to the real shops yet.'

There was no market square here, but a steep little high street, with a narrow kerb which the bottle-necked traffic overhung. They edged along it – it was congested with a Saturday shopping crowd – looking for somewhere to eat, and for those useful rarities which must be seized where one happens to see them.

'Do you want anything special?' asked Ellen. She had been silent for some time.

'Only braces, as usual. I'll be wearing a belt with my dinner-jacket soon.'

'They've got some there.'

'What, those damn-awful plastic things? Just try wearing them.'

'Neil—'

'M – m? Only waste time, I suppose, asking inside.'

'Neil, if you're really sure you want to marry me—'

'They never . . . What was that?'

'I just said I'll marry you, if you still want me to.'

Neil stepped back from the shop-window, and collided at once with a housewife carrying vegetables, who said 'Pardon' angrily.

'My dear good girl. What a place to tell me.'

'I'm terribly sorry.'

'Almighty God!'

'I know it wasn't very . . .'

'Don't keep begging my pardon, you crazy little idiot. Where on earth can we—' The outfitter's had not even a recessed doorway. 'My dear, I—' He took her hand.

'Excuse *me*.' Another human freight-carrier shoved them apart.

'Well,' said Neil at length, 'thank you, my dear. Let's go somewhere and have tea.'

14

Exposed Traverse

Miss Searle had spent the day alone. She had not at any time contemplated inviting Miss Fisher's company. The most pleasureable incident of the morning had been the arrival of Miss Fisher's new friend, by car, to call for her; he had not only fulfilled, but even surpassed, Miss Searle's expectations, and had given a sufficient demonstration of what Miss Fisher's judgment of people was likely to be worth.

The day had been a little uncomfortable for sitting about, and she had not felt inclined for a long expedition. She had taken lunch in Bridgehead. It was a depressingly typical seaside resort, except for the small fishing-quarter which she had already explored. The weather, she thought, was discouraging, with its hot, gritty little wind.

She had known from the outset that this year's holiday was only a *pis-aller*, and it had been much like her expectations. The place was peaceful and picturesque; she had fortified her health against the coming winter; and the holiday could be held, therefore, to have justified itself. Lacking congenial contacts, one could always divert oneself by a study of types. To prove it she diverted herself, for a second time, with Miss Fisher and her friend.

In spite of this determined lightness of touch, she found herself still quite upset by the debased view of life with which Miss Fisher had tried to infect her, and eager to assert herself against it. It was not enough merely to have opposed it in words; something more concrete was required. She owed it to her own standards, to human charity. She would have been surprised if anyone had told her that she wanted to assuage an inward sense of injury and loss by an act of forgiveness. She had owned to herself neither loss nor disappointment; she only felt, as she felt the weather, that it would elevate her to be kind. Clearly, only one kindness was appropriate towards a person accused of something which no one of right principle could condone: to demonstrate one's belief in his innocence.

It should not be difficult, she thought. A small social gesture could count for so much.

Circumstance smiled on her intention. Everyone, as it turned out, was in for the evening meal.

Miss Fisher was ostentatiously gay. She displayed a goggle-eyed plaster doll, and remarked that the way to win prizes at fairs was to bring someone along to do the manual work. Her lipstick was slightly smeared. She ate little; but, she explained, she had had tea late.

Miss Searle noted with satisfaction that Mr Langton and Miss Shorland behaved in a way that lent no colour at all to Miss Fisher's recent innuendoes. They made separate entrances, he quiet and casual, she, as usual, a little reserved, and joined at once in general conversation. Miss Searle had no difficulty at all in working the talk round to the subject of bridge and discovering that everyone, in some sort, played. She could never, she said, understand the mentality of people who sat down to bridge every evening; however, a game passed the time pleasantly once in a way. Perhaps if no one was doing anything after supper . . .

Miss Fisher, who had not said much since her emphatic first appearance, looked up from her plate and gazed at Miss Searle in fascinated incredulity.

'Well,' she said, 'I'm fond of a rubber myself now and again, but I don't know I'm sure if—' Her eyes wandered, with ill-concealed sympathy, along the table.

Without giving her time to finish, Ellen said, 'Of course, if you want to make up a four. Though I'm afraid I'm not very good.' She looked at no one but Miss Searle.

One of those moments passed which is not long enough to be called a pause, but long enough to make people wonder whether a pause is coming.

'Provided it isn't one of these esoteric variations,' said Neil, 'I'd be delighted.' He looked only at Miss Fisher.

The cut partnered Neil with Miss Searle, a well-balanced arrangement on the whole. Miss Fisher turned out to be a surprisingly good player, Ellen an unsurprisingly bad one. Miss Searle had a sound memory, but no cunning. Neil, whom all card-games bored to the point of illness, had had a bridge-playing headmaster at his first school: now as then, he played with dull, dogged mediocrity.

It was, as Miss Searle put it, just a friendly game; she was opposed to stakes, not only on moral grounds but because they tended to rouse unpleasant feeling. Tonight, since no one but Miss Fisher, who was keeping the score, had a very clear idea who was winning, there was a refreshing absence of post-mortems. For Miss Searle, it was enough to see everything going agreeably, and to know that her own attitude was sufficiently defined.

Neil, for his part, would have been glad to give the game his whole mind; but the habit of using half was ingrained, and he could not displace it. He looked round at Ellen, who was frowning at her cards as if she were trying to bring them in focus. Her retreat of this evening had come as a climax to the day's disturbance and strain. It had been while they were having tea that, on the point of remarking that after it they could get away by themselves, he had begun to perceive she was expecting this moment with a mounting panic, which she was trying desperately to disguise. Whatever had caused her to commit herself – quixotry, affection, or some struggle for self-mastery and decision – she was in the grip of a reaction which was almost numbing her wits, and a frantic determination to ignore it. She was going to be made love to if it killed her, and to swear it was rapture with her last breath. He had protracted the tea as long as possible, to give her time and to decide himself what to do; but things had only grown worse. In the end all he could think of was to take her to a cinema, where he had held her hand, and she had clung to his with all the passion of a frightened child begging not to be punished. After that there was not time to walk home, and they had caught the bus.

Tonight, he had thought, she would have settled down, they would go out, and he would manage somehow to reassure her. He blamed himself for a good deal of it. It had been too easy to revenge upon her shyness his physical frustration and his doubt; this afternoon had not been the only time. But had he really deserved this? It was so hurtful that he still could not quite decide that she had meant it. She had very little social sense when she was nervous, and might have been at a loss for a quick excuse; but she must surely have realised that, if she had given him the chance, he would have got her out of it.

'Your bid, partner,' said Miss Searle, with light friendly

reproach. He apologised, and switched over to the bridge department, which had been functioning, up to a point, quite independently. They made the trick.

If things got no better, what was he to do? It had been clumsy and unimaginative, he supposed, to have begun talking so soon about marriage. She had seemed, that other morning, so vulnerable and alone, so clearly unsure of where they stood, and wondering, as he could see, whether he wanted the events of the previous night laughed off or forgotten: it was then that he had known for certain that he did not. Should he offer now to let her think again? Unconscious in her essential modesty of her power, she would jump at once to the conclusion that he was having doubts himself, and, whatever she felt, withdraw. They would never get back from there ... 'Double.'

It seemed to him that they were like an incompetent climbing party which, having advanced without a proper study of the route, finds itself at a point where advance and retreat spell equal disaster, and where the exposure is beginning to tell. For her, he thought, all this could scarcely be worth while. For himself, it seemed safer tonight not to put the question. If a woman had subjected him out of coquetry to this nerve-tearing sequence of advances and checks, his experience would have seen through her and his pride dragged him clear. If she had done it out of stupidity, he would already have begun to despise her. But this continual sense of a need as great as his own reaching towards him and beaten back by forces he only half understood, the morbid inescapable jealousy against which there was no weapon and which he was ashamed to own, got under his practised self-protection, and roused a sensual reaction against which, sometimes, he could throw up no defence at all. He had been too soft with her, he thought. He ought to have learned by this time that it didn't pay.

The card-table was the folding kind, very small. He could feel as if he were touching it, her bare elbow resting on the baize a few inches from his hand. Just then he would willingly have hated her: but she was short of a hair-grip still, the loose lock was slipping back again over her eyes with the half-curl like a question-mark at the end. She was staring at her cards with her lower lip caught in, and seeing none of them. She looked in the state of which one says that the person is a thousand miles away; but she was not, and he knew it; she was only a thousand miles from the game. Against all that happened today, against even his own will to perceive it, he felt the distracting certainty of being, at this moment, her meditation and her desire.

'Five hearts,' said Ellen. She put the hair back from her face, a slow, gentle movement; as surely as if she had turned and told him, he knew that she was remembering the times when he had done it for her. He looked at his cards; he had the ace and knave of hearts himself. Her bidding was growing progressively wilder. In her movement, in her stillness, in her voice, he could feel her aware of him, and aware now, too, that their auras of perception had joined. From her place of hiding she had reached out to him. They had exchanged no outward sign at all; but he found himself waiting, with a painfully hurrying heart and a watchful stillness: the room was a forest, leaves stirred in the night wind, light feet flinched on the edge of the clearing; he drew into the shadow beside the pool.

'Having no diamonds?' said Miss Fisher in an undertone, not unkindly.

Ellen looked down at the trump she had just played, then at her hand; she stammered something abject, and knocked a couple of cards on to the floor; they landed beside his chair. Both of them stooped together, and their heads brushed softly in passing. It might have happened to anyone, except that neither apologised; but he was quite sure now.

He woke up in time to agree with Miss Searle that everyone revoked once in a lifetime, and that in any case it was only a friendly game.

He was dummy, succeeding Miss Fisher; he offered her a cigarette and lit it for her. Miss Searle did not smoke.

'Cigarette, Ellen?'

It was the only sign he could find to make her, a faint awkwardness of surface manners, to have given the other light before hers so that their ephemeral contact should not be broken. He knew that it was understood. Nothing could happen now that would not say, in one language or another, the same thing. There was only one ash-tray on the table. He gave it to Miss Fisher, and, crossing to the mantelpiece, got another and put it down beside Ellen's hand. He dared not touch her, partly because it would have been obvious to everyone; but it made no difference now.

They shared the ash-tray. He smoked at a pace he could not control; the cigarette was gone in three or four minutes. Ellen was a little longer. When she put out her stub, she held it, absently it seemed, for a moment, then moved it across the tray and laid it touching his.

He could not see her face; she had let her hair slip down again, and turned away.

Neil got up, went over to the window, made some excuse to the company about the room getting warm, opened the casement a little and looked out. There was no sign-language this time for what he wanted to ask her: whether she knew what she was doing, and how much more of this she thought he could stand? When the game was over, and its protection gone, she would run out on him again. There was a knot in the curtain-cord, a granny-knot, but old and hard to undo. He found himself with smarting fingers, and two ends of broken cord in his hands. He knotted them together, and came back.

As he sat down, she stroked back her hair again. There was something subtly different in it now, welcoming and tender, a promise instead of a reminiscence. For a moment, frightened of the current in which he was being carried, he rallied his bitterness and mistrust: he had invented everything, he told himself, and would go on thinking so whether it was true or not. But it was too late. The invisible cord was not to be broken.

Suddenly – he had no idea after how long – the cards were being stacked, the points counted, conversation was being made about how quickly an evening went. It was, apparently, nearly eleven; he and Miss Searle had run away with the score. He thanked her, and told her they seemed to be a natural partnership, or something of the kind; she appeared pleased so it must, he hoped, have made sense. All the women began to move vaguely about the room, collecting books and bags and odds-and-ends. Ellen came back to the table, picked up the bridge-marker, and flipped its celluloid leaves slowly to and fro. Mechanically, he picked up the score-pad and the cards. What did she want of him? If he kept her back from the bedtime procession, everyone would know why; if he asked her to come out, at this hour, it would be a public declaration. Either way, their silent conversation would be broken with a shout. She might refuse, or she might come, and it might well be intolerable either way. In a visitation of profound certainty, he decided to do nothing at all.

He carried the cards and pad to the fancy cabinet in which they lived, and opened the drawer. On the far side of the room, the other two women were discussing bridge-fiends, their malice and rancour, the pleasant change provided by a friendly game. Something moved beside him; Ellen put down the bridge-marker by the cards in the drawer, as he put in the score-pad. Her hand slid along to his; he covered and held it. The voices talked on, and the world was still.

'I'll come back.' She spoke in a breath of voice so slight that he had to watch the movement of her lips. He tightened his hand on hers and let her go.

The voices of the women, sleepy and perfunctory, chatted on the stairs. He could hear, at intervals, Ellen's almost monosyllabic counterpoint; then a little sentence, a run up and down on two or three notes, too far to catch words. The room was smoky and stale; he flung the curtains back, and the window wide. The hot clouds that had hung about all day were thinning; the moon came through with a vague shadowless brightness. He crossed to the doorway and turned off the light.

Upstairs a door shut, then another. He stood where he could be seen at once, against the window, so that she should not be bewildered, or afraid of being taken by surprise. A stair creaked softly. When she came in, he did not move to meet her. She stood for a moment with her hand on the door, then pushed it to. He did not hear the latch; she was still leaving, he thought, a path of escape.

Her face, as she crossed the room to him, looked dimly luminous, like the low sky outside. When she was close, she wavered for a moment, and still he did not move. There was nothing to tell her that she did not know. It was not till he felt his lips touched by the falling strand of hair that he drew her in, and lifted it back from her eyes.

Finding that she was not very sleepy tonight, Miss Searle decided to read in bed for half an hour. This, she had found, seldom failed to settle one, unless one had some definite worry, which tonight was certainly not the case; it was only that her brain had been a little over-stimulated by the game. The evening could hardly, in fact, have gone better, proving with what small effort a disinterested person could dissipate misunderstanding, smooth out awkwardness and suspicion, and put people at their ease. She wondered how Miss Fisher was feeling now. In fairness one must admit that she had borne with patience and good nature her partner's unsystematic play. No doubt she had been feeling a little ashamed of herself, which after all was only right. She must realise now that, if she had been correct in her surmises, the people concerned would scarcely have sacrificed the evening so cheerfully to a game of cards. Had some little gesture of this kind not been extended, they might well have been flung upon their own resources — and thus, inevitably, on one another's — out of sheer embarrassment. Now everything was comfortable again; the whole unfortunate episode could be forgotten by everyone concerned, and the pleasant *status quo* restored.

Cheered by these thoughts, she began to set her room in order for the night, a thing she always liked to do before undressing. What should she read? She was almost decided on *Mansfield Park*; but to make a final choice she must have her glasses. The case was in her bag; but it was empty. She remembered, now, that she had taken them off immediately the game was over, and must have left them somewhere downstairs. This showed the advantage of an orderly method; had she discovered this later, it would have meant going down in her dressing-gown. As it was, she had got no further than changing her shoes for her more comfortable moccasins.

There was a two-way switch on the stairs; but Miss Searle, a conscientious fuel-saver, did not use it; the light from the landing penetrated dimly, but sufficiently, to the bottom. The hall itself was dark, but the door of the Lounge was close at hand. It was ajar, and opened soundlessly. The switch, she remembered, was inconveniently placed behind it. She took one suede-soled step into the room; but not a second.

Outlined against pale light in a frame of blackness, a man and a woman were standing in perfect silhouette. They were in the posture of Solomon's song: his left hand was under her head and his right embraced her. Her throat was thrown back, relaxed to his support; her hair spilled through his fingers. His stooping face was a little above hers, so that he seemed to lift it like a cup, and to look down into it without drinking. Their stillness, at this moment, was absolute, so that it gave the sense of arrested time; it seemed to Miss Searle that she must have remained transfixed at the door for minutes, during which they did not move. Then she heard the man say, very quietly, 'Oh, God.' It had to her ears the sound of solitude, of deep grief and darkness. The strangeness of this voice confused and frightened her; she could not collect herself to escape.

The woman's hand slipped away from about his neck: it touched, softly, his cheek and temple, curved upward over his head, and drew it down. What followed was like the meeting of quicksilver: a pausing contact of separate shapes, a flash into identity too swiftly complete to be recorded by the eye. Now the fused shadow was almost as motionless as before; only the woman's arm stirred uncertainly, till in a movement of sudden strength it caught his waist, and clung. A different stillness now, and a different silence.

Miss Searle never knew how she got out of the room. If she had seen the back-tilted throat gripped in the act of murder (which would have offered the release of action and screams) she could have felt no more than she felt now. Often, in parks and fields, she had come upon couples in much more of outward abandonment, tumbled on the grass, and had only turned away in the distaste she might have felt for the antics of dogs, with the same absence of personal impact. But with this terrible entity, this unknown, piercingly hostile and excluding force, she had talked, sat at table, smiled. She felt nothing clearly: only (as one feels a bodily pain too blinding to admit of thought) a searing humiliation, a consciousness of being cheated, derided and alone. She knew only one thing, that she must make no noise; she backed velvet-footed through the door; seeing in imagination, as a spy eluding capture sees torment and death, the clasped shadow parting and lancing her with eyes. She dared not move the door again. Through it, as she went, she heard a light broken murmur, a wordless catch of the breath; and an answer, lower and firmer, comforting it to silence.

Upstairs, she moved about her room in the track of habit, in the sugar-pink light from the art-silk shade, undressing, folding her clothes. As she hung her cardigan she saw one of the pockets distorted by an angular bulge, the outline of her spectacles. She put them in the case, and the case on the bedside table.

When she was ready, she said her prayers. She prayed for a long time: for all such as had erred and were deceived, against the perils and dangers of this night, for the means of grace and for the hope of glory. But she could only see the hard pink sheen of the counterpane between her fingers, receiving indifferently the spreading circles of her tears.

15

Slip by the Leader

The clouds lay supine in the heavy sky, gravid with thunder and waiting listlessly for labour to begin. Meanwhile, the inertia of the air deepened till it seemed too dense to be shifted by anything; one felt that even the gestating storm must be smothered, and was contained in it already dead. In the sheltered horseshoe by the sea, walking and breathing were burdens. Neil and Ellen had struggled up through the stagnant lanes, in search not so much of privacy as of air. They had meant to go on the moors; but in the unmoving cloud-gaps the earth and sky pushed the sluggish heat back and forth between them, like plates of brass. From the cliff-top, the woods below had offered shade, and the tenuous hope of a breeze.

They were resting now on a grassy ledge below the brow.

Beyond the flat, oily sea, the Welsh coastline had the colour and weight of lead. When a twig or a leaf fell, it seemed to drop with exhaustion, and all the rest hung lax, ready to follow.

Ellen lay on the grass, watching the tree-tips which, stirring in air-eddies imperceptible to the flesh, gave some relief if only to the eyes. Her hair was spread indifferently in the thin grass and parched moss; the pale yellow of her dress was darkened with damp at the armpits and in a line round her waist where the belt, which she had loosened now, had held it to her body. She had lifted her arms to feel the dim coolness of evaporation; her hands were folded behind her head.

Neil had taken off his shirt altogether, and hung it on a spur of rock. He had worn off the sense of superiority which this advantage gives to the human male, and, propped against a mossy boulder, had started a pipe which he was too thirsty to enjoy. The boulder, soft at first touch, grew spiny within minutes to the bare back; he shifted, irritably, for the third time. There was room on the grass-patch for two; but he had already decided against it.

Vexed by some roughness in the ground on which she lay, Ellen gave a languid wriggle, and subsided again. The movement caught the tail of his eye, and drew it against his better sense. The childish down at the edge of her hair lay in dark feathers on her forehead; the clear skin between them had a fine beading like dew on ivory. Her eyelids were glossy, with dark fragile veins. The smooth-surfaced cotton of her dress, crisp this morning when she had put it on, was limp now, and if she wore anything under it at all it stopped at the waist. Her up-drawn breasts were outlined as frankly as if she had been naked: he saw that she was half asleep.

It was with some trouble that he refrained from telling her, shortly, not to be so damned inconsiderate. Knowing that if he yielded to this impulse she would not, in any foreseeable future, relax naturally in his presence again, he suppressed it, leaving his inward resentment unrelieved. He turned to contemplation of the smoke which rose from his pipe in a blue vertical line. He was aware that he was a little on edge today, which was a pity, because presently he would have to talk to her, and it was essential to set about this with unemotional detachment.

They had not talked at all last night, in any explanatory sense. It had all been too evanescent, fortuitous and easy to destroy. He had tried only to deepen and confirm it, and to avoid anything which in her next phase of reaction could bear witness against him. The innocence of her instincts had been profoundly moving; her tenderness had had undercurrents of the spirit by which she herself had seemed bewildered, disturbing him at levels which, as he realised when there was time to think, he had never till now put within a woman's reach. He had felt in it a maturity of sorrow, finding expression, blindly, through her body, as if it had never resolved itself in her mind.

There could have been – he had felt it at the time, and he thought so still – one natural and simple solution to it all. It seemed even that her own intuition, wiser than she knew, had sent her to him in search of it. To refuse it had not only been one of the most difficult things he had ever done; it had seemed, even to reason, a profitless folly. But unmaking a planned decision did not come easily to him; it never had, and, recently, the axiom that an act of will, once made, must be accepted like an external fact, had been the basis of mere survival. His returning trust in himself still climbed, so to speak, on balance-holds alone; he shrank from disturbing its equilibrium, without acknowledging his fear. In any case, whatever her own principles were in the matter (he had never asked her, since there was to be no need), she would remember he had gone back on his word. So also would he. At this point, his inner discussion had ended; but virtue had not been, altogether, its own reward.

After they had parted, and he had climbed to his eyrie in the tower, he had employed three wakeful hours in writing a poem, of the kind which one tears up next morning at sight. Having finished it, he became suddenly very tired. Some time later, he was making his way up the Col Tournanche, with a feeling that it was ill-advised to be there. The snow had that over-ripe perfection which conceals a threat; and as he noted this he heard the roar and grumbling echo of an avalanche in some hidden distance. It was better, now, to press on than to retreat; but the going was slow, a steep ice-slope masked by a fresh fall. Someone was working the slope ahead of him. It was Ellen; he caught her up. In her hands was the broken haft of an ice-axe, lacking a head; and wielding this useless rod she was trying, with stubborn futile incompetence, to cut steps. 'What's the good of that?' he called. 'Here, take mine and I'll show you how.' And he held his own axe out to her. She moved to take it, then drew back, clinging to the broken handle. 'No; I couldn't manage with that. I don't want it. This one was given me and I use it always.' Instead of his feeling the exasperation proper to real life, in the dream it was as if she had struck him in the face. He said, 'For God's sake get out of the way, then, and let me do it'; and, roping her up to him, moved past her up the slope. At the same moment the sky thickened, the wind rose, and a blizzard of snow began. He tried to work into the rhythm necessary to good step-cutting, a technique he always enjoyed; but his goggles kept snowing up, making him stop to clear them. Now he was struggling with the old dereliction and despair, the knowledge that the mountain refused him. It had grown bitterly cold, and the wind was howling. Out of the noise of it, a voice shouted, 'Say! Look behind you!' and laughed loudly. He turned; the untied rope lay trailing on the snow, she was nowhere in sight. The rest was a confusion of searching, anger and shame, the snow blinding him and his skill growing unsure, and at each failure the wind shrieking with laughter on the col. He woke to find himself, stripped for last night's heat, lying naked in the transient chill before the dawn. Between the fading of the dream and full waking, he was visited by a nightmare that sometimes came to him in this phase, that today the world would end and that he had not prepared himself and would be smothered in the universal fear.

It grew light soon after, and he could not sleep again. This was partly due to hunger; he had been awake more than half the night. His brain, made restless by his stomach's emptiness, ran back and forth, recapitulating, deducing unknown quantities, adding them up to this total or that. The upshot was that things could not drift indefinitely, subject to emotional climate and to chance. What he had been passing off to himself as tact was, more simply, funking a difficult crux on which the whole route depended. The proposition once stated in these terms, nothing remained but to do something about it.

On the way up to the cliff-top they had scarcely spoken, except to grumble at the heat and encourage one another to push on. He had been as little in the mood for sentimental exchanges as she, and would have felt them irritatingly mistimed if they had been offered; yet, irrationally, while recognising his own mood he had been suspicious of hers, and had let it link itself with all her other withdrawals in his mind. Now, sheltered from the sun's blaze and rested, he had swung back to a recollection of last night which was too vivid altogether; continuing in his reserve for altered reasons, he wanted the first sign to come from her, then began to demand it with the inner insistence of a suppressed cause. No sign had come. She had given herself up to the day's lethargy with a facile completeness which, to his present mood, spoke of evasion as clearly as print.

The yellow dress was cut fairly high at the throat, and she

had not opened it. Her raised arms had pulled up two wrinkles, converging at a point; it seemed to him that they followed the outline of the gold chain below, and met at the ring of the medal, itself too flat and close to show. As clearly as if nothing had intervened, he could see the disc lying between her breasts, the warmth and weight of the gold an accustomed pressure; he could see the enamelled wings. She seemed to lie abandoned to it, like Leda to the swan.

It would be better, he thought at this point, to have a conversation about something; but he felt angrily that to open some neutral topic would be a signal of defeat. Putting it off, he continued to look at her. Her breathing was quick and deep, labouring with the devitalised air; it rippled the muscles down the whole length of her body. Her lips were parted; she moistened them, just then, with a sliding point of tongue.

Suddenly, without a warning sign, her dropped lids lifted and her eyes met his. She gave a quick jerky twist, sat up, clasped her knees in her arms, and settled with her back to him, looking at the sea.

Unspoken dialogues of this kind did not make sense to Neil at any time, his view being that a little less false delicacy in the world would leave people more time to practise the essential kinds. His bad angel, assuming an honest straightforward air, put this precept speciously before him.

'Sorry,' he said. 'Did I give you one of those looks as if I were undressing you?'

She turned half-round, then away; he could see her struggling, helplessly, for the right answer.

'I was, of course,' he added. 'But the results were very nice.'

This turned out to be once too often. Ellen straightened, and faced him squarely. 'Sometimes,' she said, 'you just make me think of a schoolboy trying to see how far he can go.'

After the first shock, it quite pleased him to find her standing up for herself. If she had spoken with a little gentleness, or even a little humour, this effect would have lasted; as it was, his distrust returned at once to spoil it. He said with irony, 'And it was too far, m – m?'

'Yes,' said Ellen firmly. 'I think I have all I need for the moment, thank you.'

The effort required for this had left her taut and quivering all over; but she had turned back again, and in any case he was in no mood to notice it.

'I keep trying to remember,' he remarked, 'which department of that factory you said you worked in. Welfare, perhaps?'

'You don't know much about factories,' said Ellen over her shoulder. 'The girls in my shop reported a man once for a lot less than that. He was transferred to the packing-room, too.' She kicked a pebble over the edge and added, 'Everyone was very pleased.'

Neil listened to the pebble, making its way down the cliff-faces in accelerating bounds. Supplied with a new and highly legitimate grievance, he said, 'You know a stone like that becomes lethal after about a hundred feet, don't you? I thought you were supposed to have been taught to climb?'

It slipped out unprepared, leaving him afterwards with an unpleasant constriction in the chest, and a determination to face it out. There was, however, no need.

'I'm sorry,' she said at once. 'What an awful thing to do. I can't imagine what possessed me.'

'I don't suppose anyone's down there,' he said with grudging reassurance, 'but you can never be sure.' Her penitence made him, for obscure reasons, angrier than a retort. Perhaps it was only her still-averted face which gave the illusion that the apology had been offered not to him, but elsewhere. Neither of them had, at present, any more to say; and there was silence for several minutes.

Ellen's back relaxed; she turned round to him, propped on one arm. 'There's going to be a storm tonight. The air's too thick to breathe. Please don't let's be cross with each other.'

He moved over to her, pulled her backward into his arms, and kissed her. Between one reason and another, he was not as gentle as he had meant to be. She did not quite resist him, but her response stopped quickly and he could feel her tense, wary, and ready to slip away at the first chance he gave her. He let her go. She made an unhappy little movement towards him, hesitated and stopped.

'Let's have lunch,' she said.

It was too hot to be hungry, but he saw sense in her suggestion. It is difficult to feel intensely while dividing up food and rearranging it under a system of barter. As usual she slipped him a sandwich too many in exchange for the cake; but the routine argument fell flat, for neither could finish a full half-share.

'They say,' said Ellen, looking at the remaining slices whose edges had already begun to curl, 'that if we had to eat an eighteenth-century breakfast for dinner, our stomachs would burst and we'd drop dead.'

'All the same,' said Neil, who had been chiefly defeated by the liquescent margarine, 'I wouldn't mind working through one gradually, say over a week.'

After a pause Ellen said shyly, 'You might not think it to look at me, but I don't cook too badly – I mean, with what one can get.'

For a moment his mood lifted, and their eyes met in a smile. But all this came a little late; ready to detect flight in anything, he saw her preparing another bolt-hole, the labyrinthine warren of domesticity. Even when they talked about plans, this image had never presented itself to him; it carried too many associations with the past, from which he still shied away. Like most people who married nowadays, they would have nowhere in particular to live; with all its discomforts, this vagrant and irresponsible prospect had had an unconfessed charm for him. Sometime, inevitably, they would gather a home about them as a stone gathers moss. Meanwhile, the picture at the back of his mind had been of camping here and there, making a secret world in strange rooms and love in strange beds, subduing casual environment as illicit lovers do. He had not thought the thing out so clearly as to know that the picture had grown on him with her elusiveness, that he wanted her in a kind of vacuum, in order without interference to explore and possess her.

Aloud, he asked her how good she was at cooking on a gas-ring.

'Quite good. I hate these house-proud types.'

She might have read his thoughts in order to meet them half-way. It was like all her other promises, he thought, notes of hand upon securities that failed when she called them in. Desire stamped its impatience on his mind; things could not go on for ever like this, and had already gone on longer than enough. Echoing what seemed, just then, the complaint of the whole visible world, he decided that the air must be cleared. A little later, when the strain still palpable between them had settled down, but certainly today.

They had drifted, all this while, into another long silence. Ellen had got out a comb and smoothed her hair; she had managed to buy, on the way up, an imitation tortoiseshell slide, heavier than the grips she was used to wearing, which kept worrying her and needing adjustment. She put the comb away, and fidgeted with something in the collar of her dress. At the movement his anger concentrated, without warning, as if under a burning-glass, to a single point. He never saw the small prickly leaf she tracked down and threw away.

'You know,' she said, turning round, 'I think the more one gives in to this weather, the worse it gets. We'd probably feel much better if we ignored it and did something. What about that face you were talking about yesterday, the big one? It will be in the shade, by now. Let's go and climb.'

Neil said slowly, 'It's as near vertical as makes no matter.' This unattached statement committed him to nothing. The quiet world stood poised on its knife-edge, not yet moving.

'I don't blame you.' She spoke quite humbly and without reproach. 'But, truly, Neil, that was the only time I lost my nerve on rock; and it couldn't happen when you were there.'

'Good Lord,' he said quickly, 'I didn't mean that.' And with this phrase of simple instinctive decency, the poised bowl heaved, irrevocably. She was waiting now to know what he did mean. *Ruat coelum.*

'I only meant that I can't take you up rock at that angle with loose jewellery dangling about. It only needs to catch on something when you're shifting balance. Sorry, but it's up to you.'

'Jewellery?' She looked at him in perfectly blank bewilderment. 'But you know I don't wear it. You can see I've got none on.'

'I can't remember ever having seen you without it. I thought it was a fixture, perhaps. If I'm wrong, never mind.'

Her face altered; he saw the movement, quickly checked, of her hand up to her throat. She was watching him, but he could not read what was in her eyes, defiance or fear. She said, almost stupidly, 'You don't mean my medal, do you?'

He made no answer, wondering if he looked to her as he felt, and ceasing to care.

She said at last, 'I always climbed in it. It never caught on anything. It's too short.'

'Playing about's one thing, and climbing's another. Do the thing properly, or let it alone.'

The conflict in her face had stopped. It was impenetrable, and as hard as his own.

'I may not be much good myself. I don't say I am. But I was taught properly, if that's what you mean.'

'I'll take your word for it,' he said.

'You can do as you like.'

Again he did not answer, but for a different cause. He was watching the change which was transforming her into someone he did not know, a quiet fanatic, with a fanatic's uncommunicating eyes.

'You said something like this a few minutes ago.' Her voice seemed curiously dissociated from her still face. 'I didn't say anything, I couldn't believe you meant it.'

'It would probably have been better unsaid.'

'It would have been much better unthought.'

'Perhaps.'

Things moved quickly, as they do between peoples whom propaganda has wrought up into a state of furious self-defence. At the sound of the first shot, mobilisation was complete.

'If this was what you wanted,' she said, 'you should have told me before. Perhaps I ought to have known. But I thought—'

'Yes?'

'I thought truth meant something to you, and that you wouldn't want anything that came from selling it out.'

'Truth's a large loose word. If you mean fidelity, why not say so?'

'Very well. Then that's what I mean.'

'So long as we know.' In a moment's clarity, he compared the reality on which they had embarked with the delicate lines of his blue-print, the brutalities of the field with the staff college map. Noble abstractions usher in the war; human animals, wounded, threatened, insulted and bereaved, tread the bright banners in the indistinguishable rubble underfoot, careless with pain. 'You're telling me that short of a sell-out, there's nothing left, is that it? I should call that being honest rather late in the day.'

'That isn't true.' But she spoke in anger, so that she seemed to offer nothing, simply to throw off an accusation. She paused for a moment, looking at him, not in the hesitation of remorse but of one who chooses a weapon. 'I've tried to be straight with you. It's you who make it impossible. I could have been — very fond of you. You must have seen that, but it wasn't enough.' Her face, so often blurred with uncertainties, had a terrifying, abstract purity of line: the skin looked clear and bright, her eyes shone at a point beyond him. 'You want what shouldn't be given, as — as a sort of scalp. You have to have everything, and be everything. Not because you love me; to stand right with yourself.'

The abuse of an angry child, he thought; feeling the slight external pain, the deep uncomprehended injury, that signals a mortal thrust. He felt himself to be very cool and indifferent, even casual, at the moment of abandoning himself to revenge.

'I don't want the past,' he said. 'I don't even want to hear about it. All I need to know is where you're living now. You talk about truth. Lying's like charity, it begins at home. You've decided you're being fair to everyone, I gather, if you step into a living man's bed with a dead man round your neck.'

She drew herself back slowly on to her heels, then to her feet. Her clenched hand was pressed against her heart; seeing her knuckles whiten, he seemed to see the thing they covered stamping its circle on her flesh.

'I can understand now,' she said clearly, 'why your wife ran away.'

There was silence. The words hung in the air with a curious unreality, as when a child brings out some obscenity it has picked up parrot-wise, and tries over for the sake of the sound.

'You've saved this up for a long time, haven't you?' she said, as if groping her way back to language she understood. 'Now I'll tell you the truth, if you want it so much. I'd unlive my whole life, if it would bring Jock back again. Every moment of it, and forget it as if it had never been. And now you know.'

'Yes,' he said. 'That seems to cover everything, doesn't it?' This was his line, in the script as it stood; he waited, unconsciously, for some director to recognise the impossibility of the whole sequence, to shout 'Cut!' and bring them back to the beginning, with the lighting changed, new dialogue, and a not incredible plot.

She was still too, except that gropingly she put out her hand and closed it round the trunk of an ash-tree beside her. It was the tree on which it was necessary to hang one's weight as one swung from the ledge to the rocky path. For a moment he saw reflected in her eyes his own helpless incredulity, as if the tree had been a prompter, signalling her exit from the scene which, unbelievably, had been shot and left to stand. In this instant strangely at one, they expressed the same instinctive appeal, the same dawning realisation of the irretrievable, the same desolate protest. When she spoke aloud, it was in a dead, formal little voice; it sounded like a comment on an incident many years closed.

'I want to apologise. You've been very considerate, and I've treated you very badly. One doesn't know oneself how one will feel. We just have to remember it would have been worse than this, if we hadn't found out in time.'

His silence had, like her words, the quality of retrospection.

'I said a horrible thing to you just now,' she began again. 'I didn't mean it and it wasn't true. It's you who deserve someone better. I'm a drifter, you see, I realise things when it's too late. It's not much use to say I'm sorry now. Is it?' The flatness of her voice changed, on the last words, to a sharp insistence, flung at his silence as her endurance of it snapped suddenly and unforeseen.

'Never mind,' he said. 'I dare say I asked for most of it.'

'No. I—' To their half-stunned minds all this futility became for the first time audible, like the loose slamming of a door on an empty room.

Her arm bent, putting her weight on the tree, and she began to turn. At the last moment, her set face broke; her other hand groped at her neck; and he saw in the movement what he had been too fixed in unhappiness to see when she had made it once before: frustrated seeking, an unaccustomed insecurity, loss. Seeing the realisation in his face, she cried with a helpless bitterness directed nowhere, 'I knew this morning ... I knew something terrible would happen when I took it off.'

He started to his feet; an involuntary physical exclamation, without aim. She shrank back. 'No. It's no use. You know it's too late for anything. Oh, please. We *must* get away from each other now.'

As she swung upward to the path, her blindly placed foot slipped; it seemed for a moment that she would fall, and, without thought, he ran forward and put out his arm to catch her. But her grip on the tree saved her balance; she found her feet, then the path above, and went into the thick trees out of sight.

16

Straight Pull Out

The cloud-gaps had closed together, making the sky a solid grey blanket over the parched and breathless land. Giving it a moment of half-dulled attention, Neil thought the leaden light must mean that the storm was about to break, though he could neither hear nor feel the signs. He looked at his watch; it was the day itself that was failing. The cliff-shadows, reinforced by trees, caught the long autumn twilight first of all. The time he had spent here, putting off the first movement that would have its counterpart of quickening in the mind, had seemed infinite, yet he had supposed it shorter by the clock. Now the hours of inertia behind him gave him a sickened sense of defilement, like a drug or a debauch. The lunch-wrappings still lay on the ledge beside him, pointing the squalor; he screwed them up, to bury them under a stone.

Some different texture in the handful of rubbish gave him pause; he had gathered up with it the yellow cotton belt from Ellen's dress. He remembered her saying, as she threw it off impatiently, that one could fancy it weighed pounds. It seemed no heavier than the paper with which it was entangled. Separated from her, the stuff and the white buckle looked thin and cheap; the plainness of her things, and their fresh harmless colours, had deceived him for some time into thinking them good. He turned the strip over in his hand; it was, probably, essential. When he got back he must leave it somewhere, where it could be found. He stuffed it into his pocket, and put on his shirt.

The dusk, so far, was premonitory only; beyond the trees the sea still reflected, flatly, the heavy day. He threaded the cliffs by one of the wandering paths, working gradually downward; he did not mean to return till very late. Tomorrow he supposed he would leave; but from the thought of packing and looking up trains his stretched mind bolted with the furious revulsion of weariness; tomorrow could look after itself. He walked on, carrying emptiness like an intolerable burden which there was no place to lay down.

An enormous shadow stopped him, like an out-thrust hand. He looked up. Just ahead, above and below him, split in the cliff at right-angles to the sea, was its one considerable face. The near side of the cleft, on which he stood, had crumbled and broken and was overgrown like all the rest; on the far side, a hundred and fifty feet were sheer. This was the cliff of which Ellen had spoken. Seizing, then, on a pretext which had been as good as any other, he had conveniently forgotten that in no case would he have taken her there. Even if he had had a rope, it would have been criminally unjustifiable; her form was not within miles of such a climb. It would have been a thing to try with Sammy, on the right day. With vivid clearness he could see Sammy standing beside him in a characteristic pose, his weight on one hip, his head tilted back and askew, rubbing the back of his neck and saying with pleased anticipation, as he studied the face, 'Looks a bit 'aughty from here, doesn't it?'

Everywhere dark with shadow, the grey rock was streaked more deeply by oozings of water from within. Its almost vertical pitches were broken here and there by ledges, all sloping, and with evil loose surfaces. Quietly and insistently, its question sucked at his emptiness; like a lover whose word is to be trusted, it promised that the vacuum should be abundantly filled. He had no sense at all of making a decision; there was simply this, and nothing else in particular, anywhere, to do.

He climbed down the wet boulders of the gully stream, and studied it again from the foot. He had on the rubber-soled shoes he used for dry rock-climbing, worn today for lightness in the heat. Useless on a wet surface, they would restrict considerably his choice of route; but if he went back for his boots, he might meet someone, and in any case the light would be gone. Accustomed to think clearly on such matters, he confronted for a moment the facts that he had never before knowingly begun a climb with unfit equipment, and that this climb was not one for a casual approach. All this was true but irrelevant, like a time-table for some place where one does not mean to go.

Having scraped his soles on dry earth (his passage down the stream had already made them slippery) he began to climb.

The first pitch was moderately difficult; the holds, following the strata like the ledges, sloped downward, but not at an impossible angle, and rubbers gripped them well. Though the whole of his mind seemed engaged with their problems, there was still a part remaining which tested, as it always had since his boyhood, the relationship between himself and the rock. Once always met and satisfied, more recently frustrated and hungry, in the last week unconsciously content, this instinct encountered for the first time a complete nullity. The holds were there, one leading to another; the rock was of such a type, and such a formation. He climbed like a textbook, the conventional phrases for each step forming themselves in his head.

The first ledge offered a better stance than he had expected; the scree was superficial and easily cleared. With dry accuracy he marked a projection where, if a second man had been following, he could have belayed the rope. From here there was, or should have been, a choice of ways; but the narrow chimney which first drew his eye was slimy with water. He would have to work up by small holds to the third ledge, traverse along it, and get to a crack at the other end which looked clean and dry.

It was when he was half-way up the next pitch that he heard, for the first time, the roll of thunder over the sea.

In the first moment of hearing it, it said very little to him. He was not on a mountain, and carried no steel. Soon, however, he became aware of a nagging, then of an alarm-bell in his conscious thought. When the storm broke, there would be rain.

To a man climbing in boots it would have meant awkwardness, a drag on speed, discomfort to be shrugged off and put up with. To a man climbing in rubbers, it meant that within minutes his feet would encounter, not points of grip and friction, but a greased slide. Socks might have served, if he had been wearing any; but it had been too hot.

The thunder sounded again, nearer. For the first time that day, he felt an eddy of air cross his face, and in the eddy a faint touch of chill.

He was already past the half-way point. With a reasonable hope that his route would go, a total certainty that retreat would be slow and (to say the least) highly delicate, there was nothing but to go on.

The second ledge sloped steeply and was covered with friable stuff. His instincts recoiled from it at sight; with a sound hand-hold, it was good enough to brace one foot on for a rest. There was no time to rest long. Working out to a small buttress he edged up to the third ledge. This, somehow, he would have to use.

The buttress ended as an extension of the ledge itself; but as soon as he got his head over, he saw he must work round to another point. From the buttress-top to the face, there was nothing but a long steep tongue of scree; not, like that of the first ledge, a thin coating over rock, but thick, indefinite, based loosely on dry earth. There was no sign of a handhold, and he had no time to waste on digging about for one. Leaving the buttress, he made his way with some trouble to the tapered end of the ledge. The other end would have been better, but that way there were no holds.

A complete view of the ledge confirmed his worst surmises. The surface, combined with the angle, made it clearly impossible unless the handholds were sound. They had better be; he saw at once that there was no hope of a higher traverse to the crack, or any alternative way to the top.

The thunder was a good deal closer now. The first distant flicker of lightning made him realise, by contrast, how little daylight was left. A long, quiet sigh sounded across the trees.

He called 'Anyone below there?' and heard an echo slap back the last word at him, but nothing more; he tested the ledge, at once dislodging stones. The sound of the first brought back a memory, from which he pulled his mind away. The sense of urgency pressed on him, with alternate waves of disturbance and release. He was aware of being on a bad, careless, unjustifiable climb, of which all the roots of his training were ashamed; but the new unconsidered passenger within him, its vacuum filled, felt the negative pleasure which is the cessation of pain.

The handholds were there. He shifted on to the first by degrees, trying to argue with the distrust which flowed into him through his fingers. There had been no doubt, till now, of the soundness of the rock. Here it was sharper, more recently broken; it felt solid, but linked itself unpleasantly in mind with the chute of rubble on the slide. He distributed his weight with catlike circumspection, the main to the hands, the lesser to the feet.

A mounting rumour rustled in the trees. Just after the next thunder-roll a new air touched his face, cool, and damply sweet.

He tested each handhold he came to; but the thought of speed, increasingly pressing on his mind, made the tests a little less exhaustive than they had been. Now he was above the tongue that sloped down to the buttress; there were only another few feet to go before he reached the crack. When he found the next and necessary handhold, he discovered that it was an undercut.

It was a hold that must be taken from below, giving no lift, only a counterpoise, a straight pull outward from the rock, along the line of the strata: when the rock has one's perfect confidence, a useful hold enough. He gave it every test which was possible while still committing his weight to the other hand; but if he were to use it, he must put more on his feet. In the deepening dusk, his eye was gladdened by a small tuft of grass; it argued a certain coherence below. By crossing the place quickly and lightly, he could make the crack. In it, just out of reach, there was a good deep hold. The structure of the crack reassured.

Setting his foot on the grass-tuft, he pulled on the undercut, shifting his balance to it from the other hand. There would be only a second, while he changed hands on it, when it would take the whole outward pull. The moment came; and, at the point of direct tension, he felt it move. An instantaneous reflex brought his foot down on the grass-tuft. There was a little dry, tearing noise; his foot slipped downward. He flung his whole weight out against the undercut. With a motion that seemed grudging, almost lethargic, it parted from its root in the face, and came away.

As his hands left the rock, and his feet slipped lower, his efforts to grasp the receding face seemed protracted, rational, an infinite exploration of possibilities. Then he was face down on the scree, feeling it heap under him, experiencing with flat unbelief his gathering speed; while his body, which understood before him, dragged and struggled, and thrust fingers bent in violent and useless strength among the shifting stones. He thought, This is it, with the unreality of knowing that Australia is under the world; and felt his feet leave the edge.

A sharp tearing, not like pain, wrenched his right hand; his arm, among unrealised movement, felt racking tension and arrest. His body swung sideways on it, and stopped.

Among the scree, indistinguishable to the eye, projected a jag from the underlying rock. In the mind's absence, the mysterious animal he inhabited, whipped back to its primeval swiftness, had found it, clawed and clung. Obeying the creature (his consciousness so far behind that it was still trying to apprehend the fact of death) he clenched his grip, and tried to reinforce it with that of the other hand, which would not reach. His legs from the knees down hung in space. When his mind overtook his body, it was to remark that in a few seconds he must let go.

His first consecutive piece of feeling was to be angry with the animal's idiotic resource. But for this, it would already be over, without apprehension or pain. Now, in an instant more, he would have time to be afraid; and, perhaps, not time to get beyond it, the most disgusting of all ways to go. Fear, he thought angrily, was futile. It would be pointless, inconsistent.

Let him admit at once the truth concealed from himself but now manifest, that he had come to this place to die.

The strain on his fingers was becoming agony. Reduced by the pain to a scarcely perceptible sensation, he felt the warm spread of blood over his wrist and down his stretched arm. He wondered how long it would be before anyone found him: and heard in memory, like something external, his own voice saying, 'It's ten to one you'd lie here for days.'

Swiftly as his body had clutched the rock, his mind shot into an arrowy realisation which made nothing of time. He knew upon whom he was committing murder; a barbarous reprisal upon her helplessness, a massacre, a thousand times beyond the strength of her nature to bear. His dull resignation was stripped from him, like a smothering garment snatched away. The thought of dying in the act of this atrocity electrified him with a life whose force, spun out, would have kept him for a year. He did not think what he should do. It was merely inevitable that his left hand, groping among the scree, should encounter another outcrop, smaller than the first, but enough. Feeling the skin of his cut palm split again and tear with the contraction of the tendons, he began to pull.

When he was far enough up the slide to press downward against the jag, instead of hanging from it, he started with infinite care to sweep the scree away. It rattled down into the gully; the thunder, for which he had no attention to spare, responded. At first it seemed that there was nothing but sliding grit below; then he found a projection, then another. Within two minutes, he had got to the crack.

The crack was to be climbed, so he climbed it. He could not recollect much about it afterwards, except that his red hand-prints had looked odd on the rock. He used jammed hand and foot pressure, he believed, for a good deal of the way; when he clenched his hand the fingers stuck to the palm, and pulled raw flesh when he opened them. After he had lain down in dry leaves at the top, he did not attempt to remember.

The first drops of the thunder-rain fell, with a heavy and deliberate kindness, on his upturned face.

17

Summit Ridge

He was soaked to the skin, and cold. The rain had been some time in penetrating the trees; now it brought down with it the aggregate from the leaves. A sound of falling water on the face below him changed to a steady pour. He had been thinking of nothing; getting to his feet, he discovered a ravenous hunger. After one or two false starts, he got to the cart-track which traversed the upper level of the woods; it led up to a farm, where they had once given him and Ellen tea.

He had not spent much thought on his appearance till the farmer's wife, looking terrified, tried to shut the door in his face. He pulled himself together in time to call something out to her; she peered again and let him in. Dripping beside the kitchen range he followed her mild slow gaze to the rent in his trouser-knee through which a raw graze showed, the earth-patches on his shirt dissolved to mud, the bloodied handkerchief wrapped round his hand. She lent him her dead father's dressing-gown (he had been bed-ridden, she confided, for ten years before he was taken; the stuff smelled of old sickness and camphor-balls) while she dried his clothes and dog-stitched the tear. Her husband, a huge, clean, softly moving man with deep Devon eyes, offered the awkward sympathy of the sane toward afflicted aberration; there had been a lad once fallen thereabouts, a wild-like sort of a lad, birds'-nesting they reckoned he must have been. As soon as they had got a fire going in the parlour they put Neil in there; he did not deprecate this, guessing that in the kitchen he was in their way. At a round mahogany table he ate fried bacon and chitterlings and drank mugs of thick, dark tea. The fire of dry logs crackled, spurted and grew incandescent at the heart. His meal finished, he sat, his chin propped on his good hand, staring across the table at the flames.

A moment of reality, he thought, shows us how far we are straggled from our roots; exposing the false sensibility, thin efflorescence of talk and print, which presents the clumsy griefs we inflict on one another as wounds without cure. In the spirit, as in the flesh, the principle of life runs deeper; we leave it untapped, fidgeting with the surface of our self-esteem. Not in search of death, but of life, he had gone to the rock; to be measured in seconds perhaps, perhaps to be bought with death as soon as realised; life, and reality, none the less. Not for appeasement, or compensation, or forgetfulness, he had turned to a woman almost a stranger, and, after an acquaintance of days, sought a responsibility which might well have daunted him after a year. Desire, a condition inevitable but secondary, had fogged the issue. Her need, her conflict, her trapped and muted life, had drawn him like an unclimbed face which promises difficulty and exposure increasing at every pitch; but at the summit the realisation of oneself and of the mountain, union and release, a sky whose spaces humble, but no longer humiliate or appal.

He had chosen his climb and slipped at the crux of it,

through impatience and bad judgment and blindness to the weather-signs; and, in a stupid artificially civilised negativism, had accepted the end. Now, illuminated by their physical counterparts, the shock of falling, the lacerations given and received, took their proportion against the central impulse, like the torn hand on which, at the imperative moment scarcely feeling its injury, he had raised his weight and climbed. The skin would be scarred, perhaps, but he would climb on it again. He had not the arrogance, nor the defeatism, to assume in her a vitality less than his own.

When he left the farm, he had a good deal of difficulty in persuading them to let him pay for his meal; they clearly thought him one of those helpless irresponsibles for whose protection cities exist, and were ashamed to exploit him.

While he ate, the storm had passed the zenith; its spent thunder was trundling to the east, the wind had steadied under its burden of rain. Soon he was soaked again; but he had started warm and fed, and he went briskly. His hand, however, was beginning to smart and throb; finding it burn more when it hung downward, he walked with it pushed into the front of his shirt.

It was just after ten when he reached Weir View. There were lights in the upper windows (Ellen's, which faced away, he could not see) and one in the hall. He wished there were a separate way into the tower. He was getting tired; the thought of all the women clucking over his tatterdemalion entrance exhausted him in advance; they might say something to Ellen, besides. A car had just driven away from the door; he hung about for a minute or two before letting himself in quietly.

He had not, however, left it long enough. The nurse was at the hall-stand mirror, tidying her hair. She had not seen him; he half thought of going out again. The hall light seemed strong after the wet darkness. He had a moment's fresh and detached view of her; her profile looked jaunty and dubious, resolute over a quelled dejection. He took a step backward, his hand on the door.

Too late; she had turned. To his unexpected relief, she did not gape. After her first start, she surveyed him carefully, as if he were something not much out of the way, but needing classification.

'Well, Mr Langton, what happened to *you*? I suppose you fell down one of those cliffs?'

A sudden, relaxed comfort crept over him. He had felt the same when at eight years old he had returned from some silly exploit, triumphant but a little shaky at the knees, to his mother's resigned crossness and kind hands.

He said, meekly, 'Not all the way.'

'I should hope not indeed. A good job I didn't stay out any later. How much blood have you lost?'

'Only what's here.' He held it out. She exclaimed, not in horror but in disapproval and disgust.

'Don't tell me you've had that horrible dirty rag next to it all this time!'

'It was a handkerchief once,' he apologised. 'I didn't have anything else with me.'

'You ought to carry proper first aid, doing that sort of thing. Never mind, let's get it cleaned up and have a look.'

Upstairs, Ellen's door hung emptily open; no one was about. She took him to the bathroom, fetched a handful of paraphernalia, and ran the tap. 'No, don't pull it, it'll be stuck by now.' When the handkerchief had been soaked off in warm water, she took him under the light and peered, silently, into the gritty, ragged-edged, ploughed-up wound. It made him feel rather sick himself.

'You're in luck,' she remarked. 'It's missed the tendon all right.' He nearly said 'I know,' but this seemed presumptuous, so he refrained.

'I suppose, if you hadn't run into someone, you'd have gone with all this muck ground into it all night. The way people ask for trouble! Now keep running the cold over it. I've got some tweezers boiling on the ring in my room.'

She fetched them and got to work. Setting his teeth silently, he felt thankful her attention was engaged. Without looking round as she poked and probed, she said, 'I *know* it hurts. You're being ever so good.'

Lulled by her cosy realism, his pride succumbed without a struggle: next time he felt like drawing a sharp breath he did so, and was much relieved.

'Now don't watch this part, it'll set your teeth on edge.' He looked obediently at the wall while she snipped off the loose skin. 'There. That's all the nasty part finished. It just goes to show – I never go on holiday without some flavine cream. Keep it in my sponge-bag; the mess it makes if it leaks you'd never believe.' A slimy emulsion of a violent orange went on to the lint; its first contact brought smoothness and ease. She padded it over with wool and wound on a firm intricate bandage. 'Well,' she remarked, 'that ought to keep *you* quiet for a bit. Would you like a couple of tablets, just to sleep on tonight?'

'No,' he said quickly; and then, 'No, thanks, it's very good of you, but I always sleep.'

'One of the independent ones, aren't you? Now don't forget . . .' And she gave him a number of instructions which, for quite five minutes afterwards, he remembered to the letter. 'And I wouldn't waste time getting to bed; you look all in, and who'd wonder. Have you had a meal?'

He explained that he had, and started to thank her. She was

cleaning the blood from the basin with a swab of clean wool; his handkerchief, rinsed already, hung on the edge. A silly headband, ear-rings, the forgotten trappings of coquetry, framed her plain, preoccupied face as she cleaned, scrupulously, round the base of one of the taps. He had been much at strain today: suddenly he had to swallow, his pretty speech stuck in the midst of a phrase. 'Good night,' he said, 'and God bless you.' He thought she turned as he got to the door; but he was feeling embarrassed, and did not look round. As he went, it occurred to him that he could still not remember her name.

In the corridor, Miss Searle passed him in her dressing-gown. She gave one glance, and went by with rigidly averted face. It was odd, he thought, that in these all-concealing garments women should feel undressed.

The rain was finished. He lay for a long time with the door open, watching the stars skim between still-seeming clouds in the washed sky. The drowsiness he had felt by the farmhouse fire had left him. He ought to take some medinal, he supposed; he had had none for a week now, so that would be all right. He would need to be clear in the head tomorrow; before he considered what to say to Ellen, it would need some resource merely to get word with her alone. Should he write a note, perhaps, and leave it under her door early? If so what should he write? He could think of nothing. A slow, blank certainty possessed him that there was nothing. He could apologise, retract, explain for himself; it would be decent, but unmeaning. He could not retract on her behalf the position into which he had forced her. She herself might not be able to retract it; it had become, perhaps, unalterably true.

As he faced this possibility, memory suddenly presented him with the picture, two hours old now, of her open door. A new thought, insanely overlooked till this moment, struck him with

274

a force that jerked him up sitting on the bed. She might have gone already. She might never have returned.

He remembered the morning after the Phillips episode; her bathe on the wickedly unsafe beach, her stupid climb (he was hardly the one to reproach her with that). Vainly he tried to remember if he had seen anything inside the room: clothes on a chair, a pair of shoes. The light had been off; he had seen nothing. He argued with himself: if she were gone he would be helpless till morning; it would be far better not to find out. All this was useless. He had to know.

Everyone made some degree of sound in sleeping; he need only open the door a crack, listen a moment, and go. His footsteps in the passage, if anyone heard him, could be simply accounted for by walking on to the lavatory farther down.

He paused on the roof steps, his dressing-gown tugged by the cool wind, looking at the sliding stars and thinking that when he came back they would be different for him, but in themselves the same.

The passage was close after the roof, very dark, and tinged with soapy, powdery female smells, all foreign to his remembrance. He found the door. It was shut. Anyone might have shut it. He could hear nothing through it, but, with instant conviction, knew that she was there. With this knowledge came the realisation that to open it was out of the question. He imagined her waking; her horrified, tense indrawn breath; his own attempts at explanation sounding more sordid with each fresh start. When he had gone he would question his certainty of her presence, and have no peace; but that couldn't be helped.

He was turning away when something arrested him; he came back, and listened again. He had not been mistaken. It was a thin, exhausted sound, like a reflex which is wearily resisted; it must have worn itself almost out, and would shortly cease. All his thinking came to a standstill. He opened the door, and went in.

The sobbing was extinguished with a finality like death. Rigidity could be felt in the room's very air. He closed the door behind him, and, with some dim idea of proving his good intentions, put on the light.

The room was like a junk-shop. Strewn in the litter of transit, even luxurious clothes look shabby and defenceless; these looked like one of those derelict little accumulations which are quickly bundled away when someone has died. The light he had switched on was a reading lamp on a rickety, arty little table beside the bed. She had been lying flung forward; her face, turned sideways on the pillow, blinked at him with dazzled, drenched and dilated eyes. With the idiocy of strong feeling he said, 'What's the matter?'

She was slow to recover from the sudden light. He was horrified by what he had done; did one never learn? He waited for her to say 'Go away,' in order to apologise, and go. Through the glare, now, her eyes had found him. Expression returned to her face. He saw that it was the face of one unbelievably reprieved at the foot of the scaffold.

He could say nothing, and besides there was nothing to say. He crossed the room and sat on the edge of the bed, and she threw herself into his arms and clung there, choking and shivering. Her hair under his mouth was tangled into a mat from the pillow; her tears ran down between his pyjama-collar and his neck.

After some time, in which a long conversation seemed to have been exchanged without a word spoken, she said, 'I thought you'd gone.'

'I thought you had.'

'I've been here all evening.' It turned out that when he had passed her door she had been in the second bathroom, with the taps turned on. Having no handkerchief with him, he wiped her eyes with the corner of the sheet. No fresh tears came; she was wrung dry.

'You'll catch cold,' he said, and pulled the eiderdown round her shoulders. She had on a pair of pale-blue cotton pyjamas, the kind that cost five shillings at Marks and Spencer's before the war. They looked old enough to date from then; a patch was let in under one of the arms. She had put the medal on again; it hung down outside, fully visible. He saw it as a detail among other details, like the pearl button on which it had caught.

He was rather clumsy with the eiderdown. She struggled out of it, too quickly for him to hide his bandaged hand. She took it between hers and said in a whisper, 'What's this?'

'Nothing. Only a scrape. Miss Whatsit did it up for me.'

'How did you do it?'

'Fooling about. I slipped on a bit of scree.'

'Where?'

'I forget now. It isn't anything.'

She stared into his face. He tried to brazen it out, but had to look away. Still staring in silence she began to shiver again, violently and rigidly. He hauled up the fallen eiderdown, and through it patted her on the back.

'Shut up,' he said in his disciplinary voice. 'We're not having this flap.'

She was quiet almost at once. 'I'm terribly sorry.'

'I should hope so too.'

She sat up straight in bed, with the eiderdown over her shoulders. He put an arm round her to keep it there. Her eyes were puffy with crying, her lashes stuck together. She looked as if she needed a thermometer and a basin of bread-and-milk.

'Neil,' she said, looking at the tops of her knees, 'I've thought now, I see what we ought to do. I'll sleep with you when it's all right for you, when you're free I mean; as soon as you say. I don't mean,' she went on painstakingly, 'to make up for what I've done. I mean because I should like to. Then you'll get me out of your head, and you'll be all right.'

The general effect of all this was so funny that he would have laughed, if he had not also been nervous of becoming emotional. 'Of course we will,' he said calmingly. 'People do who get married. I'll send you a little book about it.'

'Please don't make fun of me.'

'I'm not, darling. Thank you very much.'

'It's just obstinacy,' she said urgently. 'You never will go back on anything. You must see for yourself that you can't be in love with me.'

'Well, I am.' This sounded like a prep-house argument, he thought.

'Oh, nonsense.' She turned round to him, with a weary kind of reasonableness. 'You? You could have anyone in the world.'

'For God's sake,' he said sharply, 'don't be such a bloody God-damned fool.' He pulled her against his shoulder. One slapped their faces for hysteria. It seemed a little drastic: he patted her again, looking away.

'You know nothing about me.' She was suddenly quite steady, and compellingly calm. 'You don't know what I'm really like, or what I've done. I've got in the way once before of a man who was better than I am. He's dead. I killed him. Now I'm good for nobody. You may as well know.'

The words seeped into his consciousness slowly. They remained quite meaningless. Staring at her, trying to make something of them, he found his eye caught by the medal on its chain. She followed his look, and made a movement of assent.

'But you told me he . . .' He stopped, helplessly. He ought to be experiencing some cataclysmic shock or change; she ought to feel different in his arm. Everything was exactly the same. 'I don't believe it. You couldn't take life. How did it happen?'

'Nothing happened. That was it. I didn't do anything. That's how I killed him.'

His mind following vaguely its lines of association, he said, 'You were climbing, you mean?'

'Oh, no. Jock wouldn't have let me kill him on a climb. He was too good.'

He said, trying to think, 'Of course he was. Outstanding, I should say . . . How *did* he die?'

'He died as I told you he did. He was shot down by a Messerschmitt, over the Channel. I don't mean that I murdered him. No one else would say so. He wouldn't have said it himself. That doesn't alter it.' She sat forward, her hands round her knees. 'It doesn't seem real to be telling anyone about it. I'm glad it's you that I've but told. Not only because it's due to you. Because it's what I deserve.'

He stared past her shoulder at the disordered room, seeing it as a vague pattern of drooping and horizontal colours. Taking his arm away he sat back against the head of the bed. He felt too much concentrated in himself to be touched. It was not against what she would tell him that his force was keyed, but for his own effort; the crucial pitch, hidden till now by a twist of the route, showed at last its first vertical and delicate holds.

He said, 'I don't know anything yet. Would it be difficult to start at the beginning?'

'No. It isn't difficult any more. It's only that I can't believe, now, that you need telling. I shall have to go through it as if I were talking to myself.'

'Yes,' he said. 'Go on.'

'We were a kind of cousins; our mothers were stepsisters. They read Cinderella when they were little and made up their minds not to be like that, and ran to the opposite; they were inseparable, like twins. It was the same when they grew up; they married safe men who wouldn't take them far away. Most of the time they managed to live in the same town. Jock says he can remember me being born, but I think he made that up, he was only two. The first thing I can remember at all is him hitting me in the bath with a red celluloid fish.

'You know, when I realised I'd made you hate him, I kept not believing it. It still seems incredible, somehow, that you can't know him for yourself and have to listen to me. I've felt it's you and he who would be going off and doing things together, and me left out.

'You know how some people get a cliché stuck to them like a label, because it's really the only possible thing to say. I can't ever remember a fresh person who didn't say Jock had a sunny nature, as if they'd found something out. The ones who were proud of not making obvious remarks used to put it in quotes. You couldn't help it. A room really looked lighter when he came into it. He was fair and brown. Not at all good-looking; you could see it in a photograph, but in real life no one took it in.

'He hadn't much in the way of intellect, either. I suppose by a lot of tests, he wasn't even very intelligent. Have you ever met a person who seemed to live purely by instinct, and yet never to put a foot wrong?'

'Yes. Sammy was like that. On a climb, and in other ways.'

'I wonder why they missed meeting ... Jock had no principles, none at all. He was straight, and nice to everybody, because he wouldn't have enjoyed life any other way. He was good like one drinks water, thinking of something else. I don't know what he thought about evil; nothing, probably. One of those things you muddle through till it's over, like fog.

'As soon as I could get about, I was always being pushed off on him while our mothers talked. He took a lot of living up to, because he took things for granted so. He'd never tell you if you were a nuisance to him, which made you mind much more. Of course we fought sometimes; but even when he was a child, he never made the sort of generalised remark that pulls people down.

'Most of his friends were older than he was, because he could do their things; but he sort of hypnotised them into taking me on trust. Of course I worked like a black to keep abreast, knowing he'd cover up for me if I didn't. When he had to, I felt bad for the rest of the day.

'I forget how old I was when I asked someone what getting married meant. They told me the kind of thing you do tell small children, about promising to stay together. So after I'd proposed to my father and he explained he was disqualified, of course I asked Jock. He said, 'I will if you ride down Brick Hill on the step of my bike,' so I did. I wasn't really much frightened, because nothing ever happened to Jock, and he never expected it to.

'He never went back on a promise, so he announced it publicly as soon as we got in. Our mothers went sort of misty – of course they must have been praying for it since we were born – but they were too sensible to give us ideas, so it just became a family joke. After Jock went to his prep-school he must have got all the dirt about things, but he never let on a word of it to me. Later on when he got to the loutish age, of course he made silly cracks about us, but never unkind. Naturally I knew the facts of life by then, but I never connected them. I suppose in a dim way I did still think we should marry sometime; but you feel being an adult will happen formally, on a birthday, and till it does there's no need to worry.

'One day when I was seventeen, I remembered Jock hadn't made the joke for a long time now, and it dawned on me that it wasn't good form any more because I was grown up. It was a solemn thought for five minutes, but when he showed up I forgot all about it and never bothered again. It was about then he got bitten with climbing, and started teaching me. The summer after that, there was the war.'

She stopped, gathering herself together. Neil had been aware for some instants of the silence, before he could come out of himself to fill it. With a sense both of shame and of danger, he put aside a moment of deep and compassionate peace. It shocked him that he had almost said this was enough.

'No one was ready,' he said. 'Go on.'

'Jock joined the RAF a month before it started. The uniform suited him terribly well. He loved flying; he used to come home all shining from inside. It was because of him, of course, that I went to make planes. All those first months when nothing much happened, I used to wonder if it was wrong of me not to be afraid of his being killed. I couldn't be. I always knew he was a charmed life. He wasn't one of the kind who flower early because they're marked for death. He was alive steadily, like the earth is.

'I suppose working in the factory ought to have altered me a lot; but it was a thing by itself, somehow outside me. I'm not good with many people at a time; I did the job and didn't get across anyone. But when I went off the shift I left it all behind me. None of it prepared me for Jock growing up as he did, all in a moment. You're a man, you'd take it for granted, I expect.

'When things really began, in 1940, he only got short leaves, but he could get over because he was stationed quite near. He had to spend most of the time with his mother, of course; his father had to go away a lot. I used to tell her nothing could happen to Jock, and sometimes she believed it. When I did see him, I used to have stray moments of wondering what I was doing, talking to this rather magnificent type as if he were someone I'd always known; and then suddenly everything would be like home again, and I'd forget.

'Then one day they had a dance at the hotel near his station, and he asked me to come. I'd never been before, and I felt like I did when we were children, that he'd got to be lived up to, only more so, because this was his own thing. You could still buy real clothes then, and I spent every penny I had. I felt sure the competition would be terrifying. Actually for some reason it wasn't – I expect all the prettiest Waafs were on duty – and I made a sort of impression. It had never happened before, and it felt rather queer, but quite fun. Jock was in tremendous form. There was a warning at one point, which was rather exciting but didn't come to anything, and afterwards Jock drove me home. This is the part that's so impossible to explain.'

'Never mind. Go on.'

'You see, Jock had often kissed me coming and going, and put his arm round me, and things like that. It sounds imbecile, I know; but somehow it had never occurred to me that if he really made love to me, it would be so very different. I—' She broke off, twisting a corner of the eiderdown. Neil effaced himself behind her, sitting very still. 'I suppose it can't really have been so sudden, if I'd had any sense. It was like a nightmare, trying to keep him from knowing how terrible it was. He didn't do anything I *should* have minded. He knew I'd always adored him. He couldn't understand. I didn't either, I never have.

'I think perhaps if I could just have taken it as it came, it would all have blown over. As it was, it seemed to stir him up

283

more. He'd always got me over being frightened of things and I'd been glad afterwards, and he wanted to get me over this one. The worst of it was, I thought he might be right and didn't know what line to take. After a while he got all caught up in it, and then . . . And the more I felt it happening the more terrifying it was, and the more he seemed like a stranger; and yet it was Jock. I got to dread seeing him, and that by itself was terrible enough.

'He tried so hard, too, I couldn't bear it. You see, he wasn't a subtle kind of person, he didn't go at things by thinking them out. It must have taken a lot out of him, trying to work out this one. He said we'd always got on, and it was only because I was shy, and a – and inexperienced, and it would be all right afterwards; and if I didn't feel happy about it, would I go away with him somewhere, once, and give it a chance? That was a lot for him to say, because he knew if we were found out it would break up his mother and mine, and he'd have taken the blame for both of us, like he always had. It wasn't that he wanted to get me easily, quite the reverse.

'We dragged on for weeks like that, and the war got worse, and he began to look different. Not warm and glowing, a sort of hard, bright shine. Then he started drinking. Only off duty of course, and no more than some of the others who had to relax sometimes somehow. But he'd never needed it before. I kept asking for more time to think, and wondering if I ought to marry him anyway, and pretend. But he'd have known. It seemed intolerable for Jock and me to come to that.

'Then, when I was out one evening, I saw him in the street with a Waaf. She was looking at him when he wasn't at her; you know how sometimes women forget there are other people. I knew more in that couple of seconds than I did later when he told me about it. He saw I'd seen him, or perhaps he wouldn't have, I don't know. Anyway, he said there were times when you had to have somebody, and he'd been straight with her about it and she knew where they stood. He hadn't needed to tell me that part. At first I couldn't think of anything but what she must be going through, keeping a light touch all the time. She was one of those girls who put a sort of hard varnish on the surface; I don't suppose she was often caught out like she was when I looked.

'Then suddenly I stopped thinking about her and looked at Jock. I never saw him look better, as a man, than he did that day. Self-reliant and alert and upstanding. I forgot to tell you, he had a DFC. And all in a moment, I saw that something had happened. Something had gone, a sort of magic invulnerability. He wasn't a charmed life any more. He was mortal, like anyone else.

'I stayed awake all night afterwards. I thought I must have been mad, to imagine I was important enough to be worth that. I thought I could make myself be in love with him somehow – I *did* love him – it shouldn't be so different, I thought. I wrote a letter saying I'd marry him. But in the morning it didn't look right, and I kept it back to write again. And then I thought I'd write a better one next day, when I wasn't so tired. I put it off three days, and the fourth day I had it in my pocket, ready for the last post. And then the 'phone went. It was Jock's mother. I knew as soon as the bell rang, before I answered it.

'My mother went straight over, of course, so I was alone. This is the worst thing I've got to tell you. You won't understand it; it's outside your kind of life. That's why I'm telling you, so that you'll see what I meant when I said you couldn't be in love with me.

'It was a beautiful summer evening, all clear and still. And I had a wonderful exalted feeling, like one has after seeing a great tragedy on the stage. It seemed everything was resolved between us, that I'd always loved him, and that now it was perfect and spiritual and he must know it too. And then a sort of shrivelling light burst in on me, and I knew what all this ecstasy really was. It was relief.

'You can't look at a thing like that for more than a second at a time. I never have. It's unbelievable I should be telling someone in words. I've never faced it for as long as it's taken me to say it now. But it's always there. There's something I read a short time after, and I've never opened the book again.'

She looked down at the twist of eiderdown in her fingers; her voice was clear, like grey glass.

> 'The many men, so beautiful,
>   And they all dead did lie;
> And a thousand thousand slimy things
>   Lived on: and so did I.'

As he looked past her shoulder, Neil saw that her hand had moved upward, and was fingering, unconsciously, the medal at her neck. A sudden illumination jerked his voice back to silence; his heart checked with a taut constricting pain. Not daring to move lest she felt it, he clenched his cut hand till he felt the blood break out against the dressing. This distraction saved him, and he made no sound.

'Afterwards,' she said, accepting his silence with quiet submission, 'I tried to prove to myself that it had been inevitable. If I couldn't do this for Jock, I thought, it must be that I was different, that it wasn't in me at all. They say some women are queer and don't want to know about it. I thought perhaps I was, only one day a woman got sentimental about me, and that was no good. So I must just be frigid, I thought. Presently I got quite convinced of it, and as I see it now, I suppose it made me feel safe, and I began to get rational about it, and pretend to myself that I must be sensible and take it in hand. That was why I took up with Eric. I know now why it really was. I must have known all the while that he'd be unendurable, and I could convince myself all over again. I hid that from myself, completely, till the morning after he'd gone, and I was having breakfast, and ...' She turned her face away. 'I was afraid of you. I suppose you knew that.'

'Not now,' he said, and, drawing her back against his shoulder, began to caress her; but he knew he was only playing for time. He felt her trying to relax and yield to it, and knew that the fear of hurting him possessed her to a point where her own sensations were extinguished; she neither knew nor cared what they were. When she began to speak again, one effort cancelled the other; she grew tense again to the touch.

'Not of you, now, but for you. It's gone too deep; I think it's become a part of me. I think perhaps ...' With a movement that she herself seemed to be resisting, she took his hand between hers and held it away. 'Perhaps if you were less kind. If you were going to take what you wanted and give me nothing, or if I could keep myself from ...' She averted her face. Over the shadowed mass of her hair, the light picked out an intricate web of threadlike gold. 'I think, and tell myself, and it makes no difference. I ...' He felt her wrestling, bitterly, with the habit and strength of her own reticence. In a voice almost quenched with shame and struggle, she said, 'I can't feel any pleasure, now, without a sense of sin.'

'Be quiet a moment,' he said. She grew slack against his shoulder; her hands folded themselves passively about his. She was taking this pause into herself, creating a memory for solitude. He let her rest.

'Wars,' he said at last, groping his way, 'are a flaw in time. We're half evolved beyond them. We're pitched off our individual points of balance, and our own rhythm of growing, and told they no longer exist except as utilities for the herd. We know it's a lie, but we're ashamed to value our souls because cowards are valuing comfort, and the coward in ourselves values it too. So we slither about between two different kinds of being, trying to find a stance. The wonder isn't that delicate adjustments are destroyed; it's a miracle that any survive at all. If I wasn't ready for it at thirty-four, what do you expect me to say about two children who weren't ready at twenty and eighteen?'

He knew, before she spoke, that this had got nowhere.

'Age doesn't mean anything. One's there, one's responsible, and one takes the results.'

'We all do. I've never talked to you as I should. Pure egotism . . . I worked out an adjustment I thought would do for me. So, good enough. I left a woman who wasn't yet fit to look after herself, with a child she wasn't yet fit to take care of. The woman became – what she need never have known she could be. And the child died as I wouldn't see a murderer die. Like you, I don't look on myself as a stainless martyr.'

She turned to him, silently. He submitted himself to her compassion, moved by it, and willing in any case to accept with grace what he had asked for. But, as he perceived, its ultimate message was still defeat.

'You did something positive, because you decided it was right. I did nothing, and decided nothing. I was just invertebrate; a total loss.'

He felt as he sometimes did when the route seemed to come to a dead stop, below an overhang. As then, he wiped his mind clear, and tried to see it all as if for the first time. As then, on one of those days when he was in luck and form, something came; he felt suddenly that the impasse could be turned. He had only been silent for a few seconds.

'What do you mean,' he said, 'that you decided nothing? Do you believe yourself that you took the line of least resistance? It isn't indecision that one clings to through punishment like that.'

He had begun, not sure where it was leading him. Now his view cleared; the truth stretched, unbroken, before him to the finish.

She had not answered; but he felt her weight lighten, as it does when the mind ceases to be listless, and draws together.

He asked, 'Have you any brothers?'

'No,' she said, separating herself to look at him. 'I'm an only child. I should have had one, but he was born dead.'

He said, quietly, 'Are you sure?'

'Of course I'm—' Her face took on a look of surprise and fear, as if some frail-looking hold, long considered and dismissed, were pointed out to her as a thing to which she might entrust her weight.

'When I was little,' she said slowly, 'very little, I mean, I used to pretend he was. To other people, who didn't know. I used to get told off for being untruthful. I'd forgotten about it for years.'

'Don't you think,' said Neil, 'it's time you remembered?'

'But, my dear, do you suppose I've never thought this kind of thing? It's the oldest alibi in the world. It's a line in a farce. It's what Victorian girls used to say sitting under potted palms.'

'What the hell does it matter who's said it? You little fool, don't you realise it's true?'

She sat up and he let her go. The eiderdown, which had slipped away long since, was tangled under her in a churned-up heap. She wrapped her arms round her breast and shoulders.

'You don't trust things you'd like to believe too much.'

'You're sentimental,' said Neil unsympathetically. He gave this a moment, recovering a knack of timing he had had at school. 'This isn't done up in lavender. It's a taboo that was real when we were savages living in caves. It's formed in the mind, not in the blood. He'd been shaken out of it; for him, what was left of it was just a longing to perpetuate something stable, when everything was rushing over the edge. It wasn't his fault, or anyone's fault, that it was love to him and incest to you.'

There was a long silence.

'Do you know now?' he said.

'Yes.' She did not move. He let her be; it was a moment at which he himself would have demanded to be alone.

'How helpless I was,' she said at last, 'what a fool, not to have seen it in time. If I could have told him, he'd have understood. He understood all the natural things.'

'At eighteen? Try and remember how it feels.'

'I don't need to. I wonder, now, if I've ever grown beyond it.'

'Oh, yes, for a long time. As Plato says in the *Phaedrus*, growing that's held in always hurts.'

'And yet . . . innocent or guilty, one's still a cause.'

'Yes, one may have to face that, if it's true. If. I knew a lot of boys, you know, who were twenty when the war began.'

'He was bound to change. I know that. It's a more concrete thing. Flying a Spitfire, everything's in split seconds. You can't afford anything on your mind, when it comes to the pinch.'

'My dear,' he said, 'if you'll forgive me, I'll take from you one of woman's pet illusions. When it comes to the pinch, a man doesn't have anything on his mind.'

'You should know,' she said slowly. 'What do you think about?'

'About what to do next, as long as there is anything. After

that, it's everyone's own business. Perhaps the man who's most alone, then, is the best off.'

She reached round, and took his hand. It was the bandaged one; he tried to give her the other, but she had known what she was looking for. She turned it over; there was a dark-brown patch, he discovered, staining the dressing across the palm. He knew now, as a hard, dry fact about which there was no time to think, that she would have killed herself if he had died. Some part of him, working by itself like the reflex which had gripped the rock, had known it at the time.

'Something nearly happened today,' she said, 'didn't it?'

'It seemed to, for a minute. But it was all done with mirrors.'

Turning round, she looked up at him; but he had seen this coming. He returned the look, straight in the eyes.

'No,' he said. 'Sorry, darling, but there it is. There simply isn't time. Till it was over, I didn't remember you were alive.'

She looked down at his hand again, and smoothed out a crease in the bandage.

'It's always like that,' he told her. 'Something to do with the glands. Adrenalin, I think.'

This improvement seemed to fail, somehow, of its hoped impression. She simply looked at the bandage, tracing the pattern where it crossed with her finger-ends.

'I love you,' she said, speaking down to it. 'I love you. I—'

'S-sh.' He brought her over. 'Don't carry on so.'

Clear and precise in the quiet, the chiming clock downstairs struck one of the little hours. Stroking her hair, he felt beneath it a harder strand entangled. She felt it too; their eyes met in a moment of question and assent.

The clasp had slid from the centre, and took a little while to find; but, found, it was quite easy. The gold disc, smooth and warm like a part of her body, dropped into his hand. Turning it over, he saw on the reverse the white span of wings. He put it down in the ring of light on the bedside table, and said, steadily,

> *'The albatross fell off, and sank*
>   *Like lead into the sea.'*

She looked at him, without wonder or surprise. 'Yes. That's true, too. After I knew how you felt about it, just for one moment I knew what it really was. A penance. But I couldn't face it. They say, don't they, there's nothing so cruel as a coward.'

'I could say the same,' he said, with the peace of a long perspective. 'But it's all over now.' For a while he consoled her in silence. Presently she recovered enough to look, rather blankly, from the chaos of the room to that of the bed. He laughed, and helped her to fish up the eiderdown and spread it out. While they were doing this, it occurred to him that, from a standpoint which it was hard to take seriously at the moment, he had been very indiscreet.

'I'm going in a minute,' he said. 'God knows what time it is. You'd better get some sleep.'

'So should you.' She turned to smile at him.

The light had begun to feel hard and strident; unconsciously he had narrowed his eyes. The pulled muscles ached draggingly in his arm and side; his hand throbbed; a variety of small strains and bruises seemed to have stiffened up. One had taken these minor mishaps in one's stride, a few years ago. Still, it had been a long day after a short night; there wasn't much in it.

'Oh, my darling,' she said, her voice suddenly changing, 'what have I been thinking of?'

'What's the matter?' This, he remembered with dim amusement, was where he had come in.

'You're dead tired. Why haven't I looked after you?'

He had begun telling her not to make a fuss about nothing; but her arms felt warm, her breast soft; it was much more comfortable lying down, and there seemed no need to protest for a minute or two. A little of this *laissez-faire* revealed an overstatement: he was tired, certainly, but he wasn't dead. That this fact had communicated itself appeared in the changed rhythm of her tenderness, deep and shy. There was a critical little pause.

After all, he thought, why this obstinacy on a point of order? It looked, in the light of the moment, merely silly, and it had become factually pointless besides. If a long arm of mischance caught up with him, perjury no longer came into it. The evidence as it stood was final; as well, then, a sheep as a lamb. He felt her hand move over his head, tentative and trusting. They were beyond the awkward intrusions of the spoken word. She was saying that it was inconceivable he should be wrong, tonight, about any of their concerns. So far he had brought her; if it seemed well to him that she should part with her virginity as a casual epilogue, after an exhausting emotional crisis, in the abrupt and flickering desire of weariness – a satisfaction as brief and trivial as the biscuit which, wakeful, one reaches from the bedside tin – then this must be the perfect, the only possible thing, and she would embrace it gladly. He had been trained for a good many years in another kind of technique which sets high premiums on tactful co-operation and the finer points of style: one did not ask a spent companion to haul one, needlessly, up the last difficult bit on a tight rope. There was a time for all things; they could, and would, do better.

Without ambiguity or misunderstanding, they settled the question between them in a wordless way; and, too tired for sharp gestures of abnegation, declined into a gentle physical sentimentality. In some late and lethargic phase of this, he felt the eiderdown wrapped tenderly round his shoulders; he had been a little cold, lying outside, and had nothing against it. Closing his eyes again, he made a mental note to be out in five minutes; it would be quite easy for someone who didn't keep his wits about him to go to sleep.

He must nearly have dropped off, he realised presently, recalled by a twinge in his arm with a sudden start. She, poor child, had gone flat out in these few minutes; from her profound relaxation and slow, quiet breathing, one would think she had been asleep for hours. Careful not to disturb her, he reached for her wrist-watch which lay near the medal under the lamp. He blinked at it, the light in his eyes. Perhaps he had it upside down. The hands stayed, however, with firm persistence, at five-forty-five.

After all, he was too drowsy to work up a panic about it. Mrs Kearsey, whose piercing alarum reached him sometimes through the roof, got up at six-thirty; and, by now, insomniacs of the earlier hours would have dropped off. He returned Ellen her eiderdown, indulged a moment of unashamed emotionalism by kissing her hair on the pillow, and put out the light as he went. The wind had got up again; somewhere a window clicked, or a door. But the passage was soaked in slumber. He went up to the roof and the iron stairs.

The cold clearness of the dawn air woke him, and he paused just below his door. After the warmth he had left, the wind struck sharply; but he was used to shelving discomfort when there was a good sky to see. This one, he thought, would be worth waiting for. Already the grey translucence in the east was paling; the moon had set; between thin bars of cloud, shadows on an upper twilight, the star of morning waited alone. It hung low, and trembled to itself in a remote soliloquy, meditating compassion or awe. As he watched, the first cloud caught the sun; its dim wreath of mist changed, slowly, to a clear and fervent profile, a pure cold incandescence growing from red to intense gold. The next cloud lit; the grey void between them was flooded with a pale, immaculate and ethereal green. Deep in this sea, Lucifer, son of the morning, faded like a liberated spirit, and died into light.

Sitting on the iron stairs, small and still among these presences, he recalled the day when he had come to Ellen on the beach with the lump of clinkered meteor in his hand. The pattern of the future, like that of the constellations, stood unchanged; but its threat of nothingness passed through him without a wound, for he was nothing, and everything, already. He was happy with the sky in its solitude, free from him and from time, and with the hills no longer troubled by his aspiration. In the remoter-seeming present, decision would be as heavy and effort as hard: but he hated nobody, he would do what he could and accept what was beyond his limit; the readiness was all. A picture came back to him of Sammy, his young ugly face tranquil in the light of a not so different morning, resting a sandwich on his knee to summarise.

We will fall into the hands of God and not into the hands of men. (The rest of the clouds were lit now, but beyond them the air, not yet bounded by its reflected blue, was transparent to the last height of space.) For as His majesty is, so is His mercy.

The gulls were waking, and, somewhere a long way off, two men shouted to one another across a field. It was too late now to get into a cold bed and count sheep; and, however he spent the time between now and breakfast, he could hardly be hungrier than he was already. Mrs Kearsey's alarum sounded, a note of inspiration. If he arrived at the right moment on his way down to the beach, she had been known sometimes to give him a cup of her morning tea.

18

Rescue Party

'I do not think,' wrote Miss Searle, drawing her dressing-gown closer about her in the seven o'clock chill, 'that I have ever been confronted, even in college, with a moral decision which weighed on me more. In fact I am not sure whether I am writing to you because I feel I *must* discuss it with someone of judgment and principle, or simply to clarify my own thoughts. In an issue like this, it is so easy to find two sides even to one's own motives. One can say, for example, that these matters are for the private conscience of the people concerned, and thus give oneself the great relief of feeling no further responsibility. But then one realises that this is simply bowing to a pagan morality; that, perhaps, it is only loose-thinking opinion, and the *personal* unpleasantness, which one fears. One could not adopt this standpoint in, say, a case of theft; the criminal law would recognise one as an accessory. Surely, then, one becomes equally so under the moral law.

'No one, it seems to me, can sufficiently condemn a woman who deliberately tempts a man at such a time; so, whatever the consequences to *her*, they can only be deserved. In the case of the man ...'

She broke off; her fingers felt almost too cold to control the pen. She warmed them in the lapel of her dressing-gown, looking over what she had written; trying to make the lines on the paper fill the inward as well as the outward eye. She wanted to use them as a barrier against memory, as, two hours earlier, she had used her door as a barrier against sight. It was useless; she could still see the face she was trying to obliterate, as clearly as she had seen it in the lit doorway in the second before the light went out, drowsy and inward-looking, blurred and yet intent. The almost unseeing eyes, the tousled hair, the marks of a profound physical weariness partly smoothed by sleep – it had all been terrible to her. It was a whole world of rejected knowledge, a mine exploding security, a shaft into a darkness full of whispers, the revelation of a shame which must never, never be understood. It was life: it was death.

'In the case of the man, one may hesitate to form a personal judgment, since one cannot enter into their very different psychology; but, after all, the authorities of the Church have always been men, and have stood firmly, and I am sure rightly, against a separate standard. It would seem the height of presumption to set up one's ignorance against their knowledge and experience.' (Considering this in some uncertainty, she crossed 'and experience' out.)

'One must ask oneself, too, what future happiness either party could hope for on the foundation of a sin which must, inevitably, prevent each of them from having any respect for the other. However, there is no real need to burden one's conscience with such questions, since the ruling both of the Church and of the civil law is perfectly clear.

'There is only *one* thing which makes me hope that, perhaps even in the interval before your reply reaches me, this very painful decision may be taken out of my hands. You will remember my telling you in my first letter about a Miss Fisher whose conversation was so trying! Her efforts to attract the attention of this man to herself have been so obvious as to be most embarrassing; so that she has naturally taken a morbid (and clearly malicious) interest in all these developments. I have no doubt she will have made it her business to know about this most recent one. The question is whether one is justified in letting her take steps (as I feel sure she will) from the *wrong* motives, and spare oneself the ordeal of acting from the *right* ones. Since she will no doubt do so in any case, one's effort would after all be superfluous. If as a result one were questioned in any investigation, of course one could only speak the truth. She loves to hear her own voice, and will no doubt make quite evident what she intends to do.

'Do please bear with this long epistle. I know how many calls you have on your time . . . '

She finished the letter, dressed, and took it out to the postbox at the bottom of the road. It was almost time for breakfast. She would wait now until she heard Miss Fisher going downstairs. Much could be learned, this morning, from a little quiet observation.

Miss Fisher, throwing odd ends of bandage and lint into her waste-paper basket, reflected that it wasn't like her to leave these messes overnight. She had brought them in from the bathroom, meaning to get rid of them immediately; but there had been something indefinably warming in their visible presence about the room. One was incurably soft, she thought. Men were a curse: careless, wrapped up in themselves, not giving a damn unless they wanted something, and as blind as bats even then. One had known all this for a good fifteen years: and still one of them had only to come along looking a bit under the weather, knocked about through his own silly fault, shiftless and guiltily casual like a kid; and there one went again, soft as tripe. You patched them up; you cared, incredibly after all this time at it, how much it hurt them; you let them see it; and if they went maudlin over you for half a minute, you felt they had done you proud. And then, the first thing you knew ...

Well, thought Miss Fisher, wiping the greasy edge of the flavine cream pot and examining the inside of her sponge-bag for stains, he might have cause to remember one after all. He must have been off his head – here in the house, when there were miles of country available all day, and with that shaky alibi for the other night which the King's Proctor could almost certainly crack up. And the walls so thin you could hear almost what people said, crying and carrying-on. Probably he'd found out about the Phillips boy. But that sort always knew how to soften a man up.

If he hadn't the sense to remember anything else, couldn't he have remembered that sanctimonious cat only just across the way? No wonder the male expectation of life was shorter; there wasn't one who'd live long enough to get a woman into trouble, if some other woman weren't fool enough to wrap him up in cotton-wool.

It was at this point of her meditations that Miss Fisher, who had moved over to the window, saw Miss Searle going down the path with a letter in her hand.

So she *had* been up to something. Miss Fisher had felt it already, in every bone. Well, now one knew where one was. Suddenly, Miss Fisher felt much better.

It was one word against another, and surely to goodness

they'd have to listen to the person with the room next door. If it wasn't enough to say one had been awake all night and had never heard a sound, there'd be nothing for it but to go the whole hog in a good cause. One had been into the girl's room at – one-thirty, two? – to ask for some aspirins, but hadn't liked to wake her, seeing her so sound asleep. Bright moonlight – well, light enough – you could see all over the room. Not that she deserved it; but there was someone else who needed a lesson much more. It would make *her* look a bit of a fool, to be shown up trying to blacken a respectable man; she might not be so sure, after that, that all the answers came out of books.

When the case was over, at the back of the court, or in one of those corridors you saw on the films with lawyers dashing about, Miss Fisher would give her a look. No need to say anything. Just a look.

As for him, there were plenty who wouldn't care to take the risk of saying Thanks; but he wasn't like that. Nothing definite, of course, he wasn't a fool. Just take one's hand perhaps, and say – oh, well, something about having appreciated it, and making all the difference to his life. They were all alike; whatever you did for them they forgot in five minutes. One ought to have more sense and, in fact, one had. And yet . . .

This was about the time she always came down to breakfast, the starched-up hypocrite. With what she had on her conscience, she was probably hoping to get away quick without meeting anyone. It would be fun to catch her eye across the table, not passing any remark, just to see how long she could take it.

Mrs Kearsey had given Neil his breakfast early, as she often did when she found him up and about. The post arrived soon after he had finished it. His single letter looked overpoweringly arid;

feeling in no mood for business, he almost put it in his pocket unopened, but, noting that it had been forwarded from Fort William already, decided that he had better see. He hoped it might not make very high demands on his concentration. In a sense, it did not. A lawyer's clerk, it seemed, had blundered; his change of address, conscientiously notified, had never been filed. The date at the top informed him that he had been an unmarried man, in the eyes of his country's law if in no one else's, for exactly a week.

Ellen was not down yet. He restrained a natural impulse, which only the dimmest promptings discouraged, to run up and tell her as she dressed; and met her presently in the garden.

She looked very tidy, well-brushed and crisp against the memory he had kept from three hours before. There was a delicate staining on her lids and under her eyes, bluish-brown; the look of transparency was oddly moving in a happy face.

She had very little to say: he himself did not feel eloquent. They smiled at one another, in tacit apology for the inhibitions belonging to the time of day. It was evident, however, without speech-making, that wherever they went from here it could only be together. Would she mind, he asked her, if he went off and saw about the licence today? Her brows puckered; he read on them, correctly, an uninformed anxiety about the expense, and kissed her.

'I'll be back by the first train tomorrow. For God's sake don't do any climbing while I'm gone.'

'What am I going to do all that time?'

'You heard me. Promise.'

'Darling, you *are* a fool. You've got me into this miserable half-and-half state of knowing just enough to know how much I don't know. What's the use of climbing alone till you get me out of it?'

'We'll go up to Cumberland. Plenty of good graded stuff there. I tell you where ...' This led from the geographical to the technical, and thence to something too nearly lyrical for breakfast-time. 'By the way,' he remembered, after five minutes of it, 'do you mind being married from a place like this?'

'What does it matter? One's married to, not from. I don't like a lot of people about, for important things. Do you?'

'No.' The picture of a different ceremony came across his mind, with the altered clarity of something forgiven, and seen through an undistorting lens of truth. 'No,' he said; 'you can have a bit too much of it.'

She was looking thoughtful; she would be wanting something to wear, he thought. He must have some coupons somewhere, probably quite a number; he was about to give her this news when she said, 'We shall have to have witnesses, though, shan't we?'

'Oh, yes; but they go out into the highways and hedges, and compel them to come in. It's all laid on.'

'I was just wondering – not if you don't feel like it – whether those two in there might think it fun. They've both been rather nice in their different ways; and they look the sort to enjoy a wedding.'

'Who – the don and Miss Whatsit? But of course; why ever not? I don't know why I didn't think of it. They're still having breakfast, aren't they? Come along, let's go straight in now and ask them.'

THE CHARIOTEER

Mary Renault

Introduced by Simon Russell Beale

Injured at Dunkirk, Laurie Odell, a young corporal, is recovering
at a rural veterans' hospital. There he meets Andrew, a conscientious
objector serving as an orderly, and the men find solace in their covert
friendship. Then Ralph Lanyon appears, a mentor from Laurie's
schooldays. Through him, Laurie is drawn into a tight-knit circle
of gay men for whom liaisons are fleeting and he is forced
to choose between the ideals of a perfect friendship
and the pleasures of experience.

First published in 1953, *The Charioteer* is a a tender, intelligent
coming-of-age novel and a bold, unapologetic portrayal of
homosexuality that stands with Gore Vidal's *The City and
the Pillar* and James Baldwin's *Giovanni's Room* as
a landmark work in gay literature.

KE 11114

virago

To buy any of our books and to find out more
about Virago Press and Virago Modern Classics,
our authors and titles, as well as events and
book club forum, visit our websites

www.virago.co.uk
www.littlebrown.co.uk

and follow us on Twitter

@ViragoBooks

To order any Virago titles p & p free in the UK,
please contact our mail order supplier on:

+ 44 (0)1832 737525

Customers not based in the UK should contact
the same number for appropriate postage
and packing costs.